1900

NORMAN THOMAS DI GIOVANNI is an American writer who has lived in Great Britain for the past four years. His father, a Socialist and anti-Fascist, left Italy after the rise of Mussolini in the 1920s.

For the writing of this novel, Mr di Giovanni spent several months in Italy during the summer of 1975.

He is also known for his distinguished translations of the work of Jorge Luis Borges, for which he was recently made a Guggenheim Fellow.

Alberto Grimaldi presents

a film by **BERNARDO BERTOLUCCI**

1900

ROBERT DI NIRO — **GÉRARD DEPARDIEU**
DOMINIQUE SANDA

and in alphabetical order
**FRANCESCA BERTINI, LAURA BETTI, WERNER
BRUHNS, STEFANIA CASINI, STERLING
HAYDEN, ANNA HENKEL, ELLEN SCHWIERS,
ALIDA VALLI, ROMOLO VALLI**

and with **STEFANIA SANDRELLI**

and with **DONALD SUTHERLAND**

and with **BURT LANCASTER**

Director of photography **Vittorio Storaro** (A.I.C.)

Music by **Ennio Morricone** Technicolor

Directed by **BERNARDO BERTOLUCCI**

A Co-production Producioni Europee (Rome),
Les Productions Artistes
Associés (Paris), Artemis Film GMBH (Berlin)
Released by 20th Century Fox in the U.K.

NORMAN THOMAS DI GIOVANNI

1900

FONTANA/Collins

First published in Great Britain by Fontana Books 1977

Made and printed in Great Britain by
William Collins Sons and Co Ltd Glasgow

CONTENTS

To the Dreamer
Dreaming the Dream

1945

Chapter 1

The broad Po, grey and clayey, was in flood; its sandbanks and
islands and willow thickets were awash. The mingled waters
of a hundred rivers, down from the still frozen peaks of the
Alps and the Apennines, flowed in a torrent across the vast
fertile plain in a ceaseless descent to the sea. All over the north
of Italy the war was drawing to an end. Partisan bands, having
harassed the enemy in mountain battles the whole winter long,
had come out of the hills in force. A weary German army was
in retreat, and, towards the final days of April, city after
city was liberated – on the twenty-first Bologna, on the twenty-
second Modena, two days later Reggio, the following day both
Milan and Venice. Before the month was out, Genoa, Turin,
Trieste had risen against the hated foe. The long, long winter
was coming to a close. Italy breathed; Italians smiled; the
countryside awoke and began to bear its fruit.

In the last few days before May, Mussolini himself was
caught fleeing. The partisans, having found him close to the
Swiss border disguised as a German, brought him to swift
justice.

All over Italy, all the length and breadth of the flat valley
of the Po, it was spring again.

Chapter 2

On the Berlinghieri estate, in the heart of the Emilian plain
midway between Cremona and Parma, men and women were
out in the mown fields raking hay and pitchforking it up on
to wagons. It was a fine sunny morning, the twenty-fifth of
April. Birds chattered in the soft young leaves of the stately
poplars that grew along the road at the edge of the field.
To the south, the range of the Apennines was still a hazy
blue.

It was warm. The men kept stopping to listen, wiping their brows under their hats. The women eyed them. In their big black skirts and broad-brimmed straw hats, they seemed somehow less bothered by the heat.

A volley of gunfire sounded in the distance from a grove of trees in which a mill was hidden. Atop one of the wagons, where she forked into place the clots of hay shoved up to her, a young woman turned to look towards the shots. The cuckoos there had stopped their plaintive calling. The others lifted their faces to the girl, expectantly, but there was nothing she could tell them.

A man bristling with arms came speeding along the dirt track on a bicycle, raising his voice to the men making hay. 'Come on,' he shouted. 'We have them bottled up.'

'Tiger!' the men shouted back, flinging down their rakes and pitchforks.

Tiger stopped his bicycle. The others drew around him, reaching out hungrily for the weapons. The partisan had a tommy-gun and six or eight rifles and a couple of cartridge belts slung over his back. 'Let's get the bastards,' he told the men, lightening his load and distributing the arms. He spoke to the contadini by name, still astride the bicycle.

A boy ran up to him. 'Give me one too,' he said, and he began tugging at a rifle.

Tiger looked at him. Leonida was thirteen, as yet in short trousers.

'Did you cut the telephone wires?' Tiger asked him.

Leonida's hands gripped the rifle butt. He nodded and began tugging again. Tiger held back.

'I cut them,' Leonida pleaded. 'I did what you told me.'

Tiger patted the boy on the back and relented. Leonida grinned and ran off the other way.

'Careful, men,' one of the women said.

'Yes, but get them,' said another grimly. 'Get every last one of them!'

'Where are you going, Leonida?' Tiger called after the boy.

'I want to kill a few too,' Leonida said over his shoulder. But he was running away from the mill and back towards the villa.

'Let's get a move on, men,' Tiger said.

The clump of trees was a half mile away. Tiger adjusted

his tommy-gun, remounted, and pedalled off, leading the way. The makeshift army, some armed with the rifles, some taking up steel-pronged pitchforks, spread out and ran after him towards the mill.

Chapter 3

'Can you see anything, Anita?' the women in the field wanted to know.

Anita, the girl high up on the hay, sharpened her eyes and looked across the plain, but still in the direction of the mill there was nothing to see. Her eyes went to a farmhouse; an old man sat in the doorway in the sun. From the grove the cuckoo called again, then was silenced by a burst of gunfire. It sounded like a machine-gun.

'What do you see, Anita?'

Anita took the hay that was lifted up to her. Then she met the look of the old woman whose pitchfork was still raised against the load. The woman's face was lined; the mouth devastated.

'I see the Blackshirts on the run,' Anita said. 'I see our men giving it to them. I see the Fascist bastards on their knees.'

The old woman's tongue worked, spittle dripped from a corner of her mouth, and in her satisfaction she crinkled her eyes in a smile.

But Anita had only seen the old man seated in the doorway. She took another forkful of hay, brushed her dishevelled hair with a hand, and went on fervently. 'I see a bunch of Fascists running away. Now one of our men is going after them. He's alone. He's got a stick, and he's thrashing them. If you could only see how he's giving it to them!'

Another of the women raised her pitchfork jubilantly into the air. 'Harder, harder!' she shouted. 'Kill them all, kill the Fascist bastards!'

'That's right,' Anita said. 'Come on, let's all shout! Let our men hear us!'

'Kill them!' one of the women wailed. 'They slaughtered our men, now kill them!' She stabbed the stacked hay with her fork.

'Let them have it!' shouted another. 'Kill every last one of the bastards!'

'The murderers! Give it to them!'

The old woman with the withered mouth cursed her age, which, said she, robbed her even of her Socialist dreams.

Anita waved her pitchfork wildly, thrashing the imagined foe. 'I see the German soldiers tearing off their uniforms and running away. They are throwing down their guns and running. They're running too.' Now Anita's vision blurred; she hesitated. What was it? What did she see?

'I see a great cloud of dust,' said Anita. 'I see a man on a white horse, coming like the wind. He looks – he looks like Olmo!'

'If only it were Olmo!' Nina said.

'Leave the dead alone,' Edda said.

There was great excitement in Anita's voice; her eyes shone, and she was filled with emotion. Olmo was her father, who had been hounded by the Fascists and had fled them and of whom nothing had been heard for seven years.

Suddenly Anita flung her pitchfork free and plummeted down the wall of hay. 'They're trying to escape!' she yelled. 'Come on, let's stop them!' Pulling the sash of her faded housecoat tight, she grabbed for the pitchfork.

'Who?' Carlotta and Riva said.

'Attila and Regina!' Anita called out. 'Attila and Regina!'

It was like a battle cry. The other women left off raking, shook the hay off their pitchforks, and followed Anita on the run, brandishing their implements like lances. There were eight of them. Old Edda clutched her skirts and started off after the rest, her eyes ablaze, the corners of her wasted mouth wet.

Momentarily confused by the burst of gunfire coming from behind him in the general direction of the mill, Attila Bergonzi had turned his heavily loaded bicycle off the path into the tall grass along the row of grapevines. His heart beat fast, and all at once he was aware that the pullover he had on under his light-blue suit – even though he wore the collar of his white shirt open – was a mistake. Following, his wife, Regina, also turned into the shelter of the vines and came to a stop.

Seeing the beads of perspiration on her forehead, Attila drew out a handkerchief, automatically, and wiped his own

10

balding head. He could see that Regina was having trouble keeping up and that the suitcases and bundles tied over the back wheel and to the handlebars of her bicycle were giving her trouble.

Regina was heavy set, a few years older than her husband, nearly fifty. She was dressed in a smart black suit and flowered blouse, carried a leather handbag on a strap over her shoulder, and her hands were gloved with white string gloves. Fear showed on her face.

Attila felt fear too. To hide it, he avoided the woman's eyes and commented on her load. She, too, had heard the gunfire, he knew, and he wanted somehow to protect her. It was she who had insisted that they leave together.

'We'll be all right when we get to the dyke road,' he reassured her.

'Yes,' she breathed.

'Once we cross the fields it will be easier,' he said.

They heard the shouts of the women who had been haying.

'Come on!' Attila said, near panic. He pushed his bicycle through an opening in the grapes and plunged into the tall grass, shielded from the hay-field – or so he thought – by the foliage of a row of mulberry trees. But he and Regina had already been glimpsed, from her vantage point on the hay-wagon, by the daughter of his old enemy.

Instinctively, as if she knew they were being pursued, Regina began moving faster and faster and glancing behind. 'Wait for me,' she called to Attila, 'wait for me!'

Attila saw their pursuers first, the howling pack of haymakers, only fifty yards behind his wife. In a vain effort to jettison his load, he tore at the knotted cord that bound the suitcases to his vehicle. He still had the grass bank of the dyke to climb before he could pedal away.

'Wait, Attila!' Regina called, struggling now to be rid of her burden too.

With a ferocity born of an old rage, the attackers came down on Regina, overtaking her with their heated faces and animal-like grunts. Then the great fury exploded; Regina stumbled and fell, dragging a couple of the farm women with her for another yard or two. One tore at her grey-streaked hair; another ripped at her skirt. Then she was turned over as a fist caught her on the cheekbone, hard. Another smashed her nose, and she tasted blood.

11

Attila, unseeing, had scrambled to the top of the bank and was just getting to his feet when he found himself staring at two or three levelled pitchforks. He tried to retreat, but two more pitchforks had him ringed in.

'Shoot!' Regina shouted. 'Attila, shoot!' She had lunged and broken free of the tangle of arms.

He heard. Yes, he must shoot. Whipping the revolver out of his belt, he began firing blindly. His pursuers went stock-still. He had emptied the gun without taking aim, without hitting anyone. Was this a dream from which he would awake? Helpless with panic and terror now, he sought his companion with his eyes.

'Regina!' he called to her. 'Regina!'

But Regina had been flung to the ground again, and, at the foot of the grassy bank, there was a writhing of bodies and a hail of blows. Attila saw his wife's overturned bicycle with their goods spilled out on to the field. There were a few pieces of treasured silver whose sale might have kept them going. He thought how pathetic were these objects now and how there was no longer anything to insulate him from his fate.

'Regina!' he cried again, desperately, pitifully, pointing his weapon to fire it, but the revolver only clicked impotently, mocking him.

A pitchfork stuck into his arm. A second ripped into his thigh.

'Kill the murderer!' Nina shouted, her teeth clenched.

'No,' Anita said. 'He's mine, he's mine!' She had thrown herself savagely at the mutilated man whose leg spurted blood, her hands working at his throat. Other hands, dirty, horny-nailed, ripped at him.

Attila Bergonzi, the Fascist bully, the ex-foreman of the Berlinghieri estate, was an animal in a trap. The third pitchfork struck his face. Anita felt it close to her ear; her hair was even caught in it. The long middle prong pierced the man's face above the jaw and came out the other side. Soundlessly, the face froze into a grotesque bloody mask.

'Enough,' old Edda said. She studied the skewered quarry impassively. 'He's *ours,* and he must be tried for his crimes.'

Chapter 4

Outside the kitchen door of the Villa Berlinghieri, where the thick dark magnolia trees pressed close to the house, Leonida wiped his shoes and raised the barrel of his rifle. Timidity and determination were at war in him. Did his set look mask sufficiently the wobbliness he felt in his knees? Respectful son of the soil and of generations of peasants and farm hands, he knew his intrusion was about to violate the sacred privacy of his age-old masters. He hoped it would do more – far more. Shoving the door open, he started to remove his cloth cap, thought better of it, and finally tugged the visor down hard. In his striped jersey, short pants, and handed-down shoes, this thirteen-year-old boy was about to bring down a world, to topple a whole order, to start the revolution.

Alfredo Berlinghieri, the master, would be at breakfast in the dining-room. Crossing the kitchen and entering the hall, Leonida was startled by his own footsteps. The dining-room door was open. The boy sprang in, half stepping, half leaping, and was immediately filled with emotion. He had never been in this room before. For a second or two, forgetting his mission, he stood breathlessly gawking.

The master, a man of about forty-five, looked up, thoughtful, from the end of a long table set for one. He had been tapping an eggshell with the back of a spoon while Zurla, the old maidservant, hovered by him, pouring coffee from a porcelain pot. Between the man and the boy stretched an expanse of starched tablecloth, white as snow.

'What are you doing with that cannon?' Zurla said in her blunt way. She was used to cuffing the farm boys and ordering them about with tongue lashings. 'What do you think you're doing, eh?'

The boy came forward, the rifle aimed. He swallowed hard and said, too loud, 'Long live Stalin!'

Alfredo raised his pained face. In his eyes was a terrible sweetness. He wore a necktie and white shirt under an open tan cardigan. His hair was thinning and he had a close-cropped moustache which was turning grey. Everything about him was prematurely old.

'Have you gone crazy?' Zurla said, wheeling and throwing

13

herself at Leonida. Her face was flat, doglike. Zurla was, in fact, the master's watchdog. Her heavy hand caught Leonida on the face with a resounding slap. He raised the gun and fired a shot.

A din echoed through the villa. In terror, Zurla withdrew, cowering by her master's side, where, oblivious of her actions, she snatched up the porcelain pot in her apron. Then, seeing that the boy was serious, she burst into tears and began whimpering like a frightened dog.

Calmly, Alfredo turned in his chair to look for the bullet hole in the wall behind him. He found it, tiny and black, only inches above his head.

Before Leonida had broken in, Alfredo had been thinking how this room had always oppressed him – even back when he was eight or nine, when after his grandfather's suicide his father had succeeded to the head of the table to govern stiffly over the family meals. The household then had been to him an overpopulated mausoleum. His mother's sister and her daughter, Regina, poor relations, lived with them then, as did an ageing great-aunt who had left the nunnery some years before. His mother's taste ran to crowded botanical wallpapers, *trompe l'oeil* concoctions of geraniums in urns and ivies entwining marble balustrades, that effected to underline the stifling human atmosphere and that gave the dark room a heavy, hothouse-like gloom. Elaborate displays of potted African violets, set in silver trays with which his mother laid the centre of the table, further accentuated the impression of encroaching, suffocating vegetation. Speaking to anyone across the table then, as a small boy, had been like addressing someone through a hedge on a sultry day.

Today, his reasons changed, even contrary, the room was still oppressive. Spare, in the once advanced taste imposed by his wife, a kind of Bauhaus-art nouveau – clinical, geometric, modern with a vengeance – it was a décor that Alfredo found as empty and barren as he now found his own life. It was too perfect, really, in the way it matched his life. It reinforced his loneliness – this table set always for one, for himself alone, this absence of friends, of family, of warmth. In the course of his life the room had gone from the florid to the sterile. It oppressed him now, because at forty-four Alfredo Berlinghieri felt himself drained, exhausted, failed. Ada, his wife, was a drunken recluse whom he no longer laid eyes on. Olmo, his boyhood friend and spiritual brother, was gone, perhaps dead – very likely dead. The room, like them, like the estate, the house, his wealth, was dead to him.

He had been born into one world, drawn to another, and had never been able to reconcile the difference. A man's character was his fate. Alfredo Berlinghieri had been doomed early to inaction, indecision, and finally impotence. Why had he allowed his relations with Olmo and Ada – the only people who had ever mattered to him – to become poisoned? Where, why, had he failed?

The farm boy Leonida was suddenly there aiming a rifle. Alfredo welcomed his young intruder. Even such company, even this rude invasion, broke the pattern of loneliness and isolation that now shaped the master's days. Even this attention struck Alfredo as preferable to the fawning indulgence, the dutiful ministerings, of the tireless Zurla. *Yes*, he thought, before the bullet whistled over his head, *long live Stalin, indeed!*

Leonida motioned him out of his chair with the barrel of his weapon and, keeping well back of his captive, made the master move to the door. The boy cast Zurla one last look, as if to say I'll take care of you yet, you traitor.

Alfredo lifted his arms over his head, though he was unbidden to do so. He wanted to please.

'Long live Stalin!' he repeated, his voice only barely ironic.

Chapter 5

In silence the man and boy, captive and captor, moved across the threshing floor of the farm's huge central courtyard towards the brick-pillared loggia that ran the length of the cow barn. Alfredo held his hands high; Leonida kept him covered with the rifle. Stopping by one of the tubbed orange trees, the boy threw a look over his shoulder, saw no one about, and prodded the man across the shadows into the stable.

There was a long aisle with big black-and-white cows on either side – the whole Berlinghieri herd of Holstein-Friesians – blowing and snuffling and chewing their cuds. The place was whitewashed – with a vaulted ceiling and columns with carved capitals that supported the upper floor, where hay was stored clear up to the tiled roof. Swallows chattered as they streamed gracefully, almost hesitantly, in and out of the small iron-grilled windows to their mud nests which were plastered high up the white walls. The stench of cows and cow dung was hot and heavy.

Alfredo heard the entrance bolted behind him. Was he locked in alone? They had entered the stable by a middle door. At the far end, beyond the windows, was the mountain of manure festering in the sunlight. The opposite end was the dairy-room, full of pails and machinery. Somewhere a chain rattled as it was loosened. Alfredo smiled.

'She was a bit heavy-handed, wasn't she, Leonida?' Alfredo referred to Zurla and the slap. Leaving the villa, he had noticed the red mark on the boy's face and his tear-stained cheeks.

Getting no answer, Alfredo's eyes sought his jailer among the feeding cows. 'With that big gun in your hand, I barely recognized you myself,' he went on, moving towards where the sound had come from. 'Who sent you, Leonida?'

A calf scampered out from between two cows, tottering on unsteady legs.

'Tell me,' Alfredo said, 'it was your own idea, wasn't it? Tell me the truth.'

The boy gestured with the gun, forcing Alfredo into the place vacated by the calf. This incarnation of the new order, it seemed, was going to chain the master among his cattle! This was no game; Leonida was carrying out the revolution. For the moment, this boy was the new power, the new order.

Leonida leaned against a cow to open up more room, speaking to it in a familiar, guttural tone. Alfredo read the cow's name chalked up on a black slate over its head: Tina. Here was Alfredo Berlinghieri wedged between the milk cows Tina and Sofia; here was the heir and master of the Berlinghieri estate staring down the barrel of an old army rifle held in the grimy hands of a boy, of one of his own cowherds. Alfredo could not piece together the logic of what was happening.

'I see the swallows are back,' he said.

The boy would not speak.

'I've heard that in America every cow has its own drinking fountain,' Alfredo said. 'They're American cows, you see;

16

they learn fast. We should change this place, shouldn't we? Would you like to go to America? Eh, Leonida?'

Alfredo raised his eyes to see what effect the remark had made on the boy. Leonida's face showed nothing. It remained cold, fixed.

'Call me Olmo,' he said.

'Olmo?' Alfredo said. 'I thought your name was Leonida.'

'Olmo's my partisan name,' the boy said.

'You picked a good name. Did you know who Olmo was?'

'I know he was the bravest.'

Alfredo's gaze went up to an iron ring in the ceiling. His grandfather had died there, he thought. His father died in this barn too. So would he. Alfredo placed a hand on the neck of one of the cows. 'Do you know how they slaughter animals over there in America? There's very little blood. Just one shot, here, in the right place.' Now he clutched the back of his own neck. 'Here. Like in America.'

Alfredo turned the other way, facing the wall, his hands thrust through the slats of the manger. 'Well, what are you waiting for? Come on, fire, kill me. Shoot your master, Leonida. Come closer and shoot your master!'

It was senseless what was taking place, and Alfredo burned in anger. It was as though he were being called on to watch his own execution. The anger, in turn, dispelled his fear. 'Shoot your master, then!' he repeated bitterly.

The cows switched their tails, flicking at the flies.

'There are no masters any more,' Leonida said.

PART ONE

SUMMERTIME

Chapter 1

Dawn came up over the Villa Berlinghieri, sharply profiling the cluster of great elms and magnolias and the lesser trees making up the park that screened the manor house from the vast surrounding acreage of fields. At this hour, if one were approaching on foot along the dusty road that led from the highway to the estate buildings (this white track was exactly a half mile long), the towering trees, flat and black against the blush of sky, were like a massive island that raised its head, neither inviting nor forbidding, out of a dull, level sea of crop-land. Slowly, as the light gathered, one made out the enormous bulk of the farm compound closer at hand on the right, its rec-tilinear roofline unbroken, unsoftened, by any contour of vegetation. The master's house, set farther along the way and hidden in its park of stately trees, emerged only later. Then you saw the tall, spiked iron palings of the gateway, with its four lamps set on four brick piers, and beyond these gates the pebbled circular drive that ended at the villa's ochre-coloured façade.

The house itself was undistinguished. Its central portion – its original extent, that is to say – stood two stories high and was capped by a hipped roof, above which shot a small bell tower. The roof, like all roofs in that part of the country, was of curved tiles, the colour of which – tans and buffs and earth yellows and reds – resembled the kernels of a ripe ear of Indian maize.

The place had been built early in the eighteenth century by one Giovanni Battista Berlinghieri, founder of the Berlin-ghieri fortune, in a sort of half-hearted neoclassical style. It was too plain, too chaste really, and its proportions too modest, to have been a typical example of that noble style. Among its few elegant decorative ingredients were pedimented windows on the ground floor (spoiled in the middle of the nineteenth century by a masking of resoundingly ugly iron grillwork); a pedimented door with stone surrounds and flat pilasters; and over this door, with access to an upper bedroom, a stone balcony.

Succeeding generations, of course, had embellished and enlarged the house. Giovanni Battista's son, Alfredo, adorned the doorway with two large granite spheres, some two feet in diameter, set on low plinths. Another Giovanni Battista added a single-story wing on the left side of the house, assuming that a future generation would prosper and restore balance to the façade by providing the right side with an identical wing. (It was traditional in the Berlinghieri family that each Giovanni Battista named his first-born son Alfredo and that in turn each Alfredo named his Giovanni Battista; the tradition had been broken temporarily by the present master, an Alfredo, who, being assertive by nature, had deliberately and perversely named his first son Ottavio, only to repent later and give his second son the prescribed name.) But on the right side, housed separately only a few feet from the main block, were the wash-houses and storerooms, and that future generation, being of a frugal bent, refused to raze these outbuildings to make way for the wing and instead, flying in the face of all symmetry, went and built straight out from the front corner of the house a long, columned portico.

This, of course, spoiled for ever any pretence to neoclassical harmony that the house once had or was on its way to having. From then on, if the Villa Berlinghieri had wings, one of these was a broken wing, and it dangled out in an ungainly way along a side of the circular drive. This miser's one concession to taste, however, was to have planted a wisteria by the washhouse door. In time, the vine came to cover the entire expanse of squat outbuildings like an all-protective canopy or second roof. Somehow, part of it had even managed to leap the distance to the main house and now clung thickly to its corner, tempering the abandonment of symmetry there with a slight note of grace.

The top of this unsightly portico (unsightly only insofar as it spoiled the whole aspect of the house – in itself it was well-proportioned and attractive) was paved and balustraded and served as a terrace where often in early summer and autumn the family breakfasted. The lower part, with its coffered ceiling, in fact proved greatly practical. Opening out from the drawing-room, it became an outdoor extension of that part of the house, and, in the present day, was tastefully and expensively furnished with potted palms and cane tables and settees. For half a year or more, the portico was shielded from a slanting sun by elegant draperies, set between the columns, that the servants would carefully lower like blinds, a foot at a time, during the course of the day.

The villa's grounds were not extensive. When it was laid out by the first Giovanni Battista, the entire estate was only half its present size, and as the man was less interested in ostentation or personal pleasure than in increasing his wealth, the area of the park had been kept to modest limits. There were grass plots and there were gardens, to be sure, but the park's best feature was its trees – elms and chestnuts and pines at the borders. Of all these trees, the most magnificent, spreading freely in an open expanse of lawn, was a massive cedar of Lebanon.

How well the garden and park were kept varied with the generations of Berlinghieri and was dependent on the whims and particularities of individual heirs. As no Berlinghieri ever cared much about lawns, these were always in a more or less shaggy state, bright green in May and yellow by August. A Giovanni Battista, after a journey to Sicily, may have acquired a taste for orange trees or lemons and, in the huge clay pots set out evenly around the circular drive at the front of the house, would have displayed these in the months of mild weather. An Alfredo, having travelled elsewhere, may have preferred a more purely ornamental shrub that, as one entered the gates, gave the eye a sudden burst of bright colour. At least one of the masters had cared little or nothing for the garden and neglected it; the present old Alfredo liked shooting above all other pleasures, especially duck-hunting in the nearby marshes, and he left the management of the park in his daughter-in-law's hands. She was both interested and capable. It was she who saw to it that the clay urns around the drive were changed twice a year – azaleas in the spring and fan-leaved palms in the autumn.

One other feature of the park was the icehouse, or cooling-house, buried in the heart of a mammoth mound to the right of the house, nearly halfway between the portico and the cedar of Lebanon. It appeared to be a hillock sprouting a dense growth of elm trees – a wild spot, a bit of savage nature left untouched, in the midst of the civilized garden. On the mound's north side, however, was a small door, looking like the unearthed entrance to the burial vault of some ancient people. Inside, the structure had the shape of a colossal beehive. It was built of brick and was eight or nine paces across, perfectly round, and quite high. Snow was packed here in winter, watered, and made into ice; year round, meats and other perishables were hung here; and it was here also that old Alfredo Berlinghieri, the present master, chilled his wines. Over this cold storehouse, ivy gripped the trunks of the dark elms, and every summer this miniature forest was the home of a pair of cuckoos.

It was unusual that a light should burn in any part of the Villa Berlinghieri at this hour of morning. It was daybreak. Nearby, at the farm, the stable hands were barely rising. The whole Berlinghieri household retired late and slept late, and none of the servants were required – or even allowed – into the kitchen to light a fire before eight o'clock. But lights blazed in the kitchen now, as two or three serving-women bustled about the great fireplace, stoking the flames and boiling a cauldron of water.

Upstairs, a softer light burned in the elegant bedroom that boasted the stone balcony. The master's daughter-in-law, Eleonora, the wife of the second son Giovanni, lay in the early stages of labour. It was the young woman's first child; she had a terrible fear of physical pain and was in total ignorance about exactly what would happen. Already none of the hands that held her arms or soothed her brow seemed to help, and her moaning became more and more frequent.

'There!' she was told in whispers. 'There, there!'

Someone slipped a small flat object under the small of her back.

Eleonora tried to speak and couldn't. She wanted to say she was afraid. She breathed rapidly, shallowly, panted until she could stand it no more, and broke out into a piercing wild cry.

'There!' they told her, over and over again like a litany. But they knew she had a long time yet. The lamp was turned down, so that the room was semi-dark.

More lamps were lit in the house. The doctor had been sent for. Nobody could sleep any longer over the sound of Eleonora's screams.

Old Alfredo Berlinghieri put his glass of wine down on one of the cane tables, got up, and strode out for the tenth time on to the pebbled drive. The doctor's horse and coach stood alongside the door. Berlinghieri was dressed in a sober grey suit with a white waistcoat and thin black tie. He was a strong man, tall, with big yellowish teeth and a thick moustache. He wore a white hat, which he frequently removed and used to fan his face.

He drew out his watch. It was after ten. For nearly two hours he had been sitting out on the portico, restlessly getting up every now and then to glare at the drawn shutters of the balcony window. After an hour or so, to overcome his nerves, he had asked one of the servants to bring him a bottle of wine. It was now half drunk. He could hear Eleonora's cries. How long was this to go on? He put his hat back on and retired to the shade of the portico, where he sat down again and picked up his wineglass.

Berlinghieri wanted an heir. Ottavio, the older son, was thirty-three and still unmarried; pleasure was his career. He liked travel, he liked Paris, he liked expensive women, and he seldom came home any more. It was on Giovanni that the old man now pinned his hopes. After five years of a barren marriage, Eleonora was bearing them a child. It would be a boy, Berlinghieri knew; it would be another Alfredo, like him, and he had bet Leo Dalcò that it would arrive in this world before Leo's widowed daughter-in-law, Rosina, had her bastard.

Alfredo laughed at the idea of besting Leo. *That shit-pile philosopher, he'll see*, old Berlinghieri thought. Then he peered out again. The bedroom shutter was still drawn tight. Berlinghieri was a man used to getting his way. What the hell was he paying that worthless doctor for?

Chapter 2

The farm compound of the Berlinghieri estate stood in the form of a great quadrangle measuring some seventy-five yards across. Two roofed gates near the north and south corners gave access to the enclosure, part of whose centre was paved with brick and used as a threshing floor. Living quarters made up the whole east side. Here, in ten or twelve separate apartments of three floors each – bedrooms on the second floor and

23

roomy half-story attics on the third – dwelled the numerous Dalcò family, who worked the farm as labourers.

The apartments were identical, with wooden stairways connecting the floors. The kitchens, at the back on the ground floor, went mostly unused, since the family had always been in the habit of cooking and eating communally. It was in the attic, whose walls and big beams were dazzlingly whitewashed, that the Dalcò stored, in burlap sacks, the part of their pay that they took in grain.

Looking up at this façade from the middle of the threshing floor, for each apartment you saw the squarish attic window just under the eaves, a long narrow shuttered window below it, and, on the first floor, a smaller window and a door. A number of brick chimneys stuck up through the Indian-maize tiles of the roof. The building was constructed of brick and plastered, but this plaster had worn and peeled off in large patches, especially about the doorways. Because it was entirely unadorned and completely practical, there was something solid and severe and pure about this structure. It dated from the same period as the manor house. Its plaster, now faded, had once been washed an earthy reddish-brown.

The south side of the quadrangle, from the gate on, consisted of brick-pillared openings under a tiled saddle roof. Here, the heavy wagons were housed, as well as empty wine barrels, harnesses, and tools such as hayforks and hay rakes and scythes. Often when the hay crop was especially abundant, some of it was accommodated here. These vast stalls were high and open clear to the under-roof. At the back of some of them, on the rear wall above the wagon spaces, nesting boxes for pigeons had been placed. A shallow pond for the geese had been dug along here too, out in front of the end stalls.

Opposite this side, on the north, the dairy herd was stabled. Architecturally, the building matched the south wing in aspect, but its interior arrangement was otherwise. At the back, and running its entire length, were the cow stalls, divided from the rest of the structure by a brick wall. Above the cows was a haymow, leaving the forward part open up to the high roof. When empty, this area formed a long, tall loggia, though usually hay was piled here too. By the brick pillars, sheltered from inclement weather, orange trees grew in wooden tubs.

The remaining side of the quadrangle had a gallery running its entire length, too, opening into which were horse stalls and pigpens. In other parts of the building were a boiler and vats for cheesemaking. Above, in one section of the whitewashed loft under the roof, trays of silkworms were cultivated. Great fagots of brushwood, lopped off the poplars and mulberries, were also stored under these roofs. Over the horses, a central portion of the building rose to a second story and accommodated hay and feed and straw. The entire gallery was supported by square columns except in the centre, where there were four round ones. As in Greek Doric, these had plain square capitals and were without either bases or plinths. In great contrast to the exposed brick and earth-coloured plaster of the bit of upper story and the buffs and ochres of the roof tiles, the walls and columns of this gallery were washed a faded blue, like a northern sky.

Year round, from sunup to sundown, according to the season, the great central courtyard bustled with activity. The children played their games here; the men and women went about their tasks and chores. Teams of horses and oxen crisscrossed the yard at every hour; wagons, loaded and empty, came and left; tools and equipment were made and mended; dogs and cats, chickens and geese, roamed; firewood was split and stacked; wheat was threshed; wagon axles were greased; tales were told and retold, oral lessons delivered and learned; and much else consistent with the running of a large farm and a small village. For, in the midst of the flat, monotonous terrain, the place was like a rural village in its buzzing and teeming and self-sufficiency.

In the quadrangle's south-west corner a square bell tower rose a couple of stories above the roofs of the sheds. The smaller children, climbing here, pretended they looked out from a castle tower. In a matter of a few years, these dreams would be left behind. Grown up at ten or eleven, they would be working in the fields, little men and women.

Rosina Coppo, Oscar Dalcò's dark-faced young widow and Leo Dalcò's daughter-in-law, gripped the brass bedstead behind her head and breathed out in a low, steady moan. Her naked legs were bent back and held by women who stood on either side of the bed. The windows were open; the curtains tucked back to let in more light. Rosina heard horses' hooves outside and the iron-rimmed wheels of a wagon crossing the threshing floor, and from the cow barn came the incessant lowing of cattle.

This was her first birth. She tried to smile at her attendants as much as she could, almost as if apologizing for the trouble she caused them. A midwife watched from the foot of the bed, giving orders.

'When you push, push hard,' she said. 'Give it everything you've got. It's the same as taking a good shit. Push the same way.'

A cat sat on the worn tiles under a chest of drawers. Rosina looked at it, its smoky fur, then looked at a piece of bread on the floor that swarmed with flies.

An old woman popped her head in the door, asking if more hot water should be brought up.

'Keep those kids quiet out there,' the midwife said.

The landing outside the door was full of waiting, curious children, who tried to peek into the room whenever anyone entered or left. One of them, a girl, with a small unripe melon under her skirt, played at having a baby. The lot of them were shooed halfway down the stairs and warned to keep still.

As the old woman descended to the kitchen, she found Rosina's brother-in-law standing there looking somewhat stunned. Rigoletto had just made it back from the next town, having spent most of the night drunk and asleep in a ditch. He was a hunchback and was called Rigoletto after the character in the Verdi opera.

'Look at you,' the woman said. 'What have you been up to now?'

'How's Rosina?' he asked.

'It won't be long,' the woman said. 'You smell of wine.'

'I want to wash up and eat something,' Rigoletto said.

Just then there was a scream from the bedroom, and the old woman rushed out of the kitchen, raising her voice for the kids to make way, as she was carrying a great pitcher of steaming water. Rigoletto followed her. On the stairway, the children greeted him with howls. He felt himself again. He grinned, playfully cuffing them right and left and holding a finger to his lips for them to be quiet.

'That's it,' the midwife said from the end of the bed, gripping the brass bedstead herself. 'It's coming, now push – push hard!'

Rosina gritted her teeth and pushed for all she was worth. The head was out, black with hair; another effort and out came the shoulders, then suddenly the whole baby slithered out with its long cord still attached. As the midwife's expert hands lifted it, the baby wailed. It was purplish in colour.

Rosina caught a glimpse of its lifted bottom, with two huge testicles hanging down. *A boy*, she thought, *a boy*, sinking back in exhaustion. Two big round tears started in her eyes.

'Silly!' the midwife said. 'You're not going to start crying now, are you?'

She wasn't, she wasn't. But the tears came anyway. Was she crying for herself, without a husband, or for her son, who would never know his father? Rosina did not know. She smiled at the midwife and dried her tears on the pillow.

'A little more now,' the midwife told Rosina. 'We must get out the afterbirth.'

There was silence on the landing. The children held their breath, awestruck, listening to the new baby's cries.

'Boy or girl?' Rigoletto called out.

The door opened. The woman held a bundle up to view. 'Boy,' she said after all the children had had their look.

'Rosina's had a boy,' Rigoletto told the flock of children, as if they had not heard for themselves. 'You hear? Rosina's had a boy.' Hurtling down the stairs, he dashed out into the middle of the threshing floor, where he leaped up and down, announcing to the whole farm at the top of his voice that his sister-in-law had had a boy. 'It's a boy,' he shouted. 'A boy. Rosina's had a boy!'

Then he ran indoors, through the kitchen, and out the other way into the vegetable garden. Nobody was there. He ducked under a row of grapes and called the news in the direction of the hen house. No one was there either. Momentarily nonplussed, Rigoletto turned his head towards the far end of the vegetable patch and the trees bordering the villa's park. A cuckoo sounded there from the icehouse elms.

A great childish smile formed on his prematurely wrinkled face. Rigoletto sang out, 'It's a boy! Rosina's had a boy!'

Chapter 3

Old Berlinghieri heard the penetrating notes of the cuckoo too, and, on the tail of them, he heard Rigoletto's voice from the farm, broadcasting the birth of Leo Dalcò's grandson. Alfredo drained his glass, got to his feet, and strode out into the sun. Good for nothing women! He'd get a stick and go up there! A bastard born before the master's son! A bastard! He stood in the drive, muttering under his breath. He'd give that doctor a piece of his mind too.

He bent down, scooped up a fistful of pebbles, and threw them hard against the drawn shutters. Clattering loudly, they bounced back, spraying the doctor's waiting coach and startling his dozing horse. Behind Berlinghieri's back, unseen, Rigoletto had stealthily crossed the driveway and crouched by one of the big potted azaleas. From there he advanced on tiptoe to the next azalea, where he got down on one knee and kept himself hidden.

'Eleonora,' old Berlinghieri called out. 'He's on his way, push! Go on, push harder; I can tell he's coming!' Standing with his legs apart wide, as if he were the one giving birth, Berlinghieri screwed up his face and strained.

Rigoletto held a hand to his mouth, stifling a laugh. Then there was a sound of the shutters opening. Before anyone could be seen, a man's voice piped out in a high pitch of excitement, 'Papà! Papà!'

It was Giovanni Berlinghieri, the old man's son. He was out on the balcony, his back against the dark green slats of the open shutters as if he were so overcome by dizziness that he needed support. In his arms was a bundle, which he rocked and cooed at. He stammered incomprehensibly, his eyes wet with tears, and was unable to remove his gaze from his blanketed armful.

The old man felt something rise in his throat, a thrill and a tightening. He lifted a hand to shield his eyes from the sun and said, 'Alfredo's born! Alfredo, named after me!'

The hunchback was out from behind the big clay pot.

'Just a minute, Papà,' Giovanni said, disappearing indoors. A servant stepped forward and closed the shutters.

Old Alfredo was about to protest, but the hunchback was

at his elbow, seeming to have materialized from nowhere, saying slyly, 'What if it's a girl?'

'A girl?' Berlinghieri repeated, as if the idea had never occurred to him. He lifted his face to the balcony again, about to speak. At the same moment, a door opened on to the terraced portico roof. Giovanni hurried to the edge to give his father a look at the swaddled infant in better light.

'It's not a girl, is it?' old Berlinghieri said.

Giovanni gave a glad laugh. 'If it's a girl, you should see what she's got growing between her legs.'

'You're sure?' Alfredo said. He needed a moment to take all this in. There were his son and grandson looking down on him. It was summer. There was the wisteria behind the pair, dripping with blossoms. He wanted to fix these things in his mind. The full summertide of life!

'Sure I'm sure,' Giovanni said. 'It's a boy, Papà, a boy!' And he waltzed around with his son in a sudden burst of joy, and, equally suddenly, whisked him inside again.

'You see, you idiot,' the master said, turning to the hunchback. 'He's got a cock on him – a real cock!'

His arm went out. Rigoletto shrank. But the old man was beaming, smiling, his big yellowish teeth showing full, and he was only trying to put a friendly arm around Rigoletto's deformed back. And then he was babbling to the hunchback, as sweetly as could be, and leading him off across the garden to the fastness of the icehouse.

'This is a great day, Rigoletto,' the master said, taking a key out of his waistcoat pocket. 'The birth of the first Berlinghieri of the twentieth century!'

'Then it's a great day for us too,' Rigoletto said.

'Why not?' the master said. 'It's destiny for them both to be born the same day. This is a great day for all of us, and that's why we're going to celebrate it now.'

The small door was open. Rigoletto felt a breath of icy air on his legs, then on his face, but it was too dusky inside for him to make out anything apart from the old man's bulky figure. He could sense the spaciousness, the volume, of the place, however.

Rigoletto was handed two icy bottles. Then, as if a veil were torn from his eyes, he saw. There were bottles of every description – some in cases, some with their necks sticking up from between cakes of ice. He gaped.

'Here.' The master handed him a third bottle.

'Hey!' Rigoletto purred. 'I've died and gone to heaven. This is the Garden of Eden. You're God, and if you let me have that key, I'll be Saint Peter!'

'What I'll let you have is a good swift kick in the ass, my boy,' Berlinghieri said. 'Now, mind you don't drop those bottles.'

He locked up as Rigoletto went on a few steps ahead of him, in his hands the ice-cold bottles of wine safely, almost fondly, gripped by their long necks.

'A great day,' Berlinghieri was saying, half to Rigoletto, half to himself. The old man was satisfied. He had lost the bet but had gained a male heir, and that was what truly mattered, that was what he had wanted more than anything else. 'Yes, a very great day for the Berlinghieri!'

Chapter 4

'Drink up, drink up, you black crow!' Alfredo said. 'If you don't seize an opportunity like this, you'll never drink good wine again.'

Don Tarcisio, the village priest, forced a smile and took the proffered glass, thanking his host. He was a small, fat-faced man, who, at that moment, under his tight collar and great black skirt, was feeling uncomfortably warm. The cold white wine was certainly welcome, but he could not say that he liked the black crow remark. Still, Berlinghieri was the mainstay of his church, the old landowner knew it, and Don Tarcisio could little afford to offend him.

Desolina, a maidservant of about seventy, all skin and bones and a wispy voice to match, had just put down a tray of glasses on one of the cane tables, and, not wanting to be dismissed without a word to Don Tarcisio first, she went to the blinds and dropped them a foot against the encroaching sun. When she saw her master filling two more glasses, she approached the priest, saying, 'He has his father's eyes, he has. And his mother's mouth.'

'And his grandfather's money!' Don Tarcisio said.

'Very witty today, Don Tarcisio,' old Alfredo said cuttingly. He supported the church because the Berlinghieri always had – it was expected of them – and he did not know how to do otherwise, but he did not like priests, whom he considered parasites. He enjoyed making this one feel it too. He offered to refill Don Tarcisio's glass now, forcing him to finish the first one too fast. Then he handed his son a glass and said, 'Giovanni, haven't you asked that doctor to join us? He took long enough over the job; he must be nursing a healthy thirst.'

Giovanni turned to Desolina, telling her to ask the doctor to come down for some wine.

'So the Berlinghieri court has a new jester, I see,' the priest said. He sneered at Rigoletto, who stood to one side looking ill at ease.

'Never fear, Don Tarcisio,' old Berlinghieri said, 'we'll never find anyone to replace you.'

The priest's face coloured an even deeper shade of red. He quickly turned to Giovanni and said sweetly, 'After all your efforts, you've finally got yourself an heir. I drink to you; I drink to him; I drink to his mother.' He raised his glass momentously.

'Just a minute. Rigoletto, won't you join us in drinking to that?' Showily, graciously, Alfredo Berlinghieri served the marvelling hunchback. 'Now let's all drink. To my son, to my grandson, to my daughter-in-law!'

'Chin, chin,' Rigoletto said.

Giovanni smiled, the priest drank in silence, and Rigoletto quaffed his glass hastily, in hopes of receiving another.

'Now I'll have somebody I can make toe the line,' Giovanni said to Don Tarcisio.

'Ah, here comes the good country doctor now,' Alfredo said, filling another glass. 'Punctual as ever.'

'Will you have something, doctor?' Giovanni asked.

'I never drink while making a call,' the doctor said. 'But this is a very special occasion, and today I make an exception.'

They all laughed because the young doctor was known to like his wine. He was also a crony of Giovanni's. Rigoletto laughed too, hoping it would get his glass filled again.

'Giovanni!' Alfredo thundered, motioning his son aside and leaving the priest and the doctor to converse together.

'Yes, Papà?' Giovanni came almost to attention.

'Have you anything to write with?'

'Of course, Papà.' He drew a pencil out of an inner pocket of the coat of his white linen suit.

'Then let's write a letter to that playboy brother of yours,' old Berlinghieri said. Stepping off the portico, he began to stroll across the lawn – his hands behind him, the better to think. His son followed, rummaging in his pockets for a scrap of paper. 'On second thought, let's make it a telegram,' the old man said. 'Take this down now. Ottavio Berlinghieri, Hotel des Bains, Lido, Venice.' He stopped and confronted his son. 'Well, aren't you writing?'

'I'm afraid I haven't anything to write on, Papà,' Giovanni said, embarrassed.

'You're thirty years old, man. Invent, for God's sake, invent,' Alfredo told him, and he began striding straight for the over-hanging branches of the cedar of Lebanon.

It was only with an effort that Giovanni kept up with his father's pace. Extending his left arm to expose the starched cuff of his shirt, he stopped, feverishly wrote on the stiff sleeve end, cantered after his father, halted, wrote again, chased again.

'Announce birth first Berlinghieri twentieth century, stop,' Alfredo dictated. 'Pray God he grows up different from you, stop. Found wife yet, question mark. Yours affectionately, Papà. Got all that?'

'Yes, Papà.'

'Read it back, then.' When he had heard his message, Berlinghieri turned abruptly on his heels and started for the distant portico. He would enjoy another glass of wine now.

'You two are staying for lunch, I trust,' old Berlinghieri said to Don Tarcisio and the doctor. He had ordered Rigoletto around to the kitchen to ask for a large wicker hamper.

The doctor agreed.

'In these matters, I am at your complete disposal,' the priest said ingratiatingly.

'You honour us, I'm sure, Don Tarcisio,' Berlinghieri said with obvious sarcasm. He then addressed his son. 'I have been thinking that we should rename this farm for our new century. What do you say to that?'

Though unasked, the priest said that Alfredo had always been known as a man who was on the side of progress. Giovanni said that he did not know what to say.

'*Novecento*,' old Berlinghieri said experimentally. 'The

twentieth century.'

'Would you spell it out or use numerals?' the doctor asked, faintly amused.

'Which should you prefer, Don Tarcisio?' the old landowner wanted to know.

'*Novecento* spelled out, I should say,' the priest answered. 'There is a certain dignity to the word, and, besides, with numerals you always run the risk of being understood to mean the year nineteen hundred alone.'

Just then Rigoletto rejoined them with the empty hamper. The master put the question to the hunchback.

'I would say numbers,' Rigoletto spoke up boldly, without pondering it.

The doctor and the priest were visibly embarrassed. Giovanni was as well, and he filled everyone's glass again. When he finished, his father took the bottle from him and poured the hunchback a glass.

'Well, come on then,' Alfredo prompted. 'Give us your reasons.'

Rigoletto took the wine and grinned from ear to ear, revealing a mouthful of stumpy teeth. 'I know the numbers,' he said. 'But I never learned to read words.'

Alfredo laughed heartily and congratulated the hunchback. 'So be it,' he said. 'We'll make it numerals.'

There was a frosty silence.

'Come along now,' he said to Rigoletto. 'I told you we had some celebrating to do today. I'll be back shortly, gentlemen,' he announced to the rest of the gathering, and, moving off at an easy pace, he and Rigoletto disappeared from sight around the wild clump of elms that were islanded in the expanse of lawn.

'As I was saying, Don Tarcisio,' Giovanni resumed, his voice controlled, deliberate, cold, 'you keep obeying and obeying, year in and year out, and one day you find you have a desire to give orders yourself.'

But he was looking at neither the doctor nor the priest. His level gaze was fixed on the mound where, every summer, faithfully, the cuckoos came to the elms.

Chapter 5

Nine or ten men in a staggered row moved across the hay-field in a steady rhythm, swinging scythes and leaving behind them a wake of sweet-smelling grass. Through the distant treetops, the villa's bell tower could just be made out. The day was sultry. The blue sky was slowly filling with brilliant white clouds which rose in high piles, mushrooming.

From the grass-choked ditch at the edge of the park, Alfredo Berlinghieri saw the mowers and turned to urge Rigoletto forward. The hunchback was coming through the trees, his head down, stooped, bearing the wicker hamper with its dozen bottles of French champagne. Satisfied, Alfredo set off in his long stride, cutting through the rich, knee-high grass. Rigoletto breasted the ditch and quickened his step.

Already, in his elation, the old landowner was waving his arms at the men and shouting for them to stop their work. All down the line, one by one the men came to a halt, leaning on the long handles of their scythes.

'Hold the work,' old Berlinghieri said. 'It's a special day. Drink up, Orso!' He waited for the hunchback to catch up, then handed Orso Dalcò an ice-cold bottle out of the hamper. With a thumb, Orso raised the hat off his brow and beamed. The neck of the champagne bottle was wrapped in gold foil. Berlinghieri took another bottle out of Rigoletto's hamper and strode to the next man.

'Here, Turo, this is for you,' he said. 'A celebration!' Turo Dalcò was given a bottle, and the landowner and the hunchback moved on.

'No work today, Censo,' Berlinghieri said to the next man, squashing Censo Dalcò's hat down on his head and laughing. 'This is a special wine. Drink up, now!'

'Who died?' one of the last men called out.

Berlinghieri flushed a lark out of the grass, wheeled, and fired an imaginary shotgun at it.

'No work today!' Censo called back.

There were three bottles left. 'Where's Dalcò?' Alfredo asked the last man in the row. The man pointed to a line of grapevines at the edge of the field where a great solitary elm raised its head, a dark green dome of foliage against the summer sky. From that quarter, the landowner heard the sound of even, exact blows of steel hammering steel. That would be old Leo sharpening the blade of his scythe. Shoving a bottle into the mower's hands, Berlinghieri repeated, mechanically now, that it was a special day and to drink up. He then quickly summoned Rigoletto forward.

'We're down to the last one,' Rigoletto said, tagging behind the master.

'There are two, you rascal,' Berlingieri said, and he reached behind him to drag the hunchback along by the arm.

'And we're three,' Rigoletto muttered under his breath.

Leo Dalcò, his legs spread wide, glanced up from the elm's green shade and saw the master and his son approach across the drying swathes. But Leo's hammer neither missed a stroke nor slowed. The old man was bent over the curved blade of his scythe, beating its cutting edge thin against an iron punch driven into the ground.

He was a big man, as tall as Berlinghieri, somewhat more slender, and about the same age. His sleeves were rolled up to the elbows, and he wore a rope belt around his baggy trousers. His face was leathery and deeply lined; he had large, quick, intelligent eyes and a thick greying moustache. He had been a handsome man and still was. There was something solid and quiet about him, something as sure as the earth he had spent a lifetime working. He had, in short, all the air of a patriarch.

Berlinghieri stooped to lay a bottle in the grass in front of Leo. 'Your grandson was born first,' the landowner said. 'I've lost the bet.'

Dalcò hammered on without looking up. Rigoletto squatted down, a hand on the hamper, his eye on the remaining bottle. He touched it, almost fondly, to see if it were still cold.

'It was destiny for them both to be born on the same day,' old Berlinghieri said.

'Destiny! That calls for a drink,' Rigoletto said.

Dalcò eyed the blade, seemed satisfied, and laid his hammer aside. Getting to his feet, he put a hand behind his back and drew a hone from a hollow cow's horn that hung from his belt. The smooth stone dripped water. Leo began stroking the blade with the damp stone and testing the edge with his fingers. 'So mine was born first, was he?' he said. 'You know how many of us that makes now?'

'I've lost count,' Berlinghieri said.

'I haven't,' Dalcò said. 'When we sit down at eat there are forty of us around the table.'

'Well, you're a lucky man, Leo, admit it. This one may be a bastard, but at least he's a boy.'

'Don't bastards eat too?' Rigoletto said.

Dalcò handed the scythe to the master and picked up the bottle, studying it carefully, with respect. He held it at arm's length and read the label: POMMERY. Then he undid the foil, twisted off the wire, and prised the cork loose between his thumbs. There was an explosion, the champagne foamed up, and Leo quickly brought the bottle to his lips not to lose any. Rigoletto scampered after the cork.

'If mine was born first, it's only natural,' Dalcò said, lowering the bottle. 'First came the peasants, then came the masters.'

'Masters, peasants – balls!' Berlinghieri said. 'When we're born, we're all equal.'

'All equal, are we?' Rigoletto said, casting an eye over his shoulder at his deformity. He held his hand out to his father for the bottle.

Leo dried his moustache on his forearm, wiped the mouth of the bottle, and passed it to the master. Berlinghieri took a long drink.

'And now there's one more master in the world,' Leo Dalcò said. 'You know, for every master born some poor peasant has to break his back working twice as hard. And working twice as hard means living half as much.' He took the bottle and drank.

'There you go again with that Socialist talk of yours,' Berlinghieri said. 'Don't you see our interests are the same? We're all bound to the soil.'

'But some of us are more bound than others,' Dalcò said. 'What you call destiny, I call exploitation.'

They had had this discussion before – many times. They had been having it off and on for years. By now it was in the nature of a friendly rivalry. Once Berlinghieri had made the mistake of saying that he was a plain man like Leo, pointing out that his interests ran to the fields, to the outdoors, to shooting fowl and hunting duck – simple pleasures. Leo had answered that as he had had to work in the fields all his life, his interests ran to the indoors, to a good rest, and to a warm fire in winter.

'But they were born together,' Berlinghieri said now. 'That must mean something.'

'It probably means the two of us will die together,' Dalcò said.

Berlinghieri shook his head. 'To hell with you, you shit-pile philosopher. I say it's destiny. They'll grow up together; they'll get along well and be friends. I want mine to study law.'

'I want mine to study thieving,' Dalcò said.

'In that case, better make him a priest,' Rigoletto said.

All three laughed. Now Berlinghieri had the champagne. He tipped it up, drank, and handed it to the hunchback. Rigoletto squinted into the bottle and turned it upside down. A couple of drops ran out.

'Tell you the truth, I prefer our own wine,' Dalcò said.

'I didn't like it either,' Rigoletto said, pointedly. 'I knew straightaway it wasn't from around here.'

Leo moved off a few paces and started mowing.

'Ottavio sends it,' Berlinghieri said, almost apologetic, speaking to the old patriarch's back. 'Visitors are fond of it. God-dammit, Dalcò, you know I like a good Lambrusco better than anything else myself.' He then wheeled around to Rigoletto, who was picking at the gold foil that wrapped the neck of the last full bottle. 'I think we've had enough drinking now. I want you to get yourself down there to the town hall fast.'

'Births and deaths,' Rigoletto said. 'I'm always the one who goes.'

'Tell them the boy's name is Alfredo, like me. Alfredo Berlinghieri, son of Giovanni Berlinghieri and Eleonora née Rossetti.' Berlinghieri broke off and called to Leo. 'And yours? What name will you give him?'

'Olmo,' Dalcò said.

'Olmo? Like the elm?'

'That's right,' Dalcò said. 'Like the elm.'

'And like the shovel handle too,' Rigoletto added.

Leo mowed on, speaking over his shoulder. 'Olmo Dalcò, son of the late Oscar Dalcò and of Rosina Coppo.'

'But Oscar's been dead for four years,' Berlinghieri said.

'That's the point,' Rigoletto said. 'You have to show respect for the dead.'

These wily contadini, they had you every time! Berlinghieri picked up the hamper and laughed. Two births on the same day, within the same hour, and only a few yards apart. All right, one was the son of a master, the other the son of a peasant; but there was no denying it – it was destiny, and destiny had to be embraced. He laughed; he laughed so hard that he had to set the hamper down. When he stopped, all his good feelings were restored.

Rigoletto grinned broadly, a face full of stumpy teeth, and handed the master the big wicker basket.

Enjoying the joke, enjoying the master's laughter, Leo Dalcò stood erect, his wrists crossed over the end of the handle of his scythe. The years had taught their lessons and he suffered no illusions; you were friends with the masters as long as things went well with them. These two boys, born in the same place, in the same hour – this was no more than coincidence. It was not to say that the padrone was a bad man. As a matter of fact, as padroni went, Alfredo Berlinghieri was a good one. The system, Dalcò knew – that was what was bad, that was what had to be changed.

But for now he shook off these thoughts. He had won the bet, and they had all drunk champagne together. It was time he welcomed his new grandson into the world.

Leo Dalcò tipped back his hat, lifted his head, and from the bottom of his long frame, he laughed at the life-giving sky.

It was the heart of summer. Larks shot up into the air, hovering blithely, bubbling with song. Swallows skimmed the mown fields, and grasshoppers fled in droves before the onslaught of the scythes. In comic rolling progress, a hedgehog regained the tall grass, where it safely hid itself.

Rigoletto ambled across the fields towards the village; old Dalcò began to swing his scythe again, rhythmically, leaving behind him a perfect swathe; and Alfredo Berlinghieri made his way back to the cool green of the park and his waiting guests.

A bell sounded from the farm tower. Each of the three men halted briefly to listen. The earth sang and the horizon shimmered. Each of them at that moment felt himself standing at the centre of the world, at the centre of creation. In the heart of the Emilian plain it was the heart of summer.

PART TWO

THE SUMMER WANES

Chapter 1

Giovanni Berlinghieri, in his customary white linen suit, matching white waistcoat, and Panama hat, brought the horse to a halt and pulled his eye goggles down around his throat. He sat there, the reins still in his left hand, momentarily imperious and self-satisfied, as the knot of men drew in around him.

'Bravo, Papà, bravo!' shouted his son Alfredo, running to catch up with the new contraption that his father was trying out. It was 1907; Alfredo was six.

The machine, a horse-drawn mechanical hay rake, was the first of its kind in the area and the first piece of mechanized equipment to be introduced into the Berlinghieri estate. It was Giovanni's particular idea, and it had arrived by train only that morning. It was a simple enough affair, consisting of a set of curved teeth, raised and lowered by a lever, mounted on to a light two-wheeled vehicle like a sulky, with a pair of shafts in front for harnessing the horse to. This model was painted a spanking bright red.

'Leo, want to try it out?' Giovanni said to old Dalcò, who stood by, curious, sceptical, distrustful.

'Yes, you try it too, Leo,' the boy said, flush with excitement.

'I'm not climbing up on that damn red devil,' the old man said.

'Orso, let me climb up,' young Alfredo begged.

'On me or the machine?' Orso said. He had picked the boy up in his powerful arms and flung him into the air. When Alfredo stopped laughing, Orso set him astride his shoulders.

'No,' Alfredo said, 'on the red devil.'

Rigoletto took the horse by the bridle, stroking its muzzle. A crownlike branch of plane leaves shaded the animal's head from the summer sun. Rigoletto was sullen.

'The two of us aren't afraid of anything, are we, Master Alfredo?' Orso said, seating the boy on one of the shafts by his father's feet. Alfredo was dressed in a sailor suit, with trousers that came just below the knee. His elegant clothes and well-scrubbed look set him apart and gave him an appearance of being pampered and delicate. Orso held him in place on the shaft.

Giovanni shifted in the seat, his watch out in his hand. 'At this rate, it will do two acres in half an hour. That would take six men at least half a day.'

Leo picked up a fistful of hay. 'What about this?' he said. 'You call this a job well done? Look at all the hay it leaves behind.'

'Let me climb up on you again, Orso,' Alfredo said.

Turo drew in. He had been spraying the grapes and still wore the copper spray tank strapped to his back. He peered at the teeth of the rake and looked at his father.

None of the Dalcò said anything. Even Orso, who knew he would eventually operate the machine, remained more or less aloof. All of them expected there would be talk about the machine around the table that night.

Giovanni surveyed the field from his perch. 'Oh, that's nothing,' he told Leo. 'Don't you agree?'

Alfredo had slipped Orso's big hat off his head and put it on his own. Orso was the boy's favourite of all the Dalcò family. Orso always carried him on his shoulders, and if Alfredo told him to, Orso would trot like a horse. Orso always let him wear his big hat too.

'Leo, Leo, doesn't the red devil do a wonderful job?' Alfredo said from high on the shoulders of Leo's oldest son.

Leo ignored the boy.

Something was wrong. Alfredo could tell by the men's faces. He could tell because Leo would not answer him. What was it about the red devil that the men did not seem to like? He wanted to ask his father, but something told him not to speak to him about it now. It spoiled the fun when the men went silent this way. *Why couldn't everybody like the red devil?* he wondered; *it was such a wonderful machine.*

Alfredo felt uneasy in the pit of his stomach, and all at once he wished he were somewhere else, where these spectres of unspoken hostility could not touch him.

He wanted to get down off Orso now and, before everything became spoiled, remove himself from his father and the men. He had caught a glimpse of Olmo and someone else playing

40

beyond the hedgerow by the irrigation ditch. Slipping down Orso's body as though he were sliding down the trunk of a stout tree, Alfredo ran towards the hedgerow as fast as he could, getting away.

Orso's big hat was still on his head.

Alfredo parted the tall grass and watched.

Nina lay sprawled on the bank, her face in her hands, motionless. Olmo was in the ditch, standing stock still in the water. The water came halfway up Olmo's thighs, just to where his frayed trousers ended, but he was wet right up to his rope belt. The sleeves of his ragged shirt were rolled above his elbows, and they were soaked too. He was hunting frogs. Neither Olmo nor Nina made a sound.

Then Olmo crouched and darted, catching a frog in his quick hands. 'Nineteen!' he shouted, triumphant.

Nina was visibly thrilled.

Wading to the bank, Olmo threaded the live frog on to a length of wire. The frog quivered and throbbed.

Nina made a face of disgust. 'How awful, Olmo!' she said. 'I want to throw up!'

Putting a finger to his lips, Olmo slipped back to the middle of the ditch. Rushes grew along the margins of the water, and blue dragonflies hovered there. Slowly Olmo went into a crouch, then made a quick pounce.

'Twenty!' he shouted. He had a frog by its hind legs in the fingers of one hand. Quickly cupping it in the palm of his other hand, he moved to the bank and skewered the animal with the wire. Then he stationed himself a few yards farther along the ditch.

Alfredo marvelled at Olmo. He wished he dared hunt frogs, but he was afraid of ruining his clothes. Lucky Olmo, he did not have to wear shoes and could roll up his shirt-sleeves, like his uncles. Alfredo's mother scolded him if his sleeves weren't kept buttoned. He did not want to let Olmo know, but Alfredo was secretly scared of frogs. They were slimy! He knew he could never have held one and pierced its throat with wire the way Olmo did.

Now Nina turned her face and saw him. He wanted her to notice Orso's hat on his head.

'Twenty-one!' Olmo called out just then.

'You look like an umbrella,' Nina said to Alfredo.

'You look like a rabbit,' Alfredo told her.

'You look like a calf,' Nina said.

Alfredo stretched out beside her on the grass, tipping Orso's big hat back on his head.

Olmo made his way to the other two, annoyed. With a forced grin, he hoisted himself out of the water and lunged at them with his squirming frog. 'Kiss it, kiss it!' he said.

But Alfredo had scampered out of reach.

'You go shit,' Nina said.

Olmo's felt hat, with its round crown, lay on the grass next to the dead frogs. He kneeled beside it and skewered his catch. When he stood up, his face had a savage look. There was blood on his hands, and that, together with his hair – a mass of tight curls, damp with sweat and limp now – accented his wildness. The wildness worried Alfredo, and he stepped back. Noticing this, Olmo advanced towards him with the string of frogs.

'No tricks,' Alfredo said, tense.

'Shitpants!' Olmo said.

'Olmo's a bastard. Olmo's a bastard,' Nina began to chant.

'That's my uncle's hat,' Olmo said.

'He gave it to me,' Alfredo said, holding his ground.

Olmo ran at him and knocked the hat off Alfredo's head, then flung himself at Nina, shoving her to the ground and straddling her. He had made a loop of the wired frogs, and now he dangled these in front of Nina's mouth.

'Eat them! Eat them!' Olmo pressed a frog against the girl's clenched lips.

'You're a bully to scare a girl,' Alfredo said, moving closer.

Olmo shook the frogs at Alfredo, stopping him. 'You're scared, aren't you?' Olmo taunted. 'You're a coward!'

'You're a bully!'

'You're a coward! Run, coward shitpants!'

'Bully!'

'All right,' Olmo said. 'Come with me if you're not a coward.'

'Where?' Alfredo said. He knew it was a challenge; he knew he had to say yes.

Olmo stared at him defiantly. He had let Nina up. Nina looked at Alfredo in wonder. Olmo put on his felt hat. Then he took up the frogs and set the ring of them around the crown of his hat, so that their fat speckled bodies lay clustered on the brim and their legs dangled in front of his eyes. Olmo glowered at Alfredo through the curtain of dangling legs.

It was repulsive. Alfredo's heart beat with fear and excitement. He handed Orso's hat to Nina and told her to take care of it. Then he faced Olmo. 'All right,' he said, defiant himself. 'I'll come.'

Chapter 2

At suppertime, the teeming Dalcò kitchen took on the combined aspect of a circus, a bawdy house, a mess hall, a tribunal, a place of entertainment, and an unorganized and unorganizable military retreat. The men, nearly forty of them, sat jammed in at long, narrow wooden tables set end to end as in a banquet hall, but in a room too small to accommodate half that number. The women sat together on the far side of the same room in a knot around the hearth – sometimes nearly singeing themselves, always overheated, alternately eating out of their laps and jumping up to ferry replenishments across to the men. Huddled on the stairway and outside in the dooryard, the children ate with the dogs and cats. Even the smells that hung in the air clashed and conflicted – cooked food, animals, unwashed bodies, cheap tobacco, wood fires, kerosene lamps.

There was always noise, a cacophony of sounds, a din of argument and complaint, a cross fire of accusations and bickering and orders to bring this or take that away, a clatter of spoons and bowls or tipped-over bottles, a wail of brats, a hen kicked under the table and raising a squawk, a cat hissing at a dog, chairs shuffled forward or scraped back. And in the increasingly futile effort to make oneself heard, everybody raised his voice.

The men wore their hats and hunched over their plates, elbow to elbow, arms on the table, at first eagerly devouring their food, assuaging both hunger and the numbing pain of fatigue, and speaking little. Some of them, so tired from the day's work, would chew and feed themselves with their eyes shut; others would doze off after a glass or two of wine; occasionally, a head went right down on the table. Even this meal, because the men were struggling to best hunger and thirst and exhaustion and even boredom, was more like work than a time of rest. All along the table there were bottles of their own Lambrusco, great serving bowls of beans with ladles sticking out, vast salads. The main food, served on round wooden platters a couple of feet across, was polenta. The men helped themselves to pieces of it that they hacked out like wedges of pie. The older women sat along the walls, isolated, spooning their food out of bowls held cradled in the crooks of their arms.

Rigoletto's head went up from his polenta. 'Anyone know how far it is from here to the Madonna dei Prati?'

'How far?' Turo said, without looking at him. 'It must be all of four miles.' He sat opposite Rigoletto, feeding a kitten on his knees.

'Well, I once saw a train as long as from here to the Madonna dei Prati,' Rigoletto said.

Reaching for the beans, Anghinoni, one of Leo's sons-in-law, said, 'Sure, and my prick stretches from here to Piacenza.'

There was an outburst of raucous laughter among the women. 'He's always bragging!' one of them said, licking the polenta from her fingers.

'He's got something to brag about,' Anghinoni's wife said.

'When it comes to trains,' Rigoletto said, insistent, 'I'm the only one here who's ever been on one.'

Censo roused himself out of a sudden drowsiness, yawned, and said, 'A train – now there's a real machine for you. Not like that contraption out there.' He jerked a thumb at the courtyard.

'I'm the one who handles that thing out there,' Orso said angrily. 'Enemies of progress, that's what the rest of you are.' He was still smarting from their argument over the new hay rake. All of them but him were against it.

Leo sat at the head of the table in his usual place with his back to a window. From there he saw everything and heard everything, but mostly he kept silent – his eyes narrowed, pensive. A hen wandered in, hunting for something to peck at by the table. Orso gave it a kick that sent it and feathers flying.

'Who pays for it, eh?' Turo said. 'Answer me that.'

'The padrone pays for it,' Orso said.

'If the padrone pays for it, that means it saves him money,' Censo said.

'Yes, it saves him money,' Orso said. 'And it saves my back. I don't have to sweat so much, and that makes me happy.'

'A happy man's a satisfied man,' someone said.

'And a satisfied man's a fool,' Rigoletto said bitterly. 'The padrone, my ass! We pay for the machines – us – with the sweat of our balls!'

From the corner by the hearth, Nella was saying to Olmo's mother, 'First he gave my Paride lice. Then he gave them to the baby. And they're so bad even with kerosene you can't get rid of them.'

'How many times I've tried to pick them off him, but he always runs away,' Rosina said.

'The lice are the least of it,' Adelina said. 'Today he made my Nina eat a live frog.'

Rigoletto raised his voice to quiet the women. 'What do the bunch of you know about it, anyway?' he said.

'And what the hell do you know about it?' Censo said.

'I know because I went to the meeting of the League,' Rigoletto said.

'You'd be better off doing more work and less running around,' Roncone, another son-in-law, said.

Up and down the table there was laughter.

'Let him talk,' Leo said. 'What did they say at the meeting?'

'They said to go around the farms preaching social justice you had to understand, and to understand you had to go to the meetings. They said the honest peasant was bled white, while the landowner got fatter.'

'Amen,' Turo said.

'We know all that already,' Leo said. 'What else did they talk about?'

'They said working by the day is for the horse and the ox,' Rigoletto said. 'They said we had to wage a battle to be paid by the hour.'

'By the day or by the hour, in the end it's still labour,' Censo said.

'Our labour is our only wealth,' one of the others said. 'We must sell it more dearly.'

'That's right,' somebody else said. 'Ottavio Berlinghieri buys French whores with the sweat of our brow. His father needs ten fancy shotguns for hunting ducks, and we can't have a goddam sparrow to eat on our polenta.'

There was nodding and agreement to that all around the table. In the pause, Leo Dalcò lifted his head like a forest animal pricking its ears. His gaze went to the corner by the hearth. 'Who's crying there?' he said.

All eyes shifted to the hearth, where Rosina sat in tears, an apron covering her face.

'Rosina wants to send Olmo away to the priests,' an old woman said.

'Why?' Leo asked.

'Because he's a devil,' the woman said.

'They want to take him away from me,' Rosina sobbed. 'Imagine making my son a priest – my flesh and blood.' And she buried her head again.

'You wanted your fun, didn't you? Now cry,' Nella said.

'Leave her alone,' Orso said. 'That's all water under the bridge now.'

'Bastards always grow up meaner than others,' another woman spoke up. 'Everybody knows that.'

A fist came down heavily on the table, tumbling an empty bottle and making a few glasses jump. There was immediate silence, and everyone turned to the end of the room where Leo sat outlined against the window frame. 'Bastard? Who said bastard? There's no bastard in my house, do you hear? Olmo's father is one of us. Is that true or not?'

No one spoke.

'Is that true or not, Rosina?' Leo said, 'Tell them, Rosina. You know.'

'We all know,' someone said.

There was embarrassed laughter.

'It's true,' Rosina said, drying her tears. 'Of course I know who his father is. How could I help but know?'

Leo looked down the table, but no one would meet his gaze. Then he wiped his big moustaches and broke into a wide smile. 'A priest in our family, eh? Father Dalcò!'

Now there was uproarious laughter from both the men and the women, and even Rosina managed a smile. Glasses were refilled.

'Olmo!' old Leo thundered. 'Hey, Olmo!'

Olmo set his bowl on the stone threshold, where he had been listening, and stood up. Clenching something tight in his fist, he shyly stepped inside.

'Olmo Dalcò,' his grandfather called to him.

The lamps were not yet lit. In the twilit room, Olmo made out the backs of the men on the near side of the table and the row of faces on the other. They stared at him. From the glowing hearth, the women stared too. Even the smaller children, hugging the banisters alongside the staircase, gaped.

More than anything, Olmo would have liked diving under the table, but only a quick cat could have made it through such a profusion of legs, human and chair, and gained cover there. Instead, head down, he just shuffled forward. Then a pair of arms was grasping him and lifting him straight up, and the first thing he knew Olmo found himself standing on the table.

'Now that you're grown – ' Leo began to say.

'Still hasn't learned to wipe his ass, though,' Rigoletto said, reaching out and pinching the boy's bottom.

'Go shit,' Olmo said, and he threw a kick in the hunchback's direction.

'Come here,' Leo said. 'Now that you're grown, remember this. You'll learn to read and you'll learn to write, but you'll still be Olmo Dalcò, son of peasants. Understand?'

'And a poor son of a bitch,' somebody piped up.

In his bare feet and short trousers that were still damp around the middle, Olmo picked his way among the plates and glasses, walking the length of the tabletop.

'You'll go off to the army,' Leo went on solemnly, as though preaching a sermon, 'and you'll learn about the world. You may even learn to obey.'

'And to eat shit,' someone else interrupted.

Leo droned on. 'You'll take a wife, and you'll work for your children, understand?'

Olmo murmured faintly. Out of the corner of his eye, he saw Nina pressed against the door jamb.

'And you'll learn to be patient,' one of his uncles said.

'And who will you be, eh? Who will you always be?' his grandfather said.

'Olmo Dalcò,' the boy said, head still lowered. He stood only a few feet from his grandfather now, his fist clenched tight, trying to work up the courage to look the old man in the face.

'You'll be Olmo Dalcò, peasant,' Leo corrected. 'You understand that? There are no bastards, no priests, in this house.'

47

With that, the trace of ironic mockery underlying the old man's solemn tones became clear. There were smiles and laughter now. Leo's words, they all knew, had been a kind of solemn blasphemy.

Leo himself smiled, then going grave again asked, 'What's that in your hand?'

Olmo put his fist behind his back.

'I know, I know!' Nina cried out from the doorway. She hopped up and down, bursting to tell.

'It's nothing,' Olmo said. 'I got nothing in my hand.'

'Oh, yes, he has,' Nina said. 'It's money. Olmo's got money.'

Leo fastened his eyes on to the boy's and held out his palm. Olmo unclenched his fist, letting his grandfather see his two coins.

'Where did you steal them?' Leo said.

'Signor Giovanni gave them to him,' Nina said.

'I earned it myself,' Olmo said. 'I sold him my frogs. It's my money.'

'Well, if it's yours, then it belongs to all of us,' the old man said.

Nina was even with him now. The whole family's gaze was on Olmo, as he stood there in dumb fear of his grandfather's wrath. Olmo was trapped, caught.

The memory of this moment was to live with Nina and haunt her into adulthood. Nearly forty years later, when they all believed Olmo to be dead, Nina would not forget the boy standing on the end of the table in the long summer twilight, the felt hat on his head, mute. And not forgetting it, not forgetting her betrayal, she would look stonily on the man she held responsible for Olmo's disappearance and, seeking atonement; want with her own hands to pitchfork this man to death.

Olmo tightened his lips and felt his chest tighten. The two warm coins passed into Leo Dalcò's outstretched palm.

Chapter 3

The Berlinghieri dining-room was luxurious. The large table, graced with embroidered tablecloths and silver baskets of Eleonora's carefully tended African violets, was always laid with crystal and old silverware and the family's finest Limoges

48

plates. The heavy wood was polished, so that it gave off a warm glow in the light of the lamps. The silver and crystal glowed softly too. The napkins were large and starched, and the men wore them tucked into their collars. The place was impeccable. Expensive French wallpapers, usually floral and somewhat dark, decorated the walls. On a console table were baskets of fruit artistically displayed with exotic leaves and flowers, and on a large silver tray in the centre were watermelon slices carefully arranged against a background of the halved melon. Three old maidservants waited on the table, and there were nearly always guests. It was expected of everyone to dress if not formally at least elegantly for dinner.

'Have some and don't act so childish,' Eleonora said across the table to her son on this midsummer evening.

'No. They turn my stomach,' Alfredo said.

The old maidservant Desolina stood stiffly at the boy's elbow, about to help him to some fried frogs. Eleonora nodded for the maid to serve the boy, and she gave her son a look of mild reproof.

A postcard was being passed around among the adults. Eleonora's sister, Amelia, read it and said to Giovanni, 'He's a clever one, your brother Ottavio. Paris! *La liberté!* Gigolos and coquettes!' While her obvious aim had been to express disapproval, Amelia could not disguise either the secret thrill or the envy that coloured her brittle voice.

Amelia was an older, faded copy of her elegant sister. Neither as tall nor as talented, she seemed always on the verge of hysteria and, consequently, once started she tended to go on too long and to say too much. At thirty-five she was still pretty, but there was something starved in Amelia, and it was starving her prettiness. The crow's-feet that radiated from the corners of her eyes were not unattractive.

'From La Ville Lumière, affectionate regards,' Giovanni sneered, angrily mocking Ottavio's message. 'Bah! My Parisian brother!' He speared a frog with his fork, then turned on Alfredo. 'Eat!' he said.

'We stay here working and slaving, never getting away,' Eleonora said, the card in her hand now, 'while *he* travels. Paris, Berlin, Vienna – the squanderer!'

Alfredo's fork toyed with the frogs on his plate, moving them about with disgust. In a peremptory manner, his father told him he would be punished.

Next to the boy sat Giovanni's aunt, Suor Desolata, an Ursuline nun. She was dressed in the sumptuous pomp of her order, and her sharply contrasting black coif and spotless white wimple accented her pinched face and bony nose. Old and kindly and mildly outspoken, she had arrived only two days earlier, having left the convent to come and live permanently in her brother's house. The nearly squared fore edge of her coif was trimmed in white.

'And my brother?' she said now. 'Aren't we waiting for my brother to come to table?'

Eleonora looked uncomfortably to her husband. 'For the last few evenings he hasn't been dining with us,' she said.

'Not dining with us,' Giovanni said, bitter. 'Why don't you tell her the truth? He makes us set a place for him at the table every night and then refuses to sit with us.'

'He's not well,' Eleonora hastened to explain.

Suor Desolata had a way of ignoring unpleasantness. She picked up a frog in her elegant, bony fingers. 'In the convent they can never fry anything properly. Mmmm. They're so good it's sinful!' And she ate, blissful and oblivious.

They had been waiting for her in the driveway when she arrived. Eleonora, considering it would add a proper touch, had invited Don Tarcisio to be present as well. Suor Desolata had stepped down spryly from the coach and, precise as ever, immediately ordered the servants to unpack all her bags. 'I'm not returning to the convent,' she announced then and there. 'The monsignor, despite one's having come from a good family, seems to prefer young girls nowadays.' She then called out for her brother and, noticing fat Don Tarcisio for the first time, said crisply, brushing past him, 'My goodness, priests even here!'

'They're good these frogs,' Giovanni said, head bent low over his plate. 'Your friend Olmo is a shrewd one. He hunts frogs and sells them. Eat now, I told you!'

'No, I don't want them,' Alfredo said.

'We'll see how you'll enjoy the food when you're a soldier,' Giovanni said, raising his voice. 'Then you'll cry for frogs. Eat!'

'Shit! All shit!' A voice, sounding mean and almost delirious, came from the adjoining room. It was old Alfredo Berlinghieri.

'My brother,' said Suor Desolata. 'What did my brother say?'

They all turned to the open door of Berlinghieri's study, which connected with the dining-room. It was where old Alfredo, alone and gloomy and afflicted with arteriosclerosis, now took his meals.

'There's the ocean,' the old man called out. 'The ocean between me and the rest of you.'

At the table, embarrassed faces and lowered glances were fixed on the plates, except for one person – Regina, Amelia's twelve-year-old daughter, who leered across the African violets at young Alfredo, trying to get his attention. She had a round, full-moon face and sly, mean eyes. Her hair hung in long curls that were pulled to the back of her head and tied with a bow.

'Who are those two?' old Alfredo called out.

Eleonora addressed her father-in-law. 'You ask me the same thing every evening, Papà. It's my sister and her little girl Regina.'

'Alfredino!' the old man called to his grandson. 'My dinner!'

'Go and come straight back,' Giovanni told his son.

Alfredo slipped off his chair and hurriedly left the room.

'You see the state the poor man is in,' Amelia said. 'How much longer can he last?'

'Just a moment,' Suor Desolata said. 'He's six years younger than I am, and you're killing him off already.'

Amelia coloured. Her sister came to her rescue, saying provocatively, 'With the excuse that he's the eldest, can you imagine how quickly Ottavio will want to flock here to act as lord and master of the place?'

'Ottavio was born a master, just as I was born a nun,' Suor Desolata said.

'When I grow up, I'm going to be a nun too,' Regina said.

'Well, I've decided not to go back to the convent,' Suor Desolata said, licking her fingers. 'And this convinces me. They don't fry a thing properly there. These little souls in purgatory – absolutely delicious!' There was a twinkle in her eye.

Alfredo was in his grandfather's study. It was his favourite room in the whole house. Over the fireplace, there was a gun rack with eight shotguns. In glass-fronted cabinets all around the room were stuffed birds, whose names old Berlinghieri made his grandson learn.

'What's this one?' he would say.

'Heron,' young Alfredo would answer.

'And this one?'

'Partridge.'

'Good, and this one?'

'Duck,' the boy would say.

'No, not duck,' the old man would say. 'All these are ducks. What kind of duck?'

'Mallard,' the boy would say.

'Would you like a shot?' the old man said to the boy now. The boy nodded excitedly. 'Here, hug the stock. Left hand under, right elbow straight. That's it. Both eyes open. Now, you see that family of vultures?'

'Yes.'

'The old black one with the beady eyes?'

'Yes.'

Every word they spoke could be heard in the next room, and everybody in the next room was listening.

'That's your target,' old Berlinghieri said.

Click! went the gun.

'You got her!' the old man hooted. 'You got her! And now for the jackal!'

'The one that looks like Aunt Amelia?' the boy said.

'Yes. Good, good. Right between the eyes! Ho, ho, look at them scatter!' Berlinghieri fluttered a hand at arm's length, and through his bushy handlebar moustache his big yellow teeth showed in a smile.

'My little girl and I – well, from one day to the next we were out on the street,' Amelia said in a sudden outburst. 'My husband, you see, went bankrupt and ran off to South America, leaving his wife and poor daughter penniless.' The woman spoke nervously and too loud, trying to drown out the voices from the other room. 'Why, if it hadn't been for all of you . . .' She trailed off, sad, pretty, faded.

'Won't I ever see my papà again?' Regina said.

'He's your new father now, aren't you, Giovanni?' Eleonora said.

'Of course. Who would support them if it weren't for me?' Giovanni blustered. 'But you go on calling me uncle, eh?' He turned on Regina a forced, benign smile.

52

'Ssh, there they are,' old Berlinghieri said in a false whisper. 'I'll take Regina.'

'No, Regina's mine; Regina's mine!' Alfredo said.

'Ready, aim, fire! Right between the eyes!' his grandfather said.

'Stop that at once, you little fool,' Giovanni shouted, 'and come back here to this table. Shame on you. Shame on you at your age!'

Young Alfredo returned to the dining-room and marched meekly to his place.

'You're the fool,' Berlinghieri bellowed at Giovanni. 'There's such an ocean between us, between me and the rest of you – an ocean! Talk, talk! Buy machines! The place is going to rack and ruin, I tell you. You'll end with that fancy hay rake up your ass, Signor Modernizer!'

Giovanni clenched a fist on each side of his plate, mouth set angrily, and stared up at the ceiling. Eleonora reached out and laid a hand on his sleeve. When the old man stopped, Giovanni jabbed at the frogs on his son's plate, saying, 'Now then, are you going to eat or not?'

'Eat your frogs, or you'll go to hell,' Regina said.

'Shitpants,' Alfredo said at his cousin, full of spite.

'Who taught you to say that?' Giovanni wanted to know, striking out and slapping his son's face. 'Who taught you?'

'Nobody,' Alfredo said.

'His friend taught him,' Regina said. 'Three Our Fathers and three Hail Marys as penance.'

Unseen, Amelia pressed her daughter's knee with her hand to quiet her.

'He didn't,' Alfredo said. Snivelling, he took a mouthful of frog, but he swallowed it without chewing.

Eleonora studied her son. He looked feverish to her, over-excited. She attributed this to his grandfather and those guns. Could all these new faces around the table have something to do with it too? Amelia and Regina had been there only a week; Suor Desolata a few days. Something was obviously troubling the boy.

His mother's eyes rested on the new suit he wore of a light, summery material. Alfredo had come home that afternoon looking wild-eyed, his sailor suit horribly soiled, and he would not tell where he had been. Eleonora did wish he could keep his hair combed. She liked it parted in the middle and brushed flat on both sides. It was all dishevelled now. If only the boy would quiet down and be neater about his appearance! And she must speak to his father about his spending so much time with the Dalcò. Alfredo was beginning to speak like a farm hand.

Giovanni was saying, 'Nobody's taking anything away from me. Not a square foot of land, not a cent! Not after the way I've waited and obeyed and spent my whole life saying yes!'

'You talk and talk and talk with your father, but it's always Ottavio who wins out,' Eleonora said, halfway between sympathy and nagging.

'The only reason I'm still here is because I want this estate to become mine and mine alone,' Giovanni said. 'Otherwise, if you want to know the truth, I've always envied Ottavio. Yes, that's right, envied him! How many times these past few years I've thought about throwing everything up and running off, enjoying life for a change – who knows, maybe squander everything in six months, a different woman every night.'

'With me ending up like my sister?' Eleonora said, and she dealt her husband a vicious slap.

Giovanni sat there without reacting, while everyone feigned not to have seen. Alfredo took advantage of the moment to slide off the front of his chair and disappear under the table. From the other room came old Alfredo Berlinghieri's booming voice, singing about burning love. Then the singing stopped, and he began talking about the ocean again, an ocean of shit.

Suor Desolata, who politely pretended to be oblivious of the goings on around her, suddenly began giggling and squirming in her chair. 'Stop that, you little rascal,' she said. 'You're tickling me!'

Laughing, she pushed her chair back, at the same time lifting the front of her habit a few inches. Where her feet had been, Alfredo was racked by a fit of vomiting. The nun's laughter stopped abruptly. 'Oh, dear!' she murmured, taking in the bits of undigested frog's legs on the floor. She tried to cover them with her voluminous skirt.

'The poor child,' she said. 'He had to vomit. You should not have forced him to eat.'

Giovanni, trying to control his agitation, spoke to her with his eyes shut. 'He's my son, and nobody's going to tell me how to bring him up. Is that clear?'

'You set him a fine example,' Suor Desolata said with equanimity.

The boy was gone. He had scurried out from under the table and run from the room. A distant door was heard banging, then feet were heard running in the garden.

'Alfredo!' his mother called, starting to rise.

Giovanni put a hand out to keep his wife in her chair. 'Don't worry. When he's hungry, he'll come back.'

'I'll get him,' Regina announced, and she was gone before anyone could stop her.

From the next room, the voice boomed again. Old Berlinghieri said, 'Between me and the rest of you there's an ocean of shit.'

Chapter 4

Ripping a handful of leaves from a branch and wiping his mouth with them, Alfredo saw Regina come out into the garden. It was dark now, and she did not see him. The still night air was alive with fireflies.

'Come inside, naughty!' Regina called, peering into the shadows.

'Go away, you ugly cunt,' Alfredo said, and off he ran behind the trees of the icehouse mound.

A minute or two later, he had wandered into the big farmyard, where a dozen or so hay wagons, waiting to be unloaded, cast long shadows across the brick-paved threshing floor. Lamplight flooded out from the Dalcò kitchen, and voices came to him from the various apartments. Alfredo crouched down by a wagon wheel, watching through the spokes. A few yards off, in front of another wagon, a lamp burned dimly. Someone was seated there on an overturned crate. It was Olmo. His uncle Rigoletto circled round him very slowly.

A ladder stuck up from the back of the next wagon. Alfredo climbed it, silent as a cat.

'These aren't lice,' Rigoletto was saying. 'They're roasting chickens, that's what they are!'

Hidden atop the hay, Alfredo spied on the two figures below him. In one hand Rigoletto held a pair of barber's clippers, in the other he held Olmo's head, which he was shearing of its nest of tight curls. Every now and then the hunchback stopped, lifted the clippers, and worked over the scalp with his fingers. Olmo wore a clean shirt. It had been stitched together from two different shirts, and its sleeves did not match the rest of it. He looked dejected.

'There,' Rigoletto said, stepping back. 'You're five pounds lighter with all that dirt and lice gone.'

Olmo's face suddenly turned up towards the hiding place, almost as if he had sensed Alfredo's presence. The two boys exchanged a long, silent glance. Strangely, Alfredo's heart tightened.

'Alfredo, where are you?' his father's distant voice called. 'Come back to the table!'

Instinctively, Alfredo ducked down out of sight. *You'll never find me again*, he told himself. *I'll run away. I'll run away with Uncle Ottavio.* He was looking up at the great constellations now, staring, and the sound of Rigoletto speaking to Olmo seemed miles away.

That afternoon Olmo had made him follow him to the railroad tracks. They had run most of the way, part of it over a field of burnt stubble. When they got there, Olmo dropped down lengthwise in the middle of the tracks. Very far away, a train's whistle could be heard.

'What are you doing?' Alfredo had said.

'Come on,' Olmo said. 'Now we'll see who's brave and who's a coward.' He lay there flat, his face up.

Without a word, as though hypnotized, Alfredo stretched out beside Olmo. He heard the cicadas all around them, then a kind of hum, and the rails began to vibrate. The train's whistle was closer now, and Alfredo's hand sought Olmo's, pressing it.

'When the train goes over us you have to shut you eyes or else you go blind,' Olmo said.

They could hear the train; it was drowning out the cicadas. Alfredo raised himself to look, and there it was, coming into the straight stretch, the locomotive belching smoke. He stared, paralysed with fear, then tried to free his hand from Olmo's; but Olmo would not let go.

'Let me go! Let me go!' he had screamed.

Alfredo tugged and writhed, but Olmo was the stronger, and he held Alfredo there, close to him.

'You see?' Olmo shouted. 'You're yellow!'

Alfredo's heart pounded even now, rethinking it, seeing it

all take place again, from on top of the hay wagon.

They were face to face; Olmo's eyes were wild. Alfredo screamed, but the train whistle drowned his voice, and then Olmo suddenly rolled to one side, letting him free. How Alfredo got off the tracks, he never knew. The train seemed to be on top of them, pounding and thundering. Alfredo lay in the burning weeds at the edge of the track bed, deafened, seeing only a rush and blur of iron wheels. Olmo had remained in place.

Then the train was gone and Alfredo found himself screaming Olmo's name and flinging himself down on the tracks by Olmo's perfectly still body. Alfredo could not move his tongue to speak. All at once, Olmo opened an eye – just one eye. And in singsong, like an incantation, he uttered something barely comprehensible.

'Ding dang! Ding dang!' he said. 'Devil sing and master hang!'

Olmo then spat in Alfredo's face and bounded off at a lope. In that moment, his admiration of Olmo was unbounded. It was some time, however, before Alfredo's terror left him.

Remembering all of it now, under the stars, Alfredo once more felt seized with that terror. Or was it his father's voice just below him, suddenly addressing Olmo, that had caused the terror?

'Have you seen Alfredo?' Giovanni Berlinghieri was saying, his tone tinged with ire.

'No, he hasn't been around here,' Olmo said.

Alfredo remained rigid until he heard his father's footsteps withdrawing across the threshing floor in the direction of the villa. Olmo had not betrayed him – even after his cowardice of the afternoon! The wonder of this was dazzling. Looking down, Alfredo saw that Rigoletto was gone and that his friend Olmo sat there alone, his hair completely clipped. His friend Olmo, Alfredo thought, for now Olmo was his friend. *I have a friend; I have a friend.* The notion pulsed through the head of the boy in the hay, and he was suddenly stirred with an emotion that gripped his throat and brought a veil of tears to blur his eyes. Into the dried grass, he said, inaudibly, breathlessly, 'Oh, Olmo! Oh, Olmo! My friend Olmo!'

After a while, for Olmo to hear, Alfredo said, 'I'm dying. I want to die. I'm dying.'

There was no utterance or any sign from Olmo.

A window shutter opened from one of the apartments and Olmo's mother called out. 'Olmo, come to bed,' she said. 'You know I can't sleep when you're not home.'

Speaking to no one in particular, Olmo said, 'If my father had been here, they wouldn't have shaved my head. He wouldn't have let them.'

'Olmo, where are you?' Rosina called from her window.

'Once I heard my father in the bottom of a well,' Olmo said, speaking to Alfredo now. 'He was calling me. I heard him in a hollow gourd too. I heard him call me.'

'Alfredo!' came Giovanni's voice from the distance.

Alfredo slid down off the wagon, plummeting, and landed in a shower of loose hay at Olmo's feet. With a hand on his shoulder to rouse his friend from his reverie, Alfredo said excitedly, 'Let's run away from home together!'

'Alfredo!' It was Giovanni's voice again, this time farther away.

Olmo brushed Alfredo's hand aside, got up, and took a few steps into the darkness.

'Once I put my ear against a telegraph pole,' Olmo said, 'and I could hear him calling me. It was my father. "Olmo! Olmo!" he said.'

'Alfredo!' Giovanni Berlinghieri's voice called.

The next moment, Olmo had dodged out of sight between the hay wagons, and at the top of his voice, into the night, he began shouting – as though he were the father he never had, the father he would never know – his own name.

Eerily, the word reverberated off the walls of the great quadrangle: 'Olmo! Olmo! Olmo!' In the dark, Alfredo saw nothing, but he listened.

Chapter 5

A couple of months later, on a very hot Sunday afternoon, a dance was in progress in the poplar grove by the river. All the farm's young men and girls were there, dressed in their best clothes. Many of their friends had come too, and as the day wore on and the men kept removing their jackets (but not their hats), still new couples arrived.

The atmosphere was festive. Music was provided by three

musicians, led by a lanky labourer named Montanaro, who sat in the centre playing his ocarina. Montanaro was a bit squint-eyed and had a healthy moustache, whose ends he twisted into fine points. Flanking him were a fiddler, who was as thin as a stick, and a blind man playing an accordion. Each newcomer, before beginning to dance, went and laid a present at the players' feet. There were cheeses and bottles of wine and baskets of fruit, all watched over by Montanaro's two children. One of the presents, a live rabbit, his daughter held in her arms. Nearby, for everyone's refreshment, stood a small wagon containing a heap of ripe round watermelons. Music, dance, and watermelon slices partaken under the cool of the poplars – these were enough to make everybody happy, content for a change to wear themselves out flying to a polka instead of toiling in the field.

An old man made his way along the nearby dyke road, tugged this way and that in fits and starts by five hunting dogs that he held on leashes. It was the master, Alfredo Berlinghieri, out for a stroll. 'Where the hell are you taking me? What's got into you bastards?' he said aloud. Then, fifty yards ahead on the left, below the embankment that he walked on, he heard the music and saw the dancing couples among the tall straight trees of the poplar grove.

Curiosity and the straining dogs led him forward. *Young people dancing and embracing,* he thought. *Before the day is out, they'll be in the grass doing something else.* He hid himself in the shrubbery along the path that led down to the trees, spying into the festivity like a conspirator. The shade was green. The poplars, with their thick grey-green trunks, grew in widely spaced aisles. The river could be made out in the background, swishing along, it too greyish-green. This was no place to be old, Alfredo Berlinghieri told himself.

'Hot, isn't it, Signor Padrone?' a girl of about fifteen said to the master's back. She sat a few yards away, at the edge of a ditch, soaking her feet.

'Who are you?' old Berlinghieri said. He had spoken after a moment of irritation, and now he took a better look at her. The girl wore her hair in two long braids.

'I'm Irma, don't you recognize me? Adelina's daughter.' She held up a pair of brand-new patent-leather shoes for the old man to see. 'Pretty, though, aren't they? The signora gave them to me. They belonged to Regina.'

Irma wiggled her toes in the water with obvious relief. Old Alfredo studied her in silence, then, as if he suddenly had an idea, he was off behind the dog pack, striding rapidly back towards the villa.

When he got some twenty-five or thirty yards along the dyke road, he halted and called the girl by name. Irma got to her feet to see him more clearly.

'Come!' he said.

It was an order. At once, the girl collected her new shoes, lifted her long skirts, and started up the embankment path. Old Berlinghieri was already walking ahead, rapidly, straining after the dogs. Soon they could no longer hear the laughter or the music of the dance. The dyke road was hot, and every now and then Irma had to break into a trot to keep the distance between her and the master from growing. Never once as she followed did it occur to Irma to wonder what old Berlinghieri might want.

At last they came into the deserted farmyard with its Sunday afternoon quiet and emptiness. Irma was panting a little, and drops of perspiration showed on her face. Old Berlinghieri had released the dogs, and when the girl came through the gate, she saw them, noses to the brick pavement, beating their tails, crisscrossing the bare threshing floor. She also saw the master slipping into the stable. Breaking step and trotting, she hurried after him.

The hot, heavy stench of urine and dung, heightened by the oven-like heat of the afternoon, made the stable so overpowering that just standing there in the long central aisle – the big cows on either hand blowing and snuffling and switching their tails – the girl broke into a sweat.

'Come here,' old Berlinghieri said, handing her a bucket and milking-stool.

It was not milking time, and the girl was puzzled.

'Can't you see how full she is?' the master went on impatiently, gesturing with his head to indicate the cow named Dacca. 'Do as I say and milk her.'

Irma dropped down, as if curtsying, to place her new shoes on the floor of the aisle, then moved into the stall to take her place on the stool by the cow's udder. Her feet pressing firmly in the ooze of straw and excrement, she placed the bucket between her legs and laid her forehead against Dacca's

60

flank. Irma's hands were expert, and the milk lashed the inside of the metal bucket in a steady rhythm.

The master removed his shoes and stepped barefoot into the deep dung of the stall. 'Splish, splash,' he said. 'Cows are full of milk and shit.'

Irma raised her face and smiled up at him.

'It's a curse that hangs over the lives of all men,' old Berlinghieri said enigmatically. 'We carry it inside us, and it gets worse with age. You know what the worst curse in the world is?'

What he said made no sense to the girl. 'Hailstorms?' she ventured.

'No, not hailstorms. They're no curse. It's milk and shit in the brain.' The old man dragged his feet in the dung the way a child does in a rain puddle, and he moved to the other side of the cow. 'What I mean is when you can't do it.'

'Do what?' Irma said.

Berlinghieri cupped his hands over the bucket. The girl aimed several long spurts of milk into them for him to drink. 'I can't do it,' he said. 'It won't get hard.' Standing from his crouch, he unbuttoned his fly. 'You see? Put your hand inside.'

The girl looked around for a moment, modestly, then slipped her hand inside the man's trousers. 'Eh, Padrone,' she said, 'nobody can milk a bull!'

'Milk and shit,' the padrone said. 'Go back to the dance now, and when it's over, tell them I'm dead.'

His face was strange in its seriousness; his jaws were tense. He wiped his moustache clean. When he addressed the girl, he seemed to be seeing not her but something beyond her. Irma had hurriedly picked up her shoes and was moving towards the open door.

'Yes, go,' Berlinghieri repeated, 'but remember, when the dancing is over, I'm dead.'

Irma slipped through the door into the cooler air of the loggia, only to have him shout after her to shut it. When she had done so, old Berlinghieri moved to Dacca's head, and, speaking to the great beast, he freed her from her chain. Then he slapped her flank and backed her into the central aisle. The bucket was overturned. The white milk puddled in an oozing hoof print. Dacca let out a moan, as if she did not know what was expected of her.

'Splish, splash,' Alfredo Berlinghieri said, breaking into an ugly leer. He spoke the next animal's name and set it free, sending it out into the aisle. 'Splish, splash, Abba.' And the third cow's chain was loosened.

His eye went up to an iron ring in the whitewashed ceiling. *Milk and shit*, he thought, *milk and shit*. There was sweat on his face, but he did not bother to wipe it away. *Milk and shit, and it gets worse with age.*

Leo Dalcò woke from his afternoon nap to hear the restless lowing of the stock. It was so unusual an interruption of the Sunday afternoon quiet and tedium that at first he thought he was dreaming. Before walking out into the big courtyard to cross to the stable, he paused by the kitchen table to pick up one of the slices of watermelon he had earlier brought back from the poplar grove.

Now, leaning slightly forward each time he bit into the fleshy melon so as not to soil his clean shirt, he made his way over the sunbaked threshing floor, spitting the black seeds. The deep throaty sounds coming from the stable, so loud now, alarmed him, and on reaching the loggia's welcome shade he threw down the uneaten portion of melon, glimpsing through the iron bars of a small window a mass of restless cattle that milled about in disorder. Cows, oxen, and bulls pushed each other, seething, slipping, as they sought footings for themselves in space that was not there. The stable sheltered close to a hundred animals.

Leo moved calmly, slipping inside and bolting the door again before any beast was drawn to the opening. The confusion among the stock was dangerous now. Everywhere he looked there was a sea of backs and tossing horns and great moist eyes. The cries were deafening, outlandish.

Working slowly, keeping firm hold of the columns and mangers, Leo began pushing and pulling each animal back to its place and securing it to its chain. It would be a long job, he knew, and already the sweat ran down his face in rivulets and his fresh shirt clung to his body, stained with his sweat and the animals' sweat and with dung. From time to time, as he moved forward and back, he cast a glance upwards over the heads of the cattle, and in his eyes at that moment, there shone a comprehension and something almost akin to a complicity. Had he been able to rest from his labours, he would have compressed his lips and shaken his head. Instead, in a half-audible monologue, he said, 'What did you have to turn the cows loose for? Why? Just to make more work for me?'

They were dancing polkas still, and Irma was whirling dizzily, so dizzily that she could not make out her partner's face. Everything was a grey-green blur to her, the trunks of the poplars, the river, even the odd sunlight that came down weakly through the filter of leaves. Five or six couples were whirling, the women's skirts ballooning out full, until suddenly, as though the world had come to a stop, one of the girls froze and threw her back against a tree trunk. It was Irma. She was paralysed by a recollection.

Her chest heaved; her braid was curled around her throat. 'The padrone is dead!' she screamed. 'The padrone is dead!'

The three players stopped abruptly. The other dancers stopped. Everybody listened to the girl.

'He said, he said –' Irma broke off, panting. 'He said, "Tell them I'm dead, but to go on dancing." '

'So the master gives orders even when he's dead, does he?' Rigoletto said, immediately making a joke of it.

They all laughed at the remark.

'And we'll obey him!' Censo said. 'Come on, music!'

They started in again, musicians and dancers. Not one of them believed Irma. But Irma held back, uneasy, until her partner pulled her by the wrist.

The girl smiled. Now not even she believed what she had said.

At first, with the milling and the turmoil and the din, he had not seen the master's body hanging from the iron ring in the ceiling. When he did, he noticed the cattle's slavering nostrils and tongues poking and sniffing at the bare feet, where the dung had begun to harden. But Leo Dalcò knew he had to chain up the animals before he could cut Alfredo Berlinghieri's body down. From time to time, as he struggled with the herd, the old patriarch kept casting glances at the master's lifeless form swaying over the sea of heads and horns, and these thoughts had come to him:

Why did you have to make all this work for me? And on a Sunday, too. If only you could see yourself now, Signor

Alfredo. This is no master's death. The trouble is when a man does nothing all his life, it leaves him too much time to think, and thinking too much stupefies him. I knew what you were, and you knew I knew. You were nothing but a useless shit who never did a goddam day's work in his life.

Chapter 6

Old Alfredo Berlinghieri's bedroom was dimly lit. The canopied four-poster bed that stood against the far wall was nearly in darkness. Over its headboard, the chart of the Berlinghieri property, with all the subsequent acquisitions since the original purchase in the eighteenth century marked in various colours, was invisible.

In the opposite corner of the room, a very old notary sat bent over a small desk, his back to the bed, his eyeglasses only an inch or so from the surface of the paper he wrote on. The man was so old and frail, so tiny and bent, that he had had to be carried in from a carriage in the arms of two of the farmhands. A single short candle lit his page.

Giovanni Berlinghieri hovered at his side, alternately casting worried looks at the bed and scrutinizing over the notary's shoulder the words the man wrote. At the bedside, clutching the withered hand of the man who lay there with the covers drawn up to his ears, Giovanni's wife struck an attitude of suitable affliction. By her elbow, in another chair, sat her sister Amelia.

'I, Alfredo Berlinghieri, being of sound mind and body,' a voice began loudly from the bed.

'What did he say?' the notary asked, looking up at Giovanni.

Giovanni reached down, shoved a metal object into the pool of light, and told the man what had been said. The instrument was an ear trumpet.

'Oh, yes,' the absentminded notary chuckled, putting the tube to his left ear and bending back to his scratchy pen.

Giovanni shot a nasty look at the bed and made a gesture with his hand for the voice to speak up.

'I, Alfredo Berlinghieri, being of sound mind and body,' the dictating voice went on, 'declare my younger son, Giovanni, as my sole heir and successor.'

'Not so fast, I'm writing,' the notary complained.

'To my elder son, Ottavio – '

'What?' the ancient notary asked.

'My elder son, Ottavio,' Amelia repeated, anxiously.

'To Ottavio, I leave an annual income of nine thousand lire, to be paid him for the rest of his natural life by my sole heir,' the voice said.

The notary's pen scratched away. It was good, he thought, that the old landowner was putting the estate in Giovanni's hands, where it would be safe and continue to prosper. It was also just that Alfredo Berlinghieri not be too generous with that notorious wastrel Ottavio.

Giovanni bent over the tiny man's shoulder, inspecting. The two sisters' eyes met uneasily.

'To Ottavio, I also leave my town residence. It must be understood that – '

The door to the room came open a crack. Young Alfredo entered in a long nightdress, rubbing his eyes with his fists.

'Go back to bed, Alfredo. Grandpa's not well,' the boy's mother said.

'Grandpa, Grandpa,' young Alfredo called out weakly. He approached the bed.

'Get out! Get out of here!' his aunt said in a harsh whisper, rising from her chair to prevent the boy from drawing near.

'Alfredo!' Eleonora admonished.

Amelia picked the boy up and carried him to the door, surprising some of the servants there, who were trying to eavesdrop.

'Is he dead or isn't he dead?' one of them asked meekly, as a sort of explanation for her presence in the corridor.

'If he's dead, why did they call the notary?' another servant said.

'Pray, pray!' a third said.

Amelia told them to put Alfredo back in his bed.

In the room, the voice from the four-poster said, 'It must be understood that the entire Berlinghieri estate, consisting of nine hundred acres of cultivated land, the villa, the farmhouses and outbuildings, the machinery and tools, and the entire livestock of cattle, horses, and pigs, goes to my son Giovanni and to his direct heirs.'

The notary called for pauses and repetitions, which, each time he asked, Giovanni assiduously supplied. The little man screwed his eye to the page and wrote at a frantic pace in a crabbed hand.

Suddenly there was a loud squabble outside the room, and the door burst open. It was young Alfredo again. This time, rushing straight for the bed, he managed to elude both his aunt and mother in their desperate stabs to halt him. Amelia actually caught the tail of the nightshirt and sent the boy sprawling. As Alfredo's face came up from the fall he saw before him, sticking out from behind a table that had been shoved by the head of the bed, two muddy peasant boots. A look of unspeakable horror came into the boy's eyes. Leo Dalcò was crouched there on his knees in the semi-dark, speaking out in imitation of old Alfredo Berlinghieri's voice.

The sisters acted together now. Striking out almost as a reflex, Eleonora slapped her son's face, hard. Amelia pounced on the stunned boy and hauled him up in her arms, a hand clasped over his mouth. As she did so, Alfredo caught the edge of the coverlet that draped his grandfather's dead body, and he yanked it free.

There lay the old man, his bare feet awry and still smeared in dry dung, his face hideous, a rope burn around his neck. It was nightmarish. The boy kicked and squirmed, but his aunt managed to hold him firm, and at last she got him to the door. By this time, to escape blame for not having been able to restrain the boy, the servants had long since fled the corridor. As he was bundled off, Alfredo saw his mother hastily pulling the bedspread over his grandfather's corpse. At that moment, Leo Dalcò was saying, 'The geese and the hens I leave to the Dalcò family.'

Giovanni Berlinghieri's eyes immediately flashed an angry glare into the dark corner.

The notary, also surprised at the sudden generosity, thought he had not heard right. 'Why is he speaking in such a faint voice?' he asked Giovanni. 'Poor man, he's really in a bad way.'

Old Dalcò repeated the bequest, and, pleased with his own cunning, he uttered a dry little laugh.

Young Alfredo was out of the room, in his own bed, sobbing. The notary had never been aware of his presence. But that night a seed was sown. The boy had understood everything.

Chapter 7

After that, Alfredo lay in bed for two days, his eyes glistening, his cheeks flushed with fever. It was nothing serious, the doctor said – just one of those things children come down with, maybe growing pains.

'He won't eat a bite, the poor thing. He won't speak,' the maid told Ottavio on the stairway.

'But what's the matter with him?' Ottavio said.

The funeral had been held that morning. The will had just been read. Ottavio, usually so jovial and outgoing, was using the solemnity of the day to mask his feelings. He was a tall man, like his father, good looking, easy in his manners, liberal in his ways. For years, the pursuit of pleasure had been the substance of his life, but there was a serious vein in him as well, which, out of a fear of self-exposure that he himself only half understood or wanted only half to understand, he kept hidden, buried. He was a master of drawing others out, of giving them his ear, but he never talked about himself except self-deprecatingly, in that limited and charming way of the mixer, the polite listener, the raconteur. He was an art connoisseur and a collector, with a fondness for *objets d'art*, but at the same time he was slightly ashamed of this interest as being too ephemeral, almost too feminine. He knew he was overly concerned with settings, decoration, and did not like this in himself, did not altogether trust it, finding it shallow and wishing he were more contemplative and intellectual. He was beginning to cultivate a serious interest in pictures. But as he was unsure of this inclination, this intellectuality, he belittled it by refusing to be serious about it to others, just as he always made light of himself as a protection and a defence. In doing these things, in immuring unshared his inner self, he also created about him that greatest of all social assets – a mystery.

The life of parties, dinners, and salons Ottavio Berlinghieri could not resist. It was such an easy life, so habit-forming; its successes were so immediate and forthcoming – the flatteries, the small kindnesses, the attentions readily given out and as readily received. But when he faced himself unevasively, Ottavio never considered the superficiality and glamour of his social life as anything more than indulgence, self-indulgence, even perhaps as a need to make up for a rural childhood – an unsophisticated upbringing – in which the peasants were hard, the earth hard, the animals hard, the summers too hot and winters too cold, and there was no softness, no excitement, no delicacy, no glitter or refinement. He knew it was easy to convince oneself, in the midst of this glitter of party-giving and party-going, that one was really living to the full; but he also knew, though he often pretended he did not, that the glitter was brittle and that depth in life is cultivated outside of drawing-rooms and salons and forged, worked for, striven after, earned, in the privacy and loneliness of one's heart and mind. And so his life provided him with much satisfaction; and so, in infrequent moments, it also provided him with deep dissatisfaction. He was torn, but not so much to change.

Ottavio was addicted to beautiful women, but he was never serious about any of them because he looked on them too, essentially, as ornaments and unworthy of a lasting attachment. Nor was he sure he was capable of making the necessary commitment to a wife, since he had devoted a whole lifetime to training himself in the art of telling a woman whatever she wanted to hear and of listening to her as though she were the only person on earth – of flattering her, in short, with these twin attentions – just to have her for that moment or for a few moments. In his circle, seriousness was unpardonable; cynicism, and even this lightly, was the sign and mark of social grace.

Ottavio was generous, a good friend to his friends, likable, reliable. But he was also easily bored, he feared loneliness, and he was lazy, undisciplined. The last thing on earth that interested him was agriculture. In some way, he thought, perhaps what had happened now was all for the best.

And yet it hurt. Not for the estate, the land, the house, the money, the prestige – all lost to him. It hurt because he had known, as natural as breathing air, that he was his father's favourite, the apple of old Alfredo's eye, and though his father had often chided his extravagances, the old man had also tacitly approved of his son's life, had perhaps even lived vicariously through Ottavio a life the old man once dimly aspired to but that had been denied him. The father had been rough; Ottavio, polished. The crates of French champagne Ottavio had shipped home and the way old Berlinghieri used them symbolized the old man's pride in his worldly son. But Ottavio had been mistaken, after all, about the nature of his father's feelings for him. It was this that made him unaccustomedly melancholy now, so unlike himself, so withdrawn. It was this that made Ottavio question – question himself, his past, the course of his life, the decisions made along the way (and the decisions avoided) that had brought him to the point where he stood today. And he realized now, too late, that he had lacked vision, foresight, having instead relied on a natural confidence, his self-assurance, to see him through.

Now the maid repeated what the doctor had told Giovanni and Eleonora. Then she said, her hand on the door of the boy's room, a finger at her lips, 'He may be asleep. Don't wake him.'

Alfredo, hearing voices but not sure whose they were, had closed his eyes, pretending to sleep. After several moments of silence he opened them again, and his uncle, Ottavio, was at his side. There was a black mourning band around the sleeve of his suit.

'What is it, little man?' Ottavio said. One look told him it was a deeper ill the boy suffered.

The boy stared at him without speaking, unable to speak. Tears welled up in his eyes.

Ottavio sat on the edge of the bed and motioned to his nephew not to move, not to try to talk. Picking a book up off the floor, he asked Alfredo if he'd like to hear an adventure story. The boy made no response.

'I know,' Ottavio said. 'I'll show you my tattoo.'

The boy, having sunk back into himself, showed no sign of recognition. Ottavio took up a towel that lay at the foot of the bed and began winding it around his head. 'This turban once belonged to a tiger hunter,' he said. 'Want to hear about him?'

'Uncle Ottavio, take me away with you,' the boy said weakly.

'But why?' Ottavio said, feigning joviality. 'Don't you like it here?'

'They're all liars,' Alfredo said. His eyes began filling with big round tears.

Ottavio took one of Alfredo's hot hands. 'Where would we go?'

'On a ship.'

'Like this one?' Ottavio rested a hand on a large model caravel with cloth sails that adorned a table by the boy's bed. The late afternoon light cast a blown-up shadow of its sails on the wall.

'Like this one?' Ottavio repeated.

But the boy was asleep. Ottavio got up and studied Alfredo's face. The sadness the uncle found there seemed almost to match his own. There was something mysterious about his nephew's ailment. The boy was full of hurt and conflict even now at the age of six.

But Ottavio Berlinghieri was not a man who liked to dwell overlong on mysteries – especially ones that might turn him inward. Having found out how he had misjudged himself, his father, his past actions was enough for one day. He would take his nine thousand a year and the town residence and make himself the best possible life with them.

He looked at himself in a small mirror by the door. The double-breasted tropical suit, cut just so, fitted his athletic body impeccably. Ottavio adjusted the arm band slightly, lowering it to better effect.

Life was to be lived, life was to be enjoyed. He had lost his claim to the estate, but he refused to mourn his disappointment. He was already smiling bravely, the glint back in his eye, when he left the room.

Chapter 8

The great storm broke in the late spring of the next year, 1908, and, in the way of such cataclysms, from one day to the next it changed to the root the lives of all those it touched.

It was May, and the earth was green and full. The grain was already high and beginning to turn to gold; the breezes hissed through the ripening heads, bending and tossing the wheat and the poppies that grew in it like a caressing hand, gently, softly. There was a big crop of tomatoes coming too; the vines were heavy with the fattening green fruit. On the Berlinghieri estate they had counted on a heavy tomato harvest and so had doubled the acreage usually planted to that crop. It had been a good spring, with much sun; the signs were for a heavy harvest, and by mid-May all the crops, including the grapes, were well advanced.

Then one day the sky suddenly grew dark, just as though evening were falling at midday. The birds stopped their singing, the insects grew quiet, and the sky turned to one great leaden mass of scudding cloud, with turbulent black wisps where some blue still showed on the horizon. Soon the whole sky began to boil in a thick black boil, and the winds whipped down to lift long plumes of dust off the roads and to force the grain flat, in waves, like the work of an invisible hand pressing down, destructive, crushing. The wind tore tiles from roofs, rocked and humbled trees. Then the clouds poured out water and the skies sent out a sound and the earth trembled and shook. The silvery flashes illuminated and rent the sky, the thunder reverberated like a thousand cannon, and the hail came down – a thick, relentless downpour of white pellets that struck at the earth and everything in its path like a rain of bullets. Some of the hailstones were the size of a boy's fist, and the clatter they made on roofs was deafening, terrifying.

Immediately, when the sky had so quickly blackened, the church bells began to peal out a warning. The bells were a violence themselves. Don Tarcisio stood by the church door, gathering his cassock around him with one hand as if about to flee for his life and urging on the village cobbler, who tugged at the bell ropes. On the estate, there had been a scurry. Servants ran from room to room closing shutters, and like eyelids they blinked shut one by one. Women ran into the back yard to take in sheets off the drying lines, where they flapped and snapped like crazed banners. The bell in the tower of the farm sent out its signal. But already the men were running back from the fields. In the threshing yard three wagon loads of hay stood waiting to be taken in. With no time even for hitching the oxen, a number of the Dalcò brothers put their backs and shoulders to the heavy wagons and pushed them, teetering, to the safety of the sheds. In the stable, the cattle were restless. They lowed and clanked their chains, and a couple of stable hands walked up and down the central aisle, trying to calm the animals, speaking out to them in low guttural tones. The hens and geese and turkeys all took cover. The hail hitting the brick threshing floor bounced three feet, and the rain came down in sheets, drowning the land.

Like a pestilence, like some cosmic retribution, the great

terror had struck from the sky.

Young Alfredo had climbed up into the loft over the horse stalls, and now he huddled there in his dripping poncho, listening to the hail that hammered on the roof tiles only a few feet above his head. He had never been up here before, and he was not sure what lured him here now, as he could easily have made himself comfortable and dry below, out of the din of the hailstones. He studied the web of great beams that supported the roof, the sacks of stored wheat, and the garlands of grapes that hung drying on poles.

Then he stepped over a high threshold into another room. It was like entering another world. The room was immaculate; the beams and walls and ceiling were spotlessly whitewashed and uncobwebbed. Aisles had been set out with posts and poles to support trays. It was full of mulberry leaves that were pierced and gnawed, and he could hear a ceaseless hissing sound coming from the leaves.

He was in the room where the silkworms were reared. The light was grey and watery, but soon his eyes made out the thousands of caterpillars satisfying their voracious appetites. Alfredo reached in and picked up a leaf to which a fat white hairless caterpillar was attached. As he examined it, it stiffened. He blew on it gently.

'Leave it alone,' a voice said. 'Put it back.'

It was Olmo. Alfredo wheeled around to see him standing in the low entrance, the rain streaming off him, his arms filled with fresh mulberry branches.

'What are you doing here?' Olmo said, throwing the branches down and shaking the water off his arms. He was drenched to the skin.

Alfredo had the silkworm cupped in his hand. Olmo tried to take it from him.

'No,' Alfredo said, in an outburst of self-assurance.

'You're not to touch any silkworms,' Olmo told him.

'I'll touch them whenever I feel like it,' Alfredo said.

'That's what you think.'

'I'm the master,' Alfredo said.

'The silkworms are mine,' Olmo said. 'And I don't want you up here.'

'Why not?'

'Because I'm the one who feeds them. Now give it back to me.'

'They're mine,' Alfredo said. 'Just as the grapes are mine, and the wheat and the cows. Even your whole family, even you are mine.'

Olmo's nostrils flared, he made his hands into fists.

They began calling each other names, angrily, provocatively, contorting their faces to back their words.

'Watch out or you'll get it,' Olmo said.

'I'll punch you one in the nose and in the eye too,' Alfredo said. He knew that Olmo was stronger, but he also knew that if he was to be Olmo's friend he would have to stand up to him.

'I can take you with one hand,' Olmo said.

'Try it.'

They flung themselves at each other, wrestling, Olmo at first holding one hand behind his back. But as he was about to tumble he dragged Alfredo with him in both arms, and over they pitched. Alfredo seemed to be without fear. Then, rolling, one of them accidentally kicked a rack holding the tray of worms, and it fell, spilling leaves and caterpillars over the brick floor.

'Come on, help me,' Olmo said, letting go of Alfredo. 'Otherwise we'll both get beatings.'

They set the tray back in place and, side by side, on their knees, they began collecting the silkworms.

'You're a liar,' Alfredo accused. He was gaining confidence in himself and did not want to back off; some inner compulsion told him not just to hold off, watching, observing, but to *do*. 'You said you'd wrestle with one arm, and then you used two.'

'If you want to try it, I'll take you on with no hands at all,' Olmo said.

'You make me laugh, you know that?' Alfredo said. 'Where are the cocoons?'

'It's too early. First they have to eat.'

Now the boys began working together, replacing the old leaves with the fresh ones.

'And then?' Alfredo asked.

'Then they begin to spit out the thread. They make a nest with it.'

'It's not a nest,' Alfredo corrected. 'It's a cocoon. I saw one once, but not a real one. It was in a book.'

Olmo looked at Alfredo out of the corner of his eye, as if he were measuring something in him. Then he said, 'I'll show you a real one.' He reached into a slot in one of the huge beams and drew out a small silk ball, which he put into the cup of Alfredo's hand.

Alfredo poked it. 'It's so light,' he said. 'There. See the hole? That's where the moth comes out and flies away.'

'I've never seen it,' Olmo said.

'I read about it in the book. I wonder if they fly off at night or during the day.'

'The minute they're born,' Olmo said. 'But nobody ever sees them.'

'You ought to get out of those wet clothes,' Alfredo said. 'You'll catch pneumonia if you don't.' He slipped out of his poncho and told Olmo to put it on.

The hail had stopped but the rain drummed on.

'No, I don't want it,' Olmo said. He was beginning to shiver.

'Don't be childish; put it on,' Alfredo said like a parent.

They went into the part of the loft where the sacks of wheat were. Olmo undressed and rubbed his body with an empty burlap sack. Then he got the poncho over him and sat on the wheat, comfortably, as though on a soft bed. The two boys talked. Olmo told Alfredo about all the birds' nests he knew on the farm, not counting sparrows and swallows. Alfredo talked about his grandfather's hunting guns and how when he was bigger he would lead shooting parties in the marshes. They spoke about trains. Alfredo said he had a book about trains, with pictures of locomotives.

Olmo sat hunched over, the poncho covering him like a blanket, his hands hidden in his lap. For a long time they did not speak. Alfredo watched, filled with a feeling he could not have expressed – a feeling of being close to the unfolding of a great mystery.

'Do you have to pee?' Olmo asked Alfredo at last.

Unsure what to answer, Alfredo said, 'No.'

'Well, I do,' Olmo went to a corner, lifted the poncho up around his stomach, and urinated into a hole in the floor.

Alfredo had followed him. He decided he needed to pee too.

The two boys urinated through the floor, looking closely at each other.

'Does it hurt you?' Alfredo said.

'Hurt?'

'It's all open.'

'Let me see yours,' Olmo said. 'Gee, it's like a cocoon. If you pull on the skin, it'll get like mine.'

Alfredo grew shy and began to hide himself.

'Try it,' Olmo said, like a challenge.

Alfredo did not want to try. They went and sat on the sacks again. Olmo showed him how. Olmo told Alfredo it would give him a thrill. Alfredo held back. He looked at Olmo's dirty fingers, now wrinkled and slightly puffed from the wet, working between his legs.

'You try it too,' Olmo said.

Alfredo touched himself. It was a rite, an initiation. He burned with interest but feared letting his interest show. He almost wished Olmo would touch him.

'It doesn't move,' Alfredo said, all hesitancy.

'Pull harder.'

'It stings.'

'Like this,' Olmo said.

'It stings,' Alfredo said.

'Too bad, then.'

'What do you mean?' Alfredo said, fearful that something was about to be taken from him.

Olmo laughed.

'I'll try, I'll try,' Alfredo pleaded, burning.

'We'll do it again another day,' Olmo said.

Alfredo was relieved. He wanted to stop for now, but at the same time he wanted to know it was not over. The thing was dark and mysterious and secret, just like the room. On fire with the secret of it, he suddenly wanted to be by himself, away from Olmo and from this dark nook, to escape from the weight of the thing. Or maybe he wanted to think about it hidden somewhere at home, alone.

'I've got to go now,' he blurted out all at once. 'You keep the poncho.' And he made a dash for the stairs.

'You'll never be a Socialist,' Olmo called after him, taunting.

'Why not?' Alfredo said from the stairhead.

Olmo grinned and said enigmatically, 'I'm a Socialist with

holes in my pockets.'

But Alfredo could not ask for or wait for an explanation – not now. He bolted, the great mystery burgeoning in his breast like the burden of a secret too big to be contained. Olmo's laughter followed him, happy and mocking, pursuing him down the stairs, and for no reason Alfredo could understand, as he reached the gallery these words of a refrain sounded in his mind:

> *Ding dang! Ding dang!*
> *Devil sing and master hang!*

Chapter 9

It was not until the next day that the men were able to inspect the devastation. The fields were sodden; the grain bent flat; the grapevines hung in shreds. Small green tomatoes, broken loose by the hail, had floated down the rows and been swept away in the ditches. By everyone's estimate, half the crops were destroyed.

Grimly, Giovanni Berlinghieri tramped about in rubber boots, inspecting the damage. Grimly, the men worked trying to salvage what they could. Tending the vines, old Leo Dalcò recalled that he had not seen hail like this since the year before he was married.

Coming up to him, nearly in tears, Rigoletto held a smashed cornstalk in both hands as though it were some delicate glass object. 'Look,' he told his father, 'look at the corn! It's all like this!'

'A man can live without wine,' Leo said. 'But without corn, without polenta – ' He could not bring himself even to finish his statement. Famine was sure.

The master approached. 'Call your people here, Leo,' he said curtly. 'The day labourers too. Call them all.'

Leo stepped out from the row of vines and put his hands to his mouth. 'Orso,' he called, 'Turo, Censo, Oreste.' He took a breath and went on with the roll. 'Moretto, Guercio, Onorato, Montanaro. All of you, come here!' He summoned them, waved them in with a hand.

As the men gathered round, Giovanni could not help looking them over like the opposition one sizes up for weak-

nesses, for an opening, for an advantage, though what he was
trying to marshall and to demonstrate was a brand of pity for
them that would cloak the words he aimed to speak. It was
the performance of the wolf sniffing the lamb for its weakness,
and, as such, it was pathetic, unnecessary, overdone, for Giovanni Berlinghieri had been born with whatever advantage
he needed to best these men – he had money and he had power
– whereas they had only empty pockets and half-filled
stomachs. As a performance, then, it was superfluous, a waste,
unmanly even; this lording it over the vanquished – especially
these vanquished, in their tatters, some of them shoeless, all
of them lean, lined, and exhausted with toil. In fact, Giovanni's attempt at friendliness and concern only put the men
off, was doomed, since, despite himself, his underlying manner
– he was short, curt, impatient, blaming – gave him away.
And so, one by one, the men's gazes dropped down, averted
the master's scrutiny, took in the trampled grass, the mud,
their own torn boots, their naked feet – anything but that
pair of wily, hypocritical eyes.

'Let's face the facts, men,' the master started, magnanimous,
'we've lost everything – wine, tomatoes, potatoes, corn. The
whole harvest.' Here, as though there were opposition to the
statement, Giovanni held up a hand to still it. But there was
no opposition, there was only the stolid, stunned silence of
those who are beaten and who know they are beaten. 'I'll see
you have corn meal. I'll see you don't go hungry. But we all
have to make some kind of sacrifice – you *and* me. Am I right,
Leo?'

But Leo would not meet his eyes, would not be drawn into
complicity.

'What's happened to you?' Giovanni said. 'Lost your tongue,
have you? Tell them how much grain we've lost.'

'At least half,' Leo said.

'So we'll have to be satisfied with half pay, then,' the
master said.

'Signor Padrone,' Montanaro, one of the day labourers,
interrupted. He spoke with his head bowed, twisting his hat
nervously in his hands.

'Take it or leave it,' Giovanni said, cutting him short.

But Montanaro persisted. 'When the harvest was double,
did we get double pay?'

'To be honest,' Giovanni said quickly, 'if I were looking

after my own interests exclusively, I'd fire the whole lot of you – especially you day labourers.'

'If we're being honest, half pay is dishonest,' Leo said flatly.

'And if you weren't such an ignorant lot you'd thank me,' Giovanni said. 'Because the one who's making the biggest sacrifice is me. We've lost everything, and I'm offering you half pay, do you hear that?'

The men muttered and grumbled among themselves.

'Starting the end of this month,' Orso said, 'according to the League, you should pay us by the hour instead of the day. That's what the League says.'

'What's the League, anyway?' Giovanni scoffed. 'What is it?'

'They made an agreement with the Landowners' Association,' Orso said.

'The Landowners' Association – that pack of fools!'

From the farm bell tower came the peal announcing lunchtime. Giovanni moved off a few yards, turned suddenly, and snarled, 'Who's the master here, eh? Who gives the orders?' Then he stalked away, brushing angrily past the group of women who were bringing the men their food.

'Rest your bones, men,' Rigoletto said. 'The hail has done our work for us today.'

The women chatted gaily, unaware of the situation, serving out slices of cold polenta.

'Your polenta,' Rosina said to Montanaro. 'Don't you like it?'

'Yes,' the man said. He had wrapped it in a napkin.

'But you're not eating it.'

'I'll eat it later.'

'Is it enough?'

'Yes,' he said after a moment's hesitation, and on the tail of his reply, he struck off across the fields.

Sullen and speechless, the rest of the men settled down to eat.

Chapter 10

Montanaro lived in a shack by the river bank. The shack had a thatched roof, and corn grew right up to the door. There was no yard, just a poplar tree along a path.

Inside the shack's single room there was a fireplace, a table without chairs, a few pots and pans, some cornhusk mattresses flung against the walls on bits of straw. The floor was dirt.

Montanaro was the musician who played the ocarina at the dance in the poplar grove. He was squint-eyed, and he wore the ends of his moustache twisted into fine points. He lived in the shack with his mother and father, who were in their eighties, and with his children, a freckle-faced girl of twelve and a boy of three.

The boy's name was Osiride. Osiride had a continuous flow of snot running from his nose to his upper lip. His only article of clothing was a woollen undershirt that did not come down enough to cover his naked bottom or his thin thighs. Montanaro's mother was small and bent over with arthritis; his father held himself erect and had a proud moustache, but his hands trembled and every now and then he would hold them out in front of him and look to see if the trembling had, by some miracle, stopped.

When Montanaro came home, the others gathered round the table, sitting on broken crates and a tree trunk. The slice of polenta was unwrapped in the centre of the table. Over it, from the ceiling, a single salted herring dangled from a piece of string. Montanaro cut the slice in five. Each of them rubbed their piece against the herring to flavour it. Montanaro rubbed Osiride's piece for him.

'Tell him,' the mother said.

'We're good for nothing now except eating,' the father said. 'Let us go to the poorhouse.'

'They pay me on Saturday,' Montanaro said. 'We'll have enough to eat then.'

Osiride sat on his sister's lap. He had quickly eaten his portion of the single slice and said he was still hungry. Montanaro gave the boy his piece. He had already eaten, he said.

'You'll be better off and so will we,' the father said. 'Let us go to the poorhouse.'

Montanaro's fist came down on the table. 'As long as these hands can work, no poorhouse. Understand?'

'Hungry,' Osiride said.

Anger burned in Montanaro's eyes, then the flame went out, leaving his gaze absent, vacant. The meal was over. Had it ever begun? Montanaro smiled, went rummaging in a sack that hung from a nail, and said, 'I'll make your hunger go away.'

He had his little yellow terra-cotta ocarina in his hand. Now he settled the boy on his lap and blew into the instrument. It made a cheery sound.

Montanaro's tune was light-hearted. They all listened. Osiride bounced up and down on his father's knees, laughing, laughing. Montanaro wagged his head to the music.

Nobody spoke of hunger.

Chapter 11

Talk of a strike went on all summer, day after day, week after week, growing, slowly spreading over the plain, passing from mouth to mouth, from farm to farm, from district to district. At the outset, when the League men had said it was time to act, even the word 'strike' had been without meaning, unfamiliar, unheard of.

Where would this strike happen? men asked.

Everywhere, they were answered.

What was a strike? they had asked.

It was when everything stopped, nobody worked.

Not even the women?

Nobody.

It was like a germ, a seed. Boys questioned men, passed the answers on to other boys, who told other men. 'Hey, Carlèn! Come here and listen to this!'

Old people thought a strike was crazy. In the first place, there had never been one before. In the second place, how could you just let the grain rot in the fields?

On the Berlinghieri estate, old Leo Dalcò told his sons, 'Strike and before it's over we'll be eating grass from the ditches.'

'That's where you're wrong,' Orso said.

'But strike,' Leo said. 'You know what that means? It means these hands won't work any more – they won't reap, they won't harvest, they won't milk. It means everything at a standstill while the land dies. And then what? A great hunger for all of us. You think you can go through with this?'

'We have the League now,' Turo said.

'The League! The League! What is this League, anyway?' Leo wanted to know.

It was night. Summer had advanced. The fields were now parched, and the men were working by lantern light along the canals and ditches, opening sluice gates. The irrigation system ran in a network through the countryside like veins in the vast body of the plain, connecting farm to farm. Iron sluice gates were quickly raised. A burst of water shot out violently from the lock of a community canal. The water flowed in a ditch, spreading to other smaller ditches. By shouts and lantern signals, families and farms came into contact with one another as they shared a precious natural wealth between them. Three or four of the Dalcò brothers and their father were on the boundary of the Berlinghieri estate, watching, giving advice about the irrigation, talking to their neighbours. Wherever men met now there was only one subject for discussion or debate or argument – the strike.

'The landowners have to respect the agreement,' a young man of twenty said. He was from the next farm. 'They have to pay us by the hour, like a factory worker.'

'Factory workers,' someone else said. 'They've got it easy.'

An old man said, 'I've worked as a day labourer all my life, and I've had a bellyful. I'm going to strike so I can become a sharecropper.'

'Half and half on everything,' one of the Dalcò men said. 'The crops, the expenses.'

'And the work?' the man of twenty said. 'Try telling the padroni to go half and half on the work.'

Leo Dalcò remained sceptical. The League was big, the League was strong, his son Orso told him, and Orso said he would be damned if he went to work the next day.

And now Leo repeated his question. 'What is this League anyway, can you tell me that?'

'You want to know what the League is, Papà?' Orso said. 'All right, then, you listen.' Orso left the others and moved off a few yards, out of the range of the lanterns' beams. Halting, he called out, clearly, at the top of his voice, 'Strike! Strike!'

From the distance, like an echo, a voice replied, 'Strike!'

It was followed by another voice, farther away, calling, 'Strike!'

Orso returned to the circle of men, while his cry reverberated, and from near and far came five answers, ten answers, each uttering clear as a bell the word 'strike'. And on and on went the concert of voices, filling miles of the night.

Orso looked for the effect in his father's face. The old man was bent over a sluice gate. When he lifted his head, he was smiling, suddenly convinced.

'If there are so many of us,' Leo said, 'let's start right now!'

Out into the field he vanished, his tall erect frame melting into the dark. There, cupping his hands around his mouth, with conviction, with loud joy, he pronounced the single living word: *'Strike!'*

'Oh, bother,' Eleonora Berlinghieri said, glancing up at the sun, annoyed.

She was seated on the roof of the portico, painting a picture, and the sun had risen to such an angle that the small parasol attached to the easel no longer shaded her work. A few steps away, still in the cool shadows of the house by the thick wisteria, her husband lingered over breakfast while reading the newspaper. Through the trees of the park and across the garden came the pained bleating of the cattle. Eleonora summoned a housemaid from the table to readjust the slant of the parasol.

'Listen to this,' Giovanni said, about to read to his wife: ' "The meetings between the Chamber of Labour and the Landowners' Association have been broken off. We shall reply to all boycotts by boycotting the League's leaders. We shall answer violence with violence. If the working class is strong, the landowning class is equally strong." '

Alfredo leaned against the parapet, staring off at the farm, listening to the moan of the cows. Since the strike began, he had been forbidden to associate with any of the Dalcò family or to leave the confines of the park. He was a prisoner, listless, bored.

Desolina, the old maidservant, sighed as she cleared the table. 'Poor things,' she said. 'It's two days since they were milked.'

Giovanni glared at her. 'What of it?' he said. 'Are maids on strike too?'

Desolina fumbled with the cups and saucers, about to leave as quickly as she could, when Eleonora summoned her.

'Desolina.'

'Yes, signora?' The old woman attempted a curtsy.

'You must go into the village and buy some milk.'

'It's insane,' Giovanni blared. 'With a hundred cows in the stable, we have to buy milk.'

'And if you meet any of the Dalcò family, don't stop,' Eleonora said. 'Walk straight on, do you hear?'

Desolina withdrew.

'There's no way of making them see reason,' Giovanni said. 'Not even the old man. This strike is an outrage, I tell you – it's an offence to all human laws!'

'Sooner or later they'll have to give in,' Eleonora said. She was painting a picture of the façade of the villa.

'Meanwhile, the cows are bursting and the grain is rotting in the fields,' Giovanni said. He spanked the newspaper with the back of his hand, rose, and paced up and down the roof terrace. He was seething. He could not help feeling that the strike was an insult, an indignity, to him personally.

Alfredo cowered by the railing, trying to make himself invisible. He barely spoke to either his mother or his father these days and longed only to see Olmo, to be able to enter the farmyard once again. Now, not wanting to look at or see either of his parents, he kept apart, to himself, uncommunicative, observing by use of his ears and his senses. He could not bear to rest his eyes on either of them.

'We must do something,' Giovanni announced after five minutes of his frantic, caged pacing.

'Yes, darling,' said his wife, holding her head back and admiring her canvas.

'Yes, by God, I have an idea,' Giovanni said, suddenly brightening.

'I'm so glad, darling,' Eleonora said. 'And perhaps you could stop that awful pacing now. It's so hard for one to concentrate when you tramp about that way.'

Giovanni turned brusquely to his son. His son turned away.

The cows mooed dolefully.

Towards sundown, Alfredo slipped away and by a roundabout route reached one of the barred back windows of the stable. Climbing up on a derelict old cart, he peered inside into the gloom. The sounds the suffering cows emitted were outlandish, like the wild howling of some tortured prehistoric beasts. Their unmilked udders hung close to the ground, enormous, swollen to a gigantic size, their teats the thickness of a man's wrist.

A shadowy form moved among the cows' hooves. It was Olmo's uncle Rigoletto. Alfredo dropped down to stay unseen and watched with one eye from the lower corner of the window.

Rigoletto was secretly milking the cows. He was talking to them. When he came close to the window where Alfredo observed, the boy could hear his words above the frantic lowing.

'Asia, I'm here,' Rigoletto said. 'Now I'll make you feel better. I know it hurts, but it's not my fault. All the same, we're not going to give your milk to the padrone, are we?'

Alfredo gripped the bars, tears of compassion in his young eyes. Why did these things have to happen? That afternoon one of the maids had said to him, 'Don't ever grow up. Just stay a child.' Oh, why couldn't everybody get along without all this bitter hostility?

The floor of the stable, in the thick ooze of straw and dung, showed white with streaks and puddles of milk.

Chapter 12

It was a perfect summer's day. Olmo and his grandfather sat back in the grass on the slope of the dyke, facing the river and watching an occasional boat sweep along. In his hands, the old man twisted some wire, bending and bending it to shape a strange object. It was to be a mole trap, he told Olmo, and now Olmo scoured the bank for telltale signs of a mole or maybe for a burrow into which to lay his grandfather's contraption.

'Hey, Grandpa,' Olmo said, all at once serious. 'What are scabs, anyway?'

'They're lousy bastards who come and work when other men are on strike,' Leo Dalcò said, eyes fast on his handiwork.

'Why, don't they like to go on strike?'

'It's not that exactly. It's because they're poor and ignorant, poorer and more ignorant even than we are.'

Olmo watched the old man's hands at their work. Suddenly his ears pricked up. He heard something – music. Olmo could tell by his grandfather's face that the old man had not heard it.

'Come on,' the boy said. 'I hear music playing.'

'I don't hear anything,' Leo said.

'Maybe there's dancing,' Olmo said.

The old man got stiffly to his feet and started to the top of the dyke. 'Not so fast,' he called after his grandson. Olmo waited at the top and took his grandfather's walking-stick. Placing a hand on Olmo's shoulder, Leo started towards where the music seemed to be coming from. He thought he heard it too now.

There was a bend in the dyke road where a leafy thicket of locust trees sprang like weeds and below which, on level ground, a plantation of young poplars was laid out with wheat growing between the widely spaced aisles. It was from this wheat field that voices came and a phonograph blared. Leo tried to move more quickly, his curiosity piqued, but he could only drag his feet along wearily. He was tired, drained, aged by these impassioned days of the strike. In some way, the present struggle was pushing and forcing his life to a culmination.

The old man and the boy squatted in the grass, screened by the locusts, and surveyed the scene below them. A group of ten or so men and women were at work, bent over sickles, reaping the over-ripe grain.

'Are they scabs?' Olmo whispered.

Leo Dalcò ignored the question. He beamed, a weight suddenly flew off his heart, and he drew the boy to him, embracing him with one arm and using the other to point. 'Look there,' he said. 'Who's that?'

'Signor Giovanni,' Olmo said. 'And Alfredo's mother and aunt.'

'And over there with the fancy clothes – that's Ottavio,' the old patriarch said.

'They're scabs,' Olmo said.

'Landowners,' Leo said, laughing.

It was incongruous, it was comic. Here was the Berlinghieri family, having summoned city friends and associates to help, all of them dressed in their finery, trying to do the work of peasants. There was Renato Vitali, Giovanni's cousin. There was Pasini, the lawyer, and his daughter. Most incongruous of all was Don Tarcisio in his biretta and cassock, looking as though he would suffer apoplexy at any moment.

Giovanni Berlinghieri himself attempted both to work and to inspire others to work. 'Courage, now. Don't give in. Don't sit down,' he called out, playing the gadfly. A moment later he told the lawyer, 'Careful how you tie the sheaves.' Next he was telling the priest that he was sorry but that Don Tarcisio had to work, that there was still some time before lunch would be served.

The women, as if attending a garden party, wore elegant tight-sleeved dresses and straw hats. There was a flurry of maids emptying hampers of food and laying out an elaborate al fresco meal. A large square of canvas had been tied up between the trees as a sunshade. Even the maids were comical, lifting their skirts with one hand, their taut faces revealing how much they disliked the unaccustomed feel of stubble under their shoes, the unaccustomed sun and heat. There were tubs of iced wine and several watermelons cooling. The party had driven out in small carts, from which the horses had been unhitched and now grazed at the margins of the field. A windup Victrola, watched over by one of the younger maids, played two or three popular songs over and over again for the reapers' entertainment.

'The rich out there sweating,' said Leo, in the manner of one recounting a dream, 'and us, the poor, lying on our backs in the cool shade of a tree. It's too beautiful, too beautiful.' A great happiness shone in the old man's eyes, like the beholding of some vision or of some long wished-for revelation.

'Don't they look funny,' Olmo said.

They did. Their movements were unsteady, awkward, clumsy. Giovanni Berlinghieri had a handkerchief wrapped around the palm of one hand where it had obviously blistered. His wife solicitously asked to have the wound shown to her every five or ten minutes. Ottavio sweated but would not take off his elegant sport coat. The priest was as red in the face as the wine he liked to swill, but would not remove his biretta. As for the grain, they trampled underfoot nearly as much as they cut.

Tomorrow morning, old Dalcò reflected, *when they wake up and can't straighten their backs, when their right arms are stiff with pain, maybe they will accord us some respect.* Leo had propped himself against the trunk of a tree. The unfinished mole trap lay in the grass by his side. 'Olmo,' he said, 'you must always remember this day, because you are witnessing things you may never witness again in your whole life. I had to wait seventy-three years to see this – a priest working, landowners working.'

'Is this Socialism, Grandpa?'

'In a way,' the old man said. 'But sooner or later this will end, and we'll be back in the fields sweating and labouring.' He motioned to the trap and told Olmo to finish it. Then he asked him to break off a leafy branch and fan him with it, saying he always loved a breeze.

Olmo sat beside his grandfather, fanning him with a locust branch.

'Seventy-three years,' the patriarch said in a faint voice, 'so don't you forget, eh.' His eyes shone as if he were weeping, but on his face there was a broad smile.

Olmo saw the peace and the joy in his grandfather's gaze, and he felt strangely moved by it, so moved that he swore to himself that he would never forget this day.

The boy did not see that his grandfather was dead.

Chapter 13

The small square in front of the country railroad station was festive with fluttering red flags and banners, and it was thronged with children, all of them scrubbed clean and in a holiday mood. On one side, a puppet stall had been set up, with benches for watching the show until it was time to board the train. But first there was icecream for everyone, served by a vendor dressed in white, whose wagon, a great swan with open wings that extended over the wheels of the cart, was the marvel of everyone present.

'Icecream!' the vendor cried. 'Free icecream for all the little travellers!'

In its beak, the swan held a long tricoloured ribbon. The fantastic wagon became so mobbed that the parents seeing their sons and daughters off had to keep the children circulating in order for those at the rear to get a chance to take their free cones.

The summer and the strike had drawn on. Between peasants and landowners there was sheer rancour, and the much-feared famine was at hand. In the midst of the deadlock, a number of the children were being sent, evacuated, to the shore for a summer holiday. Railroad and dock workers from Genoa, in solidarity with the Po valley peasants, had arranged for a train to bring a coach load of children to the seaside, where, on the other side of the Apennines, they would be welcomed into the homes of fellow workers and fellow Socialists. The banners proclaimed this and other things about fraternity and the oppressed that none of the children knew how to read.

But read or not, the children were excited. They had tasted icecream (most of them for the first time), they were about to see a puppet show (most of them for the first time), and ahead of them was a long journey on a train (most of them had never been on a train before). And in the excitement and laughter and gaiety of their children, parents had a brief taste of happiness too. Inevitably, there was also sorrow – and fear – since not a single one of these children had ever spent a night away from home.

Olmo, shy and withdrawn, would not sit on the benches with the other children but wanted to stand to one side by the fence near his mother. He was unable to tell his mother why he preferred staying alongside her now because he did not understand it himself, since at home he spent most of his time escaping from her and her tendency to smother him, to worry over him.

The boy missed his grandfather, felt the pain of the loss, sensed that the family had lost its centre, its key, was rudderless. He knew now at the station that he would miss his mother intolerably, so without quite clinging to her skirts, he clung to her still – three or four feet off.

Rosina kneeled and spoke to her son, urging him to join

the other children on the benches, licked a handkerchief and wiped the icecream off his chin, tucked his shirt into his trousers. He was ashamed to be seen by the children he knew fussed over by his mother, but neither would he turn away from her. Instead, he lapsed into silence, moodiness, loneliness. The several other children from the farm who were there Olmo carefully avoided.

Montanaro, the man Olmo knew as the ocarina player and day labourer, spoke to Rosina. Olmo's mother had urged him to send his two children to Genoa, and she had even patched together some of Olmo's old clothes for Montanaro's boy and found a suitable dress and some shoes for the girl. Montanaro smiled, thanking Rosina. Osiride and the girl held their father's hands tightly, cowering, seeming afraid even to smile. Their eyes were big with wonder, and snot still ran from the boy's nose. They had never eaten icecream before, never seen so many children before, never before been to the railroad station, let alone ridden on a train.

Now there were cheers and clapping hands and laughter as the show started. Rosina and Montanaro rushed the children to the near benches, sat them there, and then withdrew again to the fence. Olmo immediately rejoined his mother, but the other two stayed where they had been put, the girl holding tightly to her brother's hand. Seeing his children among other children who were enjoying themselves made Montanaro smile so broadly that his moustaches curled upwards more than ever and his bad eye went even more askew.

Two puppets stood out against a backdrop of violent colours, purple and pink. One of them, Sandrone, was an old peasant, with a peasant's wrinkled face and a drinker's great red nose. The other, younger and fairer, was Fagiolino.

'Fagiolino, wait a minute,' said Sandrone. 'Sandrone has to think.' The wizened puppet leaped to the edge of the stage, dropped his head to one side, and pressed his hands to his temples, concentrating.

'Remember, Sandrone,' said Fagiolino, 'the reformers say you should earn ten centesimi more an hour. The Socialists say, on the other hand, that the land should belong to those that cultivate it, that there must be no more masters and no more slaves – '

'Wait a moment,' Sandrone said, leaving his corner and approaching Fagiolino. 'Just one moment. I have thought.'

'Well?' said Fagiolino.

'Long live the Socialist Party!' cried Sandrone. 'Long live the General Strike! Long live the Revolution!'

The children greeted Sandrone's declaration with cheers and applause, and even the parents, scattered here and there at the edges of the gathering, laughed and applauded. Now, on the stage, Sandrone and Fagiolino did a kind of ballet. All at once, it broke off. Sandrone spoke out in exaggerated fear. 'Fagiolino, Fagiolino! Quick! A policeman's coming!'

'Grab your stick, Sandrone,' said Fagiolino.

From the back of the stage, a puppet carabiniere advanced in a three-cornered hat and chin strap. Sandrone and Fagiolino, armed with rolling pins, fell on him, raining blows on his head.

'There, hoo hoo! Give it to him!' shouted Sandrone gleefully.

The children shrieked with joy.

'Hurrah for the strike! Down with the cops!' shouted Fagiolino.

The children squirmed with pleasure.

'Ow, ow, ow, ow!' cried the puppet carabiniere.

From the children roars of laughter.

But from a corner of the square, before anyone had noticed, two real-life carabinieri suddenly swooped in on horses, sabres drawn, and were hacking at the puppet stall. For several moments, the audience was motionless. Was this too part of the show? The backdrop was soon hanging in shreds, the stall was teetering, as the police, in their three-cornered hats and chin straps, exactly like their stage counterpart, slashed and slashed, their horses wheeling, weaving, clopping loudly on the stones of the cobbled square. The policemen grunted and cursed and gave their horses orders, and there were sounds of canvas ripping, and the puppeteer, buried in the tangle of his smashed stall, shouted desperately for help.

A woman leaped to her feet, ordering the children into the station, herding them, urging them, sweeping them off the benches with waving arms. Rosina screamed for Olmo, forgetting momentarily that he stood only a few feet away from her, and she ran to the benches to Montanaro's children.

Montanaro, meanwhile, a cry on his lips, rushed to the aid of the puppeteer, unarmed, lunging at the first horse in hopes of ramming a fist in one of its nostrils and causing it to unseat its rider. The man, the ocarina player, the day labourer, with starving aged parents at home and ill-fed children about him, felt unleashed in him all the pent-up hate and fury of thirty years of sweat, misery, starvation, hardship, outrage, exploitation, because for the first time in his life the actual enemy was personified, he beheld him face to face. Had Montanaro spoken, had he been able to articulate his thoughts, they might have been these: *Thirty years you robbed and stole and bled me, but now don't rob my children – all these children – of this day's small pleasure. You took bread from my children's mouths, but don't steal from these innocent children now, don't rob them of this sunlight, don't, because I will stop you with my own bare hands.*

'No, no, come back!' Rosina screamed at Montanaro, tearing his children away from the benches.

Olmo clutched the fence, his back pressed tight against it, watching, paralysed by fright. He saw Montanaro rush forward as everyone else scattered pell-mell the other way; he heard the shouts, the puppeteer's cry for help. Olmo saw only Montanaro meeting the attack.

Montanaro got a hand on the horse's bit and was about to bring his fist to the muzzle when the rider wheeled in the saddle and cut the farmhand down with his sabre. Olmo saw it coming; he opened his mouth to warn Montanaro, to scream, but no sound came out. The boy saw the sabre slash down and split Montanaro's skull, like a knife splitting a melon, and he saw the man he knew fall under the horses' hooves, trampled.

Rosina saw it too, had also seen it coming. She had clutched the man's children to her bosom, shielding their faces, so that they had not seen, and for their sake ridding herself of the terror and horror she felt – willing herself rid of them – she shepherded the children through the small station and on to the platform, her own son in tow, stricken. Rosina spoke calmly to the two children, feigned calm, told them what a good show it had been and how their father would miss them and for them to look after Olmo for her.

The train was in the station, huffing and chuffing. The locomotive was decked out with banners and red flags. 'Long live the strike!' one of them read. Parents and the conductor and the stationmaster all helped the children quickly aboard, pushing them through the open windows even. The train whistled. Soon children thronged the windows, leaning out, waving their hands, shouting, waving small red flags. Steam shot out from between the wheels, and with tears from parents and children, from the platform and from the moving train, the train rumbled out of the station, its whistle toot, toot, tooted gaily, as if there had been no hunger, no strife, no carabinieri, no man's skull riven by a sabre and pounded by horses' hooves.

The holiday began.

Olmo sat on a hard bench, staring straight ahead, seeing nothing, holding on inside. He wanted to run and hide and to cry, but the coach was packed, and there was no place to be alone. He wanted not to think about what he had witnessed in the station square. But he could not help the monstrous images from flowing into his head. He felt pain, he felt, containing it, that he might burst. Where was he going? What had happened?

The train rushed forward over the rails, beginning to lull him. Had Montanaro's children seen? Olmo could not bear to think they had, was afraid to lift his gaze and look at the children and possibly, from their faces, find out. Now they too, like him, were fatherless. He stole a glance across the aisle, where they sat. Their faces were impassive. The breeze from the open window blew their hair, snarling it. The snot-nosed boy clutched his sister, both of them as mute as ever.

Thoughts of Montanaro tugged at Olmo, thoughts of his grandfather tugged at him. Death. Thoughts came to him unbidden, drifting in the same way that fluff blew down from the big poplars in April.

Fanning the old man with the leaves that day and suddenly Alfredo had sprung out of the thicket bringing Olmo a piece of meat wrapped in a cloth napkin and Olmo telling him to be quiet, not to wake his grandfather, and Alfredo had asked to be shown how to make a mole trap, and Olmo ate the meat and Alfredo, dressed in his sailor suit and straw hat, asking him why his grandfather slept with his eyes open, and Olmo noticing it and at the same time seeing an ant cross the furrows of the old man's brow and the old man not bothering to flick it off and Olmo saying his grandfather knew how to

do all kinds of things and had once seen Garibaldi, and then
Olmo got up and gave his grandfather's head a light kiss,
and next he and Alfredo were setting the trap in a mole's
lair and Alfredo saying he was a Socialist too, and the two
of them hidden deep in the thicket, their trousers open, playing with themselves, showing themselves to each other, and
at the end of it Alfredo putting a hand in his pocket and
pulling the pocket out and showing the hole in it to Olmo and
saying he was a Socialist with holes in his pockets too, and
from below in the grainfield Regina crying out 'a wasp, a
wasp,' and then pandemonium, the women screaming, and the
two boys peeped out of the greenery to see the reapers in
flight, all of them, the maids too, and the pair of boys laughed
together as though they were watching a puppet show and
Olmo wanted to wake his grandfather so the old man could
enjoy it too, maybe this was Socialism too, the wasps attack-
ing the landowners was maybe Socialism, because one time
Olmo had seen his uncle Rigoletto stung countless times over
the face and neck and arms and his face swelled and Rigoletto
was featureless and sick for four days with the stings in another grainfield, and when Olmo touched his grandfather his
grandfather was dead dead dead.

It was the train clacking over the rails, dead dead, dead
dead. The fields were wheeling by, the poplars, the rotted
grain, the ditches, the vines, wheeling, wheeling, and dead his
grandfather, dead, dead, dead, and Montanaro with his skull
split, the way a watermelon is split, and the horses' hooves
pounding the open skull on the stones of the square, dead
dead, dead dead.

And the boy heard a voice come to him; it was his grandfather's voice, and the voice was both speaking to Olmo
and calling to him, and Olmo did not know where the voice
came from, but he knew it was his grandfather's voice, or
maybe it was the voice of his unknown father, and it told
him that in his life he must take care of his mother, and
he must always help those who were weak and persecuted and
cried out for help, even if it meant stepping down one step for
others or putting others before himself. Whose voice was
this? It was not his grandfather's voice; it was the voice
of the father he never saw, never had; yes, it was his father's
voice, and now, unthinking, unbidden, Olmo found himself

across the aisle, and he had taken the little boy Osiride, roughly torn him from his sister, roughly because Olmo knew no other way yet, and pulling the shirt out of his trousers, the shirt his mother had tucked in for him, Olmo took the tail of it and looking around to be sure he was unseen by anyone except the boy's sister, who did not matter, he bent the boy's head down and wiped the rope of snot off the upper lip. Then wanting to say something to him and his sister but being shy and not knowing what to say, Olmo just blurted out that they were all going to the sea. They looked at Olmo blankly. Olmo said, 'The sea. It's as big as a cornfield. Bigger.'

Alfredo, hearing the train whistle, pressed on across the deserted fields, and when he got to the place there were tears and sweat mixed in his eyes. Around him, the countryside seemed abandoned and hostile. Alfredo stood by the tracks now, hearing the whistle again. Soon the train would round the bend and come down the straight stretch. Olmo was on that train. Even though he was a Socialist too, Alfredo had not been allowed to go with the other children to the sea. He knew he could not have asked his mother or father to let him go because they were not Socialists like him and did not want him associating with Socialists; but he would show Olmo now that he was no coward, and, some day, when Alfredo was a man, he would stand up to his father and be the Socialist he wanted to be, like Olmo already was.

He lay down between the tracks, lengthwise, face up. The pain of waiting was excruciating; the vibration of the rails became almost unbearable. Alfredo's eyes were shut tight. He tried to press his back and legs down on the ties. *Olmo, don't leave me alone*, he thought. Then he was swallowed up by the thundering mass.

At the windows of the train, the children of peasants watched places that were familiar to them wheel away and disappear from sight.

Olmo was back in his own place on the wooden seat across the aisle. He had slept. He had heard the litany of the wheels, dead dead, dead dead, dead dead, and when he opened his eyes hours later (only he did not know it was hours later), he found himself in blackness. They were in a tunnel, it was like

94

death, and then suddenly, briefly, they were in dazzling sunshine, and there was a vast flash of blue like no blue Olmo had ever seen. *What a lot of water*, was all he could think in his awe. It was the sea, except it was bigger, much bigger than he had expected, and it was like some new form of life, some new breath of life. And then no sooner had everyone rushed to one side of the coach to look out, crying 'The sea! The sea!' when they were plunged back into the darkness of a tunnel again and once more there came over Olmo a cold sense of death.

Death, life, death. How long before the cold and the dark were gone and the new life came?

Chapter 14

Seventeen-year-old Olmo Dalcò, with a light step, walked the long road from the highway into the farm. The mulberry trees were bare and the fields were brown. Everything was different now, he felt, and yet, looking around him, nothing bore this out. Everything here was the same. Perhaps it was only he who had changed. A year was a long time to be away. On a farm a year is nothing, nothing changes; ploughing, sowing, reaping, the cycle is never-ending and always the same. But to have gone away something of a boy still and seen what he had seen in this year, endure what he had endured, it is inevitable that the boy change and that if he is lucky enough to come home again, he comes home a man.

From the farmyard came the thudding of an engine, a big one, Olmo judged, from the sound of it. He knew they would be at the end of the threshing now. Straight ahead were the stately trees of the park; on his right, through the aisle of bare mulberries, he could see the mass of the farm buildings. Shifting his load slightly and getting it up higher on his back, Olmo pressed on. He knew he had been changed. How much had he changed?

He remembered the green feeling he had had the autumn before, when, on coming through that mountain tunnel, he looked out the train window at the indescribable confusion of the station. There were motors and horses and mules and streams of men clotting the roads. There was a tent on the station platform for the wounded; but they were so many

that they spilled out into the open, the stretchers lying everywhere, the Red Cross nurses' uniforms flashing white as they
fluttered here and there among the dying and wounded. Away
in the mountains, distant cannon could be heard like summer
thunder.

Olmo's mouth went dry. On the platform, right under his
eyes, dripping like oil from an engine, he saw blood leaking
through a stretcher and pooling. Then the train lurched,
hurtling the packed recruits together (now they were all silent),
crept forward thirty yards, and halted again. Olmo saw
groups of men in ragged uniforms, bound one behind the other
on a long chain. They were guarded by carabinieri wearing
steel helmets.

Uneasiness spread through the coach of young soldiers then.
Who were these men? Why were they chained? What had
they done?

'They're a disgrace to Italy,' an officer told them. 'They're
deserters, the bastards. Take a good look at them. They are
traitors to the fatherland.'

Olmo had one shoulder out of the window. The faces of the
prisoners had something familiar about them. There was no
mistaking it, they were all peasant faces, sunburnt and stolid.
Then Olmo started. The last man in line, with a dirty beard
and bloodstained bandage over his forehead, was his uncle
Turo. Olmo called to him wildly.

The man's head came up, searching for the person who
shouted his name. 'Olmo!' he cried, 'Olmo!' And he began
walking alongside the slow-moving train, making the five other
men on the chain move with him.

'They got you too, eh?' Turo said, grinning up at the
window. 'It's hell up there. They're going to kill all of us.'
He had been revived by the sight of his nephew, and he was
shouting like a man obsessed. Now he tried to cling to the
handle of the door of Olmo's coach, but a yank on the chain
brought him to the ground and made Olmo think of the way
animals were roped and brought down before they were
slaughtered. A pair of carabinieri were bent over Turo, beating
him with the butts of their rifles.

Leaning as far out of the window as he could, Olmo kept
calling his uncle's name. 'Turo, Turo!'

'Fuck the king,' Turo shouted back. 'Fuck the king and
fuck the fatherland.'

Then the train was in another tunnel, and this time when they emerged there were steep hills and mist and it was much colder. After the train, they marched, and the road ended in a wrecked village. There was shelling on the ridge above them, not much at first, and the new men could not tell if it was Italian artillery or Austrian. Not until they got to the top along the muddy road, with the wounded being taken down on stretchers, and could see across to the next ridge could they tell about the guns. Olmo saw the soft puffs with the yellow-white flash in the centre. That was the beginning of his new knowledge – of understanding death, of learning to live with it, of learning to conquer the fear of it.

Olmo walked along the autumn road now, less than half a mile from home, in his grey-green uniform with the red and white bars at the throat of his tunic. His shins were wrapped in puttees; a thin blanket was rolled in a tight roll at the top of his musette bag. Almost eighteen, Olmo was a good-looking young man, solidly built, broad in the chest. His hair was cropped close at the sides. His face had taken on a thoughtful look, inspired trust. There was something friendly and de-liberate in his eyes. He felt good now, in high spirits.

The other lesson Olmo found out from the war was about the Socialists. They were everywhere; they came from every-where, from every part of Italy. It was even understood that on the other side, among the Austrians, they were all Socialists too. The Socialists, Olmo had learned, were even bigger than the sea. This certain knowledge made him stronger, more sure of himself. There was comfort and strength in being part of something so big, so universal. It also released him, more or less, from the anxiety of being fatherless, for now he had something outside himself, outside his private plight, into which to feed his energy and thought. A social conscience had brought Olmo to manhood.

Drawing up to the gateway to the courtyard, Olmo felt his face. He needed a shave. A dog rushed out at him, snarling at his ankles. The sound of the steam-powered threshing-machine racketed off the four walls of the quadrangle.

'Stupid, don't you know me any more?' Olmo said.

The dog wagged its tail, beating it wildly, and began fawn-ing.

Inside the farmyard, they were all at work, and nobody saw him yet. Then a boy approached him shyly. Without breaking step, Olmo slipped the pack off his back and handed it to the boy, whom he did not know.

Then he could hold back no longer. He saw his mother, his legs went out faster and faster, and he was running to her.

Chapter 15

'He who dies for his country,' said Regina dramatically, 'has lived greatly.'

Alfredo lay back in the semi-dark on the sacks of grain, lifted his scabbarded dress sword, and prodded with it between his cousin's legs.

'Oh, Lieutenant,' she said in a whisper.

'You're dying for this, aren't you?' he said.

They were in a darkened loft, and, outside, down below in the courtyard, the big threshing-machine chugged away. Alfredo was dressed in the elegant uniform of an Italian officer, with riding breeches and leather boots. He was near seventeen; his cousin, Regina, was now twenty-four. Regina was plump but attractive. She had a great pile of reddish-brown hair, which she wore tied at the nape of her neck, and she always dressed well and carefully.

'Aren't you?' he repeated cruelly.

'Yes,' Regina said. 'You know I am.' She was leaning into the tip of the sheathed sword and rocking slightly, forward and back, and feeling her excitement grow.

'I can't go on,' he said. 'It's like being buried alive. Here I am hidden away in safety, while out there they're fighting.' He tried to bring the sword down, but she had grasped it in her hand and held it there, grinding into it.

'Oh, please, not that again,' she said. 'Not now. And please don't stop what you were doing.'

'Bitch!' he said viciously, 'bitch!'

'Yes,' she said. 'Your bitch. Use your bitch.'

Alfredo let go his grip on the sword. It dangled uselessly in her hand.

'Alfredo, no,' she begged.

He laughed at her. She threw herself on top of him. 'Alfredo, you mustn't act like this. I want to keep on playing.' Her hands were unbuttoning his tunic and reaching for his belt. She tried kissing him on the mouth, but he squirmed and pulled her head aside by her hair. Regina sank her teeth into his neck.

'Bitch,' he repeated, and slapped her hard, once, twice, and a third time.

'You know the more you hit me, the more you make me yours,' she said. She clung to him still, then with one hand she brushed her loose hair out of her face. The blows had stung. There were tears in her eyes.

'Enough of this stupid game,' Alfredo said.

'Let me have some fun,' she pleaded. 'I'm good at it, aren't I?'

'I'm a coward,' he said. 'Letting my family do this to me.'

'No,' she said. 'It's different for you. Your father was right in what he did. The estate needs an heir, and you might have been killed.'

Alfredo gave a bitter laugh. 'Instead, my manhood has been killed.' He had spent the entire year in uniform at home on the farm. After Alfredo received his commission, Alfredo's father had bribed a medical officer to keep him out of action.

'And me?' Regina said. 'Don't I mean anything to you?'

Alfredo covered her mouth with his, his hand worked at her breasts. He lay on her, and she ground against him, softly moaning. He kept her moaning, fingering the nipples of her breasts. Then all at once he flung her away and jerked up on to his feet.

'Don't,' she said. 'Don't leave me this way.'

'A bitch in heat, that's all you are.'

He was at the window, giving the shutters a violent kick that made them fly open. Sunlight burst into the room. Below, in the courtyard, he caught a glimpse of Olmo just as he handed his musette bag to the boy.

All of the Dalcò family, the ones who were left, were busy around the machine. It was a colossal machine of wood and iron, with ladders and catwalks, and it was mounted on wheels. The wooden parts were painted bright red; the iron, black. It was powered, in a system of belts and pulleys, by a steam engine with a tall thin stack. This engine, which looked like an early locomotive, stood several yards distant from the thresher. A mountain of wheat sheaves was stacked by the machine and fed into it by men and women whose faces were masked from the dust by handkerchiefs.

Olmo threw his arms around his mother before she knew who it was. She uttered a breathless cry and immediately wept with joy. It was him; it was her Olmo. She lifted the cap off his head and touched his hair, like some long lost admired object. Olmo took the cap from her hand and slapped it on to the head of the unknown boy who carried his knapsack. Then he hugged his mother tight to him.

But otherwise the threshers did not interrupt themselves. Those working nearest Olmo embraced him; the ones on the machine greeted him with a wave or a nod. A few questions were asked him, but the questions and answers were drowned out by the noise. Olmo saw that the women had aged and that the girls had grown into young women. He also saw how many of the old faces were missing, carried off in the storm of the war. How many of them would return? How many had died on the battlefield? No word had ever come about Turo. Doubtless he had been shot, in disgrace, as a deserter. There were many new faces about too.

And then Olmo was stripping off his tunic and joining the rest of them. Some of the men, wearing hooded capes fashioned out of burlap sacks, carried bales of straw. Others bore the filled sacks of wheat to a wagon. Olmo hefted one of the wheat sacks on to his back and, bent over under its weight, started to the loft with it.

Alfredo and Regina were at the bottom of the stairs when Olmo got there.

'Atten-tion!' Alfredo called out.

Olmo saw the officer's uniform, dropped the sack, and came to attention. He held a hand stiffly to his forehead. 'At your orders, Lieutenant.'

'At ease, you stupid shit. Don't you recognize me?' Alfredo said.

Olmo grinned. 'Fucking officer. The war's over. Nobody gives us orders any more.'

'Kiss me, my hero,' Alfredo said.

The two embraced. Olmo looked at Regina for the first time and nodded to her.

'There was no one to take care of the silkworms,' Alfredo said, gesturing with his head to the loft. 'There's nothing but rats up there now.'

'Like the trenches,' Olmo said.

'You must have a lot of stories to tell,' Alfredo said.

'Tell us about the trenches,' Regina said.

'What's it like in the trenches with the enemy shooting at you?' Alfredo pressed, boyish and eager.

Olmo had the sack on his shoulders again and had started up the stairs with it. 'You feel like a rat,' he said.

The other two followed him.

'And at night?' Alfredo asked.

The wooden stairs creaked. Olmo went all the way up to the top, where he flung the sack down in place. 'At night it's cold as hell.' He looked the pair of them in the eye. 'And you're always soaked, like bread in soup.'

The bitterness in Olmo's voice made Alfredo uneasy. Things were different now, changed, and both of them knew it. Olmo understood this and accepted it, but Alfredo could not. He had stayed home, and for him very little had changed. On an impulse, he took Olmo in a wrestling hold, and they grappled, tumbling down on to the sacks like in the old days.

But it was no good. Olmo's heart was not in it; they were not the same boys they had been a year before. Olmo had seen the slaughter, had lived through the shelling of Austrian guns, while Alfredo had stayed cosily at home. And 'hen, too, Olmo resented Regina's presence, knowing she did not like him, had never liked him.

That had started four or five years before, when Olmo and Alfredo came often to the loft and played with themselves and talked about girls and about getting them. They had talked about Regina then, about getting her up into the loft on the sacks and playing with her. Alfredo had told Olmo that he spied on Regina through keyholes and saw her naked once. He told him he had seen her naked breasts. They made an elaborate plan for her coming up to the loft and their taking turns with her, feeling her, and, if she liked it, maybe having her. But Regina, in her early twenties, already snobbish and under her mother's influence aspiring to become one day mistress of the Berlinghieri household, was not about to have anything to do with a Dalcò or with any other farmhand. Alfredo reported to Olmo that Regina would not come to the loft with them, and Olmo had understood. After that, Regina and Olmo had always been careful to avoid each other.

Alfredo tried to joke now. He wanted to remind Olmo of the times they had climbed the bell tower and looked out dreamily, imagining they saw the distant city. In the cloud shapes, they used to point out to each other the city's different tall buildings.

'Do you remember all the things we saw?' Alfredo said.

It was no good. Olmo felt the alien presence of the girl, her snobbishness, her stiffness, the way she wanted to patronize him now, and besides, after the trenches it was useless thinking that Alfredo and he could any longer view the world in the same way. Cuttingly, almost cruelly, Olmo said, 'I suppose you saw the fighting from up there too.' He then brushed impatiently past them and down the stairs.

'Olmo, wait!' Alfredo shouted.

On the way down, nearing the bottom, Olmo slowed his steps. A blonde girl with a very pretty face stood there at the open door looking up at him. From her features and from her fair skin and smooth hands, he saw she was not a peasant. He had never laid eyes on her before, and she was so pretty and slim in her long blue dress that Olmo nearly came to a stop on the lowest flight of stairs. Then, as he was about to pass her, he paused close to her face and kissed her lightly on the lips, looking at her, looking straight into her eyes.

'You must be Olmo,' she said.

'And who are you?'

'My name is Anita. Anita Foschi.'

'From the north?' he said, studying her.

'Yes. From Sedico.'

'We camped near Sedico once.'

'I'm a refugee. I lost my whole family.'

'What did you do in your village?'

'I was a schoolteacher,' Anita said.

'Come,' he said.

He led her out into the bright sunlight of the farmyard.

Chapter 16

Giovanni Berlinghieri sat at a table in the threshing yard, a big ledger open before him. He had a grizzled beard and wore a battered old Panama hat. A white waistcoat was buttoned up over his paunch.

'Hurrah for our war hero!' he called out to Olmo, who was coming towards him. The master laid his glasses down on the ledger and sat back comfortably, expansively, in his chair. It was his invitation for Olmo to stop and speak.

Giovanni introduced Olmo to the new foreman, Attila Bergonzi. Bergonzi seemed to be in his middle twenties. He was tall and lean, with a thick mop of black hair. His eyes bulged slightly, and he had a longish nose. It was obvious to Olmo that Attila was another demobilized soldier. He was dressed in black breeches and boots. The way he moved showed that he was neither a member of the peasant nor of the landowning class.

Attila flashed Olmo a big toothy smile. Olmo raised two fingers to his temple and sketched a salute. 'Hello, corporal,' he muttered.

Attila had been at work at the nearby scales, where the sacks of wheat were weighed and tallied in the ledger. Tucked into his belt were small lengths of twine, with which the sacks were tied. The man was blustering, eager, sycophantic, and unable to look you straight in the eye. He was one of a proliferating new breed that Olmo had encountered in the army, and he took an instant dislike to him.

Regina and Alfredo were in the yard now. Regina had shoved the ledger aside and sat importantly up on the table by her uncle. There was something provocative, almost lusty, in the way she perched there, her back to Olmo, the thick rich hair cascading down her shoulders.

Olmo went to the wagon to take another sack from the pile. Nina, who was standing there, shook her head. Olmo did not comprehend, and his face showed it.

'No, Olmo, no,' Rigoletto said. 'Our part is finished.'

'Have we had our half already?' Olmo asked.

'Try to understand, Olmo,' the master said. 'You've been

away, and there are a lot of things you don't know.'

Attila remained fixed by the table, hands on his hips, legs apart, nodding confirmation of the master's words.

'I know we always shared half and half,' Olmo said.

'This is an unusual year,' Giovanni Berlinghieri said. 'There was the rental of the machine and the extra hired labour. It's a bad time.'

A small crowd had gathered round. The thresher idled. All eyes were on the men clustered by the tallying table.

'Even sharing half and half is robbery, since we do all the work,' Olmo said. 'And now not even that.'

Giovanni raised his voice. 'Do you know why I had to hire extra hands? Because almost all of you men got yourselves killed in the war, that's why.'

'Papà, really!' Alfredo spoke up. 'You have no right to say that.'

'You keep quiet and play at war if you like,' Giovanni snapped at his son. 'Do you know how much I spent to keep you at home?'

'No, I don't know. How much did you spend?' Alfredo's face burned with rage.

'More than you're worth!' his father answered acrimoniously.

A number of the hands laughed openly. More of them had drawn around. They had tugged the handkerchiefs off their faces. Olmo caught a glimpse of Alfredo out of the corner of his eye, and what he saw in Alfredo's face, this public humiliation, pained him.

'First you shame me by keeping me from fighting, now you reproach me for it. Just remember,' Alfredo said, 'I was the one who wanted to go. You prevented it.'

'At your age I used to get up at four every morning to check the stables,' Giovanni said, turning in his chair to take them all in. 'You old-timers recall that. And at threshing-time, I was the first to be up and the last to go to bed. That's the truth, and everyone here knows it.'

Regina tried to calm her uncle, to soothe him. 'Uncle Giovanni,' she purred, 'times have changed. Ideals –'

'Ideals! Ideals!' Giovanni shouted. 'Property, the estate, increasing milk production, extending the farm – aren't these ideals any more? Respectability, devotion to the church, love for the land, loyalty to the family, credit at the bank?'

'Come on, Uncle Giovanni, come on!' Regina soothed, laying a hand on his shoulder.

'And respect,' the master said. 'Respect, respect, *respect!* A son's respect for his father.' He beat on the table with his fist, oblivious now of everyone else.

But Olmo suddenly sprang up on to the wagon that was loaded with sacks, drawing attention away from the father and son and to himself. He held a bayonet in his hand, and in a calm, premeditated fashion, he plunged the blade into the filled sacks, one after the other. Grain gushed out like water.

Giovanni shot Attila a glance that was a command. Attila bent down and collected a handful of the grain, then raised his head to Olmo. 'It's not right to do things like this,' Attila said. 'You heard the master. You've had your share of the grain. Did the army teach you nothing?'

The two men stared long at each other. Olmo did not speak but stood there unflinching on the wagon bed with the bayonet in his hand at the ready.

'I'm a soldier like you,' Attila went on loudly, for the benefit of all the gathering. 'The master has given all he can. He had to hire modern machines because there was no one here to work, but machines make life easy too. It's a change, it's progress. We've all got to work together and understand each other. Now come on down from there.'

Alfredo, believing Attila was about to spring up on to the wagon after Olmo, moved in, his hand on his drawn sabre. 'Watch out, Attila,' he said. 'There are two of us now.'

'Keep out of this, you idiot,' Giovanni shouted.

Now everyone had stopped working. Someone had even cut the steam engine. It was quiet, and they all stared at Attila in silence, waiting to see what move he would make. The seconds passed. The flow of grain dribbled to a stop. A flock of hens worked their way around the wagon and pecked greedily at the spilled wheat. Anita shooed them away.

'Did you hear the master, women?' she said. 'It's our men's fault that they got themselves killed in the war. It's the hired hands' fault because they work and want to be paid for it. I suppose it's our fault too because we get hungry and sick and catch diseases and two out of three of our babies die.'

'Six I've lost,' one woman cut in. 'And they used to cry because they were hungry.' She shook her wooden hayfork savagely.

Anita kneeled on the ground and began collecting grain in the folds of her skirt. 'Peasants are the thieves,' she said, 'and yet the master is content if we take only a little of our grain and leave him all the rest. Come on, women, come on!'

Attila stood over Anita, hands on his hips again. 'Miss Schoolteacher,' he said. 'Is the lesson over now?'

The women had closed around Anita and were scooping the spilled grain into their laps. Olmo had climbed down, and now Attila took his place on the wagon to see what could be done about the rent sacks.

Anita got to her feet. 'Let's give the rooster his feed,' she said. 'Here, peck at this.' She flung a handful of grain in Attila Bergonzi's face.

The other women did the same. They laughed and hurled grain at the foreman. Attila held his hands up to protect himself from the pelting. Then all the threshers were laughing and pelting Attila with handfuls of grain, and the women were imitating the *pock-pocking* sounds of hens and doubling over with laughter.

Giovanni Berlinghieri was outraged. Shoving his glasses deep into his coat pocket, he folded up the ledger and stomped off.

Olmo caught Alfredo's look, and they exchanged odd smiles, almost as if each were thanking the other for something. In Olmo there was even a flicker of admiration for his friend. He thought that maybe in some men there was a fundamental decency and sense of justice that transcended class, so that just then the pity he felt for Alfredo Berlinghieri was tinged with affection.

They all dispersed. Attila and the threshers went back to work. Alfredo went off with Regina. Olmo went off with Anita.

One world was coming to an end and another was coming to birth, that was sure. Olmo pitied Alfredo because he knew that the old peace and calm on which the Alfredos lived were finished. If times were hard, for some they were going to get harder.

Olmo went off with Anita. Things that before the war seemed impossible, even sacrilegious, Olmo Dalcò now knew were no longer so.

The long summer of the masters was over.

1945

Chapter 1

It was like the triumphal entry of a ragged army into an
ancient walled city. First came a pair of oxen drawing a
swaying mountain of hay on the flatbed of a wagon, then
behind it, a knot of shouting women. They came noisily
through the gateway into the half-deserted courtyard like a
crowd of holiday makers, like drunks at a carnival. They bran-
dished rakes and pitchforks and shouted bold slogans, and some
sang snatches of a song. Their cheeks were aflame, their faces
glistened with sweat, and as soon as the wagon came through,
a small crowd of old people and children joined them, material-
izing out of nowhere, and pushed to the centre of the commotion for a look. Then they all erupted into the big courtyard,
invading it.

At the centre, roughly roped together on the back of a cow,
rode Attila and Regina, she behind, her arms locked around
his semi-conscious form to keep him from tumbling off. Both
were battered and bruised and smeared with blood.

Children shoved through to look at them, spitting on
them, and the others kept up a barrage of insults.

Regina held her head up, rigid with anger. 'Bitches!' she
screamed at the mob. 'Stinking bastards!'

'We'll show you who's a bastard,' Nina said. 'You filth,
you murderers!'

'We'll cut out that rotten tongue of yours,' another peasant
woman shouted.

'Cut out her filthy tongue,' someone else echoed.

'Bitches, you bitches!' cried Regina.

'You won't bleed us white again, you won't ruin us again!'
others screamed.

'Don't answer them,' Attila said, barely managing to utter
the words through his ruined face.

'I'm still called Regina, and Regina means queen.' Regina
shouted this and was answered with mocking laughter.

'Lock the queen in the pigsty,' someone called out.

'With the pigs! With the pigs! Pigs with the pigs!' the crowd demanded, chanting.

'Throw them to the pigs and shit,' Anita said.

Regina's face was swollen and bruised, discoloured. Her clothes were torn, and Attila's blood smeared her. Some of the children recoiled in horror.

A couple of the women stood in front of the cow and shook their pitchforks wildly, scaring the animal, which lurched to one side, spilling the two roped riders. Attila came down hard on the brick threshing floor and was knocked unconscious. Regina piled on to him.

At once, one of the peasant women came down on Regina, tearing open the front of her skirt, snatching at her underpants, and tearing them off with a sharp rip. Regina twisted her legs to shield herself from kicks and to keep herself covered, but not before the old woman had spat three or four times on Regina's sex. Regina saw the woman's wrinkled face and raw red eyes and the pleasure that lighted up her countenance. Then men's arms were loosening the rope and lifting the fallen figures off the ground.

It was the man known as Tiger and some of the others, back from the mill. The two prisoners were borne by them to the pigsty.

They came to in the stinking darkness of the sty, in a wet concrete pen with seven or eight sows grunting and poking at them. Regina had got herself up and sat on the rim of the low concrete trough that ran the length of one wall. Her face ached. A pig came and sniffed at her feet, then scurried away. It was breathless, stifling.

She made out Attila in a heap in one corner and spoke to him. He groaned, asking for help. Regina pushed her way through the sows and knelt beside Attila on the dank, slippery floor.

'Can you stand up?' she said.

He could not answer. He seemed to be suffocating. She tried to lift his head, but he screamed in pain and began vomiting. He vomited on to her arms.

'You miserable coward,' she said to him, her voice filled with hate.

Later, regretting these words, she sat on the rim of the trough again, huddled up, her back to the wall, and cried. She could hear the guards talking to themselves, pleased with themselves, on the other side of the low door of the sty.

Chapter 2

Tearing herself from the mob that circled Regina and Attila, a young farm girl hurried into the cow barn, squatted down, and let out a sigh of relief as she urinated. Through the forest of hooves, she caught a glimpse of Leonida's face and called to him.

He had not heard her come in. He dropped to one knee, gripping his rifle, and immediately saw it was Inès. He shushed her.

Inès sprang up to join him, wanting to tell him all about the two prisoners who had been brought in on the back of a cow. But Leonida had stepped into the passageway, his rifle levelled, blocking the way.

'Halt!' he said. 'Nobody passes here.'

The girl ducked out of sight and wriggled under the bellies of the cows. Puzzled by her disappearance, the boy moved forward to see where she had gone. But she was already at the exact spot that Leonida was trying to prevent her from getting to.

A man lay in the straw, chained to the manger by one leg. When Inès saw who it was, she drew back in fright. The man seemed to be asleep.

'It's the padrone,' she whispered to Leonida.

'He's my prisoner,' the boy said.

'You haven't killed him?'

'No. He's asleep.'

'Why are you hiding him?'

She could not take her eyes off the figure in the straw. The man looked tired, haggard. He had a close-cropped moustache and wore an unbuttoned cardigan and a necktie that was open at the collar. It was the padrone, all right. His thinning hair was combed straight back.

'I'm waiting for the partisans,' Leonida said. 'When they

come, I'll surrender my prisoner to them. Olmo will come too.'

'Since when do the dead come back to life?' Inès turned to go. Leonida accompanied her to the door.

Unseen by them, Alfredo's eyes came open, and he watched them, unstirring.

'Stay and keep me company,' Leonida said softly.

'All right,' Inès said. 'You look good with a gun, you know?'

At that moment, there were shouts and cries from the courtyard. Alfredo got to his feet and tried to look out of the window, but the chain was not long enough for him to reach the opening.

'To the pigsty! To the pigsty!' chanted the voices outside.

Leonida instantly dropped down, pulling Inès with him. One of the voices he recognized as that of Tiger, but suddenly Leonida felt he was somehow not ready to turn over his prisoner. With the pointed rifle, he motioned Alfredo Berlinghieri to get back on the straw again.

The swallows skimmed in and out, chattering. With the back of his arm, the boy wiped the perspiration from his brow.

PART THREE

THE GATHERING DARKNESS

Chapter 1

Rising from the river, the autumn fog lay over the land like cotton wool, thick and white and silent. It was St Martin's day, the eleventh of November, when work contracts expired and families often moved from one farm to another. It was 1921; the war had been over for three years. All morning, along the dyke road peasant carts, loaded down with crude furniture, loomed out of the fog, creaking, pulled by oxen or a horse – old people, women, and children were installed wrapped in blankets among tables, chairs, beds, mattresses; the men trudged behind on foot – and then quickly disappeared again, in silence, swallowed up by the white shroud. It was a slow, steady exodus; it was like a primitive migration. Sometimes wagons passed and guttural greetings were exchanged.

There was a disturbance on the Avanzini estate that morning. One of the peasants, Oreste Dalcò, an uncle of Olmo's, refused to vacate his house at the foot of the embankment, claiming that his contract had still another year to run. He had gathered around him a number of friends and sympathizers, some, including Olmo and Anita, from the nearby Berlinghieri farm, and was pleading with them for support, haranguing them. Several passing wagons had been persuaded to stop and join in the demonstration. Avanzini, Oreste told the gathering, had threatened to have him removed by force by noon that day if he and his family did not leave voluntarily. But Oreste was not going to move, and no one was going to evict him from his house – not the army, not the Madonna, not the government, not even the pope! They cheered him. What they did not know was that Avanzini had sent for a detachment of a mounted carabinieri to back him up and that, at the very moment, these troops were approaching along the embankment road, muffled and ghostlike in the swirl of fog, now visible, now hidden, as it sometimes opened in white wisps then closed in again.

Avanzini himself on this morning was leading a hunt of about a dozen fellow-landowners over his property, ostensibly to shoot hare – that is what he told them – but in reality to allow him to look on the proceedings he had set in motion, conveniently armed and in the safety and company of his kind. For an hour, against the wishes of the others, he had been drawing the hunt closer to the river and the dyke road, deeper into the fog, where the party ran the danger of shooting one another instead of game. Nonetheless, single shots and from time to time volleys rang out, and the dogs brought back the warm, still quivering hares to the gunners. But Alfredo Berlinghieri was wary, and he hung back from Avanzini and his father and the others, keeping his cousin, Regina, the only woman in the party, by his side.

It was the hunting party, working its way east below the rim of the dyke road, that saw the cavalry first. To Alfredo, the steel-helmeted carabinieri seemed to be riding on rocking horses. Only the men's heads and shoulders and the heads of their mounts showed above the white bank of fog. Gliding as if over a silent carpet, some of the cavalry turned in their saddles, trying to identify the hunters' gunfire. But seeing nothing, the column rode on, two abreast, thirty men with a lieutenant at the point, all of them bearing rifles and sabres.

From the fields below, Avanzini's disembodied voice rang out, 'Well done, young men! That's it! Let them see that property is sacred, inviolable! Bravo!'

'Listen to that fool,' Alfredo said to his cousin. Holding a setter on a leash, he was dressed in checked breeches and a new Norfolk jacket. He had a cartridge belt around his waist, and a black cape hung loosely from his shoulders.

Regina wore an identical cape. She leaned back against a pollarded mulberry tree now, trying to penetrate the fog with her gaze, listening hard.

She touched Alfredo's arm. He slipped the cartridges out of his gun, placed the stock between her feet, and pressed the double barrel between her thighs. Regina's eyes closed, she threw her head back and spread her booted feet.

'You're crazy,' she said. 'They'll see us! You'll make me come like this!'

He laughed nastily. 'You come? An elephant couldn't make you come!'

She clutched the barrel in both hands, rubbing herself into

114

it. 'Don't stop! I'm coming, I'm coming!' Shivering, she let out a long sigh.

'I don't believe you,' Alfredo said, removing her hands from the gun.

'What do you mean?'

'You're frigid. You can't come.'

'It's not so,' she said. 'All I need is a real man.'

Sneering, Alfredo turned abruptly and hurried to catch up with the rest of the landowners.

Thirty yards from Oreste's house the squadron of carabinieri suddenly emerged from the mist and halted. The farmhouse was in plain view now. Before it, the peasants stood in a body blocking the road. The lieutenant left the group and rode his horse forward alone.

'In the name of the law, vacate the premises,' he ordered briskly. 'The rest of you, move on.'

Oreste rushed forward. 'And where are my kids going to sleep? Under the bridges?' He was shouting.

'They'll sleep in jail if you don't disperse,' the officer said.

Olmo had moved forward to restrain Oreste. 'Put the landlords in jail for not respecting their contracts.'

'In the name of the law – ' the lieutenant began.

'The law! The law! What law?' shouted Olmo.

'The law's on our side,' Anita said. 'Oreste's contract expires in a year. The padroni want to rob him of a year's work.'

A woman called out of the crowd, 'Thieving padroni! They want to throw us out because we're Socialists!'

A big mongrel, black as coal, barked at the horse's legs. The officer turned and galloped back to his detachment.

Olmo addressed the others. 'We ask for work, and what do they do? They send the carabinieri! Spread the word, comrades, spread the word! We need everybody here we can get!'

Leaving the women, Anita took a few steps along the road and lay down across it. Olmo went and knelt alongside her to get her up. But a half dozen other women began imitating Anita, dropping down in the road.

'Come on, you women!' Anita called.

The men looked at each other without speaking, seemingly powerless. There were fifteen women lying in the road now.

'We may be women, but we're afraid of nobody,' one of them said.

Three blasts sounded on a bugle. Then the whole troop came galloping. The women sang, drowning out the sound of hoof-beats. Behind the carpet of bodies the men closed ranks around Olmo and Oreste. They had taken up poles from a stack by the farmhouse, and they made ready to use them. On came the carabinieri, clear out of the blur of fog, clearer each moment, sabres drawn. Olmo felt something dimly familiar about the scene. The horses came thundering, then a few yards from the women they drew up short, rearing and kicking to the side. The bewildered riders struggled to remain in the saddle. Now the women were loudly chanting.

'Get back!' Olmo shouted to the carabinieri. 'Get back! Do you want to kill them? You're sons of the people, the same as us. You're being exploited too.'

The lieutenant gave the order to retreat. Quickly, the riders went back down the road, disappearing into the fog. One of the women had been hurt. Oreste rushed to pick up her limp body.

'All right, Lieutenant,' he called after the carabinieri, 'are you happy now?'

The woman's face was covered with blood. Now Olmo remembered. He saw the puppet show at the railroad station when the carabinieri cut down Montanaro with sabres. He saw that blood, heard the hooves of those horses, and his heart raced.

The procession of wagons along the dyke road had long since stopped, choking a long stretch of the road. Many of those on the St Martin's day move had left their carts to see what was happening at Oreste's house, and a number had joined the demonstrators. They had grown to close to a hundred now.

Anita was quick to move up and down the line of carts. 'Come, comrades, come down! This is the last St Martin's day you'll have to suffer! No more evictions! The land belongs to the peasants! The land belongs to those who work it!'

Some fifty yards away, half hidden by a row of vines, Regina and Alfredo followed the course of events.

'Do you hear that?' Regina said. 'Olmo and his whore. It's always them. They're always in the middle.'

'Shut up, idiot,' Alfredo told her.

'They're the worst. They're the ones who give orders.'

'At least they believe in what they're doing. They have courage.'

Regina burst out in a crude laugh. 'Look at your friend. Take a good look, because he's going to end up badly, you mark my words.'

Alfredo clamped a hand over her mouth; then, gloating when he noted the fear come over her, he slipped his hand down her body, roughly fondling her breasts. 'Shut up, I tell you, or I'll throttle you.' He finished by shoving a hand up her skirt.

Again the bugle sounded its three short blasts. Pushing Regina aside, Alfredo tore out from the cover of the leafless vines and raced across the meadow and up the embankment. The squadron had regrouped and was now coming down the road at a gallop. Alfredo waved his hands over his head, shouting for them to stop.

'You can't do this!' he cried breathlessly. 'Stop it!'

Heedless of him, the charge went past, but one of the horses grazed Alfredo and sent him spinning down the slope. He got up dazed but unhurt.

The roadway was newly carpeted with reclining women, more of them this time. Hoofbeats pounded the track. Then once more at the last moment the horses shied, twisting and rearing before the prostrate bodies. In the confusion, the lieutenant's mount turned in a narrow circle as the lieutenant, ordering his troop back, cut the air above his head with his sabre.

Avanzini and the rest of his hunting party had meanwhile made their way around to the river side of the embankment, where they had stood more or less in the open looking on the successive charges as if from a box at the opera. But for Achilles Avanzini this second failure of the carabinieri was the last straw.

'Goddam them!' he cursed. 'The bunch of cowards!' Searching the others' faces for some sign of agreement, he leaped down off his perch, the parapet of an old well, and struggled up the bank with his shotgun.

'Avanzini!' Giovanni Berlinghieri shouted after him.

The rest of them went in pursuit. Like a madman, Avanzini broke into the midst of the stampede of retreating police, who were having difficulty controlling their horses.

Running from one of them to the other, Avanzini shouted

117

insult and abuse. 'Crack troops, eh? Cracked is more like it! Good for nothings, that's what you are! Living off our money! The money of honest citizens! And we have to stand by and watch you run away from a handful of beggars!'

From Oreste's house, Olmo was leading the mob in a provocative chant. 'Padroni thieves!' they called. 'Padroni bastards!'

'Where's all this going to end?' said Pioppi, one of the huntsmen.

'They respect no one,' said another. 'They don't even give a damn for the carabinieri now.'

Giovanni pulled Avanzini away from the milling horses to the edge of the roadway. But, enraged, Avanzini broke loose and stormed up the road to take on the peasants alone. After five or six paces, he shouldered his gun and fired in their direction.

'I'll drive you out myself, I will! Criminals! Bolsheviks!'

But Giovanni was on him again, wresting the gun from Avanzini's grip. 'What are you doing, you fool? Starting a one-man war? At a time like this we need self-control.'

From the peasants came a fresh volley of insults.

The lieutenant rode up and asked for the shotgun, half snatching it away. 'That's enough, sir,' he said.

'Bravo, Lieutenant,' Avanzini said. 'We'll make you a general for this.'

'I did my duty. I had no orders to kill people.'

'You hear that?' Avanzini said, laughing bitterly. 'Did his duty. You shit in your pants, Lieutenant, that's what you did!'

'Watch your language,' the officer said. 'You can't say –'

'I can and I will say,' Avanzini barked. 'And I'm not joking. I'll kill them all! I'll kill every last one of them!'

'Come on now, let's go,' Giovanni said, trying to soothe the agitated Avanzini. With a hand, he motioned Zevi, Fornari, and some of the other hunters to form a tight ring around Avanzini. 'It's our fault, gentlemen. We needed this lesson. If the law won't defend us, we'll have to defend ourselves.'

The cavalry moved off the way they came. Alfredo started after them along the dyke road, just behind his father and the other huntsmen. The fog was closing in again. He could not see Regina anywhere. Turning for a last look back at the house, Alfredo saw the peasants waving their poles in the air and shouting in triumph. In the roadway, the women were on their feet, arms around the men's necks.

A boy had climbed up to the roof of Oreste's house, where he fixed a flagstaff to the chimney. As the grey fog drifted in from the river, a red flag unfurled.

Alfredo moved on, gladdened in spite of himself.

Chapter 2

For Giovanni Berlinghieri the time had come to act. That afternoon, returning from the hunt, he suggested to his colleagues that they meet in the village church to discuss methods of dealing with the current spate of peasant rebellions, stirred up by political extremists, that threatened to ruin them all. He also sent Regina with a message to his foreman, Attila Bergonzi, instructing him to summon a few other estate owners to the gathering.

The church was an old one. The back of an engraved postcard of its interior, which Don Tarcisio pressed on the occasional visitor, claimed that it had been built in 1399 in the Gothic-Lombard style from a plan by the celebrated architect Bartolino da Novara. The unique feature of the building, however, was its later decoration. Above the thick square pillars dividing the nave and aisles was a series of brown wooden columns, encrusted with shell-like rococo ornamentation, with niches in between containing painted figures of the martyred.

These figures – monks, knights in full armour, a pope, a brace of emperors – seemed to have been carved in wood but were really of papier-mâché they stood about four feet high and were lavishly, even lovingly, modelled and detailed. One hung by a rope from his crossed wrists; another was seated with his feet in stocks; a third was being lowered into a well by a noose around his neck; a fourth consisted of a head on a block about to be crushed by an outsized wooden mallet. These statues dated from the seventeenth century. There were dozens of them. Under each, a round plaque recorded the martyr's deeds and suffering.

Sitting here and there, widely spaced on the pews, the padroni looked like the few, sleepy faithful at an early morning mass. Those who had been on the hunt still wore their cartridge belts. The shotguns had been stacked near the entrance around the carved marble of the holy water stoup.

Regina, in the front row between her uncle and her uncle's foreman, turned and craned her neck. Satisfied, she whispered to Attila, 'Go on! They're all here. Let them see you. They must get to know you. This is your chance!'

Attila, wearing a fur-collared jacket, slid off the bench and sidled up the altar steps, where he sat facing the assembly. From time to time his glance moved to Regina, as if he were seeking her approval. Attila sucked on a toothpick. This, together with the jacket and his casual manner before the altar, lent him an air of truculence.

After one or two more straggled in, Giovanni rose to address the gathering. He was impressive in his grizzled beard and long raccoon coat. Sixteen landowners, including himself, were present. Don Tarcisio, ancient and doddering, stood at the back, rubbing his hands together and eyeing with envy a pair of hares, blood still dripping from their mouths, that one of the hunters had draped over a prie-dieu.

The State, Giovanni deliberated, was obviously too weak to be counted on any longer to guarantee law and order or to protect private property against those who would make attempts against it. Nearly all of them had seen this for themselves, plainly, only hours before. The question, then, was what could they, the landowners, do for themselves to restore order to the countryside?

Giovanni had a plan of his own but wanted a general discussion, argument even, before unfolding his scheme. For now, it was enough to set things in motion. With a show of tact and modesty, he relinquished the floor and sat on the bench.

Discussion began. Avanzini, still smarting, leaped to his feet and called for their taking an immediate united stand, armed, to be sure, and shedding blood – the same way that blood had recently been shed at nearby Rivarolo.

'But a man was killed at Rivarolo,' Lorenzo Pioppi objected. Pioppi had snow-white hair and the brilliant red cheeks of a man on the verge of a fatal stroke. 'And now the Reds have a martyr there, and they're stronger than ever.'

'You don't know what you're talking about!' Avanzini shouted.

'I know all the peasants around Rivarolo are behind the Reds,' Pioppi said. 'They even say the Socialist martyr is

120

going to have his monument in the village square.'

'I say they made a mistake at Rivarolo,' Avanzini cut in. 'That was to have created only *one* martyr.'

There was murmuring and restless stirring among the padroni. Attila watched attentively, chewing on his toothpick.

Giuseppe Fornari got up. He was a small man, with a twisted mouth and beady eyes. 'It's like my dog,' he said. 'Hit him once – it's no use. Hit him twice – still no use. But thrash him ten times and he learns the lesson!' Pleased with this pronouncement, Fornari looked all around him, then sat down.

Others got up and spoke. Some were for outright violence; many counselled against it. A few said that they did not mind blood but only wished there were a way their own hands need not be stained with it.

Giovanni Berlinghieri listened patiently, elbows on his knees and chin on closed fists. Now it was his turn. He wheeled to catch the eye of some of the last men to arrive – the ones he had sent his foreman to round up. They had already been sounded out privately, and Giovanni knew exactly to what extent he could count on them. They now gave him meaningful nods.

'May I speak?' Giovanni said, rising. He exchanged a look with his foreman, left the pew, and stood facing the others. 'It was here, in church, that we were baptized. It was here that we were all confirmed. It was here that we were married.'

Behind him, as if obeying a command, Attila had got to his feet. As he spoke, Giovanni moved slowly, hypnotically, down the aisle between the two rows of pews. All eyes were screwed to him. He raised a hand, indicating the main door. 'And it's through here we'll come, feet first, at the very end. Naturally, we all want to postpone that end, but the way things are going – ' He paused dramatically and stared at his little audience. Attila was rapt. 'All of you know what the crusades were, I trust.'

Giovanni halted. His look picked out someone standing outside, leaning idly, arms crossed over his chest, against one of the porch columns. It was his son, Alfredo, who was deliberately keeping away from the reunion.

'Young man, we're talking about things in here that concern you too.' Giovanni, having interrupted himself, now motioned Alfredo to him with a gesture of his head.

'I'm only here because you ordered it,' Alfredo said, reluctantly coming forward. 'Now leave me alone, please.'

Giovanni put an arm around his son's shoulders, drawing him to the pews. Like a defiant child, Alfredo released himself from the embrace. The moment his son sat down, Giovanni resumed his speech.

'The church!' he exploded. 'Even the church, when it was necessary, used the stick! Who are these Bolsheviks, anyway? Semi-Asiatics, that's what they are – like the Saracens. These Bolsheviks are Mongol subversives who, if things go on like this much longer, will kill us all and strip us of everything we own. Am I right or not, eh, Pioppi?'

Pioppi did not answer.

'Talk, talk, talk. Nothing but talk,' Avanzini shot out. 'I know what has to be done. Kill them all first!'

'Dead bodies,' Giovanni thundered. 'That's what you call for – dead bodies and more dead bodies. I say no. We want neither revenge nor violence; we want order. We are the new crusaders!' He pounded an open palm with his fist.

Down the length of the centre aisle, Alfredo and Regina exchanged odd looks. Neither of them had ever seen Giovanni so impassioned before.

'We must instil courage in our young people,' Berlinghieri continued, softly now, kindly even. 'They are only waiting for a sign from us. So let's give them this sign!'

Pulling out his wallet, Giovanni went back up the aisle towards Attila. From the wallet he drew a fistful of crisp bank notes, spread them open in his fingers, fanwise, and waved an arm about for them all to see.

There was excitement. Attila's eyes shone. The last man to have arrived, Bonacci by name, stood up to say that whatever sum his friend Giovanni Berlinghieri contributed he was pleased to match. Another of the latecomers was quickly on his feet, saying he would be ashamed to do less.

Don Tarcisio appeared from behind a pillar to hand Attila the collection basket. Half smiling, eager, obedient, Attila took it and held it out for Giovanni to place the notes in. Emboldened, the foreman began passing the basket along the pews. He looked menacing as his big hand held it out, almost impatiently, and he rolled the toothpick from one side of his mouth to the other. The rest of the padroni began imitating Giovanni, reaching into their pockets for their wallets and counting out the notes.

Regina pumped her head at Attila and smiled. What success! the smile said.

Alfredo observed, sneering to himself. At some point his eye moved up along the series of niches where those martyred for the faith suffered their sufferings.

'This isn't the first time we saved the country,' Attila said, swaggering. 'We answered the call in the trenches, and now we're here to answer it again!' He shook the plate under Avanzini's nose.

But Avanzini needed no prodding. 'Solidarity!' he shouted. 'Solidarity! What Italy needs is a good swing of the pickaxe!'

Avanzini was generous in his offering. Attila moved on to Fornari.

'Quite right,' Fornari announced. 'When you start a new business you need capital!'

He too had been generous. The donations mounted.

Don Tarcisio shuffled behind Attila and kept trying to peer into the collection basket. 'All that money!' he said. 'I've never seen so much money in this church before! What are you planning to do with it all, my son?'

Speaking over his shoulder to the priest, but his eye fixed on the next prospective contributor, Attila said, 'Buy trucks, Don Tarcisio. And guns, and a lot of fine uniforms for our young men.'

'And nothing for the parish?' the old priest asked. 'Not even a penny for the salvation of your souls?'

Attila laughed sarcastically. 'Without this there'd be no more parish!' he said.

'San Donnino!' Don Tarcisio said, crossing himself.

Attila drew up to Pioppi. Pioppi's face was more crimson than ever. He was hesitant.

Attila shook the basket. 'Cough up, Pioppi,' he said.

'Not on your life,' Pioppi said so only Attila could hear. 'I don't approve of your kind.' Rising abruptly, he moved crabwise the other way along the pew. Every eye followed him. Dipping his fingers in the holy water stoup, Lorenzo Pioppi made the sign of the cross and started for the door. Then, remembering something, he returned to take his shotgun from the base of the stoup.

All the other barrels were still propped there. Their tips made a reflection in the gentle ripples of the basin.

Chapter 3

'Christ, think of the fit my father would throw if he knew we were together!' Alfredo said, buoyant with good feelings.

'Respect, respect, respect!' Olmo mocked. 'Like all masters, your father's just a thief longing for respect.' He laughed.

They were in the city, walking briskly through the narrow, teeming streets of an old quarter on their way to Ottavio Berlinghieri's apartment. Ottavio was nothing like his father, Alfredo had promised. His uncle was like a young man, and he was generous and full of fun. Olmo was sure to like him. Now, as they dodged passersby in the stream of foot traffic, Olmo felt a thrill akin to uneasiness imagining the meeting.

The two young men were in high spirits and as frisky as young colts. Dressed in their Sunday best, they were out for a good time, an adventure – anything. Olmo had been feeling a lot warmer towards Alfredo recently, especially since the incident at Oreste's house the week before. A few days after the landowners met in the village church, Alfredo had warned Olmo of a punitive night raid against Oreste to be carried out by Attila's newly formed gang of black-shirted toughs. When the hour came round and the rowdies showed up they found Olmo and a rough-and-ready gang of his own lying in wait for them. The Blackshirts were soundly routed, Oreste was saved from a hiding, and once again Olmo was ready to believe – did believe – that there was something fundamentally decent about his friend Alfredo. It was this warm feeling, this renewed closeness, that they were here in the city celebrating.

'If you think he's bad, wait till I take over!' Alfredo said, ogling a couple of girls going into a dress shop.

Olmo laughed and tugged Alfredo onwards. Alfredo led them along a shortcut through an arched alleyway that pierced a tenement block. At the heart of it, familiar music poured out of a large courtyard, where a number of artisans were at work in the open air outside their shop doors. A group of children pressed around a juggler and acrobat team, who looked like brother and sister, while an older man stood to one side providing musical accompaniment on an ocarina. In the windows above, women had interrupted their gossiping to take in the spectacle.

'Wait a minute,' Olmo said, holding Alfredo still. It was the ocarina, bringing back memories. For the second time in as many weeks now, thoughts of Montanaro had crossed Olmo's mind.

'What's the matter?' Alfredo asked, noting his friend's suddenly clouded brow.

The girl was juggling brightly coloured hoops. Her brother was dressed like a harlequin. Olmo could not take his eyes off the ocarina player.

'Nothing,' he said.

Alfredo tossed a few coins at the acrobat's feet and started on. Just then a young laundress carrying a huge hamper that overflowed with damp sheets knocked into him.

'Shit!' Alfredo said.

'I'm sorry, sir,' the girl said.

She was thin, with long dark hair and a pretty face and eyes. Alfredo immediately pardoned her, saying it was his fault for not watching his step. 'Come on, Olmo,' he called, his good humour restored. 'We're giving this lovely young lady a hand.'

'Oh, you needn't trouble,' the girl said.

'No trouble at all, miss,' Olmo said, smiling gently.

They followed a few steps behind the girl. Her name was Neve. Neve laughed seeing that Olmo and Alfredo found the basket of wash heavy.

'Miss, did you know we were twins?' Alfredo said as the three of them started up a large gloomy stairway.

'Liar,' said Neve lightly. 'You're making fun of me.'

'It's true,' Alfredo said. 'We share everything. What's his is mine and what's mine is mine.'

Neve went on ahead.

'I'll bet we can both have her,' Alfredo whispered to Olmo.

'She's not that kind,' Olmo whispered back. 'She's a working girl.'

'Don't worry. I'll pay for us both.'

'You think you can buy anything you want,' Olmo said, annoyed.

'You're getting more and more like a priest,' Alfredo said. 'You're serious all the time.'

'And you – all you're out for is fun.'

'You see, father.'

125

'Cut that out.'

'Don't be sore,' Alfredo said. 'It's Anita. She's making you this way.'

'Lay off Anita,' Olmo said. 'The world is full of people suffering and in need, that's what it is. Somebody has to try to help, to try to change conditions.'

'If that's your mission, all right. Just don't try converting me.' Now Alfredo's tone was serious.

'You're beyond salvation anyway,' Olmo said, showing Alfredo a big grin.

'And when the Revolution comes, what will you do with me?' Alfredo laughed. 'The firing squad?'

'No,' Olmo said. 'I think we'll do something far worse. I think we'll make you work.'

'Olmo, you are positively evil. My daddy warned me about you Bolshies!'

Neve waited for them in front of an open door.

'Shall we put it down here?' Olmo asked her.

'No, inside. Let's give complete service,' Alfredo said with a wink.

It was a small dingy room, cluttered and disordered. Drying wash hung everywhere. On a table were stacks of folded laundry. The only other furniture in the place was a big old-fashioned brass bed, a sideboard, and a couple of rickety chairs.

'My God, what a mess!' Neve said, embarrassed.

'Ooh!' purred an old woman, rising from one of the chairs. 'Two real gentlemen in my house. Come in, come in,' she told the pair of young visitors, ending their hesitation.

'Thank you, madame,' said Alfredo with exaggerated politeness and a slight bow.

Olmo set the basket down. Neve went about straightening up.

The old lady laughed happily. 'All right then, I'm off,' she said to her daughter. And dragging a chair out on to the landing, she closed the door after her.

Neither of them knew how to begin. Alfredo, foraging in the sideboard, came up with an odd-looking bottle of liqueur and was sniffing it. Olmo hung back, playing with a loose button on his jacket. Neve noticed and offered to sew it on properly.

126

'It doesn't matter,' Olmo said shyly, retreating. The button suddenly came off in his hand.

'Give it to me,' Neve said. She went and looked for a needle and thread in a drawer of the sideboard.

'It's been ages since I've drunk homemade liqueur,' Alfredo said, slipping an arm around the girl's waist.

'Have some, if you want,' Neve said.

'Yes, but I insist on paying,' Alfredo said. He pulled a fistful of money, bills and coins, out of a pocket and put it down.

Neve gaped.

'You and your goddam money,' Olmo said with his old annoyance.

But Neve quickly gathered up the money and stuffed it into a tin box on the sideboard. When she turned around to them, she had two glasses in her hands.

'You have a drink too,' Alfredo said.

'Oh, I can't,' Neve said. 'It's bad for me.'

Olmo took the bottle from Alfredo, roughly, and poured out two drinks. 'If you're not thirsty, why don't you get undressed?' he said angrily at Neve.

The girl moved to a corner of the room, where, half-hidden behind a heap of laundry, she began drawing off her clothes.

Alfredo turned a sage smile on Olmo. 'You see, I told you she was a whore.' He watched Neve undress.

'She's not a whore, she just needs the money.'

'If she's not a whore why does she take it?'

'It's your money that makes her a whore.'

'Come off it, that's just Bolshie talk. Anyway, you can always go to confession afterwards.'

'Do you go to church?' Neve asked Olmo.

'Can't you tell he's studying to be a priest?' Alfredo said.

Olmo drank and poured himself another, then burst out in nervous laughter.

Neve stood there in her underclothes. 'Aren't you two going to take anything off?' she asked.

'You can go first,' Alfredo said.

'No, after you,' Olmo said.

'Go ahead,' Alfredo said. 'I insist.'

'But you paid. You should go first.'

'I need to warm up,' Alfredo said, drinking.

'I'm kind of freezing myself,'

127

Neve, showing gooseflesh, hurriedly got out of the rest of her clothes. They saw her naked legs and slender belly and tuft of dark hair like matted wool. Her breasts were large, flattish, and the rings around her nipples were large and a dark brown. Alfredo felt himself grow pleasantly hard in his trousers, but Olmo was a little put off by the girl's nakedness. Her slimness reminded him uncomfortably of Anita. Neve slipped into the middle of the bed and drew the covers up tight around her chin.

'Who do you want to go first?' Alfredo asked her.

'Both?' asked Neve, sheepish.

'Both of us together?' Alfredo said.

'Aren't you twins?' said Neve.

Sitting on opposite sides of the bed, each of them undressed, embarrassed and silent, while Neve peered out at them. Then they hurriedly got in on either side of her.

Alfredo placed his hands over her breasts; then, moving down in the bed, he rubbed himself stiff against her leg and with the tip of his tongue licked her near nipple. Neve shuddered deliciously.

'Who starts?' Alfredo whispered.

'Your friend,' Neve said softly. 'He's so sad.'

Alfredo took one of Olmo's hands and placed it high up on the inside of Neve's thigh.

'Don't you have girl friends?' Neve said.

Alfredo laughed.

'What's so funny?' Olmo said.

'I was just thinking about Anita.'

'Leave Anita out of this.'

'Is she your girl?' Neve said.

'Come on, have a drink,' Alfredo said. He drank from the bottle, then put it to Neve's lips.

'No, I feel strange if I drink,' she said.

'That's what's so great! Come on!' Alfred tilted the bottle up, forcing her to drink.

Neve wiped her chin. 'Are you going to marry her?' she asked Olmo.

'She's already my wife without being married,' Olmo answered. 'She's my comrade.'

They all drank.

'No marriage,' Alfredo said. 'They're Bolsheviks. They believe in free love.' He had his hand between Neve's legs, fingering her, and he had put her hand between his. He was ready to climb into her. 'Now you know what free love is too, don't you? Answer me.'

Neve had pulled Olmo's head to her other breast. 'Oh, don't ask me hard questions,' she said.

'Answer me,' Alfredo insisted. 'You play with her cunt too, Olmo.'

Olmo did.

'Now you know what free love is, Neve,' Alfredo said, sneering and almost cruel. 'Out of the way, Olmo, before I waste this coming all over her.'

Alfredo parted Neve's legs and got into her. He was oblivious of Olmo's presence now. He told Neve to lift her legs to let him in deep, and he thrust and thrust and then he asked for her mouth and made her open it big and wet, and then he came in her without making a sound. He'd let Olmo have a turn, and after that he would have a second go. It would be even better the next time, unless she were too juicy with all their come. The little whore, he'd make her tell him what free love was. Alfredo slid off her.

Olmo mounted her. She wrapped her arms around him, and he was working his arms under her shoulders, being gentle with her, about to push into her, when she began murmuring something. In his excitement, Olmo began kissing her. He was in her now, moving on her tenderly.

Thrashing about, Neve got her mouth free. 'I'm ashamed! I'm ashamed!' she said. 'Please, you must go right now! Please!' She pushed Olmo off her, imploring, and began to rouse Alfredo out of his half sleep. 'Go, both of you, quick!'

'What the hell is this?' Alfredo said.

Neve's body began to tense, her lips were drawn back, and her eyelids became very heavy. 'It's not your fault,' she said. 'Please excuse me!'

Alfredo sprang out of bed, pulling his clothes on hastily. 'Christ, she's an epileptic! Let's get out of here!'

Olmo quickly drew on his shirt and trousers.

Neve's voice was now a long groan with a wild sound in it. Her pupils were dilated and seemed to be rolling back in her head. A trembling, which she appeared to be trying to fight, convulsed her whole body. Suddenly her head snapped back, banging against the brass bedstead.

'Quick! Call her mother!' Olmo said. He was on his knees

on the bed, lifting the girl in his arms and getting a blanket around her.

'Signora!' Alfredo called at the door.

The woman burst in, about to scream. Olmo was pressing the girl to his chest. Her face was unrecognizable in its convulsions.

'We didn't do anything,' Olmo said.

The old lady made Olmo hold down her daughter's arms and she ordered Alfredo to press her ankles tight to the mattress.

'Shall I get a doctor?' Olmo said.

'That won't help. Just press down hard,' the mother said. With difficulty, she inserted a handkerchief between Neve's teeth.

'Fool,' the woman told her daughter, 'you know you shouldn't drink.'

Olmo and Alfredo exchanged an uncomfortable glance.

'Be patient for a few minutes,' the mother told them, wheedling. 'When it's over, it's over.'

They said nothing. They held the girl down and felt the force convulsing through her limbs. It was raining now. Somewhere a downpour drummed on sheet iron, and outside the window the early twilight had fallen.

Pale and exhausted, Neve lay asleep, her head in Olmo's lap. The girl's mother sat in a chair with her arms crossed over her breasts, dozing. Alfredo dozed in a chair by the table. It was as though they had all been overtaken by some epic exhaustion after battle.

Gently, Olmo placed Neve's head on the pillow, saw that she was properly covered, and went over to Alfredo on tiptoe to rouse him.

'Shh!' Olmo's finger was up to his lips.

The two young men went out without making a sound. At the threshold, trying to do up his jacket, Olmo remembered the missing button. He gave a look around the room, trying to locate it. It lay on the sideboard. He tiptoed over to it, put the button in his pocket, withdrew to the door, and quietly shut it after him.

Chapter 4

Walking half a dozen steps behind Alfredo, Olmo was troubled and uncommunicative. Both of them kept close to the walls to avoid getting wetter. The rain fell steadily now, straight down and chill. Only an occasional car passed along the streets, but there was an endless stream of dripping umbrellas. They had crossed a bridge over the river and were making their way in a wealthy neighbourhood.

Olmo felt empty, bitter with himself. What had happened to his loyalty to Anita? Anita was at home, two months pregnant. He also had a bad conscience about Neve, but he wanted to forget about her. Somehow, the epileptic girl had ruined all the pleasure of being with Alfredo, had even divided them again. Olmo knew Alfredo was irritated with him too.

Alfredo ducked into the gateway of a great palazzo, where he waited for Olmo to catch up.

'We're here!'

Olmo brushed the rain off his sleeves and looked around. From the depths, in the courtyard, he made out a white marble staircase, grand in its proportions and elegance, leading to the upper floors.

'I'm not coming,' he suddenly announced.

'What?' Alfredo said, incredulous.

'I'm not coming.'

'But we're here already. Come on.'

'No, I don't feel like it any more.'

'Christ, I bring you to the city, and you act like this. What's eating you?'

They were both drenched. Alfredo passed a hand through his wet hair.

'Come on, we'll get dry,' he said.

'I don't like the city,' Olmo said.

'Some gratitude you show,' Alfredo said. 'You're like a goddam bumpkin.'

Olmo wanted to tell his friend that there was an unbridgeable gulf between them, but he knew it was useless trying to explain that now. He did not like the way Alfredo used his money, throwing it around, buying people. It insulated and isolated him. It was a class thing, and Alfredo would never understand it. Olmo saw green plants in large pots along the elegant carved marble staircase. At the top of the first flight, where it branched in two, were a pair of sleek hounds, sculpted in marble.

Olmo's conscience about Anita nagged at him, making him unfit company. 'I don't like this place either,' he said.

'Okay, okay,' Alfredo burst out in a fit of temper, 'you don't like it. Leave then! Go on, go home! Go back to your cows!' He wheeled abruptly and started up the stairway. 'This is the last time I take you anywhere,' he added loudly, without looking back.

Olmo turned up his collar and trudged out into the street and the chill rain. *Your* cows, he wished he had said to Alfredo.

Chapter 5

Nobody seemed to be in. Alfredo pressed the bell repeated times, in a fury, but no one came. He listened. Not a sound. He tried the door, and it opened.

'Ottavio? It's me, Alfredo. Anybody home?'

Alfredo crossed the entrance hall, passing his hands over his wet suit, and entered the large salon. A welcome fire burned softly in the fireplace and he went straight to it. There, warming himself, his eye went around the room.

The atmosphere was of great refinement and taste; the décor was the current and latest phase of art nouveau – thin lines, geometric curves, and whiteness. Everything in the room, every picture, every piece of furniture, was just so, chosen and fussed over for the particular place it occupied. It was all so new, so modern, that it struck Alfredo how great (and peculiar) a courage it took to live this completely in the present. Had he thought further about it, Alfredo would have found such minute attention to detail too finicky. The drapes hung impeccably, the carpeting was thick and rich. Each object on the mantelpiece – a clock, vases, various boxes – was placed for an exact effect. The pictures, of which there were many in the room, actually baffled Alfredo. But what caught his eye now was the woman's garments, including underwear, that were strewn on a sofa. There were a hat and white dress, a coat and a handbag.

He called for his uncle again, hesitantly this time, then, in spite of himself, moved to the sofa, where he looked closely at the petticoat and held the bra up between thumb and forefinger.

He was smiling to himself, about to drop the bra, when from the doorway a woman's voice announced that Ottavio was not in. Not expecting a woman's voice, Alfredo recoiled, dropping the object that was in his hand. In his fluster, meeting her gaze, he said, 'I'm sorry, I didn't mean to disturb –'

She took his voice, his breath, away. The woman he was staring at – almost not daring believe what he saw – was the most beautiful creature Alfredo Berlinghieri had ever laid eyes on. She was wrapped in a man's green silk robe that was sizes too big for her, and she had a towel turbaned around wet hair. She was barefoot, obviously having just stepped out of a bath. Her hair was blonde, her skin honey-coloured. She had a wide expanse of forehead and large, warm eyes. Something about her manner, her self-assurance, told Alfredo that she had to be at least a half dozen years older than he.

When he had regained his composure he told her, haltingly, that perhaps he had better be on his way. She ignored him, wandering about the living-room, searching in boxes on tables and on the mantelpiece. With the hand that held the towel she gave her hair an occasional drying rub, while to Alfredo's pleasure the loose sleeve of her dressing-gown revealed her arm to below the elbow. He was burning to see more of her or at least to be able to stare openly at her. Her hands were elegant, the fingers long and tapering.

'Have you a cigarette?' she finally said.

Absently, Alfredo felt in his pockets, then blurted out, 'No – I don't smoke.'

'Damn,' she said. 'This is a disaster. By the way, I don't know you,' she added.

'I don't know you,' Alfredo said.

'You're Alfredo, Ottavio's nephew.'

'Well, actually, he's more my spiritual father than an uncle.'

'He's mine too,' she said. 'That makes us spiritual brothers.'

'Who are you?'

'I'm Ada, and I'm out of cigarettes.'

'I'm Alfredo, and I don't smoke.'

'My, such a clean-living boy!'

Ada went to the couch and gathered up her clothes. She slipped loose the sash around her waist, opening the robe. She was naked beneath it. As if paralysed, Alfredo stood gaping at her.

'What's the matter, never seen a woman's body before?' She was about to step out of the garment entirely, but at the last moment she thought better of it. 'After you've finished looking, would you kindly turn around so I can dress?'

Alfredo was stunned into silence and went crimson with embarrassment. In his awkwardness, turning away from Ada, his arm brushed an ornamental crystal obelisk off a table, but he caught it before it crashed to the floor. He wanted desperately to say something but feared whatever he said would sound foolish. Besides, his mind had gone blank. In a mirror he watched her slip into her dress. He knew he would be haunted by the glimpse he had caught of her nakedness. He had seen one of her breasts and her pubic hair. It was blonde. The breast had seemed to him some perfect golden fruit.

'Put on a record,' she ordered.

The phonograph was against the wall, a record already in place on the turntable. Alfredo wound it up, put the head down, and out of the horn came a Puccini aria.

When he turned around Ada was still barefoot but otherwise completely dressed. Her damp hair was drawn back. She smiled. Yes, she was supremely beautiful, he thought. Alfredo found his heart melting – anyway, a sweet pain in the chest like a melting heart.

'Would you like me to go out and buy you some cigarettes?' he said.

'Would a cigar do, my dear?' boomed Ottavio's voice from the entrance. Coming briskly into the room, as elegant and handsome as ever, silvery hair but an astonishingly slim waist, he held out a cigar, which Ada greedily took. Ottavio wore open a long eccentric overcoat.

'My saviour!' she sang out, throwing her arms around Ottavio's neck.

'Good afternoon, Uncle,' Alfredo said.

Ottavio held Ada at arm's length. 'Alfredo, what brings you around?' he said to his nephew, genuinely pleased to see him.

'I got drenched and have just had a hot bath,' Ada said.

Ottavio handed her his coat, offhand and familiar, and looked Alfredo up and down. 'And you? You're soaked. Let me lend you some dry clothes.'

'I've had a rotten day,' Alfredo said with boyish enthusiasm. 'I came into town to have some fun, and then I saw an epileptic – ' He stopped himself. 'Say, I think I could use a bath myself. That is, if I wouldn't be putting you out.' He shot a look from one to the other of them.

Ada and Ottavio exchanged a smile. Ottavio called to someone in the entrance.

'Mario, leave it there,' he said.

Picking up the green robe and towel, Alfredo retired to bathe.

'I spent a whole morning at that sale,' Ottavio said, half in complaint, half pleased with himself. 'God, the search for beauty can be tiring!'

'Just think if you had to work!' Ada said.

'*Quel horreur!*' said Ottavio, frowning. 'Come now, sit down there a minute and have a look at this.'

He left and was back in moments to show off his latest acquisition. Ada had lit the cigar. She tilted her head, narrowed her eyes, and studied the picture. It was of a seated nude.

'A young German painter; I didn't even know his name,' Ottavio said. 'But I couldn't resist it.'

'Collectionitis, that's what ails you.'

On his way to the salon, in the same green silk dressing-gown Ada had worn and in his uncle's slippers, Alfredo stopped in the outer hall, unseen, listening to them talk about the new picture and trying to catch a long glimpse of Ada. He did not understand much of what they were saying, but he drank in Ada's silky voice. The fire blazed now. Ada was sprawled by it in an armchair, legs across the arm, smoking her cigar and occasionally waving the cloud of smoke away from her face. Dazzled by her sophistication, Alfredo told himself he now knew what he wanted in a woman.

He entered the room and sat in another armchair by the fire. Ada was saying, 'I've fallen in love, Ottavio.'

'Again?'

'Yes, but this time it's serious.'

Alfredo was stricken and looked surreptitiously from his

uncle's face to the woman's.

'Let's see if I can guess,' Ottavio said. 'Itala?'

'Bugatti,' Ada said languorously.

'A saloon?'

'Torpedo, but it's an impossible love. It's too expensive.' She turned suddenly to Alfredo. 'Why so serious, young man? What do you think?'

'I was just thinking maybe I'd go out and buy one tomorrow,' Alfredo said, smiling brightly and trying to be witty.

'Can you drive?' Ada asked.

'Yes – well, no. But it can't be so difficult.'

'This nephew of yours is a bit glib, I see.'

'Bravo, Alfredo!' laughed Ottavio. 'Make my skinflint brother spend some of his money. How's your mother, by the way?'

'Improving,' Alfredo said, deliberately cynical. 'She doesn't seem to tell so many lies these days. Painting still occupies her – one landscape after another.'

'Ah, my lost countryside,' Ottavio said.

Alfredo winced, finding it difficult to discuss his parents, the estate, or its affairs with his uncle. He still remembered vividly the night he had come into his grandfather's room to find his mother sitting there by the bedside, clasping the dead man's hand in hers with feigned affection. The duplicity, the faked will, had haunted and plagued him from the age of six or seven, and he knew he would feel even worse the day he came to inherit the estate. Often it amazed him how a scheme in which he had no part and yet from which he ultimately would benefit had become a kind of trap and curse to him. Every time he saw Ottavio, he felt the falseness of his own position, and it burdened his conscience. Occasionally, he thought he would turn half the property over to his uncle when it came into his hands – should Ottavio survive his father. This thought salved Alfredo's conscience.

'Ottavio, do lend me the car,' Ada asked sweetly, bringing Alfredo out of his dark ruminations.

'If you're off to the concert this evening, I'll go with you,' Ottavio said.

'Mahler? For the love of heaven, no! I thought I'd like to give young Berlinghieri here a lift home.'

At once, Alfredo sprang to his feet, all eagerness and excitement. 'I'm ready,' he said, beaming. 'Let's go!'

Ottavio and Ada looked at him and burst into laughter. What were they gawking and laughing at? Of course. He laughed too, uncomfortably. He was still in his uncle's dressing-gown and slippers.

Chapter 6

Alfredo Berlinghieri was swept off his feet. Over the next few weeks, all his thoughts, his dreams, his sleepless nights had at their root Ada Paulhan Fiastri. Alfredo wanted to know everything about her, he wanted to see her as often as could be managed. After the farm girls, after the girls like Neve, after Regina, here was the woman he really wanted, and it was like waking up at last and finding boyhood behind him, finding he was a man.

And yet, she was his uncle's; he could never have her; it was doomed. The hopelessness of it burned in him like a fever, and the more the fever consumed him, the more he was in love with her. After wakeful, tortured nights when he longed for the dawn, he would wander in the fields with his setter and his grandfather's favourite shotgun, shooting an occasional hare or duck – more for the dog's amusement than his own. And he barely ate. Ada, Ada, Ada. Her image went before him on his solitary meanderings; it peopled his tortured nights. He spoke to no one but his dog about her, and he avoided Olmo and Anita because the fact that they were a happy couple only underlined Alfredo's pain. He used Regina, used her cruelly, punishing her, though never letting on why, for what he told himself he could never have with the one woman in the whole world that he wanted.

He did see her. Several times they went on long drives together in the countryside, always in Ottavio's borrowed car. Ada was mad about driving, mad about speed, mad about engines and gears and machinery. She even composed poems about these things, poems which she called futuristic and of which Alfredo made neither head nor tail. Once, on one of their outings, she had thrust on him a couple of sheets of scented green writing-paper, asking him to read aloud her handwritten words.

'Do you like it?' she said when he had finished.

'Yes – I mean, it's very modern.'

One of its lines stated that 'after the boldness of first, second, and third, fourth gear left her cold for being old, grey, and bureaucratic'. Her composition was so short that it ended almost before it began. He told her so, for which she called him an ignoramus and made him read out the other page. His only comment on it – 'Gypsy, what you rouse in me still lasts/your kiss and your smile/treacherous and sad' – was, 'Pity it isn't longer.' He was trying to be helpful more than tactful.

'That's exactly why it's so good,' she said, and, snatching the sheets from him, she let them fly out of the window. His heart leaped to his mouth – in part because she had just destroyed her handiwork, in part because she had nearly veered off the road.

'What are you doing?' he protested.

'Two of us have read them,' she said. 'That's already too many.'

He loved this nonchalance of hers. And the fact that he did not understand her poems, that he considered most of their subject matter anti-poetic, and that he cringed before her attacks made him love her all the more ardently. He loved her, in fact, for her extravagances and for being everything he was not. Alfredo even made himself believe that he would settle for loving her in secret, that he would settle for her friendship. He was courting disaster, and he knew it. Ottavio had already been stripped once of what was rightfully his, and for Alfredo to strip his uncle now of Ada – strip him this time of something infinitely more precious than an estate – was utterly unthinkable. And so Alfredo knew he was courting disappointment as well. Yet he was determined to play with fire and leave it to simple blind hope not to get burned.

Ada had been an orphan for the last three years. She was twenty-one years old – 'The worst age in the world!' she had complained melodramatically, and Alfredo immediately subscribed to this truth, for he too was twenty-one – and her mother had been French. Ada's father had designed the king's portrait on the ten-lire bank note. 'So you see,' she added with a touch of melancholy, telling Alfredo this, 'we always lived in the midst of money without having any.'

Her parents had died on Mont Blanc. They had come up with the brilliant idea of organizing Alpine expeditions for millionaires and on their very first trek lost their lives in

a crevasse. 'They died the way they lived – beyond their means.'
Ada was alone in the world now, without brothers or sisters.
'But I don't mind,' she told Alfredo. 'I'm free, I live wherever
I like and with whomever I like.'

Hearing this, he was barely able to mask his seething
jealousy. 'And now you're my uncle's mistress,' he said
neutrally, staring straight ahead of him.

She laughed at his words. 'Ottavio's like me, Alfredo. He
loves no one but himself.'

There was something unclear, ambiguous, about her laugh,
but he understood her words all too well. He questioned her
no further, fearing the pain her answer might bring.

After a while, the more he was with her, the more he
saw of her, the less able he was to predict her reactions or
behaviour or moods. Even this added to the spell she cast
over him. Once, they had been talking about women and love,
and Alfredo had asked her if she liked women.

'Yes, I love myself,' Ada said in her serious, not-serious,
way. 'In fact, I'm desperately in love with myself.'

'Well,' said Alfredo innocently enough, 'then I'm jealous.'

Her foot slammed down on the brakes, and she swerved
the car violently to the side of the road. When they had
come to a stop, she said, extremely agitated, 'How dare you
say such a thing to me? You don't know me!'

He could think of no way of hiding his distress, and he
only watched her out of the corner of his eye, unspeaking.
Finally, in her own good time, she started the car and drove
on again, plunged in silence. What old torment he had awak-
ened he never ventured to find out, but his heart fluttered
with love.

One night, on another occasion, only a few miles from
the farm, their car had to slow down behind a truck that was
taking up the whole road. It was loaded with grinning, gesticulating men who wielded canes and clubs and who were
obviously drunk. There were about twenty of them, swarming
in the back and cab and even on the running-boards. A man
on the running-board by the driver seemed to be pointing out
the way. Ada sounded the horn, and the men in the truck
laughed and shouted at her.

'Look at their faces,' she said. 'I've never seen so many
Fascists!'

Finally, as she tried to squeeze past, the man pointing out

139

the road recognized Alfredo, made the truck give way, and with grandiloquent gestures waved Ada past. It was Attila.

'Good evening, Signor Alfredo,' he called, tipping his hat as the car was alongside.

The men in the back were singing a raucous Fascist song about defending their country and bringing terror to the Communists.

'Are those thugs friends of yours?' Ada asked.

'Heavens, no,' Alfredo said, disclaiming any acquaintance with his father's foreman. 'One of them must have recognized me. I wonder what trouble they're out to make at this hour.'

'They disgust me,' Ada said. 'I don't want to see them! I don't want to see them!' All at once, nearly hysterical, she shut her eyes and swerved sharply to the left. The car went off the road, bumping over a field, where, its headlamps lighting up the stubble, it came to a safe stop.

'Are you crazy?' Alfredo exclaimed in a controlled rage.

'I can't see any more,' Ada said. 'They frightened me, and I can't see anything. I've gone blind.'

Could she possibly be serious? Was this a game? Not knowing how to take her when she was like this, Alfredo sat back and observed, sometimes amused, sometimes plainly awed. It never occurred to him to question her or to try in some other way to make her account for such erratic behaviour. It was enough that her unpredictability utterly charmed him, fascinated him.

All that long winter of 1922, whatever Ada did or did not do, Alfredo's love only waxed hotter.

Chapter 7

The words on the slate, chalked up in a hesitant, untutored hand, were: 'bread,' 'wine,' 'hen,' 'goose,' 'sun,' 'moon.' Elsewhere, across the top of the blackboard, was written, 'Communism is the youth of the world.'

The upper floor of a produce warehouse in the village had been converted into a primitive classroom, and here, in the winter months, Anita taught illiterate old peasants to read and write. The building also contained a small meeting hall. Because use of the place was for the people – peasants, farm labourers, and their families – it was known as the

140

Casa del Popolo. Such 'people's houses' were springing up in all the towns and villages around.

In the classroom, someone had stencilled on the walls, in brilliant red, hammers and sickles and silhouettes of heroic men carrying banners towards a rising sun. Copies of the *International*, a Communist newspaper, were also on hand for anyone to read. On the ground floor, at the foot of a steep wooden staircase, were great piles of potatoes and wheat in sacks, and there were crates of apples and pears. The odour of fruit pervaded the place.

Anita was teaching a class of four men, ranging in age from seventy-two to seventy-eight, when one evening Olmo slipped quietly into the room. He had a bottle of wine half-hidden in his hands. The man at the slate, who had been laboriously writing, stepped aside, waiting for Anita's verdict. His face was eager, yet at the same time showed signs of the immense effort the work had cost him.

'Any mistakes?' the old peasant, Pietro Pecorari, asked.

'No, that's right,' Anita said. 'Olmo Dalcò, you sit down with the other children. Now, Pietro, read it aloud.'

Each of the other old men concentrated on shaping with his lips the sentence Pietro had just written. They wore black capes and had black hats crammed down on their heads.

'Communism is the youth of the world,' Pietro read off the slate.

'And now Olmo will explain what that means,' Anita said.

'It means – well, what does it mean? It means I'm the only Communist here because I'm the only young person.' Olmo laughed.

'Miss,' called out Iofèn, one of the other peasants.

'Comrade,' corrected Anita.

'Miss Comrade,' Iofèn said, 'what he says is not true. I'm seventy-two years old; I'm a Communist; but in bed, I do my duty like a young man.'

Decimo, a third peasant, spoke up. 'You fool! We come here to study, not to brag.'

'I'm not bragging,' Iofèn said. 'Ask your wife.'

They all burst out laughing.

Olmo leaped to his feet, a broad grin on his face. 'All right, children, go home,' he said. 'School's over for today.' And, as if it were a prize for the students, he placed the bottle of wine on the table where Anita sat.

'We'll stay on and keep watch,' Pietro Pecorari said.

'Good, Pietro!' said Anita.

'And to study this bottle,' the fourth old man, Francesco, said, smacking his lips and patting Olmo on the shoulder.

Anita gave some last instructions, telling them each to write another sentence on the slate before they went home. Olmo held her by the hand and was impatiently dragging her out into the dark corridor. There he embraced her and gave her a violent kiss.

'I missed you so much today,' he said. 'I'm starved for you.'

'You didn't give me time to finish the lesson,' Anita said, mildly chiding him.

'You're wasting your time teaching a class of four old men. What good does it do?'

'And you? What have you been up to? In the city again with Alfredo?'

'I haven't laid eyes on Alfredo since the last time,' Olmo said. 'That was weeks ago. Shouldn't you be teaching young people at least?'

'What's the matter with you?'

'I'm fed up and bored, that's what.'

They were downstairs now. Four bicycles leaned against the sacks of potatoes.

'But everything's going so well. We stopped the carabinieri at Oreste's, we've got this place. Everyone's happy and you're in the dumps. Why don't you take me dancing?'

'You dance – with that bellyful?' Olmo laughed at her.

Anita struck out at him playfully. He caught her in his arms and held her tight.

'I know, you have another woman,' she said.

'Another woman? Me?' Olmo made a face at her.

'I warn you, you know what I'll do?' Two of her fingers mimed snipping with a scissors down by his fly. 'I'll cut it off.'

He playfully struck her wrist.

'And I'll cut off this hand,' she said. Then her hand went quickly to Olmo's sex, and she squeezed it, 'I'll squash your balls.'

'I love you when you're fierce with me,' Olmo said, his hand swooping like a bird of prey to her breast. 'I'll pinch off a nipple,' he said.

'And I'll, I'll – '

But her arms were around his neck, and she and Olmo were kissing.

'I love you, you big idiot,' Anita said.

'And I love you.'

They stood looking into each other's eyes, still hugging, enchanted with each other. Then Olmo pressed her into a dark corner, slipping his hands over her breasts and the swell of her belly and down between her thighs. She did not protest. He sat her down comfortably on some grain sacks and got his head up under her long blue dress, running his tongue along the inside of her thighs and then tasting her hair with his mouth and darting his tongue out and licking the tiny place that made her hot, that would make her come.

She never uttered a word until it was over and she had shuddered and stopped him by pushing his head away with a firm but gentle gesture.

'I feel better,' she said in a soft, soft voice.

'I do too,' he said.

Then she had his head on her lap and was caressing it and playing with his curly hair. 'What do you have in this head?' Anita said. 'What do you have in this head? Tell me, do you have another woman?'

'No,' Olmo said, serious. 'You're in my head. Only you.' His face shot up, and he looked smiling at her.

'I love you, I love you, I love you,' Anita said, covering him with quick, tiny kisses. 'I love you, and I want to have some fun.'

'Yes,' Olmo said. 'Let's go to the dance next week.'

Chapter 8

The dance took place in an enormous hay barn and was very crowded. The musicians, most of whom played horns, stood on bales of hay at the edge of the dance floor, sounding out polkas and mazurkas, loud and fast. To one side, an area was roped off where tables were set and couples could order wine and cool off. Brick pillars rose and met in round arches high above the dancers' heads. The barn, made up of a long series of these brick arches, resembled a mountain tunnel. Baled hay was banked in tiers on every side.

Olmo and Anita had arrived early, soon after he picked

her up at the Casa del Popolo, leaving the four old men again to keep watch and to enjoy the bottle of Lambrusco Olmo had brought them. It was a couple of hours later, Olmo and Anita were in the middle of a dance, whirling around dizzily, when Olmo noticed a beautiful and very elegantly dressed young woman come in with Alfredo. Unsure of his eyes in the general blur of faces, Olmo stopped stock-still. As the woman was a stranger, everyone in the place turned to stare at her, the rest of the couples on the dance floor stopped, and even the musicians left off playing.

It was Ada, like an apparition, in a Parisian gown of white satin, looking sleek and rich and as though she had just come straight from a soirée in the city. In fact, she had.

Alfredo stood just behind her. 'Some place, isn't it?' he said over her shoulder. 'Wait for me here. I'll get us a bottle of wine.'

The music started up again, the dancing went on, and, in the crush and surge, Ada was pushed to the edge of the dance floor. She had not seen which way Alfredo disappeared and now, craning her neck, she called out to him.

'Where are you, Alfredo?'

A couple circled near her, and Ada suddenly knocked into them as though they had been invisible to her. Drawing back quickly, she held her hands out in front of her like a blind person.

'Alfredo!' she called. 'Don't leave me alone!'

The dancers were packed on the floor, and before anyone could see Ada groping, hands outstretched, she was bumped several more times. Slowly, as she kept calling helplessly for Alfredo, she found herself pushed towards the centre of the dance floor. 'Don't leave me alone, Alfredo,' she said again, this time her voice revealing increased distress.

Another collision made her turn completely on herself, and, for a moment, it seemed she had lost her balance. Olmo, only a step or two away, reached out to steady her. Immediately, Ada turned round sharply. 'It's nothing,' she said. 'I'm blind; it's nothing. This music is so beautiful; please don't stop dancing just for me. Play on! Please play on!'

Olmo was just about to say something to her when Ada clutched at him abruptly.

'Alfredo,' she said, 'you gave me such a fright!' Then, holding him in the slightly hesitant way of the blind, she asked Olmo to dance. 'We blind dance very well, you know,' Ada added sweetly, helplessly.

Olmo looked to Anita, not knowing what to do.

'Don't refuse me this, I beg you,' Ada went on.

Anita made a sign for Olmo to dance with her. Olmo took hold of Ada and, desperately embarrassed, began moving with her, at the same time keeping some distance between them. Alfredo appeared out of the crowd just then, a bottle of wine in his hand. Olmo and Ada circled by him.

'Make me turn,' Ada was telling Olmo. 'I adore that! How wonderful! Faster, faster!'

Olmo managed to flash Alfredo a strange, trapped look.

Alfredo and Anita spied each other at the edge of the dance floor. He moved towards her.

'To think she has such beautiful eyes,' Anita said to him sadly.

'So do you,' Alfredo said, slightly baffled. He took Anita by the hand. 'Come on, let's dance.'

While they danced and twirled, Alfredo kept moving them closer and closer to Ada and Olmo. He could hear Ada pleading, 'Alfredo, hold me; hold me tighter!' and he could see Olmo's frantic face and plain embarrassment. Alfredo knew then that it was another one of Ada's games.

'Alfredo, can I give you a kiss?' Ada purred to Olmo. She clasped him tight and, before he could move, kissed him on the mouth. Then instantly, she recoiled. 'But you're not Alfredo,' she said, her voice trembling with indignation. 'Who are you?' She touched Olmo's face with her fingertips, then drew her hand back in horror. 'How awful! How absolutely shameful of you! You're a monster to treat a poor blind girl this way – a pitiless monster!'

Olmo remained in the centre of the dance floor, red with shame. Alfredo, having seen and heard it all, glared angrily at Ada. Anita was angry too and pushed Alfredo at Ada.

'Oh, Alfredo, thank goodness! Never do that to me again. Never leave me alone!' Ada clutched Alfredo now.

'You are terrible,' Alfredo said in her ear, dancing with her.

'I'm a woman of caprice,' Ada said.

'Well, I don't like it, so cut out this silly game.'

'Do you know him?'

'He's my best friend,' Alfredo said.

The orchestra finished playing, and the couples separated.

Alfredo eagerly brought Ada to meet Olmo and Anita. He made the introductions.

'Ah, the blind girl!' Anita said cuttingly.

'Am I condemned to be blind all evening?' Ada said, in another mood now, smiling and looking from face to face.

'You invented the game, you idiot,' Alfredo said, laughing.

But Anita was outraged. 'You mean this was an act? You came here all dressed up and perfumed to make fools of us, didn't you? What do you call us – hayseeds, hicks? You rich girls make me sick!'

'That's enough, Anita; that's enough!' Olmo said, squeezing her arm.

Anita eyed Ada up and down – the satin dress, the fancy shoes, the elegant coiffure. She fixed some strands of loose hair under the headband she wore. 'Who does she think she is?'

'Come on, Anita, have a drink,' Alfredo said. He sounded a bit drunk.

'No, thank you,' Anita said.

'I know you need a drink,' Alfredo insisted. 'I know I need a drink, so let's both have a drink.' His eyes pleaded with her. 'Please?'

Anita laughed, in spite of herself, amused now by her sudden flash of anger. Ada apologized. Anita relented. They all drank, standing. Then, while the women went outdoors to relieve themselves in the surrounding fields, Olmo and Alfredo found an empty table.

'Christ,' Olmo said. 'Last time it was an epileptic, this time a blind one. We keep going this way, we can open a hospital!' He laughed and splashed out more Lambrusco.

Alfredo laughed too. He had an arm slung around Olmo's shoulders. They sat on a bench and quickly finished off a bottle of wine, as though in relief from a disaster averted, Both of them were feeling good.

'What do you think of her?' Alfredo asked.

'Is she drunk?' Olmo said.

'No, she's not drunk – except with life. Listen, Olmo, she's fantastic, really. She smokes cigars, drives like a maniac, writes poetry. She's modern, Olmo, modern!'

'She's beautiful, I'll say that for her,' Olmo said.

'Yes, she is.' Alfredo sighed.

146

'But I feel sorry for her.'

'Listen, old friend, she's the woman I've been searching for all my life. I've found her. Ada.'

Olmo did not know what to say. He wanted to tell Alfredo that in that case he was sorry for him too. But he thought better of it.

The orchestra started up again. As the dance floor filled, the two women threaded their way across it to rejoin Olmo and Alfredo.

'I didn't want to make a fool of anyone,' Ada said, stopping the dancers. 'I'm not blind; it was a joke.'

The dancing couples were uncomprehending. To begin with, they could not hear her for the loud playing.

'It was very stupid of me. I didn't want to offend anyone,' Ada went on in a fervour of self-criticism. 'Forgive me! Forgive me!'

None of the dancers paid her any attention. They tried to avoid her, to escape her. Somewhat exasperated, Anita took Ada by the arm and led her off the floor.

When the four of them were seated and they had had more to drink, Ada said, pensive, 'Anita was right, you know. But it always happens like this. When I can't stand it any longer, I close my eyes, and then I bang into people. I hurt myself in the end, and I hurt others.'

It was vague, enigmatic. There was an uncomfortable silence. Alfredo tried to fill it, saying Ada was so original. Olmo and Anita avoided each other's eyes in their uneasiness.

'That's too easy,' Anita said finally, trying to bridge the awkwardness they all felt. 'Open your eyes, face things. Why, just look at your Alfredo – handsome, kind, and democratic. Look, what do you see?'

'I'll tell you what she sees,' Alfredo said eagerly. 'Someone who's happy. One of four – no, five – friends!' He reached over to pat Anita gently, fondly, on the stomach. 'Five friends glad to be together. Now give me your hand, and yours, and yours. Can't you feel what I feel? We'll remember this day even when we're old.'

The four of them lay their hands together in a stack, one on top of the other, and pledged friendship. They were all fairly drunk and filled with unfocused emotion.

Just then an old tramp approached, looking as though he wanted wine. 'Friend, friend!' he said to Olmo. 'I've got something to tell you! A fire!'

'What?' Olmo said.

'A fire!'

Olmo leaped up and took the man roughly by the lapels.
'Where?'

'At the Casa del Popolo.'

'Are you sure?'

'Yes.'

Olmo bounded to the middle of the dance floor, flailing
his arms and causing the music to stop and the couples to
disperse. 'There's a fire!' he shouted. 'The Casa del Popolo's
on fire! Run, everybody, run and help!'

A drunk said, 'It's the work of those Fascist bastards!
They're out to kill everybody!'

There was a stampede for the door. Voices claimed they
could see the night sky lit up in the direction of the village.
Others called out, speculating whether it was the Lazzari barn
or Reggiani stable on fire. Olmo caught Anita by the hand,
and they pushed their way to the door. The musicians had
dropped their instruments in the hay and run off with the
crowd.

The hall was empty. Ada found herself in the middle of
the dance floor, somewhat drunk and dishevelled in appearance,
turning as if in a daze. From somewhere came an enthusiastic
clapping of hands. It was Alfredo, applauding as though Ada
had just finished a theatrical performance.

'Bravo!' he called as he flamboyantly held out his arm
to her. She took it, curtsying grandly, head bowed low. Again
he praised her, laughing, for being so original, for being one
in a million. When she came up, they looked for a moment
deeply into each other's eyes, then fell into a passionate
embrace.

Chapter 9

The Casa del Popolo was a roaring inferno. Onlookers milled
about frantically before the curtain of flames, but nothing
could be done. Finally, when some order could be brought
out of the confusion, a bucket brigade was organized. But
it was too late; the fire raged out of hand, and, because of
the searing heat, it was impossible to get close enough even

to throw the water. In the end, all that could be done was to protect the nearby buildings from spreading flames.

Anita went from person to person, anguished, pained, trying to learn whether anything was known about the fate of the four old men, her pupils, who had been inside. Nobody knew a thing. Olmo did not have the heart to tell her that when they first arrived he had glimpsed through a lower window their four bicycles propped against the potato sacks.

When finally the roof caved in, throwing sparks and cinders high into the night air like a volcano, Olmo tried to draw from the water spilled passing buckets from hand to hand. Her Anita apart to get her home. Her dress and hoes were soaked exhausted face was lit up bizarrely by the flames. He took her in his arms, and, as though she were a child, she buried her head against his chest and wept openly. Afterwards, she was sobbing and sobbing and holding her belly and speaking incoherently, trying to say something he could not make out about her baby, her baby.

'Come home now,' he told her, gently, pressing his haggard face to her forehead.

Tears ran down her cheeks, reflecting the blaze, but Anita would not move.

Ada and Alfredo shuffled off the dance floor, kissing, and melted into the shadows where the hay was piled in tiers. There he pressed her against the wall of hay and ran his lips over her neck and shoulders, kiss after kiss after kiss.

She said nothing. He said nothing. The only sounds they heard were each other's animal-like breathing and the occasional rustling of the hay.

At some point, when the musicians returned to pick up their instruments, Alfredo clapped a hand over Ada's mouth to keep her from starting and giving them away. He pushed her deeper into the hay.

'If we don't begin defending ourselves,' – he and she heard one of the musicians say – 'we may be next. These filthy shits have no pity for anyone.'

'Come on, boys, let's get a move on,' another player said. 'Personally, I don't much like going home alone tonight.'

They were snapping shut their instrument cases.

'It's not my trumpet I ought to be carrying,' a third said on their way out. 'It's a revolver.'

Alfredo's hand was off Ada's mouth and he was kissing her again. Then he undid one of the shoulder straps of her gown, slowly, almost cautiously, barely touching her body.

'I don't want to,' she said.

He undid the other strap.

'I don't want to.'

'I know,' he said, 'I know.'

He brought the upper part of the gown down to her waist and fondled her naked breasts, first with his hands – his fingers pricking the nipples erect – then with his mouth.

'No,' Ada said as he slipped the rest of her clothes off her. 'I meant it. I don't want to.'

'Come here,' he said, freeing her of the heap of clothes at her feet. He got her half reclining and wedged his knees between her legs. He was still dressed, but desire possessed him and he could think of nothing – not that she was somebody else's, not that she was his uncle's – other than having her.

She felt him unbuttoning his trousers, and she said frantically, 'I don't want to – no, no, no!'

But he held her mouth to keep her quiet, one hand working between her legs, trying to get himself into her. She wriggled and squirmed, and he was unable to manage it. Something was wrong. Then he stopped struggling with her, and it made her stop struggling. She was still. Gently, almost surreptitiously, he placed his hands up under her armpits and took firm hold of her shoulders. He was stiff, burning with desire, and he could feel himself in position, just brushing her pubic hair. Then all at once, tugging down hard on her shoulders, he thrust up between her legs. This time he got what he was after.

Ada screamed, shocked. Alfredo realized then that she was a virgin.

'Why didn't you tell me?' he said softly. He held her wrapped in his arms and was moving in and out of her.

'Because you never would have believed me,' she quivered. 'It hurt, Alfredo, it hurt.'

'That's right, I wouldn't have.' His voice had gone suddenly hard, aloof, with manly pride. 'Aren't you – aren't you Ottavio's mistress?'

She was moving with him now, beginning to enjoy it, beginning to feel pleasure.

'Ottavio's mistress,' she repeated faintly. 'Oh, no! Oh, no! Oh, no!'

Ada laughed a short, hysterical laugh. 'You don't know your uncle, do you?' she said.

Later, as they were getting into the car, Alfredo remembered that during what had taken place in the hay he had not told her he loved her.

Chapter 10

Early in the morning, with the first dawn, the ox-drawn wagon rumbled over the narrow cobbled streets and into the arcaded square of the village. In fitting with its sombre task, it came very slowly, and very slowly it made its round of the long piazza. Olmo walked by the oxen; Anita, towards the rear of the cart. On the wagon's flat bed were laid out the remains of the four old men who had perished in the fire. Charred beyond recognition, they looked like so many scorched logs.

At first, at that hour, the streets were empty, desolate. Then two old women in black appeared, hurrying to early mass. Next, a baker appeared at the door of his shop and saw the passing wagon. At the far end of the piazza, a streetsweeper stood by his barrow. No one else stirred.

Was the whole town dead? Would nobody come to the window to look, would nobody come down to the street to see the work of the Fascists? Anita cupped her hands to her mouth and called out in a piercing voice, half chanting, 'Decimo Bonazzi, seventy-four years old, farm labourer from the age of eight – robbed by the landowners, murdered by the Fascists!'.

Olmo searched the shuttered windows for some sign of life, anger and sorrow in his haggard eyes. Anita and he had kept vigil at the Casa del Popolo until the fire was put out and the scorched bodies were found. By then it was dawn and neither of them had slept. Now he picked up a stone and flung it against a shutter. 'Wake up!' he shouted fiercely. 'Wake up!'

Anita continued her litany. 'Iofèn Zuelli, seventy-two years old, farm labourer from the age of seven – robbed by the landowners, murdered by the Fascists!'

'Wake up!' Olmo went on shouting, angry and accusing. His echo answered him from the other end of the square, recalling to him the time, as a boy, he had shouted his own name in the farm courtyard the night Alfredo wanted to run away. Olmo bent down for stones, firing them sharply at the shuttered windows. The town's blindness, its deafness, its indifference to the events of the night before offended him. 'Wake up and see what they've done! Wake up!'

A few people emerged from the arcades and peered at the wagon. A few fell in alongside Anita. It was growing more light.

'Ilario Zambianchini,' cried out Anita, 'seventy-three years old, farm labourer from the age of ten – robbed by the landowners, murdered by the Fascists!'

Window shutters were being flung back as the clatter of stones and the calling voices reverberated around the square. Sleepy, defiant faces looked out.

'Come down and see. Come down and join us,' called Olmo.

'Who pays the murderers?' Anita shouted to the windows. 'The landowners!'

'And who absolves the landowners?' cried Olmo.

'The priests!' both of them answered.

'Pietro Pecorari, sharecropper, aged seventy-eight,' called Anita in her funereal singsong, 'robbed by the landowners, murdered by the Fascists!'

Now windows were opening everywhere and passersby streamed out from the arcade to see what was happening. The sight of the charred bodies attracted some and repelled others. But whether they joined the procession or not, everyone appeared to be horrified, shocked.

'Let's unite against Fascist barbarism!' a voice called out of the growing throng.

Olmo led the procession, asking people to come to the funeral later that day. 'We'll show the murderers that we are one, united!' he called.

His cry was taken up and echoed, and the word spread. The oxen, the clattering wagon with its melancholy burden, plodded on.

In the afternoon there was a brass band, and behind the

band followed six or eight men carrying red flags. Then came the oxen, their backs draped in red, drawing the hay wagon and four red-draped coffins. The straggling file of mourners, hundreds and hundreds of them, wore black with red handkerchiefs around their necks and red carnations in their lapels. Their faces were dumb, dark with anger and exhaustion and impotence. Red ribbons, tied to the horns of the oxen, floated in the breeze.

The cortège wound slowly, silently, through the arcaded square. The band played not a dirge but the 'Internationale'.

Chapter 11

What was this proliferating breed of black-shirted bullies? Who were these self-styled patriots, these thugs and paid killers who called themselves Fascists?

Some of them were landless peasants who disliked hard work and lived from hand to mouth, from week to week, by dodges, by small earnings, by stealing. Others were dealers, dishwashers, wagon drivers, vagabonds, and the kind of men you saw hanging around the marketplaces of the larger towns. Usually they had no trades or – this amounts to the same thing – they had a smattering of several trades.

They were open-minded and rhetorical, violent and sentimental, and – above all – they were frustrated. They were without family, without honour, without faith or religion. They were poor, yet they were enemies of the poor.

Most of them were veterans of a victorious war, but they were unable to see that anything had been gained by the victory, and so they felt themselves victims of a national frustration. Incapable of becoming part of a world of peace and modest labour, they were ready for anything – for violence, for blind obedience to a leader, a chief.

Too weak and servile to rebel either against the authorities or the rich, they preferred cringing and fawning before them in return for the privilege of robbing and oppressing other poor – peasants, small landowners, tenant farmers – which they did under the guise of defending order and property. They were at the disposal of anyone giving orders, and in the broad, flat valley of the Po this meant the powerful landowners. By day they were humble, sycophantic; by night, and in numbers, and usually drunk, they were bold, unscrupulous.

They loved myth, and they believed in the myths of the day – action, bombast, and nationalism. These men found themselves a name in Fascism, a uniform in black shirts, and a leader in Benito Mussolini.

'I counted at least a thousand!' Serafini said, agog.

'Two thousand,' Barone contradicted. 'There were two thousand Communists parading out there!'

'Hey, Barone, what's that sad look on your face?' Attila said, laughing. 'You look like you just came from a funeral. What's the matter with you? Do you think you made a mistake?' Now his voice turned hard. 'Well, never regret anything – never be afraid of anything.'

They were in a tailor's shop along the arcade, Attila and five or six of his men. Some of them had been outside watching the cortège file by. You could just hear the last strains of the 'Internationale' fading down the narrow street leading out of the other end of the piazza. The tailor kneeled on the floor at Attila's feet, his mouth filled with pins. Attila was being fitted for a shirt of black satin.

The men were nervous, restless. They pummelled each other in play, they spoke loudly, they stomped importantly up and down the arcade and inside the shop, commenting on passersby, commenting on various cloths, feeling this, feeling that, exasperating Barigazzi, the tailor. They were beefy, thick-armed, and thick-necked. They looked exactly like what they were – a gang of overgrown bullies.

Attila stood erect, buoyant, his face radiant. Big and powerful, his eyes shining bright with happiness, he looked almost handsome. With the assurance of a man whose star is on the rise, he said, 'Don't even fear fear!'

Speaking through the pins, the tailor asked meekly, 'Shall we make some tucks? They give the shirt greater elegance, don't you know.' He pinned the cloth and put his head back to admire his handiwork.

Attila stepped aside to look at himself in the long mirror. The shirt was still open in front, and along the seams it was covered with basting stitches. He narrowed his eyes and tilted his head.

'I don't want elegance,' he said. 'I want it to be strong!'

154

'Yes,' the tailor was quick to agree. 'More manly.'

'You're not making a shirt,' Attila told him, 'you're making a flag! You'll all get one just like this too. Looks good, eh?' For a moment, Attila watched the others in the mirror, then he turned sharply. 'What's the matter with the bunch of you? You look like scared little boys. You think you did something wrong?'

Just then a five-month-old black and white kitten sauntered out from the back of the shop and scampered to Attila's feet, where it sidled up to his leg and rubbed itself against him. Immediately, Attila scooped the cat up and held it to his chest, stroking its head with a finger. 'This your cat?' he asked the tailor menacingly.

'Yes,' mumbled Barigazzi hesitantly, then, fearing he had said something wrong, he corrected himself and said no, it was just an alley cat that wandered in.

'A good man bears it in mind that Communism is smart, like this little pussycat here, and plays on your human feelings,' Attila said to his men. 'Come outside with me a minute – all of you.'

The gang followed. Attila, the cat cradled against his chest, still wore the half-made shirt with the stringy basting stitches. Barigazzi watched from the window.

Against the outside of the shopfront stood a flat wooden figure with evening dress painted on. It was a sign that the tailor took in each night. Calling for Serafini's belt, Attila deftly looped it around the wooden figure, and, holding the cat in a vertical position, its back against the two-dimensional dummy and its paws sticking out uselessly, he got the leather belt tight around the animal's middle. All the while he went about this, Attila carried on his didactic monologue.

'Communism is a disease that can destroy the world,' he said. 'Now if this little pussycat has Communism, you don't think about the pussycat, what you think about is protecting all the other little pussycats in the world. A man has to be strong. A man has to look at this little pussycat and say, "This isn't a pussycat, this is Communism!" And he's got to destroy it!'

Attila stared the cat in the eye as if it were a human enemy. He stepped back. Then, hands behind him, he hurled himself forward with a wild cry, his head driving like a cannonball into the kitten's abdomen, smashing its bones and squashing

155

it. At the moment of impact, the kitten had managed to strike out with its front paws, gashing Attila's forehead. Then it fell limp, dead.

Spontaneously, the gang of Fascist hoodlums burst out in their raucous song 'Allarmi', which was about dealing death to the Communists. When Attila turned to them, smiling brightly, radiantly, his face was streaked with blood. It had run into his eyebrows and down his nose. In the window, the tailor blanched and was nearly sick.

Intoxicated, Attila dashed out into the deserted square, the others emerging between the columns of the arcade to follow his example. On the cobblestones, a few trampled carnations were all that remained of the funeral procession.

Glaring in the direction the cortège had disappeared, shouting loudly, Attila proclaimed, 'What do we make the Communists do?'

'Shit!' shouted his band in unison.

'And what do we make the Peasant League do?' Attila chanted defiantly, grinning from ear to ear.

The gang's faces leered. 'Shit blood!' they shouted like a refrain.

Chapter 12

Smitten with love, it was only a matter of a few weeks before Alfredo precipitated the inevitable break with his family and left home for Ada.

It began a couple of days after the holocaust at the Casa del Popolo. Alfredo approached his father and, without naming Attila Bergonzi, asked Giovanni if perhaps the local Fascist band had not gone too far this time. Giovanni Berlinghieri was outraged at the suggestion that he might have had anything to do with the fire. He told Alfredo that doubtless the old men had been drinking and carelessly started the blaze themselves. When Alfredo scoffed at the suggestion, Giovanni asked him point blank why he was being sentimental over a pack of Communist thieves.

'Just what are you up to, anyway?' his father asked, accusingly. 'You're out night and day now. We never see you any more; you never account for yourself. You've got your poor mother in a state, never telling her where you're going

156

or when you'll be back.'

Alfredo looked long at his father, debating with himself whether or not to reveal what was burning inside him. 'Papà,' he said at last, screwing up his courage, 'I'm in love. Does it matter where I go?'

'In love? You – in love?' Giovanni sneered. 'You'll never support a wife if you don't buckle down and do some work around this estate, learn how to run it.'

'I'll never die of hunger,' Alfredo said foolishly. 'There's fresh water everywhere.'

'You forget this love business if you want to see another lira from me,' Giovanni said offensively, insensitively. 'You're not ready for love, you're not old enough. She's probably just after your money, anyway.'

Alfredo laughed nervously. 'Do you mean that – that you'd cut me off?'

'Yes, I mean it,' his father said. 'Just you try me.'

'You think you can buy me off the way you buy that scum to do your dirty work?' Alfredo said, his anger rising.

'Watch yourself, young man!'

Alfredo met his father's gaze. 'You're serious, I see that,' he said. And without waiting for a further reply, he turned on his heels, went upstairs, packed a bag, and left home.

It was a bit of a cheat, of course. Ada was waiting for him at the end of the drive in Ottavio's car. For some time, Ottavio had been talking about a long, leisurely journey down the length of Italy, and he had asked the young lovers to accompany him. They would be away for months, stopping in easy stages at Grand Hotels, first in Viareggio, Florence, Siena, then down to Rome, Naples, and beyond. Ottavio painted them a glowing picture of sun, fun, and, ultimately, of a whole new world of Greek ideals that awaited them in the south. 'I will teach you how to live,' he promised his nephew. 'I will give you something to live *for!*'

Alfredo was under no illusion that his father would agree to let him go, that he would see the journey as part of his son's education. In the first place, Giovanni was too miserly; in the second place, he did not approve of Ottavio or of Ottavio's growing influence on Alfredo. And as for his son's travelling in the company of a woman like Ada, a woman so modern and emancipated – that, Alfredo knew, Giovanni would never, never, never have permitted.

157

So Alfredo deliberately provoked an argument with his father that would give him a pretext for leaving home. Alfredo may have been foolhardy, but to someone still young and full of dreams what more splendid prospect in all the world than that of travelling in Italy with the woman you love?

Chapter 13

Month followed month; pleasure followed pleasure; adventure followed adventure. To Alfredo happiness was this, perfection was this, love was this – being simply and exclusively with Ada – and day after day, week after week, he prayed for nothing to intercede to bring their dream existence to an end.

Nothing did. Season followed season.

Then it was early autumn, and they lay side by side in bathing costumes on a deserted stretch of beach along the Bay of Naples.

'I don't want to go back home,' Alfredo sighed.

'Oh, swear we'll never go back!' Ada smiled sweetly at him. 'Swear it!'

'I swear!'

'Swear you'll never become a fat vulgar landowner!'

'I swear!'

'Swear we'll go a month without washing!'

'Darling, I adore you when you say things like that.'

'Swear it!'

'I swear it!'

'Swear you'll learn to drive a car!'

'I swear!'

It had the ring of the catechism to it.

'Swear you'll always love me and never marry me.'

Alfredo got up on his elbows, suddenly earnest. 'No, I want to marry you.'

Ada was momentarily disturbed. Then, as she got to her feet, she swept a handful of sand at Alfredo and scampered off towards the cliffs.

'Help!' she called out, pretending to be terrified. 'Help, a sex maniac!'

Alfredo raced after her, laughing. They entered a deep

cove that was carved, almost tunnelled, into the rock. There, in a cleft, two stark naked boys stood stiffly, trying without much success to strike classical poses. The fact that their heads were crowned with laurel wreaths did not help. They were obvious Neapolitan urchins, and the effect was laughable. Ada and Alfredo stared in amazement.

'Get away from here!' a voice admonished.

They wheeled. It was Uncle Ottavio protesting against the intrusion. He stood on some nearby rocks, fooling with his camera. Only now did he see it was them.

'Don't worry,' one of the pseudo Adonises said, 'these are artistic photographs.'

'Who are you?' asked Ada.

'Isn't it obvious?' the other boy answered. 'We're sylvan deities.'

'We're also a bit hungry,' the first boy added.

Ottavio joined them, unembarrassed. 'Now that you've discovered my hidden love for photography –' he began to say, ever jovial.

'We know how to keep a secret,' Alfredo cut in, winking at his uncle, but his laughter and his smile had dried up. He took Ada by the hand and, saying nothing, led her away.

The veil was off. Alfredo understood now what Ada had all along been suggesting about his uncle. The revelation was unexpected, nonetheless, and therefore upsetting, but, in the end, what did it really matter? Nothing mattered but Ada. As soon as they were quite alone again, Alfredo drew her to him, tight. He sought escape and found it in a long, kissing embrace.

Stepping out of the elevator, Ottavio unobtrusively surveyed the elegant lobby. He was looking for the little man with the bald head and sickly smile he had dealt with the day before. They had met along the beach then, and, while talking to each other, the man's face had been half hidden behind the leaves of a small palm tree.

'Then it's fixed,' Ottavio had said. 'I warn you not to trick me. I want it pure, absolutely pure – do you understand?'

'Professor,' the man pleaded, hurt, speaking in his broadest Neapolitan accent, 'you don't know me. I've never tricked anyone in my life.' The honorific and the wheedling tone were obligatory, part of the man's badge and his calling. So were

159

the elaborate accompanying gestures of his hands.

'Tomorrow in the lobby then,' Ottavio said simply, dismissing him.

Now his eye searched the lobby for the man. The elevator doors opened, and Ada and Alfredo appeared, happy and smiling as ever. As they approached Ottavio, the lobby was suddenly filled with uniformed Fascists who were apparently gathering for some sort of meeting. They were dressed in breeches and wore tasselled fezzes. Ada's face went ashen, and she clung to Alfredo's arm.

'Take me away,' she said to him, low-voiced and imploring.

'Won't you wait for me?' Ottavio said. 'I shouldn't be long.'

There was no sign of the bald-headed man. When Ottavio turned, Ada and his nephew were gone. There were some forty or so Fascists striding about the lobby now, full of their own importance, and they were beginning to be loud, not in the usual Italian way, but in their own special vulgar manner. Ottavio found them disquieting.

'Professor! Professor!' a voice called to him.

It was the man Ottavio was waiting for, but where was he? One of the uniformed Fascists beckoned. It was his man. They withdrew discreetly behind a column.

'But what are you doing?' Ottavio asked anxiously. 'Is this a disguise?'

The man seemed offended. He drew himself up and said, serious and pompous, 'We are making a new Italy, professor. I am a patriot, a true Italian,' he went on, 'and I never gyp anyone. Here.'

He took off his fez, plunged his hand into it, and handed Ottavio an envelope. It was prearranged. Ottavio withdrew a bundle of bank notes from his pocket and placed them in the hat. The man bowed obsequiously, replaced the cap on his head without removing the money, and withdrew.

Ottavio was elated but wary. He went to the desk and asked if there were any messages for him, but he was really watching all about him. He felt better when he saw the large party of Fascists move into one of the salons off the lobby, where someone had begun singing a Neapolitan song on a small raised platform adorned with potted palms. The man he had dealt with was nowhere to be seen. Satisfied, Ottavio withdrew to the elevators. When he got out on their floor, his elation took over again, and he quickened his step.

In the sitting-room of their suite, Ada and Alfredo were packing. They barely looked up at him when Ottavio came in. He watched them for a while, faintly amused, as they rushed like children from room to room.

'Are we leaving?' he said finally.

'As soon as possible,' Alfredo answered.

'Where are we going?'

'South,' Alfredo said.

'To Taormina,' Ada said at the same time.

Ottavio held the packet in his hands. He laughed. 'But why?'

'To get as far away as possible from those uniformed animals,' Ada said with a shudder.

'In that case, you'll have to go even farthe:,' Ottavio said. He had the packet open, had taken a pinch of something from it, and sniffed it. 'This takes you there – farther south than the south.'

The two froze at the threshold of their rooms.

'Cocaine?' Ada breathed.

'I want some too, I want some too,' Alfredo said.

They rushed at Ottavio.

'Careful,' Ottavio said. 'One at a time.'

He showed them how to inhale the cocaine. Each of them took a sniff or two.

'I don't feel anything,' Alfredo said.

'Just wait a moment,' Ottavio told him.

'Try to move,' Ada said.

'I don't feel anything,' Alfredo repeated. 'My nose is a little numb. Is that what I'm supposed to feel?'

It was late afternoon. The sun was setting. From below in the garden rose the strains of a Fascist song. Ada got up all at once and began undressing. She seemed to be ripping the clothes off with unusual, even excessive, haste.

'What are you doing?' Ottavio asked.

'I want a photograph of myself in the nude, like a woodland nymph,' she said.

'There isn't enough light,' Ottavio said, but he nodded his head with an amused air.

Ada flitted about in her underwear. Alfredo rushed about

turning on lights. Then Ada stripped and lay on a divan in the middle of the room, her head resting on one of the bolsters. Alfredo kneeled beside her in his white suit, adjusting the other bolster under her ankles. Before turning to face his uncle for the photograph, he kissed Ada's pubic hair with exaggerated affection.

There was a knock at the door. The three of them went stiff.

'What is it?' Ottavio called out, annoyed.

'Telegram,' answered a bellhop from the hall.

'Slip it under the door,' Ottavio ordered.

They watched the yellow envelope come sliding into the room. It was for Alfredo. Ottavio handed it to him. Alfredo held it in his teeth and kneeled again beside Ada to be photographed.

'Open it,' he said, spitting it out at her.

He stood up now to move a floor lamp into position, while his uncle fixed the camera to a tripod. Suddenly paling, Ada got to her feet, the telegram in her hand, and went to Alfredo. He pulled her close, locked his arms around her, and began murmuring in her ear.

'Your father's very ill,' she said, unresisting. 'You'll have to leave right away.'

Not having heard a word she spoke, Ottavio looked up from behind his camera. 'Hold it!' he commanded.

Ada and Alfredo turned their heads. *Click!* Looking more stupefied than grieved, the two were caught for ever in the camera image – Ada absurdly naked, Alfredo absurdly dressed.

Chapter 14

With its windows and doors shuttered up and with dead leaves dankly clotting the pebbled drive, the Villa Berlinghieri was cold and inhospitable. Not only was the place itself vacant, deserted, but even the surrounding fields were lifeless. Unshaven and hollow-eyed after an all-night train journey, Alfredo trudged through the entrance gate, the collar of his light suit turned up against the raw grey autumn weather. He shivered, but not so much from the cold as from a sense of encroaching hostility, of impending doom.

He knew before trying it that the front door would be

162

locked. He rattled the handle. It was. He gave the shutters a violent kick and stepped back into the drive to survey the villa's façade once again. It was then that he noticed the fresh hoofprints in the pebbles and the parallel ruts of a horse-drawn vehicle. Immediately these signs summoned up the image of a hearse. Heart pounding, Alfredo was sure that he was too late, that his father was already dead.

He wandered around to the back of the house, stricken, nearly in a panic, thinking that if only he were wrong, if only his father were still alive, he would make up with him at once, he would come back home, he would forswear Ada. *Let my father be alive, and I'll give up Ada*, a voice in him said. But the notion was so absurd, so melodramatic, that that part of him which stood outside him and observed him rejected it at once as utterly unrealistic and sentimental.

As he turned the corner by the wash building, Alfredo glimpsed an old woman under the magnolia trees at the far end of the house. There was no mistaking her dark, gypsy-like face. It was Olmo's mother. She paced nervously up and down and crooned at a bundle in her arms that could only have been a swaddled infant. Alfredo held back, unseen by her, watching as she kept looking up uneasily at the closed shutters.

Not wanting to come face to face with Rosina just then, for, if his father were dead, Alfredo wanted the news from someone else's lips, he did not question the meaning of her strange presence. Instead, he remained out of sight along the side of the house, where he noticed that one of the kitchen shutters was not drawn tight. Alfredo opened it, pulled himself up on to the sill, and slipped inside, silent as a thief.

By the odour of flowers still lingering in the downstairs rooms, death was confirmed. Instinctively, a numbness like an unnamed fear overcoming him, Alfredo backed into the twilit dining-room. On the long table were handfuls of telegrams offering the condolences of neighbouring landowners. It was enough to read one. Now the death was documented.

Standing there, cold and silent, and wishing he felt something, Alfredo made an effort to generate some emotion or sentiment – grief, pity, whatever was appropriate to the occasion. Instead, nothing in him stirred. He tried picturing his father at their last meeting, and sentimentally he cast Giovanni as the misunderstood benevolent tyrant, himself as the misunderstanding, spoiled son. *Papà, Papà, Papà*, the

163

voice in Alfredo began to say, longing for release in tears. But it did not work. The hatred he had long felt for his father weighed on him like a stone, stifling what he sought. Again his observing self took over, and he knew any pity he might feel would be self-pity, he knew any tears he shed would have been for himself, about to be saddled with responsibilities he was not ready for and did not want. In this confusion, this deadlock, was the beginning of Alfredo's inaction.

Out in the hall, his father's racoon coat hung on a coat-rack. Alfredo lifted it off the hook and put it on. He was starting up the stairs when he heard something – a metallic click, it seemed – from his father's study. Going back into the dining-room, he made out a silhouette in the semi-dark of the next room, busy at the desk. As he entered, the figure turned quickly, and Alfredo saw a pistol aimed at him. It was Olmo who held it.

'What are you doing in here?' Alfredo said.

'Nothing,' Olmo answered aggressively, laying the gun on the desk top.

Alfredo did not know what to say next. He appeared apathetic, as if he did not want an explanation of what Olmo was doing there, as if he did not want to have to judge the situation. But he was glad to see Olmo. He felt a surge of confused emotions churning in him, and he would have liked talking to Olmo about his father, about how he had hated him, about how he seemed unable now to feel the slightest remorse for his death.

The room had changed since his father took it over. The stuffed birds had been removed. New bookcases with glass doors had replaced the old ones. The room was neater, more businesslike, and portraits of his grandparents hung on the wall. Alfredo asked Olmo how his father died.

'It happened in the cow barn,' Olmo told him. ' "My legs have gone weak," your father said. "I feel like I'm dreaming." That was it. He didn't suffer at all.'

'Jesus, the cow barn! It seems to run in the family.' Alfredo sought Olmo's eyes, hoping to find a long lost brother there. 'I've been away a long time.'

'Six months,' Olmo said, his voice warmer now. 'A lot has happened since then, but it's still not too late. Get rid of Attila. Get rid of him today. He goes around bragging that he killed the four old men in Anita's school.'

'I wonder if it would do any good.'

'Kick him out, I tell you. The beatings, the murders—
they're all his doing.'

'You haven't seen Italy, Olmo. You don't know how it's
changed.'

'Things have changed here too,' Olmo said. 'I've changed,
you've changed.'

'What do you mean?'

'I mean you're the master, you give the orders now.'

Alfredo suddenly leaped towards the desk, where Olmo
had placed the pistol. He aimed it at Olmo.

'What were you stealing?' Alfredo said, menacingly.

Olmo looked at him, stupefied. 'I knew your father kept it
in that drawer. I thought it would come in handy.'

'Olmo, quick! They're coming back!' sounded Rosina's
voice from the corner of the house.

The two of them peered at her through the slits in the
shutters.

'That baby with your mother, is it yours?' Alfredo said.

'Yes, it's a girl.'

'And Anita?'

Olmo would not lift his gaze to meet Alfredo's. 'She died
a month ago – in childbirth.'

Alfredo felt his chest tighten. Unable to find words, he
laid a hand on Olmo's shoulder. Then, all at once, he hugged
his friend around the neck and kissed his cheek. When he
could speak, he said, 'Go out the back way, and no one will
see you. Here, take this. He won't need it any more.'

It was the pistol. Olmo weighed it in his hand.

'Tell the truth,' Alfredo said, a wan smile on his face.
'I scared you, didn't I?'

Olmo was already across the room. At the door, before
disappearing into the cold gloom of the house, he paused,
stuffed the gun into a pocket, and said evenly, 'It wasn't
loaded.'

Chapter 15

Coming through the gate, the funeral party looked up in
astonishment. The thirty or so peasants, in dark clothes, had
already turned off to the farm. The others, continuing towards

the villa, now stood gaping. They were Alfredo's mother, his aunt Amelia, Regina, Attila, and three servants. The sound of shutters banging open had stopped them in their tracks. The downstairs windows, closed in mourning, had all at once been violently thrown open before their eyes.

They hurried forward to the front door. As they approached, its shutters too came flying open with a clatter, and there stood Alfredo in his light suit and the raccoon coat, an enigmatic look on his face and his mouth curled into a pleased little smile.

Tears started in the servants' eyes. Eleonora lost her hurt expression and threw herself on her son. 'I prayed and prayed you would come back in time,' she murmured. 'You're all I have left now.'

Alfredo let his mother engulf him with words and tears. 'It's all right, Mama,' he said in her ear. 'I have something I want to tell you.'

He then motioned the others inside. 'I'm getting married,' he announced. 'I'm getting married immediately.' Alfredo kissed his aunt. 'Aren't you pleased?' he asked her. He kissed each of the servants on the cheeks, leaving Regina and Attila deliberately out of his effusions.

Eleonora and Amelia were like stone. At once, they stopped their tragic sighing, and their tears dried up. Mother and aunt stared at Alfredo as if they did not recognize him.

'Come on,' he said, shepherding them all along, jovial and outgoing. 'Who's going to prepare me some good hot wine? I travelled all night, and I'm chilled to the bone. Zurla, have you got out my woollen clothes?'

As soon as the servants were out of earshot, Eleonora turned to her son. 'Is this any time to joke?' she said, her voice strained.

Amelia repeated her sister's words.

'What's the rush?' Regina said nastily. 'Is she pregnant?'

Attila loomed there, embarrassed, ill at ease, a great hulk in a black suit, turning his hat in his big hands.

'Sit down, sit down, all of you,' Alfredo said, firm, decisive.

'What's her name?' asked Eleonora.

'Her name is Ada, and I know she'll please you,' Alfredo told his mother.

The three women were dressed in the obligatory heavy

black of mourning. Amelia and Eleonora also wore great black veils that draped them like cloaks. Now Amelia approached her sister, in kinship, almost protectively, lifting the veil from her and helping remove Eleonora's hat. Eleonora's face was white, drained, tight-lipped.

'Ada,' she said lamely. 'Does she come of a good family?'

'Yes,' said her son.

'Is she chic?' Eleonora demanded, raising her voice. 'Tell me she's chic!'

'She's half French, Mother,' Alfredo offered.

'Has she travelled? Has she been abroad?' Eleonora's tone was feverish, nearly hysterical. 'Does she speak many languages? Is she beautiful?'

'Yes,' Alfredo said, 'yes.'

His mother was suddenly on her feet, carried away, laughter overcoming her, hysterical laughter, mad laughter. 'We'll have a wedding feast then. We'll have a party that will make everyone die of envy. We'll show them. When? When?'

'Quite soon now,' Alfredo said, backing out of the salon and heading for his father's study. 'Tell them to bring me the wine at my desk.'

The moment he left the room, Attila stood up, and with a downcast yet faithful look, tagged along after his new master. At the study threshold, Alfredo turned sharply to the foreman and asked him where he thought he was going. 'Wait here,' he ordered. 'I'll call you if I need you.'

Alfredo shut the door in Attila's face. Like a cringing dog the foreman obeyed. He sat in a chair by the study entrance and tried to make himself unseen.

Alone at his father's desk, the light through the open shutters now pouring in to dispel the sombreness, Alfredo toyed with the large number of penholders and nibs that Giovanni had collected in some strange private obsession. Alfredo was the master now. Olmo was right, things had changed. Alfredo Berlinghieri had inherited one of the richest and most extensive farms in all that part of the Po valley, and with this land, with the inheritance, came power. Already Alfredo felt it. Now he wanted the estate, he needed it, for he believed – Ada's protestations to the contrary – that only his possession of the farm would win him her hand in marriage. Certain of this, Alfredo was determined to keep the Berlinghieri estate running exactly along the lines his father had run it. Change, therefore, would be dictated by profit and loss alone.

He was sweeping the collection of writing implements into a drawer when, without a knock, the door opened and Regina came in.

'And what about me?' she pouted. 'Don't I get a kiss?'

'Shut the door,' Alfredo ordered.

His cousin obeyed at once.

'Come here,' he said coolly, getting up as she came forward. Alfredo kissed her lightly on the cheeks. But Regina clasped him and began running her lips over his neck and face, and she ended by kissing him hard and full on the mouth.

Alfredo did not resist. His cousin, drawing some pins out of her hair, shook her head. Her thick hair cascading loose, she pressed herself against him, nibbling at his ear, gently biting it and whispering to him.

'Are you in such a hurry?' she said, her voice deep and breathless. 'Did you get her pregnant? A pity if you did, because there are so many things we could have done together – special things, all the things you like. Just you and me.'

'What special things?' Alfredo said, holding himself rigid, holding himself back, yet in spite of himself fascinated by her declaration.

'This,' she said, ostentatiously displaying her tongue and flicking it at the lobe of his ear. 'Here,' she added, her hand on his fly, poised to unbutton it.

Alfredo disengaged himself, gently, placing a hand at her neck; then he slipped it inside the collar of her black dress.

'Yes,' she said, misled. 'Take them; play with them; they want your hands.'

Now he seized the dress and tore violently, ripping the material, ripping her petticoat, tearing off her bra. Regina recoiled, fear-stricken, covering her large naked breasts with her arms. But after a moment or two, she dropped her hands by her side and waited, her breasts bare and expectant, the nipples pointing, standing hard.

'My God!' she said. 'The things you want! Help yourself, then; I know I'm part of the inheritance!'

'Just remember,' said Alfredo icily, ignoring the remark and no longer touching Regina, 'with Ada you keep your distance. Do you understand?'

Regina did not flinch. 'I've laid eyes on your Ada only

once,' she said between her teeth, 'but I got the picture right away. She's one of those women who look at the brink of death when they're having a period!'

'Why not?' Alfredo returned. 'She's not a cow like you.'

'No, she's not,' Regina said. 'She's a real lady, isn't she? Well, how long do you think she'll put up with living here among the pigs and the dung and the Dalcò family?'

Regina laughed mockingly, triumphantly. Alfredo turned her to face the door and called out to his foreman.

Immediately, the door shot open, and Attila stood there, almost at attention. Finding himself unexpectedly face to face with a bare-breasted woman, he sucked in his breath and quickly shut the door behind him. In control of himself again, he looked straight into Alfredo's eyes, making an obvious effort to ignore Regina.

'At your service,' Attila said, dry-voiced.

Regina rearranged her clothing as well as she could, having finally to hold both hands over the torn bodice of her mourning dress to keep herself covered.

Alfredo had dropped into an armchair. 'Make yourself useful and take off my boots,' he told Attila. Lifting his left leg, he extended it towards the foreman.

'Wait a minute,' Regina told Attila, angrily stopping him with a gesture. 'Look at him now, the dear cousin who used to be all sugar and honey. You were just waiting for this moment, weren't you – to give orders, to become the master!'

Attila held Alfredo's foot against his stomach. With a jerk, he drew off the boot.

'Good,' said Alfredo, lifting his other foot.

Her cousin's coolness riled Regina. 'You were so nice once,' she raged. 'You were good. Look at you now!'

Attila, knowing his place, drew off the second boot.

'While you were away amusing yourself,' Regina continued, 'who do you think defended your property tooth and nail? Yes, this provincial here, as you call him – this provincial who's always humbling himself and whom you treat like a groom. Him, him. There aren't many like this man, Alfredo. He may seem thick to you and all brawn because he hasn't had a fine education, but believe me, he's your watchdog. Don't let him go. If it hadn't been for him, you might have come back to find your Dalcò friends installed in your bed.'

'What do you mean by that?' Alfredo demanded sharply,

losing his aplomb.

'Just what I said,' Regina pronounced enigmatically.

A shadow passed over Alfredo's face. He went to the desk that Olmo had rifled and showed Attila the forced lock. 'And where were you, watchdog, when this drawer was broken into? Answer me that? What happened to my father's pistol?'

Attila's attention went from the desk to Regina to his new master. 'If I catch them, I'll kill them,' he said between clenched teeth. 'They don't even respect the dead!'

Maybe he should keep Attila on after all – for the time being at least. Alfredo did not like the foreman, but perhaps reasons for keeping him on would soon become apparent. Why, for example, had his father required the services of such a man as Attila? Alfredo would wait and find out. Besides, as he was not keen to shoulder all the responsibilities of managing the estate alone, what need was there for haste when the man could always be fired later?

'If I don't throw you out right now it's because of her,' Alfredo told the foreman. 'But keep her as far away from Ada as possible. That's an order.'

Regina burst into bitter laughter. 'Why don't you just get rid of me instead of humiliating me? Why don't you send my mother and me away – throw us out into the street?' She trembled at her own boldness.

'No,' Alfredo said coldly. 'For now I want you all here. I'll find use for you, don't worry.'

As for his long-standing resolution to restore to his uncle, Ottavio, a share of the farm, it now occurred to Alfredo that that might jeopardize his scheme to win Ada's hand in a true marriage, and that he was unwilling to risk at present. Anyway, Alfredo now knew what Ottavio was, and he was not about to stand by and see the Berlinghieri lands, or the wealth and prestige they represented, squandered foolishly on a succession of dirty little street urchins.

Regina and Attila were staring at him – dangerously he thought, as if prying into his mind. Abruptly, roughly even, Alfredo waved them to the door just as Zurla knocked and came in with a tray of hot wine.

'By the way, cousin,' Alfredo said as Regina went out, Attila dutifully holding the door for her, 'there aren't any nice or not nice masters. There are only masters, and that's that!'

Chapter 16

The Villa Berlinghieri teemed with invited guests. Relations and friends, gaiety and laughter, filled the house. Festivities had begun that morning with Don Tarcisio marrying Ada and Alfredo under a simulated bower at one end of the drawing-room. Extra tables had been laid. The banqueting itself began at twelve o'clock, and by three that afternoon – a dozen overworked servants coming and going – the last course had been served, the six-tiered cake had been cut, the twentieth toast to the young couple's luck and happiness had been drunk, and the villa stood in unbelievable disarray as the restive, boisterous guests began getting up from their tables to circulate again among the rooms and one another.

The bride was radiant, innocent, obviously pleased with the attention lavished on her, and Alfredo Berlinghieri was the envy of every man present. Ada's coiffure was of the utmost simplicity. Parted in the middle, her hair was pulled back close to her head, fully revealing her wide forehead and large expressive eyes. She wore a low-cut satin gown with tight-fitting long sleeves of a gauzy material. Even her dress was simplicity itself, its only frill consisting of two bands of tiny flowerheads – lilies of the valley – that twined the upper arms.

For both bride and groom, but especially for the bride, it had been an exhausting day. Arm in arm, the two had moved continuously from room to room and table to table, wearing bright smiles, greeting friends, being solicitous, giving thanks for presents received. Little girls, gaily dressed in satins and bows and carrying small bouquets, followed Ada everywhere, inspired by her, in love with her, already dreaming of their own wedding days.

Among the guests were a dozen or so black-booted, black-shirted Fascists, chests bemedalled and dressed in their finest. The kitchen was occupied by the Dalcò family, nearly thirty of them, who sat or stood around a large table set just for them. Children seemed to be everywhere, dodging and dashing about upstairs and down, indoors and out. Much wine and much champagne were consumed, and everyone complained about how much they had overeaten. It was a chill November

171

day, not the most auspicious time of year for a wedding, but, though continuously overcast, the sky had brightened at times, and the rain that threatened in the morning had held off. Eleonora sighed long-sufferingly, apologizing right and left for her son and daughter-in-law's haste. A spring wedding, she told everyone, in May when the azaleas bloomed, would have been ever so much grander.

In the dining-room, when a number of the others had retired, Attila Bergonzi, in high spirits and somewhat in his cups, challenged his fellows to feats of strength. The servants, trying to clear the table of plates and cutlery and soiled napkins, were abruptly waved aside. Attila got down on all fours, his face level with the table, and gripped the edge of it in his teeth. The table wobbled.

Old man Pioppi, who had had a brief verbal clash with Attila during the landowners' meeting in the church on St Martin's day exactly a year before, sat overcome with drowsiness at the opposite end of the table. He dozed with his purplish face hanging down on his chest. Beside him, his attractive wife, who was in her early forties, grew uneasy over the sudden eruption of Attila's Blackshirts into the room, which, while they made spectacles of themselves, they completely took over. She glanced around as if to count prospective allies. There were none. Regina was present, encouraging Attila along with the others. A fellow landowner and enemy of Pioppi's, the irascible Avanzini, was also present with his twelve-year-old son, Patrizio. In the midst of the noise, during which the former festive spirit of the occasion seemed to be descending into mere raucousness and nastiness, Signora Pioppi felt alone, cut off, fearful.

Attila's face contorted with the effort, for a moment he hesitated, concentrating, flexed his muscles, then half an inch, half an inch, half an inch, the legs of the long heavy table came up off the floor. Bottles and remaining glassware toppled and rolled, some crashing and breaking. One of the Fascists lifted away the centrepiece of white lilies as it slid into his hands.

It was a vulgar display. In triumph, Attila let go, allowing the table to fall with a loud thud. He grinned, bowing to Regina, as if he were laying a trophy at her feet. She beat her hands together, dizzy with the wine, flattered. There was general loud applause.

The dignified Pioppi, who had removed his shoes and undone the topmost buttons of his trousers, suddenly woke feeling naked, for the table no longer gave him complete cover. Embarrassed, he fumbled with his clothes. His wife helped him on with his shoes and led him away, both of them mortified, to another part of the house.

'Papà, Papà, you try it too!' shouted Patrizio, overcome with excitement and admiration for Attila's feat of brute strength. He was a thin boy with pomaded hair and a sickly effeminate face. Squealing his delight, he egged his father on once more, for which he received a clout before Avanzini moved abruptly away from the table and the shambles the Berlinghieri foreman had created and got himself out of the room. But Patrizio stayed put, so taken with Attila's physical prowess that he could barely contain himself.

The gang of Fascists were like peacocks. All wore black shirts and breeches and highly polished black boots. Some wore the tasselled fez, others, veterans of Alpine regiments, wore Tyrolean hats. A number of them sported medals and ribbons, and across their torsos from the right shoulder down to the left hip a few had on tricoloured sashes. Attila wore a wide leather belt, and he had a large silver skull and crossbones attached to his shirt at the left breast, and small silver fasces were pinned to the wings of his collar. At one and the same time, he appeared resplendent and sinister, attractive and repulsive. He was sure of himself, and this made him both unpredictable and dangerous.

All at once, in a single bound, he was up on the table, trampling the fine cloth and kicking the remaining bottles and plates to one side. Someone handed him a glass of champagne, which he drained at one draught, his head striking the light fixture that hung from the ceiling as he tilted back to drink.

In the next moment, beaming and calling out a new challenge to his friend Barone, Attila threw himself face down on the table, flat, one hand behind his back, ready to lock himself in an arm wrestling contest. Barone, thick-necked and bullish, a squat brute of a man, put his elbow down squarely and looked Attila straight in the eye. Barone's feet were planted on the floor; half his body leaned over the table. Attila gladly, ostentatiously, gave him such an advantage.

The two were ringed in by excited shouts. Patrizio squealed

and told Serafini, the Fascist who stood beside him cheering, that he was sure his father could arm wrestle and beat anybody. Without wasting a glance on him, Serafini gave Patrizio a patronizing pat on the head.

More guests poured into the room to see what the commotion was all about. Ada appeared, her face showing signs of exasperation. Clinging to her hand, Alfredo did not miss her expression. As he drew her aside to the French windows, Attila momentarily looked up from his contest and shouted to the master, 'Hey, Signor Alfredo, Barone and I salute you and your beautiful bride!'

Alfredo winced. 'Get off that table!' he ordered. But in the uproar he went unheard.

'Send them away! I can't stand them!' Ada told her husband, biting her lower lip.

'There, darling, there!' Alfredo said. 'Don't make a scene, just let me explain.'

What was there to explain? He hated the tasteless display of brutality as much as Ada did. And yet he held back, observing, fascinated by the naked force, by the sheer power, of these Fascist bullies. Their awesomeness was such a visible thing! Mesmerized, admiring them in spite of himself, Alfredo said lamely, 'These are country people; I've known them all my life. Don't be upset, darling, they're our neighbours. The only difference is the colour of their shirts.'

'Please, Alfredo, send them away. I can't bear them any longer!'

He ignored her entreaty. 'They're our *neighbours!*' he insisted.

'Ottavio's right,' Ada said. 'The way a person dresses means so much. Put on one of those black shirts, and you become disgusting, vulgar, evil!'

'Darling Ada, they're like relatives. You have to invite them to the wedding, after that you don't see them for another ten years.'

'Say a hundred years, darling. Promise?'

'A thousand years,' Alfredo said. 'I promise. Come on now, smile!'

She looked at him. There were tears beginning to gather in her eyes, but his words stopped them. Ada smiled. Just then a shout of victory went up as Attila bested his opponent.

Holding Ada's hand, Alfredo nervously opened a way through the throng.

The moment they entered the kitchen, they were greeted by gentle applause.

'A long life to the happy couple!' a chorus of peasant voices rang out.

'To the newlyweds!' others echoed.

The room was hot and crowded and cheerful. The table was covered with lidded pots and so many plates, glasses, and wine bottles that scarcely any of its surface was visible. A number of the men ate off their plates while standing, and there was a good deal of gesticulating with their forks as they spoke.

'Are they really all one family?' Ada asked Alfredo under her breath.

'Before the war, there were at least twice as many of them,' Alfredo told her.

Ada caught the eye of someone she had not seen previously. The woman was also watching her.

'Who's that striking woman by the fire?' she asked. 'She looks more like a gypsy than a peasant.'

'That's Rosina, Olmo's mother. Where is Olmo? Goddam him for not showing up!'

'Ottavio, too,' Ada said. 'I'm furious with him. I'll never forgive him!'

'Fine friends we have!' Alfredo said.

They were shaking hands with their guests and smiling and nodding and trying to squeeze their way around the crowded table.

'I knew him when he was this high!' Rigoletto told the bride, getting to his feet to press her hand.

At last they had made a complete round and were about to retreat into the drawing-room.

'To the bride and groom! To the bride and groom!' the company shouted with genuine cheer.

'Still, I wonder,' Eleonora Berlinghieri said. 'The wedding feast so soon after the funeral. It hasn't been a proper mourning period at all. What will people think?'

'Tongues will wag, you can be sure of that,' Amelia said, trying to console her sister by agreeing with her.

175

'Nonsense,' counselled the aged Don Tarcisio. 'A great estate like this one should not be a day without its mistress. Young Alfredo has done well to marry, and may he be blessed with many children! His father would have approved. I'm sure not a single other landowner feels otherwise. They know how much the health of an estate depends on the health of its women. We all know how much you contributed to the welfare of this land, signora,' he told Eleonora, 'and we also know how devoted you were to your late husband's father.'

'Ah, Don Tarcisio,' purred Eleonora, 'how kind of you to say these things. It is always good to learn that one's sacrifices have not gone entirely unnoticed.'

The two sisters detached themselves from the old priest and sat on a sofa. A minute later, Regina came in, dropped between them, and fanned herself with her hands. They all watched the bride, their faces fixed in frozen smiles, as she entered the drawing-room on Alfredo's arm.

'She's too pretty, far too pretty, for a wife,' Amelia said out of the corner of her mouth.

'She'll never make a wife,' Eleonora said. 'Ada's a mistress.'

'Mistress!' Regina pronounced with a smirk. 'She won't be any good in bed!'

'Regina!' her mother chided. 'What a way to talk!'

'My place is no longer here,' Eleonora sighed. 'You heard Don Tarcisio's valedictory. I only feel in the way now.'

'Personally, I give her one year,' Regina said.

The troop of little girls caught up with the bride again, and, unabashedly, all giggles and piping voices, they were telling Ada how lovely her gown was, how lovely she was. Overhearing them, Regina fumed. *I hate you, I detest you,* the voice in her said of her cousin's bride. *It's I who should be in that dress today, who should be in your place!* Regina's torment registered itself in her face.

'In any case, it's settled,' Eleonora was saying to her niece, who had not been listening. 'Your mother and I will move into town. They've a right to be alone.'

'Oh, when I think how fond I am of this house!' Amelia said dreamily, nostalgically.

'What about me?' Regina burst out.

'You're young. You'll stay here,' her aunt told her. 'We want somebody close to Alfredo, to keep an eye on him.'

176

'Yes, and you're so good at dealing with him,' Amelia put in.

'You're leaving me here to be his nursemaid, is that it?'

'Not his nursemaid,' Eleonora snapped, 'but to look after things. Otherwise, who'll protect our interests now that a stranger has come into the house?'

It made Regina suddenly uneasy when she lifted her gaze and saw that the bride and groom were studying her from across the room. Breaking out into nervous high laughter, she sprang up, declaring, 'Oh, I've had so much to drink. Air, I need some fresh air!'

She was quickly face to face with Ada, planting two loud kisses on her cheeks and telling her how pretty she looked. 'Just divine. Divine, divine, divine. That's what I was telling my mother and my aunt only a moment ago!'

But her effusions were too showy, too patently false to be convincing. Then, without the slightest sign to Alfredo, Regina moved breezily off across the hall to the dining-room door.

Ada, puzzled, followed her with her eyes. Attila seemed to give Regina, or to return to her, a meaningful glance, after which she became lost to sight, swallowed up in the sea of sweaty red faces and black shirts that milled in the hallway.

Ada let her glance wander freely over the guests nearer at hand, then she turned to the French windows leading out on to the columned portico.

'Ottavio! Ottavio!' she gasped, close to a scream.

Ottavio opened the door, smiling boyishly, extremely elegant in his formal clothes. He wore an immaculate white tie, and there was a fresh white carnation in his buttonhole. Ada dashed to him; he came towards her. The guests parted, opening a way, exclamations on their lips, great wonderment in their eyes. Ottavio, striding to the middle of the drawing-room, led behind him a magnificent white horse. There were surprised cries of 'Superb! Superb!' and applause.

'Your wedding present, my dear,' said Ottavio, handing Ada the reins. 'Sorry I'm a bit late.'

Ada hugged her friend tight to her, not wanting to release him, clasped him around the neck, and covered him with kisses. She was moved by the gift, moved by Ottavio's presence, and she suppressed tears. 'Is it for me?' she barely managed to say. 'Oh, thank you!'

Amelia shot her sister a look of disapproval. The embrace was entirely too spontaneous, too familiar for her liking.

'It's a mare,' Ottavio said. 'She's called Cocaine.'

As excited as a child, utterly delighted, Ada kissed the horse's muzzle. 'She's so beautiful!'

All of the animal's gear – bridle, reins, saddle – were white. The effect of white-gowned bride and white horse there in the middle of the room was stunning. As more heads pressed into the room for a look there was renewed handclapping. Ada led the horse to a table and wheeled it around. Alfredo helped her on to a chair, Ottavio lifting the hem of her gown.

'One, two, three, up!' said Alfredo.

Ada stepped on to a table and mounted Cocaine side-saddle. A stir, then a hush came over the room, and all at once cheers went up.

Alfredo gave his wife the reins. 'You want to have a little go, don't you?'

Speechless with joy, Ada assented with a nod of her head.

Alfredo ordered a servant to bring his wife a cape as he led horse and rider out on to the portico and into the garden. Carried away by an exuberance of high spirits and plain awe, everyone followed.

For a moment or two, from the back of the crowd, Attila looked on in silence. The house quickly emptied. Watching for the servants, the foreman turned and slipped down the hall in the direction in which Regina had vanished. In his hand he held a bottle of dessert wine that was still corked. Only the boy Patrizio saw him start up the stairway with it.

Chapter 17

Regina waited for him in the attic amid the cobwebs and the jumble of discarded furniture. When he came in, he found her standing in the light of a small dormer window. They looked at each other across the room, greedily. Unspeaking, Attila drew a corkscrew out of his pocket and opened the bottle of wine.

'I thought you might like some of this,' he said, extending the bottle to her.

'No, not just yet,' she said.

Attila drank a mouthful and lowered the bottle. 'I've waited for this a long time, Regina,' he said.

'How long?' she asked, shaking her hair back.

'A year.'

'St Martin's day, the meeting in the church,' she said.

'That's right.'

His eyes went around the big room. Her eyes followed. There was a dusty mattress tumbled to one side.

'You're going to take me,' she said, low-voiced and dreamy.

'Right again.'

Attila swallowed another mouthful of wine, moved closer to her, and made Regina drink from the bottle. She laughed.

'We all know the man you are with your beastly friends,' she said. 'Now show me the man you are with a woman.'

'I don't have two faces like some people around here. I'm one and the same man in my work and in my private life.'

'I'd like very much to find that out for myself,' Regina said.

'You will. I'm going to fuck you. I'm going to fuck you hard, and I'm going to fuck you right here.'

She did not flinch. 'Yes, you're going to make me come, here in this house. This is my house too, you know. I'm part of the inheritance.'

She took the bottle out of his hand and sucked hungrily at it. Then she got down in front of him on her knees. Attila stood perfectly still, almost at attention. From his feet, Regina lifted her eyes to him and said, 'The day of the funeral I felt sorry for you standing there taking his insults. Why did you? Why did you grovel at your master's feet?'

'I'm his watchdog, remember?'

'Then bite! Bark! Don't let him treat me that way.'

'He had no right doing to you what he did,' Attila said.

She reached up now and began stroking him, gently but firmly, talking all the while. It was almost as if she thought he would not notice if only she kept up the conversation. 'Why did you let him?' she said. 'What kind of man are you?'

'Never bite the hand that feeds you,' Attila said. 'As long as you need to be fed, that is.'

She felt him harden under her caresses, and it excited her. She saw the bulge growing right before her eyes. 'He's rotten,' she said. 'Alfredo's rotten!'

'He's your cousin,' Attila said. He was listening to her more than he was paying attention to what she was doing.

'That bitch!' she said, gesturing with her head towards the window. Now with both hands, delicately, she unbuttoned Attila's trousers. Her hand went inside as she kept on talking. 'Just married and already she's running away from him.'

'Running away?'

'On a horse.'

'It was her wedding gift from Ottavio.'

They were silent. Regina, feeling his naked flesh, his bigness, was too excited to speak. Words seemed to dry up on her. She had it out now, holding it straight in front of her, her fingers at the base of it, taking in its length and shape, drinking it in with her eyes, and then – her breathing audible – she took it in her mouth, which was full of love and desire.

Attila laid a hand on her thick rich head of hair. For a moment, he watched her lips at work, saw her cheeks pulsing in and out, then he looked off, unseeing, into the middle distance.

'You don't know me,' he said. 'I gain my strength from insults and humiliation. Italy is my master. I serve her. That's why we marched on Rome.'

Regina rolled her head from side to side, sucking on him, her eyes closed now.

'The rich take and steal and eat,' Attila went on. 'They eat well, and they are rotten, and we Fascists eat crumbs and gain strength. But Alfredo Berlinghieri and all the other parasites will pay the bill for the Fascist Revolution, and it won't be cheap! Everyone will pay, rich and poor, owners and peasants! They'll pay with money and land, bread and cattle and cheese – and with blood and shit too.'

'Oh, I want you, I want you,' she said, looking up at him, her eyes pleading with him, almost in fear that he might not let her stop what she was doing. She was of two minds herself, wanting to go on with it, with what she had her mouth on, and wanting something else done to her with it.

'Get over there on the mattress and take your clothes off,' he told her.

Regina quickly scuttled across the floor to the mattress without getting up.

'Take them off slowly,' he said.

Attila drank, put the bottle on the floor, and removed his boots, never taking his eyes off Regina. Regina obeyed, peeling languorously out of her clothes. When she was down to her underclothes and her silk stockings, he said, 'Now very, very slowly.'

Finally she was white and naked, and her whiteness seemed to light up the dim attic. She was a handsome woman, if slightly over-ripe. Her breasts were large, her flesh was soft and unmuscular but firm. He drew her to him, touching her, touching her, making her tremble with desire; then he forced her down on to the mattress and quickly got out of his own clothes. He wanted her to inspect him. He stood naked in front of her as she leaned back looking. Attila was tall and broad in the chest. His muscled flesh spoke of power. *My God*, she thought, *a man – he's a real man!* But staring at his hard penis, she suddenly felt fear.

'What are you going to do?' she said as he lowered himself on to her.

He did not answer. He spread her legs and was between them, up close to her on his knees, rubbing himself into her, just the tip, slowly, firmly, like stirring something with a stick.

She was breathing very hard in short snatches of breath. All at once, her panic growing, yet utterly enthralled with what he was doing, she blurted, 'It's going to hurt!'

'Of course it's going to hurt,' he said. 'And you're going to like it.'

'No,' she said faintly. 'No.' She went dumb with fear.

'And you're going to like it, aren't you, Regina?' he repeated, his tone hard, authoritative.

'Yes, Attila.'

She screamed when he rammed himself straight and deep into her without warning.

'It hurts, doesn't it?' he said.

'Yes.'

'Yes,' he said. 'Tell me how it hurts. Tell me, and enjoy it.'

'I'm not quite ready for you and it splits me.'

'And you love it.'

'Yes, I love it.'

'Tell me you love it. Say you love it.'

'I love it.'

'Say you love it to hurt.'

'I love it to hurt.'

'Why do you love it to hurt?' he said.

'Because I want to please you, because I want to give you pleasure.'

He noted that the way she uttered the word 'pleasure', her lips drawing back over her teeth, seemed to give her pleasure.

'Fuck,' he said, 'fuck. What are we doing?'

'Making love,' she breathed.

'No. What are we doing?'

'Fucking.'

'Yes. Say it.'

'We're fucking. Attila, we're fucking.'

'Why are we fucking?'

'Because – because we love each other.'

'Say what you are to me. Say we're lovers.'

'Yes, we're lovers.'

'Say it.'

'Lovers.'

'Lovers and fuckers, say it.'

'Lovers and fuckers.'

'Say you love prick.'

'I love your prick.'

'Say prick.'

'Your prick.'

He was ploughing her very hard now, and Regina responded with rhythmic throaty sounds that were halfway between moans and grunts.

'Oh, make me come!' she burst out at last. 'Tell me to come. Look at me and tell me to come.'

'No,' Attila said. 'You don't come until I give you permission to come.'

'But I want to come.'

'No.'

'I want to come. Please. Let me come.'

'No.'

'I'm going to come, I'm going to come.' She was frantic.

'Not without permission.'

'Please, Attila,' she pronounced huskily. 'I'll do anything you ask.'

'Yes, tell me what you'll do.'

'I'll crawl to you. I'll lick your prick. I'll let you hurt me.

Let me. Let me come. I want to come.'

She was nearly crazy with it. He saw that she was nearly crazy with it.

'Yes,' he said. 'Yes. Want it. Want it. Yes. Come now, come!'

'Ah, ah, ah, ah,' she moaned in short breathless animal-like sounds. 'Ahhh!'

He came too, both with her and on the tail of her, and then against her protests he kept on, forcing her to come again – a thing she never thought she would be able to do.

Afterwards, exhausted, they lay in each other's arms, and he felt her thunderous heartbeat, he felt his own heart knocking at his rib cage. Then, slowly, everything grew quiet. He dozed.

His head was buried near her ear, she was talking to him. He kept trying to rouse himself out of sleep to listen to her words.

'Sometime will you order me to suck you?' she said. 'Will you let me kneel in front of you while you stand and let me open your fly and take it out and suck you? Will you make me do it, will you make me like it?'

'But you did it,' he said. 'That's exactly what you did to me.'

'But you didn't order me to do it, and you didn't make me keep on till the end. Tell me you will. You'll order me, and you'll make me like it, won't you?'

'I love you,' he said, lifting his head to her other ear and kissing her neck gently.

'Attila,' she said in a whisper, calm but strangely alert. 'Listen to me. Don't move. Someone's been watching us at the door. We've been spied on.'

Attila sucked in his breath and tensed, ready to spring. He let a few seconds pass, then without warning leaped up and with a bound was at the door, which he had accidentally left ajar. Before Regina knew what was happening, Attila had returned to her holding a boy at arm's length by the scruff of the neck. It was Patrizio, and he whimpered like a scared kitten.

'Were you watching?' Attila asked menacingly.

'No, no, don't hurt him,' Regina cautioned. She sat up, holding her petticoat over her naked breasts. The boy was pale, frightened. She recognized him now. 'Bring him here,' she said, a new bright note in her voice. 'We'll teach him how to have fun.'

Attila shoved the trembling boy forward. 'Have you ever seen a woman? Well, I'm going to show you one. She's pretty, isn't she?'

'Our best man!' said Regina. 'Have you ever played the wedding game? Have you?'

She lay back. Attila threw Patrizio down and, taking him by the hair, wedged his face between Regina's thighs. Gagging, the boy tried to push himself away from her sex, but Attila prevented him.

'He's tickling me! Oh God, I'm going to die with laughter!' Regina giggled and squirmed, then grew angry. She got her hands in Patrizio's hair and hauled him up on her body. 'Let's have him bareback too,' she said to Attila. 'Undress him!'

With a tug, Attila had the boy's trousers down around his knees. Regina locked her legs around him.

'We're going to baptize you. Let yourself be baptized, come on,' she said.

Attila stood back and laughed at the incongruousness of it, his lusty lover there on her back seeming to swallow up the frail boy; then, all at once, he threw himself on Patrizio as if to sodomize him.

'Complete baptism, front and back,' Attila announced.

Patrizio let out a shriek, but quickly Regina clapped a hand over his mouth.

Chapter 18

The black cape wrapped tight around her wedding dress, Ada gave the reins a jerk, and Cocaine moved into a trot. Ahead, through an opening in the small grove of poplars which the horse was about to enter, she saw the villa nestled in the trees of its park, and the sight of it thrilled her. She was glad now to be married to Alfredo, and she knew she was going to be happy here in the country.

She was just about to bring Cocaine to a walk again when from her left a figure suddenly sprang from cover and ran at her, shouting something. She heard the word 'net'. The next thing Ada knew, she and her horse were stopped short, snared in a large trap strung between the trunks of two trees. Though she had nearly been unseated, it happened so quickly that she had not had time to be frightened.

'Keep still! Keep still!' It was Olmo shouting at her. 'Don't tear it, just keep still!'

'Get me out of here,' she said, momentarily indignant. 'What are you waiting for?'

Olmo had taken hold of the horse's bridle. 'Let go of the reins,' he said. He spoke to the horse, gently, and patted its muzzle. Once he had calmed the animal, once he too was calm, he looked up at Ada with an amused glance and began freeing her from the net.

'What on earth is this net doing here?' she said, somewhat amused herself now.

'It's a trap – a trap for brides.' Olmo grinned broadly.

Pleased to see him, feeling safe, Ada fell into the spirit of it. 'And do you catch many?' she said.

'Well, thrushes and quail are a lot easier game.' His strong fingers worked deftly at the tangle. She watched them. 'There you are,' he said at last. 'You can get down now.'

'Help me.'

Taking her by the waist, Olmo easily lifted her to the ground.

'Doesn't the bride get a kiss on her wedding day?' she asked, unable to suppress a happy smile.

'Of course!' He kissed her lightly on each cheek. 'Here, help me free your horse now. She's a fine animal.'

As he worked, Olmo spoke quietly to Cocaine, praising her, soothing her. 'Easy,' he said, 'easy. We'll have you back in the stable in no time.'

'Is this land all ours?' Ada asked.

'All yours,' he said. 'Nine hundred acres.' He folded his net, picked up his game bag, and slung it and the net over his shoulder.

'I went as far as there,' Ada said, pointing to a distant line of trees. 'Is that ours too?'

They set off, Olmo leading the horse by the bridle. Ada walked beside him.

'I have a feeling I'm going to be happy here,' she said. 'And I always thought I hated the land.' She stooped to pick up a clod. 'I love the smell of earth.'

'That happens to be cow shit,' he said bluntly.

Ada quickly dropped the dry lump and brushed her hands together. 'There's a lot of work here, is there?' she said, trying to recover her composure.

'Too much,' Olmo said. 'There are barely thirty of us two-footed beasts now, and that's counting the women too.'

They went on another fifty or sixty yards in silence.

'Would you mind helping me up now, please?' Ada said. 'Everybody was at the party today – except you.'

'Yes, except me.'

'Alfredo thinks of you as a real friend, do you know that?'

'To me he's just the master,' Olmo answered.

'Master, masters,' she said impatiently, 'you're wrong. Alfredo was offended that you didn't come and so am I, since I'm fond of you.'

'All right, I know then. But Alfredo and I are different.'

'You mean maybe you're not such friends after all?'

The two stood close together against the flank of the horse. Olmo hesitated but brought his eyes to meet hers. 'If he and I are friends, tell him to get rid of Attila. Tell him before you change and become one of them too.'

Looking pained, Ada lowered her gaze. She had already reached a compromise with her husband. From the next day forward, the foreman would not be allowed in the house wearing his black shirt. She had settled for that. Ada said nothing now.

Olmo put his hands on her waist to help her into the saddle again, then on an impulse clasped her to him, kissing her on the mouth.

In panic, Ada struck out and caught Olmo a blow on the face. Her action surprised her. Unhesitating, he lashed out, striking her back. Her hand went up to her cheek. 'You've hurt me, do you realize that?' she said, and she broke into a nervous laugh.

'You hurt me too,' Olmo said. He laughed and felt his face.

'Patrizio!' came a man's voice calling across the fields, interrupting them. 'Patrizio!'

Olmo dropped his hand. Avanzini approached, walking very fast. Still several yards off, he asked, ready to explode, 'You haven't seen my son, have you?'

'No, and he wasn't down that way in the poplars,' Olmo told him.

'He's going to catch it from me when I lay my hands on him,' Avanzini promised. Abruptly, he turned the other way and stormed off, shouting his son's name ahead of him.

Ada was still smiling when Olmo lifted her on to Cocaine. Olmo went by the horse's head, the reins in his hand.

'Patrizio! Patrizio!' Other voices, some closer, some farther away, were calling now.

'What was I saying?' Ada resumed. 'Oh, yes, the wedding party. Would you like me to tell you about it?'

Chapter 19

Regina lay sandwiched between Attila, who was taking her from behind, and Patrizio, who was pinned under her to the mattress. As she felt Attila's excitement mount, her own mounted, and with her mouth open, big and wet, she kissed the boy's cheeks and mouth and forehead. Then Attila let out a savage cry, and his pumping subsided. Regina took her mouth off the boy's, suddenly fearing that he might be suffocating in the crush of bodies. With the man still clinging to her back, she untangled herself from Patrizio, lifting herself off him.

The boy stirred. Attila drew himself off her. Regina gave Patrizio a shove and sank down in exhaustion on to the mattress.

'Patrizio, you going to tell anyone on us?' Attila said, his chest still heaving. He looked at the boy and sneered. 'Are you?'

Patrizio cowered, whimpering.

'You don't tell anyone, understand?'

Then they heard a distant voice calling the boy from somewhere out in the park. Patrizio wriggled free of the mattress and tried to get to his feet.

'Stop him! Stop him!' shouted Regina. 'He'll ruin us!'

'Let me go!' the boy cried out, trying to make a break for the door. 'Help!'

But with two big steps, Attila kicked the boy's feet out from under him and sent him flying on his face.

'Help, Papà, help!' Patrizio screamed in his high-pitched voice.

'Don't yell, you ugly little prick!' Attila raged, seizing Patrizio by the ankles.

'Make him shut up!' Regina said.

The room went round and round and round. Attila whirled the boy in circles, gripping him by the ankles as if he were a weightless object. Then everything went out of control. With a sharp cracking sound, Patrizio's head bumped into a heavy wooden post that stood in the middle of the floor. After that, each time he went around, Patrizio's head cracked the post. It was a sickening sound.

Regina's eyes went up. The post was spattered with blood and hair and cerebral matter.

Attila stopped. 'I told him not to yell,' he said.

Chapter 20

Everyone had apparently joined the search for Patrizio. When Olmo and Ada reached the villa, the garden was empty of guests. Even the servants were nowhere to be seen. But from various parts of the farm came a chorus of voices calling the boy's name.

Olmo tied Cocaine to a corner of the washhouse and was about to take leave of Ada when she pressed him to wait there with her until Alfredo returned.

'I don't feel much like seeing him now,' Olmo said. 'I'll come back tomorrow. But I'll leave him some of my catch.' Olmo kneeled by his game bag, reaching inside for a handful of small birds.

'What are they?' Ada asked. She held the cape away from her face as she peered over Olmo's shoulder.

'Thrushes,' he said. 'Alfredo likes them. Wait a minute and I'll string a few together.'

Olmo went around the corner and entered the washhouse's unused end room. He was looking for something he could use to tie the thrushes together. Dusk was falling fast now. Ada, her face at the grating of the open window, saw Olmo rummaging in the dead leaves that mouldered cn the earth floor. Then, for no apparent reason, he leaped back two or three feet, recoiling as though in horror.

'What is it?' she cried out in alarm. Not waiting for a reply, she dashed around the corner to see for herself.

As she barged in on him, Olmo was backing out, his eyes fixed to an odd heap of leaves on the opposite side of the room. He seemed hypnotized.

'What is it?' she repeated, her tone gone shrill with fear.

'Get back!' Olmo breathed, waving her away. 'Get back!'

But by now Ada's eyes had grown accustomed to the failing light. There on the floor, under the tatter of leaves, she made out an inert form, then a hand. Patrizio's. On closer inspection, his mouth and eyes were wide open, gaping through the bloody pulp of his face.

Letting out a scream, Ada threw herself on to Olmo, seeking comfort, shelter almost, in his arms. Olmo clutched her, stricken himself, and backed out into the passageway and then into the garden. Ada would not let go. She clung to him and wept hysterically.

When they lifted their glance from the huddle of their grief, Alfredo was coming towards them across the lawn, a strange wild look akin to anger in his narrowed eyes. In blind terror, Ada simply bolted, starting for the villa. Then, coming to her senses, she turned back and ran screaming, hands outstretched, into her husband's arms. By now the guests had heard the cries and commotion and began to stream back, some of them on the run.

'The blood!' Ada kept repeating, still hysterical, her tears uncontrollable. 'Alfredo, the blood!'

'Come quickly,' a voice summoned. 'There's been an accident!'

A beggar, dressed in rags and tatters and with long straggly hair, came furtively out of the trees and, dragging his feet, approached the kitchen door. When he got there, he found it open. Poking his head inside, he saw a large table loaded with food and drink. *A feast for gods*! he thought. Cocking an ear and finding no one about, he shuffled to the table and began helping himself. He gnawed at uneaten bits of pie and drained the dregs of two or three wine bottles. Then he undid the dirty bundle he carried with him and scooped food and two unopened bottles of wine into it.

It was here, as he knotted up his packet and stuffed his mouth with more pie, that the beggar heard the screams from just outside the kitchen. His eyes went frantically around the room. His first thought was that he had been apprehended. But when he saw that he wasn't, he moved quickly to the door and listened.

'How did this happen?' Ottavio insisted. 'How did it happen?'

Someone had gone into the washhouse and brought Patrizio's disfigured body out. It lay on the lawn; a crowd had assembled around it in a great ring, and they were filled with agitation and terror. Women shrieked and wept; men cursed. Regina too was shaken with sobs.

'What have they done?' she repeated over and over again. 'What have they done to him?' Her mother and aunt each held her up by an arm and tried to lead her back indoors, but she resisted.

Ottavio was unable to control any of it or to make sense of it. Nor could he get anything out of anyone with his questions.

Avanzini wandered about aimlessly, vaguely, repeating mechanically, 'Look, it's my son! My son! It's my son!'

'This must have just happened,' one of the Fascists put in loudly. 'The murderer can't have got far.'

Another Blackshirt stepped up to Olmo. 'You. Where were you? I didn't see you at the wedding.'

'That's right,' Attila said, taking over. 'Did anyone see this man at the wedding party?'

'It's him, I tell you,' a third Fascist announced.

'He wants to see all of us owners dead,' Fornari's wife said. 'He'd kill us all if he dared.'

The hysteria spread.

'I know him,' Serafini, one of the Fascist bullies, said. 'He's a Communist! They want to kill us all!'

Under the shouts and threats, Olmo kept backing away from his encroaching accusers. The whole crowd, in fact, had soon moved halfway across the lawn towards the icehouse mound. Rosina and Rigoletto hung close by the edge of the circle, ready to come to Olmo's aid should he require it.

'Olmo Dalcò, don't move!' shouted Attila. 'Don't move! I accuse you of the murder of this child.'

Fornari's wife, so encouraged, threw herself at Olmo in a fury, spitting in his face. It was like a signal. Five or six of the Blackshirts waded right in. Now Olmo did not budge.

'Hit him! Hit him!' one of them called out.

The gang came at Olmo in a flying wedge, raining blows on him. When he slipped and went down, they kicked him savagely. Then they picked him up again, trying to drag him around to the blind side of the island of big elms, where they could work him over unseen by the other wedding guests.

'Women back to the house, go on!' commanded Attila, his arms up as he tried to herd the women the other way. He took Ada by the arm, but she angrily tore herself free.

'Get your paws off me, you brute!' she snapped. She hurried to join Alfredo, who stood apart arguing with Ottavio. 'Do something,' Ada said desperately. 'Don't you see they want to kill him!'

'What would you have me do?' Alfredo said, cold. He observed. Three of the Fascist toughs held Olmo fast; another punched him about the face.

'Brave bastards!' Rosina screamed. 'Five against one! That's the way you scum fight, isn't it?' She kicked at the men who beat her son, but another two Blackshirts reached in and took her by the arms. Attila motioned for them to keep an eye on Rigoletto too. The hunchback huddled close to Rosina, pleading with her to stop.

'Kill him, go ahead!' Olmo's mother shouted. 'The shit has reached the altar. This is how the landowning class behaves now. Take it, Olmo, take it and show them! Be strong and it will pass! It will pass!'

The man punching Olmo was exhausted. He stopped to catch his breath. The other let Olmo fall to the ground. But fearing they would kick his face again, Olmo struggled to get to his feet. He kept sinking down and trying to rise on all fours.

'Olmo had nothing to do with it!' Ada screamed to her husband. 'He was with me!' She shook Alfredo violently, trying to get him to listen, to respond. 'Alfredo, do something! Please do something! He was with me, make them stop!'

Ottavio intervened, putting himself directly between Olmo and his Fascist attackers, trying to call them off. But the thick-necked Barone laid his gloved fists on Ottavio's lapels and pinned him to one of the ivy-clad elms.

Just then a voice called out, 'Let go of him! He didn't do it! I know who killed the boy! It was me!' The beggar hobbled forward, serene, leaning on his stick. 'It was an accident,' he added.

Olmo bled from the nose. His right eye was puffed up so that he could hardly see out of it. The Fascists stood around him, immobile, confused by the absurd confession. Attila was beside himself. The beggar was spoiling everything. The foreman, fuming with rage, took the man by the shoulders. 'You filthy vagabond! You killer! Killer! How could it have been accidental? I saw the boy's head.'

He delivered a resounding blow to the beggar's face. When the man went down, Attila ordered him up again to take more.

Now Alfredo sought to take the situation in hand. He shoved the beggar into the arms of Barone and Serafini, who stood glowering over Olmo. 'That's enough,' Alfredo said. 'Enough, do you hear! What are all of you waiting for? Take this man to the police.'

As they dragged the beggar off, he held fast for a few moments, turning his head over his shoulder and staring vacantly at the company. Then a great slow demented grin filled his face. Tugging at his guards, he said, his voice changed now, plaintive and pitiful, 'I didn't do it! It's not true! I just said it to see what would happen! I've never harmed a fly!'

'Get him off to the police,' Alfredo barked.

'I didn't do it,' the beggar went on. 'I was joking. I'm a little crazy; everybody knows that.'

Rosina and Rigoletto were crouched beside Olmo. His mother wiped the blood from Olmo's face with a fresh handkerchief.

One of the Fascists tore the beggar's knapsack from him and spilled its contents out on the ground.

'Look! He's been stealing! He's a thief!'

'No,' the beggar pleaded. 'Not my food. All that would last me a week!' He continued his futile pleading as they dragged him off.

'Ladies and gentlemen,' Alfredo announced, 'the wedding is over. It's getting dark, and it's beginning to rain. I suggest we all go back inside.'

The crowd broke up. A number of guests hovered over Avanzini, who knelt by his son's corpse, weeping openly. Ada and Ottavio went to comfort Olmo, but he shook off their solicitude and, helped by his mother and uncle, he limped back towards the farm buildings and home.

'Look at the state Olmo's in,' Ottavio said in reproach, wheeling to address his nephew. 'Why didn't you put a stop to it?'

'What about the state Patrizio's in?' Alfredo said acidly.

'But Olmo's innocent,' Ada said. 'I told you he was with me.'

'Yes, I'm well aware of what you told me,' Alfredo said ambiguously. 'We'll talk about that a little later on – privately.'

'Alfredo, surely – ' Ada began to say.

'Later on, I told you.'

'You're becoming like them – worse than them,' Ottavio said in exasperation.

Alfredo made no reply. Abruptly, he gave his uncle his back and walked towards the house. Ottavio stood there, pained, feeling utterly alone, and sadly shook his head.

'Ottavio, don't go now. Stay, please,' Ada begged.

'I'm sorry, Ada. I'll never set foot here again,' Ottavio said, and he too moved off into the faint mist in the direction of the house.

All around the darkness fell. As she watched Ottavio's slim figure recede into the gloom, Ada trembled. Her eyes filled with tears. Now only Cocaine stood out in the dying light. Head down, the mare cropped the grass by the corner of the washhouse.

PART FOUR

THE LONG WINTER

Chapter 1

1928. Six years had passed. Olmo had chosen to leave the employment of the Berlinghieri estate, to leave the land and take up a new trade. Working now as an itinerant hog butcher, he travelled the length and breadth of Emilia, going from farm to farm and from sty to sty, accompanied much of the time by his young daughter Anita.

Hog butchering, which each year came with the beginning of winter, was like a pagan rite. In it, there was something age-old, sacrificial, epic, and the man who carried it out, pitted in a cruel struggle with the victim, was looked on as a rustic Hercules performing one of his set labours. Taking place when the first snowflakes began to fly, inevitably the occasion had about it an air of festivity, of exhilaration.

The slaughtering itself was always quickly done, always violent. The great beast screamed its short, sharp, almost human screams and thrashed about in desperation, snuffing, gasping, trying in vain to save itself, to escape, while it slipped and scrambled about absurdly, incongruously, on feet too tiny and ill-designed to support its massively disproportionate body. Three or four men usually assisted the butcher. The pig's snout was held in a homemade device, a kind of tourniquet on a stick, that was twisted by turns so as to control and subdue the animal. The peasant onlookers, their heads grouped or jammed close together in the doorway of the pigsty, were mute, excited; they held their breath, they stared wide-eyed at the unfolding spectacle, awaiting the fated moment.

As the helpers kneeled on the upturned animal, gripping its legs and spread-eagling it, the butcher sank a thin, ice pick-like spike into the pink flesh – right up to the cuff of his sleeve. With blood spurting out in hot jets, the butcher then expertly turned the point to the heart, delivering the final stroke. The animal kicked and kicked in spasms of diminishing force.

'By God,' someone was always sure to murmur, 'did you see how he did that – one, two, three!'

'I've never met a man who killed as cleanly as you!' someone else would say, clapping Olmo on the back.

'Nobody kills a pig like my father!' Anita piped this proudly as her father handed her a small glass of wine and told her it would warm her up.

Anita charmed the peasants, especially the women. She was bright, alert, talkative. She was also her father's best friend and his favourite student. Into her, Olmo poured everything – all his knowledge of the world, his loves and hates, his hopes and fears.

'Tell them your name,' he would urge his daughter.

'Anita.'

'Who were you named after?' he would say.

'Mama.'

'And who was Mama named after?'

'Garibaldi's wife!' the little girl said to everyone's delight.

In all the farmhouses of the region, Olmo was known as the best pig butcher in the business. And, in spite of the fact that Attila Bergonzi had spread the word that Olmo Dalcò was an enemy of the regime and that anyone who hired him would be answerable to the Fascists, Olmo was also the most sought after.

Olmo made no secret of it that he was an adversary of the Fascists, and everyone knew that he was persecuted by them. But people liked Olmo, and, in spite of Attila's threats to them, they called him in to slaughter their animals and to butcher them and to help prepare the sausages and salami and hams that the region, the Po plain, is famed for.

Many people were willing to run the risk of hiring Olmo for another reason too. They liked discussing political ideas with him, wanting to hear what he had to say about the Fascists and what should be done to combat them. It was in conversations like these, carried on warily in low voices, that hope for change was kept alive, that anti-Fascism was kept alive, throughout the Emilian countryside.

But the years had drawn on, and change did not come. The Blackshirts remained solidly in power. Olmo went from farm to farm, preaching his word, butchering pigs, educating his daughter, making an example of himself, trying often to bury his own feelings of hopelessness and inadequacy as he gave

196

others cause to hold hope. But for everyone, the troubled times, full of outrage, full of pain, full of sorrow, were like a long, oppressive winter.

In these same six years, life had changed for the new master and mistress of the Berlinghieri estate as well.

Sunk into idleness, Alfredo had turned into just the sort of landowner he had once sworn to Ada he would never become. He did not get fat, but he was very rich, and he more or less gave over the management of the farm's affairs to his foreman. Alfredo's time now was spent chiefly in the entertainment of his father's old colleagues. Increasingly, there were hunting parties and endless billiards matches that went on into the night.

Alfredo had never cleared Olmo's name satisfactorily in the matter of Patrizio's murder. This had been the cause of great friction between Alfredo and his bride, the cause of her gradual disillusionment with her husband and, ultimately, in the last two or three years, of her withdrawal from the life of the house.

At the outset, Alfredo laid the blame for Ada's state on the fact of a violent murder having taken place on her wedding day and in her house. When after a few months nothing seemed to cheer Ada and she wandered listlessly about the house, growing more and more morose, her aspect pallid, her manner vague, Alfredo began cultivating other pursuits, seeking out the company of his fellow landowners. Ada's resentment of him hardened when Olmo left the farm. This in turn made Alfredo more set, more stubborn, less inclined to go out of his way to comfort his wife, to look after her, to help get her past the shock Patrizio's murder had occasioned in her.

She lived now on the upper floor of the villa, over the years increasingly reclusive, occupying a little suite of rooms of her own, where she came and went as she pleased and lived the life of busy idleness that suited her. Ada was a dabbler, an amateur. Her bedroom was like a refuge, a little world decorated to her particular taste. It was always in disorder, piles of books and musical scores cluttered the piano, along with a whole battery of vases that were filled, according to the season, either with fresh flowers or dried arrangements of weeds and leaves. All the furniture was lacquered white –

tables, cane chairs, dressers, wardrobes.

She was the bane of the servants, of course, who grew to consider her, under Regina's prompting, a mere interloper. Ada kept very irregular hours – irregular even in a household notorious for such behaviour. She refused to allow the maids to clean her rooms, and it annoyed her when she saw them looking askance at her because of the number of empty wine bottles that she accumulated in her quarters and that they were foiled in their attempts to remove. For, in her private anguish and despondency, Ada had turned to drink.

Chapter 2

One night, as he switched on the newly connected electric light, illuminating the great chandelier in the middle of the drawing-room, Alfredo found his wife sitting in an arm-chair.

'What were you doing there in the dark?' he said, adopting a tone of surprise to cover his annoyance. 'Is something troubling you?'

He did not want her to answer, for he was quite sure that something was. Something always was, and Alfredo no longer wanted to listen to it. He approached her, leaned over the chair, and kissed her lightly on the eyes.

Ada blinked and tightened her eyelids against the sudden intrusion of light. She got up abruptly to avoid her husband's lips.

'I want to change all the furniture,' she said grandly, and with a sweep of her arms, she indicated the entire room. 'I want to change the carpets, the curtains – everything. I want everything to be new!'

Alfredo smiled. 'But you'll go easy, won't you, darling? Otherwise, you'll ruin me!'

Ignoring him, ignoring his remarks, Ada picked an old oil lamp up from one of the tables, examined it in her hands, then threw it suddenly to the floor, smashing it to pieces.

'Have you gone mad?' Alfredo said, going rigid.

'It served no purpose any longer,' Ada said dreamily, distant. Quickly, she seized another lamp and threw it hard at the wall. The lamp crashed to the floor in bits. 'New things, only new things,' she added, vehement now.

Unpremeditated, as if she had unleashed something in him, Alfredo bounded across the room and swept two more lamps off a table, dashing them hard against the wall. They broke.

'Yes, all right, then,' he said, extremely agitated. 'Change everything, go ahead.'

Alfredo glared at his wife, having all he could do to restrain himself, to keep himself from tearing the pictures off the walls, from overturning the tables, from tumbling the very pillars of the house. In Ada's face there were neither signs of ageing nor of maturity, but where before she radiated beauty, a freshness and kind of harmony, now she reflected weariness and dishevelment. He saw faint shadows under her eyes, her clothes were rumpled, her hair unkempt.

All at once, she seemed to shake herself erect, alert. Shards of glass lay at her feet. Ada's excitement had vanished, its place taken by an air of gravity.

'Alfredo,' she said, 'I want a baby. Why can't you give me a baby?'

Chapter 3

That same week, while working at a nearby farm, Olmo left Anita with his mother, and each night he came home to stay with the two of them in the old house where he had been born. Four pigs had been slaughtered. They had been doused with pails and enamelled pitchers of boiling water and their bristles scraped off. Then they had been stretched and hung in a frame of wooden poles, which was raised to rest at an angle against the brick wall in the portico of a cow barn. This facilitated the butchering.

Olmo in his customary dress – a cloth cap, a red scarf around his neck, and a white apron – was surrounded by his helpers and the usual group of peasants who loved to look on and talk to him. It was something of a celebration. The pigs belonged to a large family, numbering some fifteen if one counted old people and children, and they were all participating, melting fat in a great cauldron, passing around and eating handfuls of crackling, drinking wine. Among them was a young seminary student who wore a black soutane. But Olmo, who was thinking about something that had occurred the day before, was not in a celebrating mood.

'Be careful, Olmo,' a woman named Eugenia warned in friendly tones, handing him wine. 'Attila was here last week and told us not to give you work.'

'He said you became a hog butcher just so you could go from house to house preaching subversion!' Eugenia's husband put in.

'They kicked you off the estate, but a man has to live somehow,' Eugenia said.

'I quit the farm myself,' Olmo said curtly, almost irritated, as he worked with a knife on a stretched carcase. 'The decision was mine, not theirs.'

Olmo drank his wine at a swallow and gave the glass back. He carved away in silence, preoccupied, not inviting further conversation.

Late the previous afternoon, as they were bleeding one of the freshly slaughtered animals, Olmo, who was squatting in a crouch, had suddenly found himself staring at a pair of shabby shoes and the figure of a man dressed in rags. Until that moment, Olmo had not been aware of the man's presence.

'You don't remember me,' the man said shyly. 'There was an amnesty and they let me go. I've been walking for months. You're Olmo, aren't you?'

'You've come back!' Olmo said.

'Yes,' the tramp said. 'I walk and I walk and I walk and I just can't stop.'

Olmo was on his feet. 'I've never understood why you got yourself mixed up in it that day.'

'You were down on the ground. They were all on top of you. They were trying to beat you to death!'

'You've spent all these years in jail for nothing,' Olmo said, marvelling at the man who had confessed six years earlier to Patrizio's murder. Olmo was trying to fathom what sort of being he was under the tatters and straggly beard and savage head of hair.

'In jail, in a barn, under a tree,' the beggar said philosophically. 'What's the difference? I stay wherever I find myself.'

Olmo moved closer to him. Where did the man's madness end and his wisdom begin? The tramp stepped back.

'But someone killed the boy,' Olmo said. 'Who?'

'I didn't kill him. You didn't kill him. It was one of those

200

men with the black shirts on!'

'Who?'

'I saw one of them come out of the house carrying something.'

'You saw him? Why didn't you say anything?'

'He rubbed the blood off his hands.'

'Who was it?'

The tramp looked at the spike in Olmo's fist, backing away. 'That's enough. That's enough now,' he said.

Olmo lunged at him, gripping his frayed coat. Under the coat, the man's frame was spare. He stank.

'Let me go,' he said. 'The sea is waiting for me at Genoa.'

'You must speak out!' Olmo pleaded. 'The murderer must be brought to justice!'

'Justice! What justice?' the man scoffed, tearing himself loose. 'Killers and innocents, saints and sinners! What difference does it make? I walk and I walk and I walk, but where is Socialism?'

Then, as suddenly as he had appeared, the man was gone.

The next day, Olmo was still troubled by the unsettling, unresolved encounter. Were the tramp's enigmatic ways no more than a dimension of his madness? Who exactly had he seen? Why had he kept it to himself?

'Quite a change from the seminary this, eh, Carlino?' someone was saying to the boy of thirteen at Olmo's elbow, pulling him out of his thoughts.

'You enter the seminary a cock and come out a capon,' someone else chided Carlino.

Carlino's mother kissed her son on the forehead. 'Tell him we aren't that stupid,' she said. 'The priests feed you and make you study; then in three or four years' time you give them a good kick in the ass and viva Lenin!'

Carlino looked away, sheepish.

'What Lenin?' one of the men scoffed. 'Can't you see what they've done to us? No more Casa del Popolo, no more newspaper, no more membership card!'

Though the remark was not addressed to Olmo, everyone waited for him to reply to it. Olmo's attention came off his work. The others were passing around tobacco and cigarette papers. Ordinarily, he would have leaped at this opportunity to speak his mind, but today, still puzzling to himself the tramp's statements, Olmo felt cold, at a remove. All eyes were fixed on him, however, searching, and this told him that for the moment he would have to put aside his private concerns and not let these people down.

'Look at this,' he said, rallying himself. 'There still is a newspaper.' Out of Olmo's pocket, folded small, came a copy of the clandestine *International*, its pages well worn. 'There are comrades still willing to risk a prison sentence writing and printing this. Look how many hands it's already passed through.' His audience made appreciative murmurs. Olmo partly unfolded the paper, then put it into one of the men's hands. 'Here. Take it and learn it by heart, because when it falls apart and is no longer legible it will be your job to tell people what it said.'

'All right,' another of the men spoke up. 'I'll memorize it – fine. But without the League, without anyone to speak out, where do we stand? Tell the truth, Olmo. Where is the League now? There is no more League. There is no more Party.'

'We can't use that as an excuse,' Olmo said. 'The Party is you, Micio. It's Eugenia, Enzo, Armando, Martino, Gelindo – all of you. It's the family on the other side of the river; it's the next family here at the end of the road. Wherever there's a working peasant, there's the Party. There are five thousand comrades behind bars. That's the Party, that's where the Party is.'

There was a moment of silence, broken only when Eugenia took the copy of the *International* and began reading it aloud to the rest of them.

That afternoon, while they were all engaged in making sausages, a woman named Stella came on the run from the next farm and burst wildly into their midst. She was so distraught she could barely speak. Her eyes were red and swollen with crying, and she wailed something unintelligible about her husband and her husband's brother.

Olmo knew the two men. They were comrades. His hands went mechanically about their work now, but his attention was fixed on the woman. She was in her early thirties.

'What is it, Stella?' Eugenia asked, making her sit down. 'Why are you crying like this?'

Someone handed Stella a glass of wine. Someone else helped lift the glass to her lips. Through tear-filled eyes Stella saw Olmo.

'They've taken them,' she said, broken with sobs. 'Orlando and his brother Camillo. They've taken them!'

'Who did?' Olmo said sharply, wiping his hands on his apron.

'Carabinieri,' Stella said. 'Just now. In chains.'

'They're comrades; we've got to free them,' Olmo said. He had ripped off his apron and in his hand was a pistol. He checked the chamber. It was loaded.

'Get rid of that gun,' a man named Raboni said, closing in on Olmo. 'You'll get us all in trouble!'

'Give it to me; I'll hide it in my drawers,' an old woman said.

Olmo pushed them all aside. 'Not this time,' he said. 'Chaining people up, are they? We'll see about that!'

'Have you gone mad?' Enzo said.

'Hide that pistol!' Raboni repeated.

Olmo waved the barrel of the revolver. The circle around him immediately widened. He took Stella roughly by the arm and lifted her to her feet.

'Who's coming with me?' Olmo said, studying their faces. No one answered; no one stepped forward.

'You're all big on talk, then, is that it?' Olmo accused. 'Take a good look at them, Stella!' He shook her alert. 'Get to know your neighbours!'

'He's crazy!' Enzo said.

Still brandishing the gun, Olmo pulled Stella away with him. When they got to the edge of the yard, he turned around and said, 'You're the ones who ought to be chained up! You look like people, but you're nothing but animals!'

Hurrying, stumbling, Olmo led the way along the river bank, several paces ahead of Stella. The river was wide at this point, and, in the waning light, the whole expanse of grey-green water slid along silently, without a ripple. Olmo scanned the other bank for a glimpse of the carabinieri and their two prisoners. There was no sign of them, but he knew they were sure to come into view once he and Stella rounded the next bend and gained the high dyke road.

A dog howled distantly.

'That's our Prince,' Stella said, halting momentarily to listen. 'He followed them.'

Olmo ran on ahead. The moment he reached the road he

203

made out the tiny figures across the river. There were six of them. They walked single file, stick-like, the chained brothers in the middle. A dog trailed the procession, skulking and occasionally whimpering.

Screened behind a big poplar, Olmo called out the two men's names at the top of his voice. 'Hang on,' he told them, 'we'll get you out of this!'

On the other bank, Orlando and Camillo stopped. The Fascist carabinieri stopped and looked nervously around.

'We're here, we're with you!' called Olmo. 'We're all here!'

A jerk at the chains that bound them and a blow or two with rifle butts made the prisoners move on.

'Stop! You'll only make it worse!' Stella cried out to Olmo as she caught up. 'The carabinieri are brutes.'

'Release them, goddam you!' Olmo continued to call, ignoring Stella. 'Let them go!'

'What are you trying to do? Don't you see you're alone?' Stella pleaded.

Olmo shoved her away. He raged as if possessed. 'There are hundreds and hundreds of us. All the prisons in Italy won't be enough.'

It was apparent that the carabinieri could not tell where the voice was coming from. They cast looks around them in all directions, holding their rifles at the ready and lengthening their pace. Olmo kept abreast of them running along the slope just below the roadway, where he was out of sight.

'Camillo! Orlando! Hold on! The Party won't abandon you!' the strong voice went out across the breadth of water.

Without slackening pace, Camillo held his chained wrists above his head. He appeared to say something, but Olmo could not make it out. He pulled the revolver out of his belt.

'Do you want to ruin them? Is that what you want?' Stella said, and she threw herself at Olmo, grappling and tumbling with him down the slope.

They were free of each other as they came to rest. Stella quickly scrambled to her feet and reclimbed the bank for a last look at her husband and her brother-in-law.

Below the slope, Olmo stood in the ploughed field. Gripping the pistol in both hands, he fired into the ground, emptying the chamber. At the same time, hearing shots, the carabinieri spotted Stella on the dyke road, in the open, outlined against the evening sky.

'Who can that be?' one of them said to his fellows.

'I don't know,' the carabiniere in front of him said, 'but sooner or later we'll lay our hands on them!'

Standing still now, in tears, not knowing which way to turn, Stella felt utterly cast down and helpless.

Olmo was in tears too. He had thrown himself on the freshly ploughed ground and in a frenzy of frustration rubbed his face into the earth, sobbing.

'There are so many of us!' he said, inaudible. 'We're so many; we're so many!'

Chapter 4

Furtively, Attila and Regina climbed the back stairs and slipped into the dark attic. Going straight to an old table, she bent to remove some undergarments, then sat on the table and spread her legs. It was all done routinely and in silence. Attila stood in front of her with his trousers unbuttoned and began to enter her.

'Tell me,' he whispered to her.

'Use me. Use your cunt,' Regina said, low voiced and breathless. 'Use it, Attila; use it.'

He clutched her but felt her detachment, felt she was not taking part.

'Tell me,' he said again.

'You treat me like a woman,' Regina said. 'That's why I love you. You know how to use me. I like it when you make me want it, when you make me do things I don't want to do and like it.'

'Yes, yes,' Attila said, his excitement growing.

Suddenly she stifled a scream, and a look of utter horror paralysed her face. She clung to him now, not as a lover but the way a child clings to a parent.

'Oh, Jesus!' he said.

'Did you hear that? He's there!' Regina whispered.

'Shut up!'

'Over there! He was moving! Look, look! He's moving! He's come to spy on us!'

'Be quiet, for God's sake!'

'It's him, Attila. Do something. Patrizio, go away. Leave us in peace!'

'Regina, stop that!'

'Do something, please do something!'

Attila freed himself of Regina's grasp. Staggering and in a slight daze because of his interrupted coupling, then nearly tripping over his dropped trousers, he managed to get to a pile of old grain sacks that rested on the feet of an overturned armchair by the wall. Angrily, violently, he pulled the sacks down and shoved the chair to one side.

'You see? There's no one there. Are you happy now?'

Regina watched in near hysteria. 'I dream about him every night,' she said. 'He's all covered with blood. I hate him; I hate him!'

'You're making me crazy with that talk!' Attila exploded. 'I'll never come back here again! I hate this goddam room!' He pulled up his trousers and buckled his belt. Feeling all at once exhausted, he turned the broken chair right side up and sank into it.

Regina came and sat beside him. 'Don't be angry with me,' she said. 'I'm fed up too. Whenever we want it, we have to behave like a couple of thieves coming up here, hiding. It's not fair.'

'You're right,' Attila said. 'We need a house of our own, a place where we can do as we please.'

She slipped a hand into Attila's fly and began stroking him, at the same time licking him around the ear. 'Let me do it this way,' she whispered. 'If you're left up in the air, you get nervous; I know you.'

He leaned back, shut his eyes, and said, 'Of course, you could change things around here if you wanted to. He's as weak as a jellyfish, she's drunk all the time, and you've got the keys to everything. You're the one who gives the orders around here, my love.'

'No, I deserve a house of my own – like a real lady,' Regina said dreamily, her hand still pumping away. 'A house fit for somebody like me.'

'I know one.'

'Where?'

'The Villa Pioppi,' Attila said. 'They're up to their ears in debt.'

'Yes, and Alfredo holds the mortgage,' Regina said, her voice soft and full of pleasure now. 'A year or two more and he'll have to foreclose.'

Attila smiled and stopped her hand. 'Can't you just see us sitting there on our own furniture, in Chinese dressing-gowns, listening to the radio broadcast from Rome? A servant knocks and comes in with two glasses of Marsala.'

'Marsala for you,' Regina said, half indignant, half thrilled. 'I want champagne!'

'Champagne, then,' he said, and again Attila lay his head back, relaxed, peaceful. Then, absently lifting an arm, he upset a large tin box, which nearly crashed to the floor.

'Careful, you animal!' Regina snapped. 'They'll hear us!'

It was silent. He started her hand moving again; then, after half a minute, he ordered her on her knees in front of him.

'With your mouth,' he added superfluously.

Chapter 5

There was tension in the smoke-filled room. The balls clicked, split apart, roamed the green expanse, miraculously came together again, clicking, and now there was an uproar among the onlookers. Alfredo and six or seven neighbouring estate owners were gathered in the billiard-room of the Villa Berlinghieri.

Bertoli, the winner, had flung his cue stick aside, let out a triumphant cry, and, as if diving into bed, thrown himself on to the broad table.

'I adore you, I adore you!' he cried, fondly kissing the green baize and moving his loins as though he were coupling with it. Then he roared with laughter. The others roared too – all except the loser, who emptied a glass of wine at a single gulp.

The men circulated around the room, talking loudly and gesticulating. Most of them went to a table that was laden with food and helped themselves to sausages and bread and wine.

'And now where will you find the courage to go home to your wife?' one of the older men said to Ferrari, the loser.

Ferrari put his glass down angrily. 'I want a return match!' he announced.

Alfredo, who had been watching in silence, stepped in. 'I hardly think that's wise,' he said. 'Calm down, Ferrari, you've just lost a stableful of livestock. What else can you stake?'

'You want to end up like the little Fascist mayor of Mantua?' a man named Orsini said, leering.

Alfredo threw his head back and laughed. Orsini winked at him.

'Yes,' Alfredo said, 'Mayor Grossi has loads of honour but very little money, so he puts his wife up as stakes! *Viva l'Italia!*'

But the wink was a sign whose meaning only Alfredo understood. A year or two before, having beaten Orsini badly at cards, Alfredo discovered that the loser had no money to pay.

'Quite all right,' Alfredo had said calmly, sportingly. Then taking the man aside where no one else could hear, he added under his breath, 'You can pay me in produce if you like, or else –'

Orsini's heart had skipped a beat. 'Yes?' he asked, dry in the throat, fearful.

'Your foreman's daughter – Teresita, I think her name is. Maybe you could arrange a meeting between her and me.'

Orsini was dumbfounded. He stammered, 'But, but, she's a half-wit.' He meant it seriously. Teresita was twenty, but she had the mental age of a girl of nine or ten.

'Aren't they all?' Alfredo answered cynically.

Orsini saw that his friend was serious. 'Done!' he consented, relieved, even managing a smile.

From then on, Alfredo had been meeting the girl regularly in an abandoned shack at the edge of his property. To give her a pretext for her absences from home, he paid her to dig worms for him out of the slimy bank of a nearby ditch. He would hand her a few small coins and afterwards throw the worms away.

Bertoli had climbed off the billiard-table and was in the corner gorging himself on salame, which he packed into his mouth with chunks of bread that he tore off with his fingers. Ferrari, his voice a bit thick with drink, called across the room to him, saying, 'I don't need the advice of friend Alfredo here. I want another match!'

Bertoli wiped his mouth with the back of his hand, then,

208

picking up a long salame, he went to the table with it. Using it like a cue, he hit a ball. By now he had swallowed his food. Beaming, he turned to the impatient Ferrari and said, 'What makes you think I want your wife?'

The roomful of men guffawed. Ferrari reached for Bertoli across a corner of the billiard-table and took him by the collar.

'You're going to give me this game, do you hear? Because if you don't, I'll pay you all right – but after that I'll kill you on the spot!'

'You'll get your return match another day, Ferrari,' Alfredo said with a finality that made Ferrari remove his hands from the other man. The rest of them had grown quiet. Just then, the door opened and Attila came in stiffly. 'I'm sorry; excuse me, gentlemen,' Alfredo said, going to his foreman.

'Signor Alfredo, Cavaliere Pioppi would like a word with you,' Attila said, his voice low, his eyes not straying from his master. 'What shall I say to him?'

'I thought I told you not to enter this house with mud on your shoes!' Alfredo snapped.

Attila looked down. 'The soles are clean,' he said.

'Well, they're dirty to me! Send Pioppi in!'

Attila summoned Pioppi, holding the door open for him. Alfredo had not expected the man's wife as well. Signora Pioppi stepped into the room and looked immediately uncomfortable in the presence of so many men standing around in their shirt-sleeves. She fanned the smoky air with her hand.

'You all know Cavaliere Pioppi and Signora Pioppi,' Alfredo said, turning to the room. 'The Cavaliere is the only honest man among us. Now, if you will excuse us for a few minutes – '

'Don't forget about the return match,' Ferrari spoke up.

'Don't worry, don't worry, you'll have your return match,' Alfredo said pleasantly. 'All you lost was a stable of livestock. You can thank God you still have your health!'

Alfredo indicated the door to his guests. Attila opened it and followed the little party into the hallway outside.

'Lucky you that you can enjoy yourself with your friends,' Lorenzo Pioppi said, cocking his snow-white head of hair and crimson face back towards the billiard-room. 'We, on the other hand – that is, I – I don't seem to be able to get ahead any more. We had a bad harvest this year. The earth just doesn't seem to give the yield it once did.'

Pioppi saw that Alfredo was waiting for him to come to the point. 'Your father and I were very close,' the old man went on, 'and he always told me, "Watch out, Pioppi, if you don't manage your affairs properly, you'll end up in straits." But he helped us.'

'Yes, he helped us!' Signora Pioppi put in, unable to contain herself. 'He helped us sign so many mortgages there's not a piece of land left in our name!'

Attila turned discreetly away, but he listened intently.

'Really, I didn't want to come here now,' Pioppi said nervously. 'It was my wife's idea. You see, once – once we were very close, your father and I. A thing like this, you understand, is so embarrassing.'

'How much do you want?' Alfredo said straight out.

'Oh, I knew you'd understand! You're a better man than your father,' Signora Pioppi gushed.

'Do you have anything left to mortgage?' Alfredo asked.

From the back part of the house, a door opened and Olmo's face was framed in it. He seemed slightly hesitant. Involuntarily, somewhat surprised to see him, Alfredo called out his name.

'The house,' Signora Pioppi answered.

'The house?' Alfredo repeated absently. His attention was on Attila, who had sprung forward to bar Olmo's entrance.

'You're not allowed in here,' Attila was saying roughly.

'Out of my way!' Olmo told him.

'You don't learn easy, do you?' Attila said between his teeth. 'You've been told you can't come in here, so don't try shoving me. Some day somebody's going to teach you a lesson you won't forget. Now get out!'

Alfredo abruptly left the Pioppi and came forward. 'What's going on here?' he asked his foreman.

'His shoes are dirty,' Attila said.

'What is it?' Alfredo said neutrally to Olmo. 'What do you want?'

'I was told my daughter's here. I'm a peasant, a Communist, a thief, and a murderer, and I want her!' So saying, Olmo pushed his way past Alfredo and Attila and started down the hall to the stairway.

Bewildered, the Pioppi stepped aside. Attila made a move towards Olmo, but Alfredo snapped his fingers and called the foreman off. Olmo could feel Alfredo's eyes on the back of his head as he reached the stairs.

Attila was dismissed with a wave of the hand. Then, returning to Pioppi and his wife, Alfredo mumbled an apology for the interruption. In a hurry now to terminate his business with Pioppi, he watched Olmo disappear along the second-floor landing.

Anita sat in one of the white cane chairs, holding a book open in her lap. From another chair, Ada leaned over her and helped her read the page.

The little girl was thrilled to enter this special world, where the walls and all the furniture were white as snow and the rooms, which were as big as a whole house, were filled with so many interesting things to look at. For a whole week now, she had been coming here every afternoon, and Ada taught her lessons just like real school. Once, when Anita told Ada that her mama had been a schoolteacher, Ada burst into tears. Anita knew that Ada was very lonely and that she wished she had a little girl of her own. Ada was always very kind to Anita. She showed her all her books; she let her sit and play the piano; she told her all sorts of strange and wonderful things. The things Ada knew about weren't at all like the things her papà knew. Anita didn't want Ada feeling so sad. That's why it was good for her to visit Ada every afternoon. It was as her papà had told her – 'we must always help those who have less than we do.' Ada was so beautiful and so lonely and so sad.

Ada and Anita were studying a large brilliant blue butterfly that was mounted in a glass case that Ada had taken down from the wall. The door to the room flew open. The woman and the girl looked up in surprise.

'Papà!'

'Anita, come home now,' Olmo said.

'Is it all that urgent?' Ada asked.

Anita got up and ran to her father. 'We haven't finished yet,' she explained.

'I don't like you to come here, you know that!'

Downcast, but without another word, Anita collected her coat and scarf.

'She has to learn to read and write,' Ada said. Her voice betrayed a pleading note.

'That's my affair,' Olmo said curtly, looking past her.

211

He helped Anita into her coat, then led her off by the hand, not even bothering to close the door behind them. In the minute or two that Olmo had been in Ada's presence, he had not once let his eyes wander about the room, let alone meet her gaze. His behaviour, his determined sternness and single-mindedness, struck her as inexcusably impolite.

Ada found the experience disconcerting; she found herself wounded by it, and immediately after father and daughter had disappeared down the dark corridor she went to the piano, where she drained a bottle of its last drops of wine. Glass in hand, she collapsed into the cane chair again, utterly drained of strength or willpower.

She had been staring vacantly ahead of her for some minutes before her eyes fixed on the encased butterfly. She picked it up, propping the case upright, and imagined the beautiful creature vainly beating its wings against its imprisonment. Absurdly, she rested her chin on the table, gazing soulfully at the blue butterfly and feeling an infinite moment of empti-ness, of absence.

Her reverie was interrupted by her husband's arrival. Alfredo stopped at the threshold, glaring at her before he spoke. To his annoyance, Ada did not acknowledge his presence.

'You know he's right,' Alfredo said. 'What the hell is this missionary urge of yours? Who asked you to take her under your wing?'

'I love that child!' Ada said. Her eyes still rested on the blue butterfly in the glass case.

'I don't care whether you love that child. She's out of place here, and I wish you'd leave other people's children alone.'

Ada leered at him nastily. 'Yes, from now on I'll devote myself to *our* children!'

'Why not just devote yourself to me?' Alfredo said in disgust. 'Why don't you get out of this room once in a while and look after your husband's friends, eh?'

Ada stood up, a forced smile on her lips. She was about to answer him, but Alfredo was no longer there. She heard him on the stairs, going back to the billiard-room.

Chapter 6

Ada was running, running in the dark, running she knew not
where across the garden and into the trees. Her face smarted,
and she felt herself on the verge of tears. When she stopped,
gasping for breath, she heard a hateful voice pursuing her
in the night.

'Go drink in a tavern if you want to soak it up! We're
respectable people in this house, don't you know that?'

It was Regina.

Chest heaving, heart still pounding, Ada moved on, more
slowly now, drawn by a glow of lantern light that came from
the stables. *Stinking bitch!* she told herself, stumbling in the
black. *Cheap whore!*

She had hurried down the stairs and then down another set
of stairs to the cellar and tried to open the grillwork gate.
She could see the barrels and demijohns and the racks and
racks of bottles, but the gate was locked, and, even reaching
through the bars, she could not lay her hands on a single
bottle, a single drop of the precious juice. Hearing the players
upstairs in the billiard-room, laughing, laughing, she rattled
the gate, seething with anger and frustration. Then there was
a noise, and Regina was coming down the stairs, a huge bunch
of keys at her waist. *Ah, here's the real mistress of the house*,
she told herself, and Regina was laughing her loud, insulting,
vulgar, Fascist laugh. She rushed at her then, mounting the
stairs two at a time and grabbing for the keys but really
wanting to grab for the throat to quell that vulgar, bitchy
mocking laugh. 'Bitch!' she screamed, 'whore! slut! turd!'
And Regina stood there haughty, immovable, laughing. 'The
key, just give me the key,' she said, almost begging. She knew
now she shouldn't have said that, shouldn't have begged. She
shouldn't have let Regina see how desperately she needed
that key, nor should she have descended to Regina's level.
Regina wouldn't give up the key and struck out at her, claw-
ing her face with her nails. She tried to bite Regina, maybe did
bite her; she couldn't remember now, but Regina was stronger
and took her by the hair, and she felt the roots ripping and
she stopped struggling and was forced down on her knees.
'The key,' she had said again.

'You'll get the key up your ass!' Regina said, and she laughed her throaty laugh, triumphant and gloating. 'Guzzler,' Regina said, 'guzzler, guzzler, guzzler!' And then she found herself flung away, flung back, and her face was burning, smarting with pain and burning with shame. And the hateful voice was taunting her, saying, 'How stupid I am, how stupid I am! Why shouldn't you drink? You're the mistress of the house, aren't you? Of course you are. Of course you must have your daily guzzle. Guzzle yourself to death. Drown in it, mistress. Help me and drown in it. Help me, have a bottle, have a demijohn. Here, take the key.' And Regina opened the gate for her and pulled it back, and it squeaked on its hinges. Then the gate was wide open and the key was in Regina's hand, and Regina extended it with a grin on her face, about to break into the vulgar laugh.

'No,' she had said then, 'no, I don't want it any more.' And she was climbing the stairs, fast, almost on the run, and at the top she looked down, looked back, and said, 'I baptize you, my slovenly slut!' And after that she was outside, the cold air striking her burning face like a slap, running and running in the dark.

A number of peasant families sat around on bales of straw in the warm central aisle of the cow barn, the animals on either hand stirring, clanking their chains, softly lowing. This was the farm people's winter night's entertainment. They sang and told stories and worked at various household tasks – caning chairs, sewing, spinning wool, making brooms of faggots of brushwood. Some slept. When Ada slipped through the door, her hair wild, her face stricken and scratched, a sudden silence descended.

'Tell me, pretty one,' an old woman said after a while, 'have you come for your horse? Have you come to ride?'

Ada stood stock-still, not daring to go forward, not daring to go back. The lot of them stared dumbly, insinuatingly, casting her looks at once shy and knowing. Then a chorus of voices, male voices, started up.

'Come for a ride!' they said. 'Come with me!'

Her heart beat faster. The rhythm and volume of the voices rose.

'Ride, ride, ride with me!' they said, and it reverberated from the vaulted ceiling.

Then there was a quick movement from the other end of the

aisle, and a small girl was running at her. Anita. Ada dropped to her knees and scooped the child into her arms, hugging her hard and picking her up.

Anita had seen the moment of terror in Ada's eyes, and now she led her outside and made her sit down for a moment. Ada obeyed in silence. She sat on an abandoned stone trough by the doorstep of one of the peasant apartments. Anita spat on the hem of her dress and dabbed at the scratch on Ada's cheek; then, with her small hands, she tidied Ada's hair.

'You were crying,' the child said.

'A little,' Ada said.

'Me too, I cried. Olmo is nasty.'

'That happens sometimes when someone is bad.'

Behind them, the door opened, and a long shaft of lamplight flooded the great courtyard and lit them up, huddled together. Olmo stood there on the threshold, peering out.

'Come on, you two, come inside,' he said, his voice changed, warm. 'It's going to be a bitter night.'

The kitchen was comfortable. A wood fire burned in a potbelly stove, beside which Rosina slept in an old armchair. The remains of the evening meal were still on the table – a long knife and cutting-board, a foot-long salame, and empty bowls and glasses.

Ada joined Olmo at the table, and he poured them out two glasses of wine.

'To your health!' he said.

'To your health!' Ada said.

'A drop now and then does you good.'

'Or two or three,' Ada said ironically.

'All right, to bed now, little witch,' Olmo said to his daughter. And he reached out with his hands and took her face and kissed it.

'Good night. Good night, Ada,' Anita said. She raised herself on tiptoe to give Ada a kiss too. Ada clasped her tight to her bosom, overcome with emotion.

'Good night,' Ada said, watching the girl mount the stairs to her bedroom. On the left side of three or four of the steps, pairs of shoes were neatly laid out.

In the room there was silence except for a clock ticking on a shelf and the occasional sound of singing that came from the stable.

'It's nice here,' Ada said after a while.

'What do you like about it?' Olmo asked, amused.

'I like the way Anita said good night to you. I like the smell of your supper. I like your mother sleeping there by the stove. I like the way you're all together here.'

'If that's what you want, I should make you up a bed in the corner. Then every night the master could come and shut you in. I remember there used to be a key – it was as big as this – and at night the peasants were kept inside, like in prison. We could dance, sing, make babies, die, but we weren't allowed out till daybreak. Then the master sent a servant to unlock the gate. This isn't the Middle Ages I'm talking about – it was only a short time ago, when my grandfather was alive and I was small. One night Alfredo slipped in, and he got locked inside with us. Now the doors are open, but Alfredo doesn't come any more.'

'What do you think of Alfredo?' Ada asked.

'The masters are our enemies, and we want to destroy them. Alfredo is a master.'

'And me?'

'You're a master too – of sorts.'

'You really believe in class war then?'

'I do.'

'Olmo, Olmo, Olmo. I may be the master's wife; but I'm no master, and you know it.'

'You belong to the class.'

'I'm classless. I always have been and always will be.'

'You aren't a conformist, I'll admit that.'

'Well, I'm glad to see you have something good to say about me.'

'I was wrong this evening,' Olmo said. 'I should have thanked you. You know, Anita really loves you.'

'Don't you think her mother would have wanted her to study?'

'I don't want to send her to the Fascist school.'

'But she still has to learn to read and write.'

'If you were the teacher maybe, but not with the Fascists.'

Olmo's mother murmured in her sleep and stirred restlessly. Then, her eyes fluttering open, she called her son's name.

'Oh, Rosina, we woke you up,' Ada said.

216

'I had a terrible dream,' Rosina said. 'I flew to the top of a mountain. Your grandfather Leo was there, and he told me, "Look, Rosina, look down there. Those are the years." "What years?" "The years to come," he said, "lined up like a procession." Then I saw them, all in a row – a lame year, a blind year, a year that was hunchbacked, a year without a head, a year without ears, and on and on.'

Olmo got up and went to her. 'Maybe you should go to bed,' he said affectionately.

Rosina took her son's arm and stood up. 'Olmo, go away. Take another road. There's nothing but bad luck here. Pack your things, Olmo. Take Anita and go away.'

She moved to the stairway. Olmo and Ada stared at her, then at each other, dumbstruck.

Alfredo peered through the windowpanes at his wife and Olmo. He held a stone in his hand and squeezed it so tight his knuckles whitened. With half a mind to fling it through the window, he stepped back several paces.

There was a noise, and Alfredo made out an approaching shape in the dark. 'Who's there?' he asked.

'It's me, Togno.'

Togno, one of the Dalcò brothers-in-law, was surprised and even embarrassed to meet Alfredo in this place at this hour. He said nothing.

Alfredo drew him to the window. 'Do you see who's in there?' he said. 'Go and tell her I'm waiting for her at home.'

Togno obeyed at once.

Alone again, Alfredo hurled the stone savagely into the dark.

Chapter 7

Regina stood on the doorstep of the Villa Berlinghieri, along with a battery of servants, to greet the arrival of her mother and aunt. A sedan had driven up, and a chauffeur in dark livery opened the rear door for Eleonora and Amelia. Stepping out spryly, the sisters were effusive in offering their cheeks to Regina's cheeks.

It was three years later, on the afternoon of Christmas Eve,

1931. The visitors had come to spend the holidays together as a family. There was snow on the ground, and the weather was cold.

Aunt and mother, after the ritual kissing, narrowly scrutinized Regina. Regina scrutinized them. The servants rushed forward to relieve the chauffeur of his armful of parcels and packages. Regina found Eleonora's face and her mother's more wrinkled, more lined. Eleonora herself she found lively and suspicious.

Then, full of false good spirits, they all went inside. Two of the servants took the baggage upstairs. Two others, obeying Eleonora's instructions, showed the chauffeur into the dining-room, where the presents were to be laid at the foot of the Christmas tree. The sisters hurriedly removed their fur coats, eager to follow the others and to see the decorated tree, but, with her first look into the room, Eleonora's show of cheer at once vanished.

'Oh, no!' she murmured, aghast, fists pressing her temples. Since her last visit, the furniture had been completely changed. The Louis Philippe décor – the dark, heavy furnishings of nearly a century before – had given way to the streamlined elegance of Art Deco. Eleonora was scandalized, offended. Her beloved floral wallpapers were gone, replaced or covered over by an endless expanse of blank white walls. In the middle of the room, the new dining table, a rectangular slab of wood resting at its centre on heavy square supports which in turn rested on a plain plinth, was a monstrosity. What was the meaning of such austerity? It was tasteless; it was ugly.

'No, no, no, I don't recognize my house any more,' Eleonora said with an audible sigh, turning melodramatically to Amelia for sisterly confirmation and comfort.

Amelia, who had been about to join her sister in bemoaning the barbaric scene, suddenly held her tongue. The room reminded her of something. What? After a moment or two, it came to her. The exhibition of Art Deco held in Paris in the summer of 1925. One Sunday, six years before, Eleonora and she had opened the rotogravure pages of their newspaper, which featured the Paris show, and, on the spot, both of them had been enthralled by the new style of furniture and furnishings. It was all so twentieth-century, they had oohed and ahed – so French, so effortlessly chic! Amelia realized now that the dining-room that her sister was ridiculing and that she too was about to condemn could easily have come out of the pages of that very Sunday supplement. Screwing up her once pretty face into a suitably pained, yet comforting expression, Amelia turned it on Eleonora, but she said nothing.

'You see what happens when *she* takes over!' Regina said, gloating, venomous.

'And Alfredo?' her mother asked, feeling she ought to put in something.

'Him? He pays for it. He gets out his billfold and just peels off the notes,' Regina said.

'And the uglier it is, the more it costs, you know,' Eleonora pronounced. She was visibly shaken. 'Don't tell me they've sold our old furniture to buy these monstrosities!'

'Sold!' Regina snorted. 'They *gave* it away!'

'Gave it away!' Amelia said breathlessly, in an effort to sound appropriately horrified.

'Do you remember the glass-fronted cabinet with the liqueur set?' said Regina, taking exquisite pleasure in her disclosures. 'Well, it now adorns the Dalcò house.'

'But have they gone mad? Those were valuable objects — all of them!' said Eleonora Berlinghieri.

As if her aunt's distress were not great enough, Regina perversely led her into the drawing-room. There Eleonora's shock was compounded. She felt her heart beating and her mouth go dry. The armchairs and sofas had unappealing curved backs and spindly tapered legs. The curtains, a bold stylized floral print in dramatic colours, were vulgar, unbearable. Gone from the mantelpiece were Eleonora's marble and gilt clock and attendant vases. She reached for her sister's arm, wanting to weep on her shoulder.

Regina relented. For now, punishment and horror enough had been inflicted on her aunt. Regina directed her to a settee by the fire, where a servant waited to pour tea. The tea service was old and treasured, and just now it was the right touch.

Amelia, ever sympathetic, cast a wistful look at her sister and patted her hand. 'There, there!' she cooed. 'One simply can't come home again. It's too, too heartbreaking!'

Eleonora smiled bravely. She restricted her gaze to the fire and to the things on the tea table.

'Well, then, tell us all the gossip!' Amelia said brightly to her daughter, hoping by this that they could snatch her sister from the melancholy mood she had been plunged into.

219

Before Regina could speak, Eleonora's laughter all at once tinkled among the teacups. 'You won't imagine what extraordinary thing happened to us just now as our car turned into the drive!'

Amelia laughed a piercing little laugh in encouragement and in relief.

'We were cut!' Eleonora said. 'As our car slowed for the turn, we saw Maddalena Pioppi at the edge of the road, and we greeted her through the window. She seemed to be muttering something to herself. "Merry Christmas, dear old friend," I called to her.'

'And I said, "Best wishes, Signora Pioppi," ' Amelia put in.

'And what then?' asked Regina.

'Why nothing,' said Eleonora. 'She didn't reply. She didn't even look our way or acknowledge our existence. We were cut, my dear, cut!' She laughed cruelly.

'Poor thing!' Amelia sighed, tapping her forehead with a finger. 'They say since her husband died – '

Regina squealed with laughter. Her mother poured more tea.

'Well, here's the latest on her,' Regina said when her laughter subsided. 'Last week she went to confession with a dead cat in a bag and thrust it in the priest's face. The poor man was nearly frightened out of his wits!'

'Dead cat?' said Eleonora in disgust.

'Yes, the widow Pioppi, it seems, is suffering from a bad case of imagined persecution. She said her cat was killed on purpose by people who wanted to hurt her. "Love thy neighbour as thyself," the priest told her. She thinks she's about to be cheated out of her house. Of course, she's mortgaged way above her head.'

'It was her husband's fault. Mismanagement. Giovanni warned him many a time,' Eleonora said.

'Well, she's obsessed – completely obsessed! Imagine dragging a dead cat into the confessional!'

'Poor, poor woman!' Amelia clucked.

Eleonora cast her eyes around the room again, in disbelief, and sighed. Her gaze came to rest on the carpet, whose tone was plain, neutral, and, to her, utterly devoid of interest.

'Yes,' Regina said, noticing. 'It's enough to eat one's heart away. And try to imagine my fate here in this wretched role of regent! Oh, aunt, you've barely touched your macaroon!'

Alfredo had started down from the upper floor, buttoning himself into his overcoat, when Regina's voice reached him. He hesitated on the staircase now and listened to her holding forth.

'Alfredo indulges all her whims,' Regina was saying. 'If I weren't here, it would be an even worse disaster. And what do I get for my pains? Scorn, abuse, insults – all because I've been careful to keep the wine under lock and key.'

'Why, it's positively –' But Eleonora broke off. She had spotted her son at the bottom of the stair and leaped up to intercept him.

'Merry Christmas, Mother!' Alfredo said, wriggling out of Eleonora's embrace as he hastened to the front door.

'What? You're going out? And your mother –'

But he was gone.

Regina ran to the window, where she was immediately joined by her aunt and mother. All three watched Alfredo quickly cross to the far side of the circle before the house and get into his car.

'Where on earth is he going at this hour?' Eleonora asked.

'Where do you think?' said the maid Zurla, who was clearing the tea things. 'Into town to look for the signora. I had to tell him, even though it's Christmas Eve. For all her ways, at heart the signora is kind.'

Regina glared at Zurla for her impertinence.

'Oh, for the Christmases of yesteryear!' breathed Amelia nostalgically as she returned to her place by the fire.

'Personally, I'm used to all this carrying on,' Regina snapped.

'Wouldn't you think they had everything to make them happy – beautiful, young, rich!' Amelia said, speaking to no one in particular.

At the window, her sister dabbed at the tears in her eyes. The sound of Alfredo's car could be heard starting down the dark drive. Amelia got up quietly, crossed the room, and went to Eleonora's aid.

'Yes,' Eleonora Berlinghieri said in a hushed tone, as though her heart were about to break, 'everything but an heir!'

Chapter 8

The shop windows glittered, full of shining goods, but traffic in the arcaded centre of the city had thinned to a trickle, and only the last remnants of the afternoon crowds made their way along the fast-emptying streets.

Slender and elegant, Ada came into a large square that was still crisscrossed by small groups of people, some of whom greeted her with a touch of their hat brims. Certain of the passersby wished each other a merry Christmas, at the same time extending their arms in the Roman salute taken over by the Fascists. This was the twelfth Christmas of the Fascist era. Ada walked without purpose. Ahead, framed in marble, she saw the lighted windows of the Grand Café. Now that the Christmas Eve vigil had begun and the town was beginning to take on a deserted look, the café seemed a haven, a warm promise. She quickened her step.

The maître d'hôtel exchanged a meaningful glance with an old waiter as Ada entered and went to a small round marble table at the far end of the salon. The place was more than half empty. A couple of young men turned around to look at her.

Ada had just come from Ottavio's apartment, where no one answered the bell. She had been disappointed. Ottavio was the one person in the world she would have enjoyed seeing at this moment. She had rung the bell twice, impatiently. After that, she had groped in her handbag and taken out a tube of lipstick, with which she wrote a short Christmas greeting on the white wall beside the door, signing her name to it. She smiled a brief smile as she descended the palazzo's broad staircase, but once out on the street again she felt overwhelmingly melancholy and desolate.

She lifted her eyes now to see the waiter approaching with slow steps. When he got to her table, he bent his flabby, sunken face close to hers. He knew Ada and wished her a happy Christmas.

'A double cognac,' she said.

The old waiter lowered his voice and said apologetically, 'We can't serve you, madame. We have our orders. It's not my fault.' He rolled his watery eyes and, putting his face even

222

closer, said in a tone of complicity, 'I could give you a little in a cup of coffee perhaps.'

Without a word, Ada got up and recrossed the café. Again the men stared. The old waiter followed her.

'I'm so sorry,' he whispered to her at the door. 'It's not my fault.'

Chapter 9

The half-open door swung on its hinges, back and forth, back and forth, as Olmo stood behind it, testing his work. He was installing a lock.

'A key now, like we were padroni,' Rosina chided. 'We've nothing to hide here.' Her voice came from the far end of the kitchen, where Anita crouched naked, receiving a bath in a tub of hot water.

Olmo had just bored a hole through the stile of one of the leaves of the door. He worked at the opening with a hammer and narrow chisel now. This was the first lock in the history of the Dalcò family. Peasants' houses, since they seldom held objects of value, never needed locks.

'It's not for that,' Olmo answered his mother over his shoulder in his own good time. 'It's to keep others out.'

'Well, whatever it is, hurry up or Anita will catch cold!' Rosina said. She was a bit put out with Olmo because he would not allow Anita to go to midnight mass with her.

Olmo shut the door tight and turned the key in the lock. It worked perfectly. Not quite satisfied, he unlocked the door to try it once more. When he opened it, Stella's smiling face greeted him on the threshold. Olmo was speechless with surprise.

'Hello!' Stella said.

'Stella!' Olmo exclaimed.

'Are you going to keep us out here?'

'No, no. Come in. Come in, all of you. Anita, come and see who's here!'

Stella was accompanied by her three boys, aged six to nine, who trudged in after their mother. Anita rushed forward, naked and goose-pimpled, and laughed at them.

The oldest boy, Giacomino, laughed at her. 'You're skinny!' he told Anita.

Anita glared at him, about to strike out, when her grandmother came and caught her by the arm. 'Aren't you ashamed?' Rosina said. 'Cover yourself! And you,' she told Giacomino, 'what are you looking at?'

Rosina drew Anita aside and slipped a dress on to her.

Stella's once beautiful face was lined, and she had put on weight. She explained to Olmo that she had felt lonely and wanted to come and spend Christmas in the company of friends. 'We were alone, we knew you were alone too,' she said.

Olmo's pleasure showed in his face, and it made Stella feel welcome. She took a basket out of the hands of her middle son so that Olmo could see she had come provisioned. 'Happy Christmas!' she called out to Rosina.

'It's a strange Christmas,' Rosina said, grumbling about the lock, which she motioned to with a nod of the head. 'A strange Christmas,' she repeated. 'Shut in like prison!'

'Like my papà,' Giacomino said.

Olmo shut the door again, first looking out into the cold, starry night. He gave the lock one, two, three, four, five, six turns of the key.

Chapter 10

She found a small bar down an arched alleyway in the old part of town and sat there, a bottle on the table, drinking grappa. It was a dimly lit, dingy place whose front window was steamed up and opaque. Only a few people had been gathered at three of four tables when she arrived. They had been gay and noisy and apparently knew the barman, for they had exchanged loud, affectionate farewells with him on leaving. Now they were gone. The only other customers in the bar were two coal men, one old, the other young, with grimy clothes and faces, who sat at a nearby table and kept wishing Ada a merry Christmas and lifting their wine glasses and drinking toasts to her.

It was in fun and Ada enjoyed it, but the drunker she got the more morose and removed she felt. She had drunk half a bottle of grappa.

Unknown to her, out on the street Alfredo peered at her through the steamed window, waiting for the other customers to leave. It was cold, and in his vigil he stamped his feet to keep warm. When after several minutes the two coal men were still there, he entered and, without being seen by Ada, silently approached her table.

Ada lifted her glass, which was so full it spilled over the sides and ran down her hand, and wordlessly toasted the coal men. They watched her, this time without saying anything, fingering their glasses of wine. Ada brought her dripping glass to her lips.

A blow from behind knocked the glass out of her hand and sent it flying. Unmoved, Ada looked up. 'Merry Christmas, young man,' she said to Alfredo.

Then she was down on her hands and knees in the sawdust under the table, searching for her glass.

'Do you know how long I've been looking for you?' Alfredo said, seething.

Still kneeling among the tables and chairs, her reactions slowed now by excessive drink, Ada said, 'Signora Berlinghieri can no longer drink at home because the wine is locked up. Signora Berlinghieri can no longer drink in smart cafés because her husband has given orders against it. So Signora Berlinghieri has to make the round of dives like this.'

Alfredo winced, half in pain, half in a rage. 'I'm going to have you put away, do you understand? Now get up!'

'But I like this place,' Ada said playfully. 'I even like it under the table. I can fall under the table here, and nobody takes any notice of me!'

'Get up from there! Look at your face!' Alfredo stripped off his gloves and stuffed them into his coat pockets. 'You're as swollen as a sponge, and you reek of alcohol! You're disgusting, do you hear? You stink!'

She raised herself and looked at Alfredo as if she were seeing him for the first time. 'Do I disgust you?' she said. 'Am I swollen and stinking? Who are you anyway? I took you for Alfredo, but you're not Alfredo, you're my husband.'

She sat down clumsily, producing the glass and banging it down heavily on the table. Without even wiping it out, she began to fill it from the bottle.

The two coal men got up to leave. As they moved to the door, the younger one stopped by Ada's table.

'Need any help, signora?' he asked.

The older man pushed in front of him. 'Come on, don't

play the hero. We're going.'

'I know why you don't want me to drink,' Ada said, her attention still on Alfredo. 'It's because it gives me the courage to tell you the truth. You don't like me telling you you're different, you're changed. Well, you have changed. You've surrounded yourself with a pack of arrogant, vulgar bullies and murderers. And you're even worse than they are because they don't know any better.'

All at once, as though coming to her senses, Ada held out a hand to the two coal men, who still stood beside her table. 'Come on,' she said to them. 'Sit down and have a drink with us. My husband wants to meet my friends.'

Alfredo lowered his head in embarrassment. 'Stop it! Stop this right now!' he spat out between his teeth.

The young coal man was ready to accept Ada's offer, but the older one tugged at him. 'Come on, it's late,' he said.

Ada clutched at the younger man's coat. She made a half-hearted attempt to get up but found she couldn't. 'Wait a minute,' she said thickly. 'You can't refuse a drink!'

'Let us go, signora,' the old man said.

Ada let go the young one and took the other man by the wrist. 'I warn you, my husband will be offended!'

Now the two coal men began to grow embarrassed.

'Besides, where are you going anyway?' Ada pressed them.

'To wash,' the old man said.

'Why?' Ada said in genuine bewilderment.

'Ada, for God's sake!' Alfredo said.

'Why?' she repeated.

'It's Christmas,' the young coal man answered her.

'Oh, no, for heaven's sake don't wash,' she said, imploring. 'You're much more beautiful the way you are.'

Somehow managing to get to her feet now, she pressed her cheek to the old man's and began fondling him. Then she put an arm around the young man and tried to kiss him.

Physically repulsed by the sight of this, Alfredo took a backward step. But he could not stop observing, nor could he stop telling himself she was being grotesque.

'Can I have your cap?' Ada asked the young coal man.

But the old man had parted them and was dragging his friend off. The door was open, and a stream of cold air blew in. The men buttoned up their greasy, blackened coats. The young man was about to close the door behind him when, from the threshold, he raised his cap to Ada and said, 'You really want it?'

'Yes. To remember you by.'

The young man tossed her the cap, turned, and vanished into the dark street. Unsteady on her legs, Ada leaned awkwardly against the table, deliberately keeping her back to Alfredo. In a sudden violent fit, Alfredo clutched her shoulders and began shaking her hard.

'But what have I done to you? What have I done to you?' he shouted at her.

At the other end of the room, the barman shook his head. 'Ladies and gentlemen, we're closing soon!' he announced. To him, they looked like entwined lovers.

Finding himself watched, Alfredo released her. 'We'll be going then,' he said. 'I'll get your coat.'

The barman disappeared into a back room. Ada suddenly lost her balance and crumpled gently to the floor, where she found herself in front of her husband on her knees. Alfredo bent down to her. Ada's face and dress were smudged black with coal grime. He drew a white silk handkerchief out of a pocket and began wiping his wife's face with it, patiently, grimly, without speaking a word. While he dabbed at her, Ada put the cap on her head. She giggled.

'Coal! Coal for the winter!' she called out, mimicking. The expression on her face was at once impudent and pathetic.

'You slut!' Alfredo said, exploding. He picked her up and made her sit on a chair. Then, exhausted himself, he dropped on to another chair. 'You like fooling around with everyone, don't you? Even with Olmo! Yes, don't give me that look. You fool around with him too, I know. I want you to tell me everything, everything!'

'Olmo!' She laughed in her husband's face. 'So that's what's eating you, is it? Olmo! What an imagination!'

'Imagination!' Alfredo raged. 'Is it my imagination to have seen you two together? Is it my imagination that I can even smell him on you?'

'Do you think Olmo would have anything to do with the wife of a Fascist?'

'You call me a Fascist? I am *not* a Fascist. And I'll kill you if I catch you with him again!'

'Why don't you have the courage to admit we can't make love together any more?'

At that moment someone came in. It was a young woman, dressed in a huge coat. She stood just inside the door, listening to Ada and Alfredo as she unwound a scarf from around her head and unbuttoned her coat.

'Fighting, eh?' she said familiarly. 'Lucky you! At least it means you love each other!'

They turned to see who had spoken. With a graceful gesture, the young woman stepped out of her coat and slung the scarf over her arm. Alfredo recognized her at once. It was Neve, the epileptic girl. The years had left their marks on her too; she was older and somewhat worn, but Alfredo knew he was not mistaken. She approached them, but her step faltered the moment she saw it was Alfredo.

'How are you?' she said simply, remembering him.

'You know her?' Ada said.

Alfredo returned Neve's half smile.

'Yes,' he said. 'In a way.'

Ada gave the woman a long look now. 'Sit down,' she said to her, motioning to a chair.

'May I?' Neve asked, addressing Alfredo.

Alfredo introduced them. He seemed weary.

'I'm glad you remember me,' Neve said. 'What about you? You're not from around here.'

'No,' Ada said.

'You look like a lady. You are a lady, aren't you?'

Ada said nothing.

'She's my wife,' Alfredo said.

'You know, after that day I never had another attack,' Neve said to Alfredo. 'God knows what was going on in my head. A short time later, I met a man, a good man. I liked him, I really loved him. When my mother died, we got married. He was a hard worker. We settled down here, right on this street. I still live here.'

'What happened to him?' Ada asked.

'He disappeared one day, and I never saw him again. But even if he's taken up with someone else, I'm happy for him. He taught me how to manage, and now I can get along fine on my own. We never had any kids. That's the only thing I miss. I never knew if it was my fault or his.'

On an impulse, Ada reached a hand across the table and clasped Alfredo's arm. It was as if she wished to reassure herself that everything was not over between them.

Neve abruptly got up. 'I almost forgot. I've got something to cook out back.' She went off behind the bar, and, almost as an afterthought, before ducking into the other room, she said, 'Why don't you stay and eat with us? They're nice people here. And anyway, where else can you go at this time of night?'

Alfredo and Ada were alone now. She took his hand. 'Shall we stay?' she said.

Alfredo lifted her hand and kissed it, long and gently. Ada looked at his tousled hair and scraped her chair closer to him. She placed her other hand on the back of his neck and played with his hair. After a while she leaned over, pressing her lips to where her fingers touched him.

'Alfredo,' she said softly, her eyes far, far away, 'I want a child.'

Chapter 11

Along with everyone else – peasants, shopkeepers, landowners – Attila and Regina, walking arm in arm, were bound for midnight mass. But rather than accompany Eleonora and Amelia in the car, they had chosen to set off for the village on foot, a bit earlier, wanting along the way to play at a little game they shared when feeling particularly affectionate and close to each other. Passing by the Villa Pioppi, they liked to stand and gaze at it, fondly dreaming and imagining that they occupied it, living there together as man and wife, a pair of real property owners.

It was an understandable dream. Neither of them was really comfortable at the Villa Berlinghieri – Regina because she always felt the poor relation and Attila because, as foreman, despite the prestige his strong-arm activities increasingly lent him, he was still a servant. There was snow underfoot, and the air was cold and clear. What better night than this, the eve of the day celebrating the birth of the Christ child, to indulge their private dream?

The Villa Pioppi stood only yards from the highway, screened on the left by a small stand of trees. A single light burned in a room on the ground floor, but the lamps on the gateposts were unlit. The frugal widow had doubtless left for church already. Attila and Regina approached the spiked iron gates with caution, peering through them at the house. The snow cover seemed to illuminate every detail.

'Excuse me, signora,' said Attila, play acting. 'I wonder if you could tell me who the owner of this fine villa is.'

'Ah,' said Regina, adopting a lofty tone, 'it belongs to Attila Bergonzi. There's a man who has really come up in the world!'

'Does he live here alone?'

'No, sir, he lives with his queen, his beloved Regina. They're the most envied couple in the whole of the valley!'

'Oh,' said Attila.

'Yes,' affirmed Regina.

Then Attila broke it off, pointing to the trees at the left side of the garden. In his normal voice, he said, 'Tear down those trees. What we need there is a paved terrace of some kind.'

Regina agreed. 'Yes, modern, like in town,' she said. 'One more year and it's ours!'

'A year's a long time. And we'll have to see what Alfredo thinks. You never know with him.'

Regina threw herself passionately on Attila's neck. They embraced.

'You don't know how much I love you, do you?' she said. 'Do you? That's our house. No one is going to take it away from us.'

Suddenly, the lamps at the gate went on, flooding them in bright light. At the same time, the villa's front door opened. Attila and Regina were frozen to the spot.

'Merry Christmas, Signorina Regina!' the widow Pioppi called. Finding the pair at her gate seemed to cause her neither alarm nor surprise.

The two drew apart, speechless.

'What are you doing out there in the cold?' the widow went on, kind and strangely ceremonious. 'Don't be formal, come inside, both of you.'

'Merry Christmas, Signora Pioppi,' Regina answered, scarcely able to conceal her nervousness. 'We don't want to be late for mass.'

'Nonsense,' the widow insisted. 'We'll have a little drop to warm ourselves; then we can all three go together. Come along now.'

Attila looked at Regina in puzzlement and shrugged his

shoulders. Regina appeared reluctant, uneasy. With a glance back at the road, Attila opened the gate narrowly and helped Regina through ahead of him. The widow was outlined in the open doorway, beckoning them inside.

'She's really crazy,' Regina said to Attila over her shoulder. 'The other day she cuts me dead in public, now she invites us into her house.'

'She must want to make up to us,' Attila said. 'I wonder why. Anyway, it's a chance to see what the inside's like.'

'All my good wishes, Mr Mayor!' the widow said to Attila with an odd smile on her lips. Then, as she stepped back to usher them inside, she raised her right arm in the Fascist salute, executing it as smartly as it was unexpected.

Attila, almost as a reflex, responded in kind, adding a click of his heels. He looked closely at the widow. She was haggard, with dark hollows under her eyes, and her greying hair was unkempt. She still wore mourning, but her clothes were queerly rumpled, as though they had been slept in. Utterly bewildered, Attila asked, 'Surely you're not making fun of me, signora?'

'Not at all, not at all,' the widow said breezily, shutting the door. 'They'll elect you one of these days. You're young yet, young and strong!'

Preceded by the mistress of the house, the guests were led down a long corridor.

'Everything is so artistic here,' Regina said, her eyes about her. 'It's just like being abroad. Really, this is a perfect house for a lady like you.'

'Yes,' Attila said, he too avidly taking everything in, 'very refined, very elegant, very tasteful.'

'Do you really think so?' the widow said demurely. 'Come and see the parlour.'

Attila and Regina barely entered the room when the door closed behind them. For a moment or two, their curious eyes roaming over the contents of the little parlour, they thought nothing of it. Then they heard the key turn in the lock.

'What's she doing?' Attila said, whipping around.

'I told you, she's mad,' Regina said.

'Caught you, haven't I?' said the widow, speaking to them through the door. 'Now you'll have to listen to me. You want to get out? Then you'll have to sign a paper saying this house remains mine.'

Leaning close to the door, Attila and Regina stared at each other in disbelief.

'You got that mortgage from my husband with threats, with political blackmail,' the widow went on, her voice high-pitched and hysterical. 'But I've got you in my power now, and I won't let you go!'

Attila rattled the doorknob, but it was useless. Regina, who began to appear more annoyed than worried, dropped into a chair.

'Let her rant,' she said. 'She'll calm down. What are you doing?'

Attila had left the door and was studying a wooden lamp. Peering under its base, he said, 'Made in Czechoslovakia.'

'You won't get out of there!' the widow screamed. 'You won't get the best of me! This house is mine, and it'll stay mine! Rogues! Sinners! Concubines!'

'You see, I told you,' Attila said, turning on Regina. 'She called you a concubine. If we don't get married soon, we'll be the laughingstock of the whole countryside!'

Regina was amused by the remark, and, to show Attila her indifference, she turned aside and played with the knobs of a radio set. 'This radio doesn't work,' she said.

'You've harmed me for the last time!' the widow raved. 'What did my poor cat do to you? Murderers! That's what you are – murderers! Murderers! Murderers! Murderers!'

Hearing that word, a flash of fear passed over Regina's face, leaving her pale. Quickly, she was on her feet by the door. 'Signora Pioppi,' she said, serious now, 'calm down and open this door. You're hysterical; you don't know what you're saying. All these silly accusations – why don't you open the door so we can talk things over?'

Regina listened for a reply.

'Murderers!' shouted the widow.

'Why don't you open the door?' Regina repeated, supplicating. 'We're respectable people!'

But Attila, his fists clenched, lost control and pushed Regina aside. He had removed his hat. Now he swept a hand over his receding hairline. All at once, readying himself for what he was about to do, his big body seemed even bigger.

He dashed at the door, raging, one shoulder lowered like a battering ram. With two heaves, he broke through.

Chapter 12

Racing through the night, the car's headlights flooded the deserted countryside and occasionally picked out drunks weaving homeward on bicycles. Alfredo was at the wheel. They had just passed through the village and were speeding along the highway to the villa.

'Admit it, I looked nice in the coal man's hat,' Ada said.

'Stunning!' Alfredo laughed. 'Absolutely irresistible! But I prefer you in mine!' And so saying, he lifted off his hat, reached over, and squashed it down on his wife's head.

Ada laughed and handed the hat back to Alfredo, then pressed close to him. The road curved, and Alfredo raised his foot off the gas pedal.

'I know it will please you,' Ada said. 'Let's go wish Olmo a merry Christmas.'

Alfredo stiffened. 'But it's late. Surely he's asleep.' His foot went down hard on the gas.

'So what? We'll haul him out of bed!'

Her excitement was irritating, but at the same time Alfredo was pleased that Ada was in better spirits and full of enthusiasm. She was like her old self, and he did not want to kill it. Maybe they could make a fresh start together.

'All right,' he said. 'We'll wake the stubborn old mule if necessary. Where's that wine?'

Ada moved to the open window and stuck her hand out. 'It's keeping cool,' she said. She felt the neck of the bottle. It was wedged into a bed of snow on the front fender, behind the spare wheel.

'All those people up ahead,' Alfredo said. 'I wonder what's going on.'

They were approaching the Villa Pioppi. The road appeared to be blocked by a milling crowd. Ada sat up straight.

'They must be returning from midnight mass,' she said.

Alfredo was forced to bring the car to a halt by the side of the road. A small crowd, kept back by three or four carabinieri, pressed in front of the villa's gates and spilled out across the highway.

'What is it?' Ada said.

'Stay here,' Alfredo ordered, getting out. He had caught

a glimpse of Attila and Regina among the spectators.

'What thieves?' someone was saying. 'She was up to her eyes in debt.'

'Poor thing,' someone else said, 'all she had – house, land, everything – was mortgaged.'

'Who to?'

'What a question! To the Berlinghieri, who else?'

It was then, after forcing his way through the throng, that Alfredo saw the body. It lay face down over the top of the gate, impaled on the iron spikes. 'Oh, my God! Oh, my God!' he murmured, horrified by what he saw. The widow's head hung down on the other side; her legs, this side. The palings, where the blood had run down them, were red with gore. Alfredo could not take his eyes off the ghastly sight.

Standing alongside the carabinieri and a priest, Attila saw Alfredo coming forward and began opening a way for him. At the same time, the foreman raised his voice over all those around, saying, 'What's a mortgage got to do with it? It was obviously a sex crime. She was still an attractive woman; she must have been carrying on with someone.'

Alfredo recoiled, disgusted by Attila's words and by the assurance and familiarity with which Attila now took his arm. Then, in the next moment, having spotted someone else in the crowd, Attila dropped Alfredo and went in search of the new quarry. In spite of himself, Alfredo turned to see who it was.

'Your Honour!' Attila said obsequiously, tipping his hat and ushering the local judge through the crush of spectators.

'Bergonzi, Signorina Regina,' the Fascist judge said gravely, dipping his head as he came to the fore. He recognized Alfredo and made a respectful bow to him too.

Regina greeted the judge but ignored Alfredo.

With each passing minute, Attila seemed more and more sure of himself, more and more sure of his own power.

'It wouldn't surprise me if this were the act of a crazed, jealous lover,' he went on. 'It could have been anyone, possibly even someone right here. She probably led him on, then spurned him. His lust aroused – ' Attila broke off dramatically and turned to the corpse. 'We will probably discover that he raped her. After all, there are plenty of depraved types around these days – maniacs, Communists, perverts!'

'May I, your Honour?' said Regina, taking a step or two

towards the dead woman. With a brisk, theatrical gesture, she lifted the widow's skirt, pulling it up high over her waist. Then, without bothering to recover the body, she turned around triumphantly, her eyes agleam with satisfaction. 'There, you see! No underwear! And why does a woman take off her underwear?'

A hush had gone over the crowd. There were embarrassed smiles. Attila's face sought corroboration from Alfredo, but Alfredo looked away.

Now, from somewhere at the rear, a single voice sounded, shouting wildly, 'Cowards! Cowards! Cowards!'

It was Ada. Alfredo wheeled and fought his way to her, but when he reached the road he found the car empty and Ada gone. 'Ada!' he called, looking frantically up and down the highway. There was no sign of her. Then, seeing footprints in the snow, he set off running through the fields, but he soon realized that the tracks he was following were not a woman's.

He turned back. Up ahead, in the island of light at the villa's entrance, was the pack of townspeople, still growing, avid to drink in the details of the lurid crime. Alfredo felt desperate, impotent. Everywhere else in the cold night was the darkness.

'Ada!' he called one last time.

Chapter 13

The children were asleep, all in the same bed. On the other side of the room, Olmo was in bed with Stella. They had made love, and now they lay close together in the dark, talking in low voices.

'I wrote my husband today and told him I was going to spend Christmas with you,' Stella said.

'Like this?' Olmo said.

'I always tell Orlando everything.'

Olmo stirred restlessly.

'It makes me feel bad going to bed with the wife of a comrade who's in jail,' he said.

'It's different for me,' Stella said. 'I've been alone three years now, working like a slave to feed my kids and keep clothes on them, trying hard to be both a mother and father to them, giving, giving, giving all I can. Well, the day comes when you feel you need something too – a certain kind of affection and tenderness they can't provide. I knew you could give me that, Olmo.'

'Yes, I understand,' Olmo said. He had known loneliness too, agonizing loneliness – endless, sleepless nights of it. He was about to tell Stella this, when all at once there was a knock on the downstairs door. It was loud and insistent, and only the new lock prevented whoever it was from getting in.

Stella looked across to the children, but they slept on, oblivious. Olmo jumped out of bed, quickly drew on shirt and trousers, and, before going to the stairs, felt under the mattress for the pistol he placed there each night.

'Olmo! Olmo!'

The voice was familiar. It was Alfredo's. He was outside, calling up to the bedroom window. Olmo crammed the gun into a drawer, then stumbled to the door in the dark and opened it.

'A lock?' Alfredo said when the light went on. 'What is this? What have you got to hide? Why have you locked yourself in?'

'Nothing!' Olmo answered. Alfredo was obviously distraught about something, but Olmo did not appreciate his stream of questions, did not appreciate his barging in at this hour, and he was short with him. 'I'm not locking myself in, I'm locking others out,' he added.

Alfredo heard a movement on the stairs and at the same time, looking there expectantly, he blurted, 'Where's my wife?'

Olmo went at him bodily. 'Get out of here!' he shouted. 'Get out!'

From the top of the stairway, Stella shushed them. 'You'll wake the children,' she called down in a loud whisper. 'What does he want?'

'His wife,' Olmo said.

Alfredo sank down in a chair at the kitchen table. 'I'm sorry,' he said wearily. 'I'm not well. I think it's my heart. Listen, Olmo.'

'Your heart!' Olmo said, sneering at him with pity. 'You're just sick in the head!'

'Maybe you're right; I'm going crazy. I don't know what to do. Ada's disappeared.'

'And you come looking for her in my bed?'

'What's so strange about that?'

Olmo sat down. The two glared at each other across the bare table.

'What do you mean?' Olmo said.

'You know exactly what I mean.'

'Go on, then! Say it!'

'I mean it's quite possible—' Alfredo broke off, starting again after a moment or two in calmer voice. 'You like her, don't you?'

'Yes, and she likes me,' Olmo said. 'We fuck. You see this?' He reached out and tore down a salame that hung from a nail. 'We fuck all night. But that's not enough, she asks me to stuff this salame up her ass. All right?'

'You son of a bitch!' Alfredo said, not without a trace of affection. 'If you knew what a night I've been through, you wouldn't talk like that.' He squared himself in his chair, rested his arms on the table, and described what he had just seen on his way home. 'Oh, God, Olmo! She was stuck up on that gate like a slaughtered animal!'

Alfredo's head slumped down. Olmo brought a bottle of wine and two glasses to the table. He filled them and told Alfredo to drink.

'It had to happen tonight too—just when Ada and I were feeling close again after I don't know how long. All that blood, then Ada running away as if it were my fault! What the hell did I have to do with it?'

They both drank.

'Who gets the widow's house and property?' Olmo asked. But he did not need the answer. Since old Pioppi had died, it was well known around the farm that Regina had been putting pressure on Alfredo to foreclose on Pioppi's widow. 'I suppose they'll do their best to put away some poor innocent bastard and call him a Communist,' Olmo went on. 'When are you going to wake up, Alfredo? There've been a lot of killings, and there'll be a lot more! There are a lot of people in jail, and it's you and your kind who wanted it this way!'

His voice had risen dangerously. Now Olmo poured Alfredo another glass of wine.

Alfredo held his glass up to the light and looked through

it at the colour of the wine. 'I'm glad you have a woman in the house,' he said. 'Your daughter needs a mother.'

'She just came for Christmas,' Olmo said. 'Her husband's in jail.'

'Has it ever occurred to you why so many of your friends are in jail and not you – especially when you should have been the first to be thrown inside?' Alfredo's voice betrayed anger. 'Well, has it?'

Olmo stared, his jaw set, ready to spring. Instead, he said nothing.

'I was the one who stopped Attila every time,' Alfredo said. 'It was me who made him drop his bone.'

'If you protect me, it must be in your interest,' Olmo said, unrelenting.

'Insult me, insult your old friend. I've always cared for you, you know that. Don't you remember when we used to catch frogs together and how beautiful those summers were along the ditches?'

'I caught the frogs, and you ate them,' Olmo said.

'Come on, you hole-in-the-pocket Socialist,' Alfredo laughed. 'Can't you remember anything?'

'Yes, I remember. I remember your wedding day, nine years ago. I remember I was beaten up. I remember you stood by and watched.'

'Do you also remember when you crept into my father's study and stole his gun?' Alfredo said aggressively. 'Why haven't you ever used it? Why don't you use it if you're so courageous?'

'Maybe now you're beginning to be afraid too,' Olmo said.

'Attila's becoming more powerful every day.'

'If that's so, you have yourself to thank.'

'We've got to stop him. What do you think I gave you that gun for? Use it, for Christ's sake!'

'Sure, and get myself killed. Is that what you want?' Olmo gave Alfredo a hard look. 'Enough talk, Alfredo. Go home and I'm sure you'll find Ada there.'

He stood up to signal the end of their conversation. Alfredo got up.

'Do you really think so?' he said.

'I'm sure,' Olmo told him. 'Take this just in case.' He indicated the salame.

Alfredo was unsure whether to laugh or to take offence.

The two were at the open door, staring at each other, a strong tension between them, a sense of something unresolved.

Only as he moved off into the night did Alfredo manage to spit out, not quite angry, not quite amused, 'Fuck you!'

Chapter 14

Another six years passed. It was 1938. Attila and Regina, who were now married, lived in Maddalena Pioppi's house. Following the widow's death, her property had come into Alfredo's hands. In the event, Alfredo saw an unparalleled opportunity to rid himself of Regina and, at the same time, to curb Attila's power. It had long since been agreed that the house would one day go to his cousin; but now, before acting on his old promise, Alfredo delayed and delayed, wanting Regina to come to him. When she did, begging and pleading and on the verge of tears, Alfredo squeezed the last drop out of her.

It was a cunning performance. She and Attila could take over the Pioppi house, Alfredo announced, but he would hold the mortgage on it, for which he would demand only a nominal rate of interest. In exchange, Regina would remove herself permanently from the Villa Berlinghieri, where, her cousin lost no time informing her, she had meddled too much, spying on him and interfering in both his private life and domestic arrangements. Further (and this was more important to Alfredo, though he did not tell her so), Regina from that day on would restrain Attila in his strong-arm activities, political and otherwise. A particular, grave emphasis had been placed on the last word as it was pronounced. The meaning of this clear to her, Regina averted her eyes. At the same time, she agreed to the terms without demur.

Attila took great pride and interest in the little nest he had long sought and now shared with his beloved wife. He continued to work as foreman of the Berlinghieri estate, but he grew older, mellower, and middle class. (He was now quite bald except for a fringe of hair at the sides and back of his head.) Slowly, pretentiously, he and Regina redecorated and refurnished their new house, acquiring more and more comforts and trying to imitate the living style of the gentry. Alfredo's arrangement served to pull the lion's teeth. For a number of years, because this seemed to suit everyone, it worked.

But once again, after the shock of the widow's murder, Ada lapsed into reclusion and drunkenness, driven to it by the carabinieri's inability to bring anyone to justice for the crime and by her husband's silence on the subject and apparent indifference. The source of her sole pleasure during these years – apart from the oblivion she sought in wine – was Anita, whom she continued to tutor, sporadically and haphazardly, by tacit agreement with Olmo and Rosina. What Ada did not know was that while Alfredo refused to press the matter of the widow's murder with the authorities, he exerted all his influence on Attila, through Regina, to prevent the Fascists from wrongly pinning blame for the killing on anyone unconnected with it.

Regina's removal and Ada's reclusion left the way open for Alfredo to install Teresita in the Villa Berlinghieri as a sort of unofficial servant. Without fixed duties, the feeble-minded girl enjoyed a peculiar run of the house, which the other servants easily accepted, attributing it to a combination of the master's laxness and goodness, for it was quite obvious that Alfredo had taken on the poor Teresita out of sheer generosity.

His attachment to the girl was purely and morbidly sexual. Teresita was as good-natured, pretty, and well-made as she was brainless. Alfredo loved her submissiveness and her instant availability that was nonetheless innocent. Mostly, he made love to her in an angry, desperate fashion. His favourite way was to take her from behind as he leaned her over the green baize of the billiard-table. Sometimes, cynically, he showed her how to hold the stick and hit balls while he covered her, pumping and pumping to his climax, with the soft clicking sound of Teresita's inexpert play in his ears. Sometimes he had her while playing a game himself. Later, entertaining friends in the same room, he would make jokes to them – which only he understood – about his practice sessions. One such was to claim that somehow he never played quite so pleasurably on any other table as he did privately on his own.

For her part, Teresita liked occasionally to be allowed to dress up in Ada's cast-off clothes and to parade in them before Alfredo, during which time, while she insisted that he call her by his wife's name, he was not allowed to touch her. What pleasure or meaning this held for Teresita, Alfredo never learned; but he complied, for the charade strangely excited him. Playing Ada, Teresita managed at one and the same time to look charming, almost beautiful, and grotesque. In a woman, the mixture of sound body – which in Teresita's case was a healthy body that had a touch of earthiness to it – and impaired mind absorbed and fascinated Alfredo. In Teresita, he had found himself another and better Neve.

Chapter 15

One sunny winter's day that same year, six or eight men were at work in the great quadrangle of the Berlinghieri farm compound. In the middle of the brick-paved threshing floor, a half-dozen hay wagons were tipped on their sides like careened boats. A blacksmith, repairing shafts, hammered strips of metal at an anvil. Other men removed the heavy wheels and lined them up in a row to be painted while the wagons' axles were smeared with grease. Children played at the edge of the work, and women sat in the welcome sun, their backs to the faded reddish-brown walls of the living quarters. Opposite, before the Doric columns of the blue-washed west side of the enclosure, Eros Dalcò was grooming the farm's three stallions.

A new feature of the big yard was an outsized Fascist slogan, stretching the length of five of the apartments and painted, just under the long second-floor windows, in letters a foot tall. Carefully executed in black on a white ground and framed in a neat black border, the lettering was in the style favoured by the black-shirted sons of Rome – an elegant Futuristic without capitals. This sign, hated by the Dalcò family, was Attila's pride. It read: 'it's the plough that traces the furrow, but it's the sword that defends it.' The line was divided midway by a stylized emblem of the fasces.

All at once, without warning, the sweet *ping-pinging* of hammer and anvil that echoed off the walls was shattered by a deafening uproar. Attila had come driving at a reckless speed through the gateway on a brand-new tractor, the first seen on the farm, and he swung it sharply and showily on to

241

the threshing floor. A few yards behind him, on a motorcycle with an empty sidecar, came his friend, the thick-necked barrel-shaped Barone. Barone pulled up alongside the bright-green tractor and cut his motor. Attila, eager to speed up the new Landini's running-in period, left the tractor engine going and jumped down with a big self-satisfied grin on his face.

The men at the wagons looked up from their work, awed by the new machine, but none of them made a move towards it or left off what they were doing. Only the children approached, grimacing, their hands pressed over their ears to cut the din.

From a second-story window Olmo peered out to see what was causing the racket. Directly below, he saw his fifteen-year-old daughter join the small children who gawked at the tractor. He also saw Attila swagger towards the group of men. Olmo leaned out, straining to hear what the foreman was going to tell them.

'Hey! Hey, all of you, take a look!' Attila said, waving his hands for attention. 'This is what's known as the Fascist Miracle. We don't need those cart-horses any more. We've put the power of fifty horses in one machine!' His arm shot dramatically from the stallions back to the Landini. 'That's progress!'

The men eyed each other and the machine with worried faces.

Attila turned confidentially to Barone, who stood at his elbow. 'There they are, Barone,' the foreman said, gesturing to indicate the three stallions drawn up in front of the stable. 'Take your horses.'

Barone beamed with pleasure.

'Eros,' Attila barked, 'bring Mariolo here.' Eros stood no more than ten steps away, but Attila was not one to pass up an opportunity to show off his power both to issue commands and to be obeyed.

Eros brought one of the horses forward. 'They've sold you, Mariolo,' he said to the huge beast, choking back tears. 'We had good times together, you and I.'

Barone, who heard, gave Attila a raised-brows look that suggested that the man might be crazy.

'Have you finished your lamentations?' Attila asked curtly.

'No, just beginning,' Eros said, stroking the horse's muzzle. 'I've loved this horse, and now that you've sold him –' His voice faltered. The tears came.

242

'Don't cry, Eros,' Attila said for all to hear. 'You're leaving with the stallion.'

'What?' Eros said in disbelief.

'A horse is useless without a stablehand,' Attila said. 'You need a stablehand, don't you, Barone?'

'He seems fit. Make me a special price,' Barone said.

'I'll give you the best price in the world,' Attila said.

'I'm sold then?' Eros said weakly.

'Let's say I've forfeited you,' Attila said. He smirked.

'They've sold me. Me, Eros, they've sold me like a beast.' Eros's face was distorted; his eyes shone with tears. In desperation, he raised his voice, speaking to the other Dalcò men, who laid down their tools and gathered around.

Anita slipped away to tell her father what was happening. Sensing trouble, Olmo met her in the doorway, heard her out, then started across the yard.

'But I'm not an animal; I'm not a beast; I'm a man,' Eros went on pleading, as if to convince himself.

'Barone's a good man, Dalcò,' Attila said. 'You'll be happy with him.'

'But what am I – a parcel?'

'You're part of the contract,' Attila said. 'Horses, horseman, horse manure.'

The tractor engine went dead. There was a long, exquisite moment of silence. Olmo had reached into the Landini and switched off the ignition.

'Olmo, they've sold me!' Eros called out in a voice that begged for deliverance.

They all turned. Olmo came forward.

'You heard,' he said. 'Eros has been sold like an animal. But Eros doesn't give milk. Eros doesn't eat hay.'

In a fury, Attila took a step or two towards Olmo, as if he were about to throw himself at him; but Barone quickly interposed himself between the two men and held Attila at bay.

'Let it go, Attila,' he said. 'I'm not sure I can do anything about accommodation, anyway.'

'I'm in charge here,' Attila trumpeted. 'I say I've sold him, and that's that.'

'We're men, we're labourers, not animals,' Olmo went on, haranguing the others. 'Is it right for them to sell us? Is it right for them to buy us? I ask you in the name of justice.'

'Let me at him,' Attila said, straining in Barone's grip.

By now all the women had drawn around too. Even some of the men who had been working indoors joined the large circle of onlookers. Attila backed off.

'An honest working man can't be bought or sold,' Olmo told them. 'Only the kind of scum that goes around at night beating and killing people can be bought! A peasant can't be bought! Only a Fascist can be bought!'

They looked at Olmo mutely, intently, liking what they heard. None of them dared speak out, but the faces that turned to Attila had hatred unmistakably written on them.

Attila sought Eros. 'Tie the horses to the back of the motorcycle,' he told him. 'Then gather your things and get out.'

'You don't have to go, Eros,' Olmo challenged. 'You can come with me. I'll make you my assistant.'

'And you take your daughter and get out too,' Attila said to Olmo.

'Horse manure to you, Attila Bergonzi!' Anita shouted out.

Attila wheeled around. The spectators opened up so that the foreman and the girl stood confronting each other.

'Get out!' Attila ordered.

Anita faced the man squarely, holding her ground and wanting to say something, but she was trembling from head to foot, and no words came. Then, without thinking, her last utterance still ringing in her ears, she stooped and reached her hands into a pile of horse dung that was so fresh it was still steaming.

'Shit, *porca madosca!*' one of the men near her cried out like a signal.

'Shit!' 'Shit!' 'Shit!' circulated the cry.

And then Anita was flinging wet, steaming balls of horse manure at Attila, and there was a commotion, an eruption, and the whole yard went collectively mad. 'Shit!' they shouted. 'Shit, *porca miseria!*' 'Shit!' 'Shit!' 'Shit!' 'Give it to him, give it to him!' 'Let him have it!' 'Shit!' 'Shit on him!' 'Shit on the shit!'

And all of them were bending down, the men, the women, the children, to pick up horse dung and cow dung, fresh dung and dried dung, and to fling it at the foreman, pelting him with it. It rained shit, it hailed shit, it snowed shit, the shit flew thick and fast, and Attila Bergonzi, vainly weaving and bobbing and shielding his face, was soon smeared and stained with it. What was this carnival, this jubilation? It was the spontaneous expression, outburst, outpouring, of rage and resentment, a tidal wave of it, against this man and the regime this man symbolized and more than symbolized, for, to these peasants, Attila and Fascism were all one. It was an outcry, a rising up, against the twofold yoke of repression and humiliation they had shouldered and suffered – at his hands for twenty long years, at the hands of his black-shirted bully-squads for an even longer and more nightmarish fifteen years – while all their own best and most human impulses had been stifled and suppressed and crushed. For this moment, they awoke.

Of them all, only Barone and Olmo refrained from throwing dung at Attila. Barone, while not fleeing, tried to stay out of the line of fire and to make himself inconspicuous. Olmo just watched. *No use measuring the good or the harm this might do,* he told himself. *We all needed this, so let them have their fun.* Already he felt pride at what his daughter had unleashed, and now, looking on her fury, he saw another pretty young woman reaching down and picking up handfuls of grain and saying, 'Here, peck at this!' And in a rush it all came back – a score of years before, the threshers pelting Attila with handfuls of grain, Anita's mother urging them to give the rooster his feed, and then the farm women doubled over with laughter, all imitating the sound of hens. Olmo's throat tightened; his eyes misted over.

'Barone! Barone!' Attila called, blind and groping.

The dung-slingers had run out of ammunition. Barone stepped gingerly forward to his friend's aid. Now the rest of them, bent over double, roared with laughter.

'The veil is off, Attila,' Olmo declared. 'We know now what your promises to the peasant and your Fascist progress amount to. We know now what a swindling bastard Mussolini is! We know the king is nothing but a little asshole! We know that your Fascism is rotten! And you remember our red flags, Attila? Well, we still have them, lots and lots of them, some of them even lay over the bodies of men you murdered. They're hidden away now, but the day is coming when those flags will fly again!'

Barone led Attila to his motorcycle and helped him into the

sidecar. Someone brought the three stallions forward. Olmo followed, the crowd swarming around as he continued to speak.

'Thanks, Attila,' Olmo said. 'This has opened our eyes.'

The motorcycle nosed its way through the circle of grinning onlookers. Tied to the sidecar, the horses lumbered behind, one after the other. They left the yard and picked up speed. With Anita beside him, Olmo went straight to his bicycle.

'I'm going to have to go away,' he explained to her.

'Take me with you, please. I want to go with you,' the girl said, gripping the handlebars.

'I'd like to, but I don't know how long I'll be,' her father said. 'It's better if you go to Stella's with your grandmother. Be good and don't worry.'

Anita burst into tears.

'It may not be for a long time. Here, take the key. It's yours. The rest of you,' Olmo said loudly, walking his bicycle to the gateway, 'keep your doors barred, and don't go out alone! Be prepared for the worst!'

He turned to embrace his daughter for the last time.

'No, Olmo, no!' she pleaded through her tears. 'Please don't go! Please!'

One of the farm women bustled forward to separate them and take Anita into her own arms. 'Please, Olmo, go now and go quickly,' the woman counselled. 'You know they'll take revenge on you for this.'

A man pressed a fistful of crumpled money into Olmo's hands, at the same time making an apologetic gesture that said it was all he had. He then gave Olmo a rough kiss and shoved him off.

Without looking back, Olmo pedalled down the long dirt track between the leafless mulberry trees.

Chapter 16

'Signora, signora,' Teresita said, breathless, 'the things that happened today! I've so much to tell you!'

'Wait a moment! Wait!' Ada said, looking up in an alcoholic daze from the sheaf of yellow paper she was scribbling verses on.

Teresita had come bursting into the room, startling her.

246

Lost in her writing, lost in her private fantasies, for a moment or two Ada did not know who this girl was or what she wanted. 'Just a moment now!' Ada told her, trying to shake off her boozy stupor. The fog lifted. It was Teresita, bringing her news from out there. Ada listened.

'Attila wanted to sell Eros, but Olmo –'

'Sell Olmo?'

'No, Eros, I said. But Olmo wouldn't let him. You see, it's all because Attila brought this new big tractor and said they didn't need the horses or Eros any more. A man was with him to take away the horses and Eros too, all together, but Olmo wouldn't let him.'

'What happened then?' Ada asked anxiously. 'Was there a fight?'

Teresita burst into a laugh.

'Was there a fight?' Ada repeated. 'Did anyone help Olmo?'

'Everybody,' the girl said gleefully. She laughed again. 'And then it began to snow.'

'It what?'

'Yes, signora, it began to snow horse shit. Horse shit! You never saw so much shit fly! They covered him with it – everybody! His eyes, his mouth, his hair. Head to toe, really. And oh, that ugly bald dome of his!'

'And Regina? Nothing for Regina?'

'No, too bad. Regina wasn't there. Otherwise –' The girl broke off into a fit of laughter. When she calmed down, she said, 'Even the horses helped. They kept shitting! The horses shit and everybody, all together, pitched in to give that Attila a mask of shit. Then afterwards everybody was afraid for his sake, Olmo's, and he had to go away. Anita cried.'

'Olmo went away?' With a shaking hand, Ada poured herself a glass of wine and drank it down.

'Yes, because Attila might come back. You should have seen the way everybody cried, signora. First they were laughing, and then they cried. I like Olmo. I cried too.'

Ada drank another glass of wine. Teresita told her that Olmo had sent Anita away as well. Ada gripped her glass so hard her knuckles whitened. Olmo gone! Anita gone! Her only friends, the only people she cared about! Gone! How could Alfredo let this happen? She felt her hands trembling and made an effort to control herself.

'But Olmo was happy,' Ada said now in a changed voice.

Having shed her desperation, she spoke almost gaily, light-heartedly. 'Didn't you see how happy he was, you silly girl?'

'No, I didn't.'

'But you're blind – blind and stupid! I tell you, he was happy!'

'Poor Olmo,' Teresita said, 'having to go off without his daughter or his mother and father or his house. He wasn't happy at all, signora.'

'But you can't understand, Teresita, with that bird brain of yours. I'm leaving too, and I'm happy. I'm radiantly happy.'

And now Ada was up on her feet, whirling about clumsily and smiling in a parody of careless joy.

'You're leaving too, signora? My, everybody seems to be leaving!'

Ada began rummaging in a wardrobe, pulling out clothes and throwing them on the floor.

'I don't need these,' she said. 'You can have them. These too! Take these! And these! And these! And these!'

Ada madly tore her clothes from the hangers and scattered them about in piles. Teresita fell to her knees, her eyes shining, and buried her face in Ada's clothes. When she raised her head, there was a look of adoration in her eyes.

'Last night I had a dream,' she said. 'I dreamed you gave me a kiss. Will you give me a kiss before you go, signora? As a gift?'

Ada stood still, studying the half-witted girl as if for the first time. 'Come here,' she said, extending her hand.

Chapter 17

Looking over a servant's shoulder in the dining-room, Regina fussily supervised the polishing of the silver. During the last years, she had grown noticeably stouter, and her broad jaw had begun to sag. On this day, working about the house in preparation for dinner guests, she wore her hair tied up in a kind of turban. This, together with her bright-red lips that were painted smaller than her mouth, emphasized her dowdiness. Glancing up, Regina once more admired the room's new curtains, which filled her with solid satisfaction. They were a plain material, sparsely printed in red and black with the figures of playing cards – hearts, diamonds, spades, and clubs. Her husband had chosen them.

Now, hearing familiar steps in the entrance, she called out sweetly, 'Is that you, my love?'

Attila did not reply, but she knew it was him. A moment later, she caught a glimpse of him passing the doorway in a blur, then she heard his hasty footsteps climbing the stairs. She sighed, for she was far too busy to attend to him, but the house was her dream come true, and it pleased her to be so busy. Paying no further mind to her husband's apparent brusqueness, Regina turned her attention back to the silver polishing and the evening's preparations. Tonight, for the first time, they would eat off their new glass plates.

It was nearly an hour after that when Regina opened the bedroom door and found Attila standing before the wardrobe, his back to her, getting into his black satin shirt.

'What on earth happened to you?' she said. 'You left the bathroom such a mess.'

Attila did not answer.

'I'm trying so hard to get the house in order for tonight,' she went on, reproving him as she might a child.

Her husband, fastening his belt, turned on her a sinister smile. 'You'll find out soon enough what happened,' he said, half to himself.

Attila's face, stricken and severe, almost gaunt, filled her with alarm. 'What is it?' she demanded. 'What's happened?'

'Defending your cousin's interests just now, I was insulted and humiliated before the whole farm,' he said, barely able to contain his anger. 'Now the responsible party is going to pay for it.'

'But, dearest, can't this wait until tomorrow?' she said lightly, in an effort to placate him. 'We've people coming tonight, and you want to be at your best.' Then she added, 'You look so nice, so manly in your black shirt.'

She went to him and tried to put her arms around him, but he shoved her away. Just then a voice outside called Attila's name. The two went to the window together. Below, where there had once been trees and there was now a driveway, were Barone and five or six of his comrades. Regina's heart sank. They all wore black shirts.

'When do we get started?' one of them shouted.

They grinned up at their chief and jostled each other, eager to be on their way.

'Like the good old times, eh?' another called out.

Attila told them he would be right down.

'Please,' Regina said, strangely out of breath, 'don't do anything rash, I beg you.'

'We'll give them a lesson they won't forget!' Attila said, his spirits lifted now.

Regina clutched at his clothes. 'No, Attila, don't. Please don't.'

'Out of my way!' he ordered.

'No, Attila, don't; we'll lose everything,' she pleaded.

'Oh, no!' he said, wrenching himself free. 'Oh, no!' Then, casting a last look at himself in the mirror, he stormed out.

Regina threw herself on to the bed, where she dissolved in tears of hurt and frustration. She knew he would have struck her if she had persisted. Why didn't he understand that they were older now and that if they were to get anywhere he could no longer afford to make a vulgar spectacle of himself?

From the bottom of the stairs, she heard him shout, 'This house has tamed me!'

Chapter 18

Wielding wooden truncheons, the six men formed a wide semicircle around Attila as he approached Olmo's door and proceeded to kick it in. Then, with a last furious look about the deserted courtyard, Attila made a sign for them to wait there, and he burst into the house.

'Where are you, you cowardly shit?' he bellowed up the stairs.

Without waiting for a reply, Attila hurled a chair against the wall and brought down a framed photograph of Olmo's grandparents. The picture glass splintered, but the chair did not break. Attila picked it up again and smashed it to sticks against the table, then he overturned the table and went to some wall shelves and swept the plates and glasses to the paved floor, where they broke to pieces. He even danced on the pieces to grind them smaller under his heavy boots. Next he gave a flour bin three or four kicks until he split it and flour spilled out in a white cloud.

He smashed another chair, then started up the stairs to the

bedrooms. On the second floor, he threw open one of the long shuttered windows. His black-shirted associates had their faces turned up to him expectantly. There was not a sound, not a sign of life from any other part of the great courtyard.

'It's a waste of time,' Barone said. 'Why don't we just turn him in and have him put away?'

'Because I want his hide and I'll have it, that's why,' Attila crowed. 'Watch your heads now!' he warned, gesturing to them to stand back.

Furniture, even very heavy objects, began to cascade out of the window, smashing and splintering on the ground below. Whatever he laid his hands on, Attila hurled through the window with tremendous physical force. From outside, the house seemed to shake to its foundations.

'These Reds – they've forgotten all the blood I've made them shit,' he muttered half aloud as he overturned a chest of drawers.

A book fell out. Attila picked it up, tore out a fistful of pages, and flung the volume out of the window. After it, a whole drawer went out. Then he rifled the contents of another drawer.

Showing himself at the window, Attila flung down a small packet of the clandestine *International*. 'Look at this, Barone,' he called, smiling broadly. 'We've got the bastard now – harbouring subversive literature!'

He returned to the chest of drawers, gave it another kick, and heard a heavy object fall out. It was Olmo's pistol. Attila quickly bent over to pick it up and at once he recognized it as the one missing from the villa since the day of Giovanni Berlinghieri's funeral. The foreman's face lighted up. He turned the revolver over and over in his hand, his mind racing, triumphant. This find, this accident, was the best thing to have happened to him in years! It gave him power, it gave him control! He almost sang aloud as he juggled the pistol from one hand to the other. An unusual calm came over him. How much more than the humiliation he had just undergone was the worth of this lucky find!

'Attila!' a voice called sharply from the yard below.

It was Alfredo. For a moment the foreman froze, then he strode to the window, put his hands on the sill, and leaned out as if he were about to address an audience. His face shone with pleasure. The revolver was tucked into his belt.

'Come down here at once!' Alfredo ordered.

Ignoring the master's obvious rage, Attila's eyes went around the ring of Blackshirts. 'Look! Show Signor Alfredo the bundle of newspapers, Fanfoni.'

As Fanfoni complied, Attila thought better of it, did an about face, and hurried down the stairs to reveal his findings to Alfredo himself.

At the bottom, he found Alfredo standing there, inspecting the destruction. A couple of the Blackshirts stuck their heads through the smashed door.

'Signor Alfredo,' Attila began excitedly. 'I suppose you've heard he's run away, but don't worry, he'll show up – '

'Who asked you to do this?' Alfredo said. 'Who gave you the right to come here and destroy this house?'.

'Right? My job is to keep order among the peasants. If one of them makes trouble, I get rid of him.'

'You're not getting rid of anybody. On this estate, I make the decisions, and I'm sick of your hotheadedness! Just you remember, mounting a member of the family doesn't change a servant into a master!'

The remark made Attila wince. He squirmed and spluttered. 'But you saw. He's a Communist organizer.'

'Whether he's a Communist or not is no concern of yours! He's a friend of mine. How dare you – '

'A friend, is he?' Attila drew the revolver from his belt and, like playing a trump card, shoved it at Alfredo. 'Look at this! Olmo's had it for fifteen years! He stole it from your father!'

Showing contempt for the discovery, Alfredo waved the pistol aside. 'Well, it certainly took you long enough to find it,' he said. At the same time, he saw on the floor the photograph in its smashed frame.

'What?' said Attila. Dumbfounded, he shot a glance at his associates, who were pressed together in the doorway. They gawked, their faces blank.

Carefully, almost tenderly, Alfredo had lifted the photograph out of the debris and was picking away from it some splinters of glass. The man in the picture was Leo Dalcò. Alfredo blew the dust off it and returned it to its nail. Suddenly, as he regarded Attila again, Alfredo found that something had been unleashed in him. He knew now, after all these years, that he had the strength to strike out, to act.

'You've done your job,' he told Attila, his tone deliberate, final. 'Your services are no longer needed here.'

'Barone!' Attila called out feebly, as if he were stricken.

But the Blackshirts, embarrassed for their chief, had withdrawn from the doorway, and neither Barone nor any of the others was there to respond. Alfredo walked out into the yard, into their midst. Standing by the heap of ruined furniture, the group appeared to be undecided between skulking off and waiting for Attila to reappear. They stepped aside now, sheepish.

From the edge of the threshing floor, where he halted, Alfredo flashed a look of contempt at them. Then he lifted his head to the shuttered windows of that whole side of the compound.

'I've fired him!' he announced to the hidden tenants. 'Attila's no longer your boss!'

The words gave him an immediate sense of release, of freedom, and the bold sound of his own voice, reverberating around the yard now, pleased him. Ada would be pleased too. He would hurry home to tell her.

At the gateway, he turned. The Blackshirts had apparently made up their minds to wait.

'I've fired him!' Alfredo shouted again. 'Attila's through! He's finished!'

Chapter 19

The next three days it rained. It was the winter rain, with leaden skies and a relentless downpour that drenched the land and turned the roads and farms into quagmires. For two days, Attila sent his squad scouring the countryside for Olmo, but, despite their threatening and bullying, the Blackshirts found no sign of him.

It was Barone's guess that Olmo had fled the province, either going north to Milan or south over the mountains and on to Genoa and the sea. Smarting more than ever, Attila argued otherwise and refused to give up the search. Olmo was in hiding, he maintained; there must be people who knew where, and he would get it out of them. On the third day, in the company of his six henchmen, Attila revisited the Dalcò farmyard.

As if it were a police or a military operation, everybody occupying farm quarters was turned out into the central courtyard, where Attila planned to interrogate them in the steady chill downpour. There were thirty or more of them, men, women, and children, and the Blackshirts made them line up, not on the brick threshing floor, but on the sodden ground by the duckpond. While they assembled, Attila looked on, dry and comfortable, from the gallery in front of the abandoned horse stalls.

Even after everything was ready, Attila kept them waiting, deliberately, as his men, slick and sinister in their black shirts and breeches and boots, strutted up and down, as if on promenade, pistols in their hands, unspeaking. The peasants, for their part, were also silent. The tension mounted. Despite the hats and scarves and coats and ponchos they wore, they were soon soaked through. But they stood stolid and silent, thinking this was Attila's retaliation for what they had done to him a few days before. If it was, they were determined to take it.

Attila too was sheathed in black, and now, when he was good and ready, he opened a large black umbrella and stepped out into the mud of the yard and crossed to the assembled peasants. In his hand, ostentatiously, he gripped the recovered revolver.

'This is not a personal matter,' he began addressing them in a grand manner, the pistolled hand gesturing expansively, the rain nearly deafening on the umbrella. 'I am not a petty man, and so I'm letting you know at once that our presence here today is only coincidental with what happened a few days ago when I was transacting business in the name of this estate.'

The peasants, their shoulders hunched, hands in their pockets, stared at him, cold and untrusting.

'We all want to forget about that unfortunate occurrence and let bygones be bygones. I come to you today about a more serious matter, a criminal matter. A man has been living in your midst and, perhaps unknown to you, has been engaged in a conspiracy against Fascist authority. That man, Olmo Dalcò, is a Communist organizer. In his house, we have found concealed weapons and subversive literature, the circulation of which has been forbidden by law.'

The children huddled close to their impassive parents.

'We wish none of you any harm, nor do we wish to implicate any of you in this man's crimes. Tell me where he is hiding so that we may bring him to justice, and the rest of you will be considered free and blameless, and you will be allowed to go about your work in peace. We appeal to you in the name of patriotic duty!'

Attila reached into his coat and drew out a few copies of the *International*. They were the ones he had found hidden in Olmo's bedroom.

'Here is the evidence, plain for you all to see. Now, who can tell me where this wanted man is hiding?'

There was no sound but the sound of the pouring rain.

'You aren't our boss any more, Attila. We don't have to answer you,' Censo Dalcò spoke up.

The others assented, nodding their heads.

'We know nothing!' one of the women said, speaking loudly, in competition with the rain.

Now that one or two of them had spoken out, some of the others were emboldened. Eros, the man Attila had tried to sell along with the stallions, stepped out of the straggly line and examined his kinsmen's faces, as if seeking strength or encouragement or approval there. Then he said, 'Even if we knew we wouldn't tell you!'

The rest of them laughed. They were becoming defiant, and Attila saw it. It was Alfredo's dismissal of him that made them this way. Attila's patience was becoming exhausted. They were challenging his authority.

'All right, then,' he shouted, spanking open a copy of the newspaper with the hand that held the revolver. 'All right, there's enough evidence here to send every last man of you to jail. Is that what you are forcing me to do?'

'You can't order us around any more, Attila,' Niso Dalcò said. 'You can't buy, you can't sell, and you can't order us!'

From somewhere along the line one of the boys began whistling a Communist song. Whipping around, Attila caught a glimpse of him and told Fanfoni to haul the boy out. Attila was through with sterile argument. He dragged the boy by the arm to the margin of the pond and roughly pulled him around to face the others.

'I don't want to make an example of this boy unless I have to,' he said. 'Now, where is Olmo Dalcò?'

The peasants remained mute. Attila repeated the question,

and this time raised his revolver to the boy's temple. There was a stir. A man stepped forward and said it was he who had whistled the song. One of the Blackshirts shoved him back in line. Once more, Attila asked where Olmo was in hiding. Once more, the peasants answered with silence.

Attila summoned Barone to his side and said something to him. Pumping his head and grinning, Barone seized the boy by the arm, flung him into the shallow pond, and rushed in after him. Before the boy could scramble to his feet, the barrel-chested Barone was upon him, plunging his head in and out of the water.

Attila allowed the ducking to go on for a full minute, then raised his arm for Barone to stop. Barone lifted the choking, gasping boy out of the water by the scruff of the neck.

'Where is Olmo Dalcò?'

When there was no answer, Attila gave a signal, and Barone plunged the boy's head down again. This time he did not let him up. The boy's father rushed at the nearest Fascist guard and grappled with him. Attila stepped forward and fired point blank at the man's head. The echo of the shot, somewhat muffled by the sound of the rain, bounced off the enclosure's four walls. The man fell dead, face down in the mud. Two of the Blackshirts quickly dragged him to the pond and threw him in. Attila kept his eyes on the crowd, umbrella raised high, pistol hand out straight, ready to shoot the next person who disobeyed.

The children cowered in ter.ɔr, clinging tightly to their mothers' drenched skirts. Some of the women shouted curses, some wailed and wept.

'Who's next?' Attila called out in elation, stirred by the shedding of blood.

Barone came out of the pond, leaving the boy behind, face down in the water, lifeless.

'Eros!' Attila exploded.

Eros froze. Two Blackshirts hauled him out of line and dragged him, slipping and sliding, to Attila's feet.

'You didn't want to go with Barone, did you?' Attila said to him. 'Olmo promised you work, but where is he now? Where are his Communist promises?'

Attila fired straight into the man's stomach and watched him grovel in the mud. Writhing and moaning, Eros managed to lift himself on to one arm.

'Attila,' he said in as loud a voice as he could muster, 'you're a pig like Mussolini!'

Barone kicked Eros's supporting arm out from under him and, dragging the wounded man by the hair, flung him into the pond. Eros thrashed about helplessly, drowning. His blood, running into the water, stained it a coppery colour.

A woman rushed at Attila, and he shot her dead. The rain came down. This time Barone didn't dump the body into the pond.

'Maybe they're telling the truth,' he said to Attila behind his hand. 'Maybe they don't know where he is. We can't butcher them all!'

'Why not?' Attila said.

Barone, his hair plastered to his skull, rivulets of water pouring off his face, turned to the other Blackshirts for support.

'Barone's right,' one of them put in.

'Maybe he went over the mountains like Barone said,' Fanfoni added.

Attila surveyed the field. There were four bodies, one in the mud at his feet, three in the pond.

'All right,' he said, loading the empty chambers of his revolver. 'Let's make an example of a few more of them and call it a day.'

And before any of the Blackshirts could oppose or otherwise prevail upon him, Attila turned and levelled the pistol. Taking careful aim, he fired at the peasant ranks as if they were no more than targets. He fired six shots. A woman, a child, and two men dropped to the ground.

'Your resistance will be made known to the authorities!' he shouted wildly. 'We have plenty of evidence against you! We have your subversive literature, we know you are concealing a fugitive from justice, and I have six witnesses who will swear to it that you publicly slandered the name of the Duce! A full report will be drawn up!'

Quickly now, Attila turned to his henchmen. 'You all saw, men. I gave them a fair chance, but they slandered the Duce's name. You all heard them slander the Duce's name, didn't you?'

In fear that he would begin firing again, the Blackshirts, acting as one man, all at once rushed headlong at the peasants to scatter and drive them back into their homes

1900 I

before more harm could come to them. And they, seeing that the Blackshirts were now protecting them, instantly turned and fled.

'Well done, men,' Attila shouted after his associates, beaming. 'This is a lesson in respect for the law that they'll never forget! And, to boot, we've rid the world of a few more Communist rats!'

He held the umbrella high, laughing in triumph.

'Come,' he said then, 'the drinks are on me!'

The sky wept.

Chapter 20

Olmo had fled. He had gone south, first on bicycle and later on foot, climbing through the beech woods and then up into the mountains. For the most part, he was helped by comrades, who fed and sheltered him and passed him on to other comrades.

In the Apennines, a woodcutter with the almond-shaped eyes of an Oriental led him behind a string of mules through chestnut forests to snow-clad mountain meadows nearly three thousand feet above the sea. There, he pointed behind them to several distant villages.

'You see those villages,' the woodcutter said. 'All in the hands of priests. Why, the priests there keep the people in such ignorance they've never even heard of Lenin! That's right, Lenin or Stalin!'

Then, preparing to take leave of Olmo, the man indicated a valley ahead, which led to the sea. There were white patches like long triangles on the slopes of the mountains.

'It looks like snow, but it's marble. Keep to the path. When you hear the quarriers singing, ask for Ambrogio. He's waiting for you. Goodbye.'

'But one day Stalin will come and preach them a sermon and convert them all,' Olmo said. 'Even the priests. Then we'll plant red flags beside the crucifixes.'

The man, his face wizened, laughed with pleasure at the idea.

It was warmer on that side of the mountains. Coming down into the trees, Olmo heard the blast, waited to watch the dust settle, then pressed on. Long before he saw them, he heard

258

the quarry men's song. It was wild and primitive, and it spread out into the valley. Then Olmo saw the block of marble, dazzling as snow and larger than a house, that was being cut from the mountainside.

Ambrogio, a short Tuscan with a generous smile, led him down and down until the hillside was covered with olive trees. In front of them, far away, was the sea. It looked near enough to touch. There was a small harbour, filled with boats.

'The boat's called *Virginia*,' Olmo's guide said. 'She leaves tomorrow at this time. You say Ambrogio sent you, and they'll know. Tonight you stay with me.'

'Marseilles is a long way from here,' Olmo said.

The Tuscan set off down the path without another word. Olmo followed. Later, when the path entered a yard, Ambrogio said, 'This is my house. I've never been away from these parts.'

The little port bustled with activity. Boats were tied up the length of the landing wharf, ready for the night's fishing. The last but one in line, close to the harbour's entrance, was the *Virginia*. Olmo strolled the pier unhurriedly, relieved now to see his boat ahead. With a last glance over his shoulder, he quickened his step. But his heart raced. He looked back again. Four carabinieri were coming on the run.

Fifteen or twenty yards separated Olmo from the boat. On its deck, a man cast him a frantic look to warn him off. Suddenly, from the very end of the wharf, several more policemen appeared.

Olmo stopped in his tracks. From either hand, the police closed in. His only way out was the sea.

'I wouldn't if I were you,' one of the carabinieri said. 'You'll find the swimming cold.'

'Papers?' said another, unsmiling.

Olmo was taken into custody. He had left home eight days before.

1945

Chapter 1

Over and over, monotonously, obsessively, the guard outside the door repeated the same two verses:

'I'm content to die but I regret it, I regret dying but I'm content . . .'

Attila and Regina were on the damp concrete floor of the pen among the sleeping pigs, she sitting, he crumpled up. It was hot, breathless, and the odour of excrement burned the nostrils.

'Help me,' Attila groaned weakly. 'I'm sick, help me.'

Regina listened but said nothing. The dirge-like chant of the man beyond the door made her head throb and swim, oppressing her more than the semi-dark and the stench around her, and, when she could bear it no longer, she screamed out at him to stop. Almost to her surprise, he did. But at the same time she heard him call, 'Who goes there?'

Three or four voices replied. One said, 'Liberation Committee – Sausage Division,' and they all laughed.

The door to the sty flew open with a kick, and against the blinding light Regina saw four men silhouetted in black. One of them rushed forward and threw himself on to a huge sow.

'My love!' he cried. 'My great big beautiful love!'

'Hands off, Cornelio,' another said. 'We count them first!'

Two of the men were partisans, the other two, Manzolone and Robusto, were Dalcò.

Attila let out a long groan. 'Help me!' he pleaded.

'Call a doctor, you bastards!' Regina said. 'Have you no pity?'

'What are we going to do about this?' Cornelio said, still jocular. Regina recognized him now as the man who had been standing guard.

'I've had experience as a vet,' Manzolone volunteered.

'That was always cows,' Robusto said.

'Hell, in a case like this I'm willing to be a pig doctor too,'

Manzolone laughed.

'Leave us in peace at least, you vultures!' Regina exploded.

'I count fifteen,' Cornelio said.

'And these two make seventeen,' Robusto said, grinning at the prisoners.

'Bastards!' Regina snarled.

Then the men argued about the division of the pigs. Cornelio said they should be split so many to each family. Robusto said that wouldn't work out, since his family had nine and maybe the other man's had five.

'And who's going to get the biggest and who's going to get the smallest?' Manzolone said.

'It's all a question of patience,' Cornelio said. 'The little ones will grow big, and the big ones will grow into sausages.'

'Just a minute, comrades,' Tiger interrupted. 'The abolition of inherited property – that's what we're for.'

'You mean these pigs don't belong to anyone?' Cornelio said, scornful.

'I mean they belong to everyone. That's Socialism,' Tiger said.

Regina scrambled to her knees. 'I can see you're a man of feeling,' she said to Tiger. 'Look at him. Can't you see he's dying like an animal. Help him in the name of humanity.'

'Socialism is humanity,' Attila said.

Tiger gave Regina his arm and helped her to her feet. Then, sliding his tommy-gun around into position, he pointed it at Attila and told the others to get him up. Were they going to shoot her husband right there? Regina let out a wild scream.

Manzolone seized her roughly by the wrists and dragged her through the low door into the sunlight. 'Shut up!' he told her. 'Shut up or I'll kill one of these pigs and make a sausage three yards long and stuff it down your throat till it comes out your asshole!'

The others pushed Attila out. Stumbling, he collapsed at Regina's feet. The front of his shirt was dark red with blood and excrement. His facial wounds, thickly crusted with dirt and vomit, made him look monstrous.

'You bastards!' Regina howled at her captors. 'You sons of bitches! You shits, you scum of the earth, you goddam fucking bastards!'

Robusto gripped her hair so hard it made tears spring to

her eyes. A crowd of farm people flocked and swarmed around. Once again, Attila was lifted to his feet.

'Come on, then,' Tiger ordered, motioning them all forward with the barrel of his tommy-gun. 'Let's get this finished!'

Chapter 2

The cherry trees were heavy with blossoms, the April sun was warm and bright, and the village cemetery, usually a clutter and chaos of sombre marble and granite, crosses and tombs, flowers and memorials, was almost gay.

A score or so of men and women, only a few of them belonging to the partisan band recently down out of the hills, had accompanied the prisoners the mile and a half from the farm. It was they, the women who had captured Attila especially, who had insisted on marching the ex-foreman and his wife to this place and confronting him with the graves of those whose blood was on his hands.

How would the Fascist braggart and bully react? In their guilelessness, the farm people hoped to hear Attila confess to the murder of the old men who had been burned to death in 1922 and to the massacre of the eight members of their family in 1938 and perhaps to other killings for which his guilt was rumoured and long suspected but for which clear proof was lacking.

They dragged him from grave to grave, pressing tightly around to see and hear better. Some of them, wanting to scrutinize his face, climbed up on surrounding tombs. Would Attila drop to his knees and defend himself, claiming he was a victim of the times, a victim of men above him to whom he was a mere tool, an instrument? He was so weak he had to be held up. He said nothing. Regina said nothing. The witnesses remained hushed, expectant.

At the Dalcò graves, simple wooden crosses, eight of them in a row, bearing the names of Eros and Niso and Denesio and Censo and the others, together with the fatal date, 1938, a number of women broke down and silently wept.

Anita stood in the fore of the witnesses, astonished by the restraint the others showed. Attila had murdered their kin in cold blood, before their eyes, and here at the hour of justice they neither cursed him nor cried out for the sweet revenge she felt was their due. And yet, lending them dignity, was not this behaviour of theirs admirable? Anita pondered it. For her part, for what Attila had done to her – causing the separation from her father and his probable death – the young woman felt she could easily have torn him limb from limb with her own hands. The man was the personification of Fascism; he was evil itself, and in her hatred of him, only his death, no matter how cruel or how violent, would satisfy her.

Now they had hauled Attila before the elaborate memorial to Patrizio Avanzini, who had died the year Anita was born. She read the inscription to herself:

PATRIZIO AVANZINI, AGED 12
A TENDER FLOWER PLUCKED BY THE CRUEL HAND OF DESTINY
1910-1922

Attila's head hung low. He showed no sign of recognition. Regina was dragged alongside too. Her left eye was black from the farm women's blows; she looked somehow bloated, and her hair was greying. Her nose had bled. It was swollen, and her upper lip was smeared with dried blood. Regina looked powerless and pathetic.

They moved on, coming to a halt at Maddalena Pioppi's tomb. The widow lay beside her husband Lorenzo. Anita had not known her, but now, along with everyone else, she read the carved inscription on the headstone.

At last Tiger broke the silence. 'Have we seen enough?' he asked.

The witnesses felt cheated, for Attila had not yet uttered a word, and they began to grumble.

Tiger brought his tommy-gun around in front of him, levelling it. To the ring of onlookers, that signalled the start of the awaited execution. Forgetting themselves now, they dashed to take up positions out of the line of fire.

'Look at you, you scum!' Attila suddenly spoke up. He stood erect, unsupported, seeming to have regained his strength. 'You're the new order, are you? You're the new society! Well, you're shit, that's what you are! You're pigs! The whole world is falling apart, and you're like a pack of animals running wild, without a master!'

He stopped and looked around him, searching their faces. Tiger stepped back and let him go on.

'The padroni, those miserable bastards, were the first to abandon us,' Attila continued. 'And tomorrow, you'll see, it will be the priests. They'll bless the red flag. Even our chiefs – they'll all desert us!'

'And what about you?' Anita said. 'Weren't you getting out?'

'With suitcases full of silver,' another woman added.

'Stolen,' said a third. 'And you stole so much you couldn't even carry it!'

Attila shook his head and spoke now as if his honour were injured. 'If this is what's going to happen, maybe in the end it's better this way. I don't give a shit any more. All these years of hard work and sacrifice – what for, what for?'

'For the land you stole,' Manzolone said.

'For the widow's villa,' old Edda said.

'For trying to be a padrone yourself,' Carlotta said.

'To get where?' Attila went on, ignoring their remarks. 'To see cowards like you called heroes?'

There was a commotion. Two or three women had seized Regina, forced her to sit on a tomb, and were shearing off her hair with a pair of scissors.

'Regina, they're cutting your hair!' Attila burst out in an almost tender way. 'Don't cut her hair!' he snarled.

Now, something unleashed, unstoppered in him, Attila took a step forward and stared angrily, accusingly, into the wall of peasant faces. Then he shot out an arm and, with a finger pointed, swung it here and there, indicating the nearby tombs. 'I want to see if I can find a single one of you who would have had the courage to accuse me yesterday. Who killed that one? you want to know. Who killed this one? Who killed the widow?'

He stumbled and reached out to take hold of one of the stone memorials.

'Patrizio Avanzani, tender flower plucked by the cruel hand of destiny!' Attila said sarcastically. 'Well, the cruel hand of destiny is my hand! Yes, these hands, these hands here! Maddalena Cantarelli Pioppi, good and saintly woman, offended by the cruelty of time. I am that cruel time – me, Attila Bergonzi, man and Fascist; I killed that little turd Patrizio, I killed that cunt of a widow! And you all knew it.

If there's one of you who didn't know it, let him step forward if he dares!'

His arrogance was absurd, demented. He seemed to have finished and moved to join his sobbing wife, perhaps to comfort her.

'Look at you, you pigs!' he went on in a final outburst. 'Climbing all over the tombs! This isn't a dance hall! Stop it! You have no respect for the dead!'

A single shot rang out. A revolver had been placed at the back of Attila's neck, and somebody had pulled the trigger. Attila fell blindly, a yard from his wife's feet. Regina broke free and threw herself at him, clutching his shattered body to her.

'Who did that?' she screamed. 'Mob of cowards, I want to know who shot him!'

Everyone pressed forward for a glimpse of the pitiable Fascist pietà. Then the circle of spectators opened up. Any one of them could have fired the shot.

'You've taken my man from me, and I don't know who his murderer is. You won't give me a name, will you? Or at least a face to spit in. With so many thieves and whining traitors running loose, why him? Is he to pay for everything? For all Italy? Do you think he was any different from the rest of you?'

Regina held the body tightly, cradling it in her lap. Her hair was savagely clipped. She glared up at them like a madwoman.

'Yes, he fired the shots, that's true; but my Attila was only obeying orders. Don't you fools know who profited from everything he did? Alfredo Berlinghieri, that's who!'

She had shouted out her cousin's name with all her remaining strength. Then she buried her head against Attila's, sobbing and sobbing, overcome by her grief and unable to get out another word.

When at long last she lifted her face, she found herself strangely alone. Sunlight played on her; over her head, the cherry boughs were in profuse bloom; and beyond them shone a clear blue sky. Everyone had departed in silence. Craning her neck, Regina glimpsed the final stragglers filing out of the cemetery.

'Where are you going?' she called to them. She made an effort to stand but found herself pinned under Attila's weight.

'Wait! Don't leave me like this! Kill me at least!'

From the gate, Anita alone gave a backward glance. In her bitterness, she thought to herself that the disrespect they had shown the dead lay not in trampling on their graves but in killing a vermin like Attila Bergonzi in their resting place. Anita saw Regina, like a tattered rag among the jumble and clutter of the tombs, and she heard her crying out.

'Kill me!' Regina's voice came to her, wailing. 'Kill me, kill me, kill me!'

Cold, unmoved, almost at peace, Anita turned to rejoin the others.

Chapter 3

Why were there no fresh flowers outside her door? Every morning one of the farm boys picked flowers for her, lilac or tulips or irises, and Zurla left a vase of them outside her door. Was something wrong today? Ada recalled the sounds like far-off gunfire, bursts of it, that had disturbed her sleep. There had even been a noise like a gun going off inside the house. What was happening?

It was mid-afternoon when Ada got out of bed and drew back the curtains, letting the full tide of April sunlight flood in. Distantly, she saw the swathes of drying hay, but the fields were strangely deserted. In her room, Ada was surrounded by flowers. Her room was full of them – fresh flowers, fading flowers, dead flowers. They were like memories; she cherished and preserved them even when they wilted, and she couldn't bear throwing them out when they died.

Ada sensed something different about this day. It was as if she stood on the threshold of an immense revelation. She was not always in the stupor everyone believed her to be in, though it was useful letting others think so, since it made them leave her alone, insulating her and ensuring that she was free to think her innermost thoughts in peace.

Her thoughts. They flocked, they vanished. Thoughts of Olmo and his fate. The day Olmo left the farm she was drunk, but it was still clear in her memory. Alfredo had burst in, apologetic and full of boyish enthusiasm, to tell her he had fired Attila.

'I've done it! You can be happy now! I've fired him!'

She had lifted her head and gazed vacantly at her husband, completely drunk.

'Happy?' she said, as though the word had no meaning. 'Is it true Olmo's gone?'

'He'll come back now,' Alfredo said.

'They'll catch him and jail him.'

'He'll come back, I tell you.'

'He'll never come back now. What you've done is too late – as usual!'

Alfredo had remained there for a few moments, obviously hurt and saying nothing. Then, in anger, he stalked out, slamming the door behind him.

Should she have gone away too, should she have made an attempt to follow and find Olmo? She might have helped him escape to another country. Occasionally, she daydreamed of having run away with Olmo, of having dramatically crossed the mountains with him and then organized secret passage for them both to the south of France. But mostly she thought of him rotting in jail. It was the certainty of this that had made her shut herself up in one room for seven years now. If Olmo were in prison, she would become a voluntary prisoner and share his fate.

And if Olmo were dead? That was the unthinkable, and she refused to think it. When she did, sometimes the wine erased her pain, or at least made it bearable. But mostly Ada found that wine was a great magnifier of pain.

Today, however, was different. Ada felt fresh, despite her broken sleep. In fact, she tingled with excitement. Today something calamitous or something wonderful was imminent. She was not sure which, but, after the years and years of numbness, it was like being fully awake again.

Chapter 4

Leonida, hearing new voices and renewed commotion in the courtyard, hoisted himself to peer through the barred window. In the middle of the threshing floor he saw an unknown man being flocked by a small group of farm labourers, both men and women. Everybody seemed to be greeting the stranger at once. There was a lot of animated talk and gesturing, and some of the older women embraced and kissed him. The man, who wore a beard and the obvious dress of a partisan, pointed to a corner of the yard hidden from Leonida's view and gave an order.

'Who is it?' Inès asked. 'What's going on?'

It was not easy to hear over the sounds of the cows, blowing and snuffling and switching their tails. Leonida turned his head to tell her to be quiet. Alfredo was looking up from the straw at him, expectant. Now, in the yard, several men were running enthusiastically across the brick pavement carrying ladders and paint buckets. The new man, the partisan, Leonida figured, had told them to paint out the hated Fascist slogan.

The boy smiled to himself as he dropped down to allow Inès access to the window opening. Was this the man to turn his prisoner over to? Leonida set his face and glanced at Alfredo. The closed stable was hot. There were beads of sweat on the padrone's brow.

'They're coming back from the cemetery,' Inès announced. She hesitated, then said, 'Attila and Regina aren't with them!'

'They had it coming to them!' Leonida said almost gleefully, noting the sudden fear in Alfredo's eyes. The boy pulled Inès down so he could have a look for himself.

She was right. A score or so of people had straggled in through the gateway opposite – Anita, the handful of partisans, and the others who had trooped out to the cemetery. Everyone had returned but Attila and his wife. Then, as Leonida was about to drop down again, he saw Anita suddenly bolt and dash to the middle of the threshing floor, where she wildly flung herself at the man with the beard. From her lips, the boy heard her cry a single word – the man's name.

Leonida was immediately down, his feet planted hard in the straw and dung, his old army rifle levelled.

'Unfasten his chain and stand aside,' he ordered the girl. When she had done so, he told Alfredo to get up.

Alfredo obeyed, automatically raising his hands over his head. Leonida pulled his cap down hard and quickly wiped his mouth with his hand as though he were about to make a speech. Then he pressed the barrel of his rifle into Alfredo's spine and, with a prod, started his prisoner marching. Ahead of them, Inès pulled the big door open.

Standing tall, his shoulders back manfully, rifle sticking straight out from his left hip, Leonida moved from the shaded loggia into the bright sun. Inès, in a floppy blue dress handed down from her mother and clodhopper shoes with her socks rolled down to a bulge around her ankles, fell in beside her hero.

'Stupid! Out of the way!' he said to her under his breath, for he refused to share with anyone the honour of handing over his prisoner to Olmo.

Seeing the unexpected trio appear, the gathering in the middle of the yard opened up and arranged itself in a double file, forming a passage down which Alfredo, Leonida, and Inès made their way. At the other end, Olmo and Anita stood fixed, as dumbstruck as everyone else.

'Good Christ, look at that,' one of the row of onlookers marvelled, 'the padrone!'

'We'd forgotten all about him!' said another.

'Bravo, Leonida!' said one or two of the women.

One man slapped his forehead with the palm of his hand and declared, 'These youngsters – they can teach us a thing or two! Bravo!'

But another man savagely struck out at Alfredo, catching him a blow at the back of the neck. 'Excuse me, Signor Padrone,' he said sarcastically, 'but I was holding that in my hand for a long, long time, and it got away from me.'

Alfredo faltered. At once, the weapon was at his back like a cattle goad.

Someone else gave him a kick, saying, 'And I was holding that in my foot!'

Now Olmo stepped forward to take charge. He had aged, and his face told that he had suffered privation, hardship. His forehead was lined, his beard showed patches of grey, and his curly hair had greyed. Condemned to prison for life, he had only two months earlier been liberated by the partisans.

Alfredo was a couple of paces distant. Olmo saw the lined, weary face of his old friend, a face he had not laid eyes on for seven years, and in it he read Alfredo's suffering and his long private anguish. How helpless Alfredo appeared – helpless, lost, and alone! Olmo felt no personal animosity. He pitied Alfredo for his wasted years, the wasted life he had been born into, but Olmo allowed himself to betray neither recognition nor emotion. As if Alfredo were transparent, Olmo looked through him to the stern-faced boy who stood at his back with the pointed gun.

'Are you Olmo?' Leonida asked, his voice deadly earnest.
'Yes.'
'Then I turn my prisoner over to you.'

Olmo praised the boy for all to hear, then asked him his name. The boy told him.

'His partisan name was Olmo,' Inès said.

Leonida stood there, unsmiling, every muscle in his body rigid with concentration, his duty done. For a moment, Olmo wished he could pat Leonida on the head or give him a fatherly hug, but all eyes were on them, this was a public occasion, and Olmo knew it required something else. With military precision, he stepped within reach of the boy, extended his arm, and gave Leonida a reserved and somewhat formal handshake.

'Leonida, take charge of the prisoner until we are ready to deal with him,' Olmo then said. He pointed to a chair at the far edge of the threshing floor, telling the boy to keep the master there with the rifle trained on him.

'March!' Leonida commanded, and off he and Alfredo went.

Olmo, his daughter, Tiger, and the other partisans conferred. The Fascists were routed, and the Berlinghieri estate was taken over. It was agreed that they would try Alfredo that afternoon and that in the evening they would hold a victory celebration.

And then everybody swarmed Olmo again, covering him with embraces and with questions.

'Not now, not now!' Anita called out joyously. 'There's plenty of time for that later! We've work to do!'

Across the brick pavement, Alfredo sat hunched in his chair, his back to the crowd. What had this world come to? All these years of separation, and he and Olmo – the man who was almost a brother to him – had not yet exchanged a word. How had all this come about?

The proceedings were simple and straightforward. Anita sat with a notebook and pencil at a table set out on the threshing floor. (It was the same table Alfredo's father had used years and years before when tallying the sacks of wheat.) There were a couple of chairs. A red flag had been decked out. The defendant, still covered by Leonida's rifle, was brought forward. Olmo signalled the start of the trial by firing a shot

271

into the air. At once, with the great enthusiasm and fervour of the newly liberated, everyone on the farm began assembling.

'So you came back,' Alfredo said from his seat.

'Are you surprised?' Olmo said.

'I'm glad. Ada will be glad.'

'Maybe she ought to be standing trial with you,' Olmo said coldly, putting an end to the exchange. He then looked around and, satisfied, held up an arm for quiet.

'I hereby declare open the trial of Alfredo Berlinghieri, landowner and therefore enemy of the people,' Olmo went on, his voice raised now. 'Today, the twenty-fifth of April, 1945, the people in revolt have decided to bring to justice those who collaborated with the Fascist regime during the years of tyranny. We, the peasants of this estate, are about to examine the record of Alfredo Berlinghieri, master of the lands we work. Even if the accused cannot be directly implicated in the many crimes and acts of violence and injustice that have taken place on this farm, we must still determine the degree of his responsibility for them. You are all witnesses; I call on you all to testify.'

'What are you writing, Anita?' one of the women said. 'This isn't a classroom.'

'That's right,' someone else said. 'This is a people's trial. What is there to write down?'

They all laughed.

'This is a record, and it will last,' Anita said. 'What we are doing is worthy of being written down, and what's written down is worthy of being read.'

'Look,' one of the old men said, 'I know we're ignorant about these things, but whoever heard of a trial without a lawyer? Excuse me.'

'I've presented you with the accused and you're asking me for lawyers,' Olmo answered. 'What is it you want?'

'But we're the ones who caught him, not you!' someone else spoke up.

'That's not true!' Inès shouted. 'The one who put the padrone under arrest was Leonida – with his rifle!'

'Shut up, stupid,' Leonida said, turning red.

More laughter broke out.

'What about the judges?' one of the partisans asked.

'Aren't we all judges?' Olmo said. 'Our courtroom has no walls, true, but that's because our anger has destroyed them.'

He waited a few moments. The crowd murmured and spoke back and forth to each other, but no further questions or objections were addressed to him. When they fell silent, Olmo said, 'For twenty years or more our voices haven't been heard. Speak up, comrades, speak up!'

They stirred. The first to come forward was the old man who had raised the question of lawyers. Seeing Alfredo lift his eyes to him, the man found himself about to remove his hat in respect. At the last moment, he didn't. Instead, he came right up to the master, pointed an accusing finger in his face, and moistened his lips to speak. But a surge of emotion constricted his throat and no sound came forth. He stood there for long seconds, paralysed, his finger out, his eyes glued to Alfredo. Everyone watched, hushed. Finally, the man gave up and stepped back into the crowd.

Olmo tried to bridge the embarrassed silence. 'When the mute begin to speak they have many things to say,' he told them, 'but it can be very difficult because the tongue is tied. Speak with your hearts, comrades!'

Another old man came to the fore. 'These two fingers that I lost reaping your wheat, who'll give them back to me?' he said, shoving his mutilated hand under the master's eyes.

An old woman took his place. 'Look here,' she said, opening wide a toothless mouth. 'Not a single tooth left, but him – he has all his teeth. He chews all day!'

'You're clean and we're dirty!' a voice shouted out of the crowd.

'You have everything, we have nothing!' came another.

'You rest and we slave!'

'You eat and we suffer hunger!'

It was like a litany.

'No more masters! No more masters!' went up a general cry.

'We want to eat chicken!' others clamoured.

Now many of them began to approach Alfredo, each with something to say, to fling in his face, after the years and years of silence and repression. One woman complained of her rheumatism and rambled on about a foreman on another farm many years before who wouldn't let her work because of her association with the peasant league. 'You're a criminal,' she told Alfredo, 'but your grandfather was worse!'

'That's right,' another chimed in, 'and the time of the great hailstorm you tried to get rid of the day labourers!'

'That wasn't him, it was his father,' old Edda said.

'Father or son, what does it matter?' a woman named Carmelina said. 'The padrone is always the padrone.'

'I say that peasants are necessary, otherwise the land would die,' Robusto said expansively, as if about to launch into a speech, 'but the padrone – what's he good for?'

'Without him the grain grows all the same, and so do the grapes and tomatoes,' Manzolone said.

'The cows don't ask the master's permission to give milk,' one of the partisans added. 'All right then, what's he good for?'

'Nothing,' someone else answered. 'Zero plus zero!'

'He's good for exploiting us, that's what!' Carlotta cried out, shaking a fist in Alfredo's face. 'For sucking our blood dry, for killing us off young!'

Alfredo leaped to his feet, unable to hold back any longer. 'I've never hurt anyone!' he shouted. 'Never!'

'That's what every landowner in the country is saying right now,' Olmo lashed out at him. 'And you are all such hypocrites you believe it!'

'I've never harmed anyone and you know that!' Alfredo insisted excitedly.

But Olmo went right on. 'It was to be able to say that that you padroni took criminals out of prison and got them to do your dirty work. That's how it was, comrades. The Fascists aren't mushrooms that sprouted up overnight. It was the landowners, the masters, who sowed the seeds of Fascism, who wanted the Fascists, who paid them, and then hand in hand with them stole and stole and stole, piling up more and more money for themselves until the time came when they didn't know what to do with it or how to invest it. So they invented the war, and they sent us to it – in Africa, in Russia, in Greece, in Albania, in Spain! And it is always we who pay, with our blood and our sweat – the peasants, the workers, the down and out!'

A chorus of shouts arose from the crowd.

'Enough! Enough!'

'Kill him!'

'Death to the padrone! Death to the exploiter!'

'Do you hear them, Alfredo Berlinghieri?' Olmo's voice rang out over their cries. 'Do you hear the voice of the people? We, the downtrodden, the half-starved, the rabble, the vermin stuck here at the bottom, at the world's asshole — it's we, all of us, who condemn you to death!' Olmo's extended arms embraced the whole gathering. Now, for the first time, he smiled. 'It's all right! It's all right, comrades! The padrone is dead, the padrone no longer exists!'

Olmo's voice had trembled with emotion. Alfredo, in a state of exhaustion, sank into his chair. There was dumbfounded silence. An old man stepped forward and placed the point of his stick against Alfredo's chest.

'So,' he said, 'if I've understood properly, this one, right now, is already dead.'

'Yes,' Manzolone clarified. 'He thinks he's alive, but we know he's dead.'

An old woman drew close and laid a hand on Alfredo's forehead. 'He seems alive to me,' she announced. 'The dead are cold, but he's burning hot.'

'Olmo, you've learned to speak well, I'll say that,' Riva cut in. 'But there's something about your words I don't understand. There's a certain confusion underlying them.'

'The padrone is dead, but Alfredo Berlinghieri is alive and we mustn't kill him,' Olmo said.

'Why not?' Riva pressed.

'Well, because — '

'Because he's the living proof that the padrone is dead!' Robusto said.

'Nonsense!' some of them began to rage. 'He's alive! He's alive!'

'He's dead!' others countered. 'The padrone's dead!'

Now Anita was on her feet, notebook in hand, shouting for their attention and pleading for quiet. 'Listen, listen to what I've written! Alfredo Berlinghieri, the people's tribunal condemns you to everlasting death. The execution will be postponed indefinitely so that you may serve as a living example to our children, our grandchildren, and all our descendants that the exploitation of man by man is once and for all finished!'

275

There were a few expostulations; there were nods of approval; there were signs of jubilation. They had dug the master's grave but put off the funeral arrangements. From behind the table, Anita scrambled up on to her chair.

'And now let's take a vote!' her voice rang out. 'Those in favour, raise their hands!'

Chapter 5

A large suitcase lay open on the bed, and Ada was arranging her things in it. Pale and still shaking, Alfredo stood inside the door, his back to the wall, watching her. He had told her about Attila, he had told her about his own capture and the trial he had just undergone, and it had all been met with silence. Only when Ada learned that Olmo was back had her expression altered. She smiled very briefly, very distantly, and said that all afternoon she had sensed something momentous in the offing.

'I'm so glad,' she told her husband. 'I'm free now.' And she had gone back to her packing. The fact of the farm's having been taken over by the contadini seemed not to affect her in the least.

The little smile had been mysterious, and it surprised Alfredo that Ada could still arouse his jealousy. She stood there like a vision now, in a pair of black and white shoes and a pale blue dress – clothes he had not seen her in since she locked herself away seven years earlier. Her face was sad again but it was also very gentle, almost at peace. Alfredo thought to himself that she was lovely, lovelier than she had ever been, and he felt a wave of affection for her surge through him. He had just escaped death; Olmo had returned from the dead; Ada was rising from the dead. He was overcome with emotion.

'I can't go on,' he said softly. 'I think, I think –'

Tears streamed down his face. He wept, sobbing without restraint, as if the great knots in his chest, the knots he had felt there since childhood, were all coming undone.

Ada went to him now, took him in her arms, and pressed her head gently against his shoulder.

'Oh, Alfredo,' she murmured. 'Alfredo, Alfredo!'

For long minutes they held each other close.

'We may have had something once,' she said wistfully, 'but you lost it. Separate lives – that's what we lived – for never having made ourselves one.'

Chapter 6

Evening fell over the farm, a limpid iris-blue evening. In the courtyard, violins and accordions played. There was wine and food and dancing. They were celebrating the end of Fascism, the end of the war, and the first day of the new era.

Olmo stuck his head outside the entrance of his house, dabbing at his face with a towel. Anita waited for him by the door. He had just finished shaving off his beard.

'Now you're Olmo again!' she said.

On the threshing floor an energetic mazurka was in progress. Olmo laughed and told her he would be right out to dance with her. But just then Ada appeared in the gateway, saw Olmo, and made her way straight to him. Without a word of greeting, with only the faintest trace of a smile on her lips, she reached for his arm to lead him to the dance. Amused, almost uncomprehending, Olmo flung the towel to his daughter and capitulated.

The music was extra fast. Immediately, the two began turning and whirling dizzily, dizzily. They wove a path to the middle of the floor, mixing and brushing with the other couples, and then danced back to the edge of the brick pavement. All at once, Ada came to a stop. The music played on, other dancers whirled and whisked past them. Ada lifted a tentative hand and began passing it over Olmo's face.

'But you're not Alfredo!' she said, breathless. 'Who are you? I don't know you.'

Then she drew back, simulating fear, exactly as she had the night they first met many years before. Olmo laughed. Ada laughed. He ushered her off the dance floor.

'Let's have some wine.' he suggested.

He felt Ada's grip tighten on his arm.

'I'm going away, Olmo,' she said. 'I came to say goodbye.'

'You won't drink a glass of wine with us?'

'No, thank you. The dance was lovely.'

'You're going alone, I hear,' he said.

'Yes, I've been liberated too.' She smiled.

The music stopped. The players rested. Before the couples could leave the floor, a man climbed up on to a chair and, inspired by drink, began making a speech. Olmo and Ada, perhaps having little more to say to each other yet unwilling to part for another few moments, both turned to listen.

'We have passed through hell and come out the other side,' the man said gravely. 'Fate has been propitious! Death has spared us! Let us give eternal thanks!'

Someone else playfully tugged him off his pedestal and took his place. 'The time has come to build Socialism, to build the future!' the new speaker declared. 'We will create miracles from which all will profit except the padroni, the dead, and the buried!'

There were shouts and cries of approval, then insistent calls for more music. The players struck up.

'Well, this is no place for you – not now, anyway,' Olmo said, turning once more to Ada.

By now, Anita was at her father's side, tugging at his elbow and importuning him to dance with her. He could not finish what he had started to tell Ada.

'Maybe it never was,' Ada said.

As the two were being torn apart, Olmo made a sudden attempt to clasp Ada's hand. She smiled bravely. At the same moment, she backed away, so that their fingers met only briefly in what was not even a handshake.

Then she was gone, and Olmo, already touched by the many joys of that day, was now touched by its many sadnesses. Both Rosina and Rigoletto, he had learned only hours earlier, had died, Olmo's fate unknown to them, while he had been in prison. The music swept him along, and Olmo was only half aware of the brick floor under his flying feet. Around him, Anita spun crazily. Somewhere, Olmo thought, there might be a place for Ada. Somewhere – not here – perhaps the new society that it was his dream to build might find a useful place for her. That is what he had wanted to tell her.

When the dance ended, Olmo caught a glimpse of Alfredo, seemingly at a loss, wandering along the loggia that fronted the cow barn. What was he looking for? Olmo wondered. What had he ever been looking for? Alfredo halted by one of the tubbed orange trees, half hidden, watching the dancers. In his new shyness, he seemed barely visible.

'Olmo, Olmo!' a young girl called excitedly, racing in from the gateway. 'There's a big black car outside! It's the CLN!'

Olmo wheeled around, instantly pulled out of his thoughts. 'The CLN! Well, ask them to drive in!'

'They said they want to talk to you,' the girl added.

'Comrades, it's the partisans!' Anita announced. 'It's the CLN! They're here!'

The long sedan nosed into the courtyard and stopped. An expectant crowd swarmed around, some of them clapping their hands, others raising their fists in salute. One of the car's windows rolled down. For a moment, those inside appeared to be conferring. Then the doors opened, and four men stepped out.

Chapter 7

Three of the men, including the driver, were carabinieri. The fourth was a distinguished-looking white-haired old man who wore a white suit and on whose lips was fixed an ironic smile. From the way the others in his party deferred to him it was obvious that the man in civilian clothes led the delegation from the Comitato di Liberazione Nazionale.

With a quick glance ahead of him, the man moved forward into the middle of the applause and, still smiling, halted in front of Olmo. Olmo stared at the slim figure, immediately aware that there was something familiar about the man's slightly frivolous elegance. The old man extended his arm and, as a mark of respect, prolonged the handshake. To Olmo, it was like confronting a ghost, for this man, whom he knew, came to him out of the distant past. He was Ottavio Berlinghieri.

He drew Olmo aside and apologized for having to come straight to the point when there were so many personal things he would like to say. 'I'm here on a delicate mission,' he explained, and he linked an arm in Olmo's and began walking up and down with him. 'I'm here to pass on an order agreed upon jointly by the Partisan Command and the Allies. All combatants are asked to hand over their arms.'

'They won't like it,' Olmo warned.

'I know. That's why we appeal to you.'

Olmo hesitated. 'Maybe I don't like it either.'

Ottavio strode a couple of paces more, then gave a look over his shoulder to ensure that they were out of earshot. He now turned to Olmo, face to face.

'I'm appealing to you personally,' he said.

Peering out from the shadows of the loggia, apart from everyone else, Alfredo watched Olmo and his uncle speaking together. After several moments, Olmo lifted his head and nodded in agreement. Then he turned towards the crowd of peasants and, in a voice in which the anger was undisguised, addressed them.

'Comrades,' Olmo began, 'the firing is over!'

Olmo Dalcò and Ottavio Berlinghieri stood side by side, un-speaking, and watched the operation.

The peasants filed slowly past, piling rifles and hand guns at the feet of the carabinieri. Most of the men displayed sullen faces, since the order, which they had all protested, was one they understood neither the reason nor the necessity for. One partisan openly wept as he laid down his rifle. An-other, before delivering up a pistol, lifted it to his lips and kissed it. But for all the angry silence, the command was carried out in good order.

By one of the brick pillars near the gateway, still alone, Alfredo looked upon the scene with indifference. The events and emotions of the day – the trial, Ada's departure – had left him emptied, drained. But now his eye, which had been passing absently over the faces and forms there at the edge of the threshing floor, came to rest. Several yards distant from the others and midway between them and him, Leonida was staring at Alfredo with implacable hardness, with intense hatred. Alfredo observed. The boy had not yet relinquished his rifle. Its butt was planted on the ground. Rigid, almost at attention, Leonida gripped the barrel in his left hand.

Nearly all the peasants had passed in review and the laying down of arms was coming to a close.

'Well, then, have we finished?' one of the carabinieri asked.

'There's still that boy over there,' the driver of the car said. 'Bring him here.'

Hearing them, Leonida snatched up his rifle in both hands,

but, instead of obeying, he began retreating towards the gate.

'Aren't you turning in your gun, little man?' the third carabiniere said, his tone friendly.

'It's mine, it's mine!' Leonida shouted.

He moved quickly now, resolutely, and passed within a few feet of Alfredo. Alfredo raised a hand, gesturing for the boy to stop.

'Leonida!' Olmo called in a booming voice.

Several of the others took up the cry and bellowed to the boy by name. Inès started after him, but Anita was quick to restrain her. One of the carabinieri swiftly detached himself from the group and ran towards Leonida, who halted abruptly in the gateway. There, in sight of all, the boy turned and without taking aim pulled the trigger of his rifle. The pursuing carabiniere folded up. From the ground, writhing, he brought up a bent leg and squeezed it in both his hands. It had been grazed by the bullet.

Leonida lit off through the gate, rushed down the road a few yards, and headed across one of the newly mown fields. Alfredo rounded the corner and dashed after him.

The shots came in a rapid, murderous burst. Alfredo heard them, like a machine-gun, behind his back. They had been fired by the carabiniere who had driven the car. Riddled with bullets, Leonida plummeted to the ground.

Alfredo was the first to reach him. Down on his knees, he leaned over Leonida and received the boy's last gasp, his last look. It was a look that did not forgive.

Stunned, Alfredo dropped back weakly in a sitting position on the dewy grass. They were coming, all of them, on the run. Alfredo Berlinghieri's face went up. The sky was dotted with stars.

Two old men walked wearily along the track of a dyke road, advancing in silence. There was a bend ahead. On one side was the river, on the other a plantation of poplars. The men had white hair, wrinkled faces, and sunken cheeks. If it had not been for the difference in their clothes, they might have passed for brothers. One wore a white suit, elegant in cut but now slightly yellowed with age. The other was wrapped in a peasant's dark cloak.

'Those are wild flowers, but they're beautiful,' the man in the cloak said, halting. He indicated a clump of daisies that gleamed on the lower part of the bank.

'Would you like them for her grave? I'll get them for you,' the other man said.

He moved cautiously down the slope, picked his way through a network of acacias, and for an instant vanished from sight. The other man remained on the road, listening to the sound of snapping branches. Then there was a rustling sound and a splash. Beyond the acacia thicket, the man in the white suit looked up, smiling. He stood ankle-deep in slimy ditch water.

'I slipped on the wet grass,' he said. 'Give me a hand.'

'I should leave you there to croak!' the other man said, and he burst into wild laughter. Then he climbed down the bank and held out a hand to his friend.

The man in the white suit started up the bank, using branches and stones for handholds. In so doing, his weight pulled a stone loose, uncovering something.

'Look!' he said, taking the hand that was stretched out to him.

He held up a strange, rusted object. It was a cage made of twisted wires. Inside it was a tiny skeleton, a kind of white hieroglyph. The two men examined it.

'It's a mole,' the man wearing the cloak said. 'Who knows

when it went and finished in this thing.'

The man who had found the trap suddenly dropped to his knees. 'Do you remember that day?' he said faintly.

The other man nodded thoughtfully but said nothing.

'My head's spinning. Help me, I'm not well,' the kneeling man said.

His friend reached out and, with unexpected strength, lifted the other man and dragged him up the bank.

At the top, both men laboured to draw breath, unspeaking. When they were ready to move on, the peasant smiled and spoke.

'Listen here, we were born the same day. You don't want to go and die before me,' he said.

They walked on a long way in silence.

At last, the man in the white suit put out his hand to bring his friend to a stop. He looked at him. 'The time has come,' he said. 'Help me, give me a hand. It's all over. Seeing this trap again – it's a sign, a sign, I tell you. The postponement is over.'

There was a distant rumbling sound. It grew, and a moment or two later it became a clatter. A few hundred yards off, beyond a hawthorn hedgerow, they spied an approaching train.

'Help me to die,' the man in the white suit said almost obsessively.

The other man watched the train momentarily disappear from sight. All at once, he brightened. 'Come on, I want to see if you're still as scared as you were when we were small!'

The two old men climbed the embankment to the tracks.

'Let's play a game,' the man in the cloak suggested.

But the other man did not let him go on. He got stiffly down on his knees, then stretched out across the tracks, his head resting on one rail, his feet over the other. The approaching engine whistled.

The man on the tracks smiled as he stared up and saw his friend standing against the blue sky.

'Close your eyes!' the peasant shouted, his voice about to break with emotion. 'Close them or you'll go blind!'

The sound was deafening. The locomotive pounded and thundered as it came closer and closer. Holding each other in their gaze, the two friends exchanged a long, reflective look. It was as long as a century, as long as a life.

H. H. Kirst

Sometimes very funny, often bitingly satirical, Hans Hellmut Kirst's novels describe Germany and the Germans, from the Nazi era to the present day. 'Kirst's oblique, deadpan gaze is deeply revealing, deeply compassionate.' *Sunday Times*

Camp 7 Last Stop

Hero in the Tower

A Time for Truth

A Time for Scandal

The Return of Gunner Asch

What Became of Gunner Asch

Officer Factory

The Night of the Generals

The Wolves

 Fontana Books

Simone de Beauvoir

She Came to Stay
The passionately eloquent and ironic novel she wrote as an act of revenge against the woman who so nearly destroyed her life with the philosopher Sartre. 'A writer whose tears for her characters freeze as they drop.' *Sunday Times*

Les Belles Images
Her totally absorbing story of upper-class Parisian life. 'A brilliant sortie into Jet Set France.' *Daily Mirror*. 'As compulsively readable as it is profound, serious and disturbing. *Queen*

The Mandarins
'A magnificent satire by the author of *The Second Sex*. *The Mandarins* gives us a brilliant survey of the post-war French intellectual . . . a dazzling panorama.' *New Statesman*. 'A superb document . . . a remarkable novel.' *Sunday Times*

The Woman Destroyed
'Immensely intelligent, basically passionless stories about the decay of passion. Simone de Beauvoir shares, with other women novelists, the ability to write about emotion in terms of direct experience . . . The middle-aged women at the centre of the three stories in *The Woman Destroyed* all suffer agonisingly the pains of growing older and of being betrayed by husbands and children.' *Sunday Times*

 Fontana Books

Fontana Russian Novels

A Country Doctor's Notebook Mikhail Bulgakov
'Based on his experiences as a young doctor in the chaotic years of the Revolution. About 1000 miles from the lecture theatre and 30 miles from the nearest railway, he was faced with a bewildering array of medical problems and the abysmal ignorance of the Russian peasant.' *Observer*. 'Wryly funny – and fascinating.' *Sunday Times*

The Master and Margarita Mikhail Bulgakov
'The fantastic scenes are done with terrific verve and the nonsense is sometimes reminiscent of Lewis Carroll . . . on another level, Bulgakov's intentions are mystically serious. You need not catch them all to appreciate his great imaginative power and ingenuity.' *Sunday Times*

The White Guard Mikhail Bulgakov
'A powerful reverie . . . the city is so vivid to the eye that it is the real hero of the book.' *V. S. Pritchett, New Statesman*. 'Set in Kiev in 1918 . . . the tumultuous atmosphere of the Ukranian captial in revolution and civil war is brilliantly evoked.' *Daily Telegraph*. 'A beautiful novel.' *The Listener*

The First Circle Alexander Solzhenitsyn
The unforgettable novel of Stalin's post-war Terror. 'The greatest novel of the 20th Century.' *Spectator*. 'An unqualified masterpiece—this immense epic of the dark side of Soviet life.' *Observer*. 'At once classic and contemporary . . . future generations will read it with wonder and awe.' *New York Times*

Doctor Zhivago Boris Pasternak
The world-famous novel of life in Russia during and after the Revolution. '*Dr. Zhivago* will, I believe, come to stand as one of the great events of man's literary and moral history.' *New Yorker*. 'One of the most profound descriptions of love in the whole range of modern literature.' *Encounter*

 Fontana Books

Eric Ambler

A world of espionage and counter-espionage, of sudden
violence and treacherous calm; of blackmailers, murderers,
gun-runners—and none too virtuous heroes. This is the
world of Eric Ambler. 'Unquestionably our best thriller
writer.' *Graham Greene*. 'He is incapable of writing a dull
paragraph.' *Sunday Times*. 'Eric Ambler is a master of his
craft.' *Sunday Telegraph*

Doctor Frigo

The Dark Frontier

Judgement on Deltchev

The Levanter

The Light of Day

The Mask of Dimitrios

Dirty Story

A Kind of Anger

The Night-Comers

The Intercom Conspiracy

 Fontana Books

Fontana Books

Fontana is a leading paperback publisher of fiction and non-fiction, with authors ranging from Alistair MacLean, Agatha Christie and Desmond Bagley to Solzhenitsyn and Pasternak, from Gerald Durrell and Joy Adamson to the famous Modern Masters series.

In addition to a wide-ranging collection of internationally popular writers of fiction, Fontana also has an outstanding reputation for history, natural history, military history, psychology, psychiatry, politics, economics, religion and the social sciences.

All Fontana books are available at your bookshop or newsagent; or can be ordered direct. Just fill in the form and list the titles you want.